RAVES FOR ADAM HALL . . .
AND HIS MAN QUILLER!

"The unchallenged king of the spy story!"
—*Buffalo News*

"Quiller by now is a primary reflex."
—*Kirkus*

"Hall tops ninety-nine percent of all writers of spy books." —*St. Paul Pioneer Press*

"Quiller is tops!" —*Charlotte Observer*

"Splendid . . . a masterpiece of espionage!"
—*St. Louis Post-Dispatch*

"Brilliant!" —*Harper's*

Continued . . .

"Better than Bond, more interesting, more real."
—Minneapolis Tribune

"A model of breathless entertainment . . . tense, intelligent, harsh, surprising."
—The New Yorker

"The best of the new spy thrillers!" *—Life*

"Gem-hard style, unflagging action, unrelenting suspense!" *—Buffalo News*

"White-hot intensity!" *—Washington Post*

"Such stuff as nightmares are made of."
—Sacramento Bee

"Fast and deadly!" *—Omaha World Herald*

"Quiller is the greatest!" —*New York Times*

"A relentless cliffhanger!" —*The New Yorker*

"Breathless entertainment!" —*Associated Press*

"Fast-paced, hard-hitting and surprising."
—*Chattanooga Free Press*

"Hall's new nonstop thriller is compelling . . . shocking suspense!" —*Publishers Weekly*

"Ingenious . . . What a finish!"
—*San Francisco Chronicle*

"Worth reading in a single burst!"
—*Buffalo Courier-Express*

"Bristling with tension . . . enough plot twists and turns to keep us involved until the very last line."
—*Waco Tribune Herald*

Also by Adam Hall

THE QUILLER MEMORANDUM
THE TANGO BRIEFING
THE MANDARIN CYPHER
THE KOBRA MANIFESTO
THE SINKIANG EXECUTIVE
THE 9TH DIRECTIVE

THE STRIKER PORTFOLIO
(coming in June!)

ADAM HALL

QUILLER'S RUN

JOVE BOOKS, NEW YORK

QUILLER'S RUN

A Jove Book/published by arrangement with
the author

PRINTING HISTORY
Jove edition/March 1988

ISBN: 0-515-09540-0

Jove Books are published by the Berkley Publishing Group,
200 Madison Avenue, New York, New York 10016.

PRINTED IN THE UNITED STATES OF AMERICA

10 9 8 7 6 5 4 3 2 1

For
JONQUIL
Always

CONTENTS

1	Smoke	1
2	The Worm	8
3	Ducks	20
4	Party	29
5	Yasma	42
6	Katie	54
7	Johnny Chen	66
8	Flight 306	79
9	Ash	91
10	Voices	99
11	Shoda	108
12	Slingshot	118
13	Zabaglione	128
14	Countdown	138
15	Whistling	149
16	Toyota	161
17	Crucifix	168
18	Moon Drop	182
19	Colonel Cho	191
20	The Rat	205
21	Water-Bed	215
22	The Clinic	228
23	Obsession	238
24	The Birdbath	248
25	Silence	259
26	Kishna	264
27	Pink Panties	272
28	The Deal	284
29	Treble-Think	298
30	Mr Croder	307
31	End-Phase	318
32	Kiss	328

1

SMOKE

The whole place was tight with tension when I got there, people huddled in hushed groups along the corridors and hanging around the Signals Room, Croder standing outside Codes and Cyphers with one of the cryptologists, his eyes pinning the poor bastard against the wall and his voice like a knife being sharpened—*"Then why the hell didn't you get me on the phone, I don't care what time it was, you ought to know that by now."* I went on past them and thought for God's sake if *Croder's* lost his cool then something big must have blown and the fallout was still coming down—but the thing was, the thing *was,* you know, I couldn't have cared *less*.

Loman had asked me to meet him at six in his office but he wasn't there and I had to stand listening to Radcliffe talking on the phone with his mouth tight and his face pasty under the lights—

"Fensing is no longer in service." He glanced up at me and gave a nod and went on talking. "No, officially we're calling it suicide."

Now *that* was spelling it out, wasn't it, not pretty but at least honest—"no longer in service" was one of those coy little euphemisms coined by the bureaucrats on the third floor; why couldn't they put us down in the records as *dead* when we came unstuck, or was there something offensive about the idea, something not quite nice, not to be talked about?

"Of course we are." His pale fingertips drumming on the desk. "We've called Howatch in from Belgrade and Johns from Rome and they're trying to locate Hockridge through his director in the field."

I stood with my raincoat dripping—it'd been drizzling the whole day again, bloody spring for you—they'd called *Johns* in, what on earth for? The last I'd heard of him he'd been passing the hat round to the sleeper agents right across the Communist bloc for any leftover scraps of information they could give him because there'd been five red-sector contacts supporting *Sable One* when it had come apart and left them "terminally exposed," as those snotty-nosed twits on the third floor called it.

"No," Radcliffe said, "he's still unaccounted for."

I got fed up with waiting and went outside and along the corridor to see if I could find Loman anywhere, and if I couldn't I'd check back at his office and if he still wasn't there he could go to hell. But when I got to the stairwell I saw him standing against the banisters on the floor above, talking to someone. Then he suddenly looked down and saw me.

I stood with my hands in the pockets of my raincoat, staring up at him, waiting. If the bastard wanted to talk, he'd have to do it now.

Calthrop was with him and they came down the stairs together. "I'm sorry I wasn't in my office," Loman said, "but there's a lot going on." Short, dapper, smelling of shoe-polish, I could have killed him on the spot and he knew that. "Let's go in here, shall we?"

It was a room next to the janitor's closet, no number on the door, no name, just like all the other doors in this anonymous building. No one was in here; it was used to store things in by the look of it—empty filing cabinets and some worn leather armchairs and a coffee urn inside a torn cardboard box, someone's bike with the tyres flat and the chain hanging slack.

Loman shut the door and turned to look at me. "It was good of you to come."

I didn't answer, didn't look at either of them. Calthrop was here, I knew, in case Loman needed protection. He might.

The room was quiet, with only the rain dripping on the windowsill outside.

"Why don't we take a pew?" Calthrop, very smooth, almost jolly, pouring lots of oil. He slapped the dust off one of the armchairs and dropped into it, crossing his legs, looking up at me with an amiable smile.

Loman went to sit down but stopped when he saw I hadn't moved. "We feel we owe you an apology, Quiller. We—er—deeply regret the circumstances that obviously prompted you to hand in your resignation, and very much hope you'll reconsider."

The rain dripped, dripped on the windowsill.

From his chair Calthrop added gently, "You mustn't think you're not still among friends, you know. We're—"

"Friends?"

Loman flinched, though I hadn't shouted or anything.

He recovered fast, annoyed with his show of nerves. "Oh, come now. You know perfectly well that every shadow executive *has* to be considered expendable, in justifiable circumstances. After all, you signed the clearance forms as usual before the mission."

His face made me sick and I turned away and looked at a picture on the wall instead, a faded photograph behind cracked glass, the Queen at the Trooping of the Colours, sidesaddle, upright, plumed, and in full scarlet. There was a dead moth lying on the top edge of the frame. When I was ready I turned back and looked at Loman again with a dead stare.

"Yes. I signed the forms."

I said it quietly but he knew my ability to keep control, to contain even rage if I had to, with none of it reaching the eyes. It was what they expected of us, wasn't it, the shadow executives? Total control. We're required to behave like deadly reptiles out there in the field and then turn up here at the Bureau and comport ourselves like civilised people. And we do.

"I signed the forms. I also defused the bomb. And if I'd known you'd had it planted for me I would have brought it all the way home at the end of the mission and blown this whole fucking building apart."

Loman turned and took a pace or two with his bright polished shoes, his black onyx cufflinks glinting under the light, his short arms held behind him. "The necessity," he said thinly, "was agreed upon, and at the highest level, as you may well imagine. The fate of nations was at stake. We—"

"It's *always* at stake. That's the type of operation you always give me."

He shrugged. "There was the risk of your breaking under interrogation if you were caught."

"I had a capsule."

"We can never be absolutely sure, of course—" He shrugged again.

"That we'll use it?"

"Quite so."

"Do you know how many missions I've completed?"

"I acknowledge your experience, but—"

"You've directed me in the field yourself."

"That's correct."

I took a step towards him. "And did you find me to be the type of spineless wimp who wouldn't even suck on a peck of cyanide to protect the mission? *Did you?*"

The cracked glass of the picture on the wall vibrated and the little bastard flinched again, and I felt sudden compassion for him, because he was locked into a system that sometimes demanded that Control deliberately condemned a first-class shadow executive to death, somewhere out there where the people in London couldn't see him, where they couldn't in fact make absolutely certain that his death was essential, unavoidable, with no choice but to order it done and cut off a career and leave a corpse somewhere in hostile territory where it'd be found and treated as trash and tossed onto a rubbish dump, a feast for rats.

But there was one thing worse, perhaps, even worse for the people in London, and that was to have the intended dead come back alive, and curse them to their face.

"We have to do," Loman said in a moment, "what we have to do."

I didn't answer that.

Calthrop spoke, gently. "On what terms, Quiller, would you perhaps consider staying on?"

"None."

Loman said, "We would offer you rather good ones, Quiller. Your sole discretion, for instance, as to backups, shields, signals, liaison, contacts, and so on."

I didn't say anything.

Calthrop took over smoothly—"Including your presence at mission planning, with Chief of Control. And of course"—he tried to soften the crudeness of the next tidbit with an apologetic smile—"a more appropriate retainer."

The rain dripped on the windowsill.

"How appropriate?"

Calthrop glanced at Loman, who said quickly—"Double."

"What makes me so valuable, suddenly, considering you tried to get my guts blown into Christendom out there in Russia?"

Loman looked trapped, but got out fast. "I'm sure the Directorate would feel—as indeed we do—that some measure of compensation would be in order. After all, they—"

"*Bullshit*. You think they'd try and *buy* me back?"

"I wouldn't put it quite—"

"If you left the Bureau," Calthrop cut in quickly, "what would you do? Have you thought of that?"

"There's a life outside this bloody place, don't worry."

"For someone like you?"

"Yes."

"You won't find it easy," Loman took over. "And once you've gone, we can never ask you back."

"That's a bloody shame." I took a step towards him, and I suppose there was something in my eyes now that made him inch back before he could stop himself. "You could never send me into another mission with any guarantee that you wouldn't do the same thing again, if you had to. So I'd always be looking behind me for some bastard with a knife—or a bomb. And it wouldn't work. I've got to know where my friends are, and I've none here. They're outside, and that's where I'm going." I went to the door, and heard the creak of leather as Calthrop got out of his chair.

"Quiller?"

I turned to look at him, and he brushed the air with his hand. "Sorry."

I pulled the door open and it swung wide and hit the rubber stop with a little thump as I went into the hall.

On my way through the building to the rear exit I tried to avoid people, but Charlie saw me through the doorway of the Caff.

"I thought you'd chucked it in."

I went over to him in case he tried to get up: his last mission had left him with a smashed thigh and a few other things.

"Just covering traces."

"You'd never be sure, would you?" Charlie said, a burned hand hooked round the teacup.

"Of what?"

"Never be sure they wouldn't try it again."

"That's it exactly." I touched his shoulder and went out to the corridor again. Michalina was going into Signals with a file, but she didn't see me. A door came open near the staircase and Holmes came out, passing me absently and then stopping, looking back.

"Someone said you'd resigned."

"Yes."

"You'll go mad out there."

"That should be interesting."

I went to the end of the passage and through the narrow

doorway of the screened rear exit into Whitehall and splashed through the puddles on my way to the Jensen, not looking back at the building, not looking back at anything at all as I got into the car and started up and took it westwards through Kensington and Chiswick and out to the M4, turning the phone off and switching the wipers to high and flipping the radarscope on, pulling the slack out of the seat-harness and letting it snap back, putting the lights onto high-beam with nothing in front of me now but the steel-grey veil of the rain as I pushed the throttle down and kept it there, wanting only to put distance between myself and London, and the bitter, acrid smoke of a burned bridge.

2

THE WORM

"I can't," she said. "I've got to be up bright and early."

"Are you flying?"

"Not till noon." She kissed me for the last time, her hair falling across my face, cool and scented.

"Then why not stay the night?"

"I've got an interview at nine. I'm trying to get onto the Concorde—wouldn't that be fantastic? I mean apart from the pay, I'd have the name on my uniform. All the other crews *look,* when you go through the airport. Talk about *prestige.*" She slipped off the bed and looked across the room. "Which door is it?"

"That one. Guest towels on the left."

"God, I can hardly stand up. Are you normally like that?"

"No. It was the way you kissed."

She stood looking down at me, the light from the street catching the sweat on her skin, turning it to satin.

"I always kiss like that, but it doesn't normally set up a tornado."

"Then it should."

She stood smoothing her thighs, maybe considering staying. That would be all right: I was feeling intolerably lonely.

"What are all those bruises?" She'd only just noticed them.

"I looped a motor."

"Sounds expensive."

"If you'll stay, I'll cook up some eggs and bacon."

"That's not what I'd stay for, but anyway I can't. Tomorrow's the chance of a lifetime." On her way to the bathroom she said over her shoulder, "But I'm based in London."

I got off the bed and put some clothes on, with strange thoughts coming into my mind—should I look for someone to marry now, someone like this girl? Settle down, open some kind of business? I'd been getting ideas like those since last night when I'd got back to London in a hired Porsche, but they were alien to me, not because a wife and a normal job wouldn't give me a certain amount of satisfaction but because ideas like that belonged to other people, not to me. It was like having a total stranger trying to get inside my head, and if I started to lose my sense of identity I could finish up in the funny farm.

You'll go mad out there.

Holmes. And possibly that was what I was doing. But marriage wouldn't work, or a normal life. I had to have absolute freedom. Satisfaction wouldn't be enough: I wanted risk, occasional terror, life at the brink. And you couldn't share a life like that with anyone.

"What do you do?" she asked me when she came out of the bathroom.

"I'm between jobs."

"Are you an actor?" She was watching me in the mirror.

"No."

"There's something different about you." She combed her long hair and then began putting it up into a chignon. "I mean you looked after me absolutely marvellously in the restaurant, but I had the feeling there was something on your mind all the time. Have you been fired?"

"Close. I resigned. Leave—"

"What from?"

"Government work. Terribly dull. Leave your number, will you?"

"If you like."

It was gone midnight when we went down to the street; the rain had stopped at last, and I managed to flag down a cab straightaway.

"I hope you get the Concorde job."

"God, so do I. *Imagine.*" She reached up and we kissed, while the cab's diesel went on idling. "Thanks for such a good time, Martin. Give me a ring if you feel like it—I'll be back in London next week. Next Tuesday."

The flat felt deserted when I went back, which was odd, because I normally enjoyed its space and its silence. She'd scribbled her phone number on the back of a British Airways check slip; it was lying on the dressing table under the lamp, next to a blond tangle of hairs, and I picked it up and tore it in half, and then in quarters, dropping them into the waste-paper basket and turning off the lamp. I wouldn't be in London next week, next Tuesday. God knew where I'd be, but it wouldn't be here.

"Well, well . . ."

It was Pepperidge, hunched over the bar with a glass of mescal in front of him, the worm curled at the bottom.

I didn't want to talk to him, or anyone else; I'd come to the Brass Lamp to be alone, as a change from being alone in the flat; but I couldn't just walk away now that he'd seen me. I asked the man for a tonic and bitters, and looked at Pepperidge.

"How are things?"

He squinted under the brass-shaded light. "I suppose they'll work out somehow."

I hadn't seen him for months; he specialised in picking up classified info at ground level—cryptographic key lists and cards, message traffic, communications data, operations orders, whatever he could get, working mostly at the Asian desk at the Bureau.

"What happened?" I asked him.

"Bastards fired me." He watched me with cynical eyes, his thin hair lying untidily across his scalp, his moustache at a kind of angle, sloppily trimmed, his shoulders hunched. "I'm like you, old boy—sometimes I won't obey orders." His hand shook a little as he picked up his drink. "And I don't regret it, you know that? I don't bloody well regret it. Is that all you're going to drink?"

"For the moment."

He sat gazing into his small amber glass. "For the moment. I suppose that means you're working."

"Not really. I walked out."

He swung his head up to squint at me with his yellow eyes, taking time to focus. *"Walked out?"*

"A little disagreement." I didn't want to talk about it; the whole thing had been tearing at my mind for the last ten days like a pack of dogs.

"Walked out of the *Bureau?"*

"It can happen to anyone, for Christ's sake."

He went on watching me. "But you're one of their top shadows."

"Tell me about yourself."

He ignored that. "You'll go back, of course. I mean, after a while. Won't you?"

"No." I picked up my drink. I'd give him another three minutes for old times' sake, and then *out*.

"When did you leave?" he asked me.

"Ten days ago."

"You must have been going mad."

"Probably."

"That's what *I* should've done, before they had a chance to fire me. I know what it feels like. I mean I know what it feels like to *me*. What's it feel like to you?"

"None too funny. Aren't you afraid of swallowing that bloody thing?"

He looked into his drink, rather fondly. "But I always do, old boy. He's my little friend, you see. Poor little perisher, died of drink, and you know something? So will I.

Eventually.'' He straightened up on the stool, making an effort, glancing across my eyes—''Of course I don't really mean that. But Christ, you know what I did the day I walked out of there? I put down half a bottle of Black Label and went along to the fun fair and bought every bloody seat on the roller-coaster and tried to see if I could hop from the front to the back before it came in again. Fucking near fell off—there's a really rotten bend on that thing. The *next* day I took a .38 up there with me and had a go at shooting out the bulbs on the tower in the middle. Got most of them. Arrested for public endangerment, or some such thing.'' He gave a short laugh that turned into a cough. ''You should do something like that, you know, get it out of your system.''

''I did.''

''Jolly good show. Stick a piss-pot on top of the palace gates or something? I've always wanted to do that, you know.''

''Nothing so fancy.'' The cop hadn't been able to put the actual speed down on the ticket because the needle in the Jensen had been tight against the 120 mark when the front end had started aquaplaning on the wet road somewhere past Windsor and the whole thing had taken off. I'd been lucky the cop had found me: there was a bit of concussion involved.

''I suppose Scobie's after you, is he?''

''What?''

''Scobie.''

''Yes.'' I'd got the letter a week ago, three days after I'd left the Bureau. Scobie worked fast. There was an official crest at the top of the paper, and the name of a department which didn't in fact exist: *Coordination Staff—Foreign and Commonwealth Office*.

It has been suggested to me that you might be interested in a discussion with us about appointments in government service in the field in foreign affairs, which occasionally arise in addition to those covered by the Diplomatic Service Grades 7 and 8.

The letter was signed illegibly over the title: *Recruiting Officer*.

Scobie ran an undercover staffing operation for the British Secret Intelligence Service from Warwick Square, and he'd picked up the vibrations at once when I'd walked out of the Bureau. The next thing would be an invitation to lunch at the Travellers' Club in St James to sound me out.

"You won't take up with that gang, of course." Pepperidge was watching me steadily now. "Will you?"

"Not really."

"Too much bloody red tape." He finished his drink, and I looked away. *He's my little friend, you see . . .* "But then, where else is there? There is *nowhere*, of course, or I wouldn't be sitting here . . . sitting here wishing to *Christ*"—he squeezed his eyes shut and sat rocking gently on his stool for almost half a minute, then let his shoulders go slack, giving a short laugh—"wishing to Christ I wasn't. Because *I* had an offer, too. Not from Scobie." He swung his head to look for the barman. "Not from Scobie."

"Same again, Mr Pepperidge?"

"Yes. That is to say, no." He looked into the shadows behind him and touched my arm. "Let's go and sit over there."

Every table had a small brass lamp on it, burning dimly; between them it was almost dark. You didn't come here to be seen, or to see anyone. I nearly said I'd got to go, but changed my mind, in case there were any small thing I could do for him—because in the last ten minutes I'd been chilled, appalled. Pepperidge had been first class in the field before he'd come home to the Asian desk. He'd never touched booze, he'd kept in training at Norfolk and he could take on anything they gave him—a totally shut-ended checkpoint situation without papers or contacts and get away with it; he could stalk, infiltrate, kill if he had to and get out with the product. Ferris had run him in *Sapphire*, Croder had run him in *Foxtrot*, two of the major ones, and now he was sitting here with his thin blued hands restless on the polished oak of the table, his eyes needing time to focus, his memory slow, a burnout, finished, and not yet forty.

This wouldn't happen to me, I knew that; but I'd have to find a good reason for going on, a new direction. And it would have to take me back to the only life I could live with.

But there is nowhere, of course . . .

Pepperidge had his shoulders against the panelled wall, even this dim light bothering his eyes. The attempt at wry humour was done with now; it had been an act I'd seen through, and he'd dropped it. "Not from Scobie, no. This came from Cheltenham."

Government Communications HQ, out in the West Country, the nerve-centre for international classified traffic. So he'd been keeping his ear to the ground, at least.

"It was offered to me personally," he said, "under the desk."

"When?"

"Last week." His yellow eyes watched me steadily, defiance in them. "It surprises you, of course, that anyone should offer this . . . this ship-wrecked fucking sailor any kind of *mission*. I see that. I quite understand. But—"

"Spare me the violins," I told him, and finished my drink. *One* more minute, and *out*. I'd joined him here at the table because the poor bastard had started talking business, but it couldn't add up to anything; he was just wandering in the wastelands of the lost, to pick over the shreds of his pride.

"I will spare you the violins," he said with heavy articulation, "yes, of course." There was a light in his eyes now that carried a warning, and I noted it. But if the poor devil tried coming at me in his besotted rage I'd only have to subdue him, and that would make things worse, humiliating. "It so happens, you see, that a certain party knew of my accomplishments out East, and thought this one might catch my interest. It's for me to accept or turn down, as I think fit.'' He sat with his back straight again, watching me with a dreadful steadiness, waiting to see if he was getting the message across—that he was still on his feet, still in the running, well thought-of.

''Then you're in clover,'' I said, and tried to make it sound genuine.

There was a moment's silence and then he gave a kind of sob, squeezing his eyes shut and just sitting there without moving, his fists pressed onto the table to keep him upright, their tremor conveying itself to the brass lamp and setting up a vibration. Then it was over.

Not much above a whisper—''Don't humour me, you bastard. Spare me that.'' Aware suddenly of his clenched fists, he opened them and brought his hands slowly together, as if for comfort. ''Of course you're perfectly right. There's no kind of action I could take on now without getting killed.''

In a moment I said, ''Dry out somewhere.''

''I'm sorry?''

''Go into a clinic and dry out. Then do a bit of training. You'll soon get it back.''

''Yes. Yes, of course. I shall do that. One day.'' He drew a slow breath. ''Meanwhile I shall find someone to take this thing over, because it's too good to miss and I'm buggered if I'll give it to the Bureau. They couldn't touch it anyway; it's too sensitive. Have another drink, if that's what you call it.''

''I've got to be going.'' It wasn't the first time I'd seen a wrecked spook pushing his doom. He was only just this side of a breakdown, and I didn't want to be here when he pulled something out and blew his head off with it, as North had done.

''You've only just come, for God's sake.'' He lifted a hand for the barman. ''You know Floderus, don't you?'' he asked me.

''Which one?''

He gave a wintry smile. ''Good question. Charles, of course. Charles Floderus.''

The other one, I remembered, had broken up a courier line through Trieste and wiped out a Queen's Messenger before the Bureau caught a whiff of something rotten: the man had been doubling for five years before he blew his own cover because of a woman. Charles was different; they were distantly related but the blood was thin, and Charles was known for his total integrity throughout the secret services. He was also a very high-echelon director of operations for the SIS.

"What about him?" I asked Pepperidge.

"He was the one who made me this proposal." He watched some people coming in, behind me. "I'd done him a bit of good, you see, at one time. Decent of him to remember."

I'd begun listening. *Floderus* had approached him? That had been decent of him, yes. He was very cautious, very demanding.

"I got it over the phone," Pepperidge said. "We didn't actually meet." His eyes dipped away. "He didn't know I was . . . not quite at my best. Just the main drift, you see, over the blower, no names or anything, absolute security." When the barman came over he asked for the same again, and then told me, "Also, as I said, he knew I'd done quite a bit in Asia." His head swung up. "You were out there too, weren't you, a couple of times?"

"Yes. Are they anyone we know?"

"What? Nobody *I* know. Are you worried?"

"No."

"It's just a man and a woman, holding hands across the table."

"As long as you're happy."

He frowned. "Am I talking too loud?"

"Everything's relative." If Floderus had really offered him an operation then he should keep it well under cover. A lot of people who came to the Brass Lamp were from the corridors of Codes and Cyphers, together with a few second or third secretaries of foreign embassies.

Pepperidge kept his eyes on the other table for a bit

longer and then said more quietly, "They're just spooning. But anyway, old boy, this one isn't for you." The barman came with their drinks and Pepperidge said, "Cheers. What've you got, an ulcer or something?"

"That's right."

Reflectively he said, "It'd mean working for a foreign government, you see, and I'd hardly imagine you ever doing that."

"Which one?"

"Friendly to the West. Does it matter?"

"Not really." I shook a few more drops of Angostura into my tonic and watched it fizz. Working for a foreign government would be totally strange. I was used to the ultrasophisticated services of the Bureau: meticulous briefing, prearranged access to the field—even across the Curtain—a signals board in London with only my name on it and a twenty-four-hour staff, and a director in the field who could get me anything I needed: contacts, couriers, papers, limitless and progressive briefings as the phases of the mission changed, and liaison through GCHQ Cheltenham with the Chief of Control in London and his decision-making authority, which gave him immediate access to the Prime Minister, wherever she might be.

"Fabulous money, of course," Pepperidge said.

"That's what Loman told me."

He gave a derisive grunt. "Loman? He couldn't get you enough to buy a bag of chips. I mean the real thing."

"I wouldn't know what to do with it."

"Buy some more Jensens. Aren't they what you use?"

"I mean apart from toys."

"Then give it to the dogs' home and do it for kicks." He was watching me steadily again. "You've got me interested, you know that?"

"What in?"

"Handing this thing over to you."

"Forget it." I wouldn't work for Floderus or a foreign government.

"Have you got a card on you?"

"No."

"Well here's mine."

I took it out of courtesy, and pushed my chair back. I wanted to be out of here before he got down to the bottom of his drink again and swallowed that bloody worm.

You'll go mad out there.

Holmes.

Dead right.

It was eight o'clock and a lot of the options had run out: *Giselle* was playing at Covent Garden but I'd never get in without booking. It'd be the same thing at the theatres: the only shows I could get a ticket for wouldn't be worth seeing. I didn't want to go down to the club because the only people I'd see there would be talking shop, and I'd just had a gutful of that with Pepperidge. Eating out alone was a bleak enough thought: food was a celebration of life and had to be shared. Moira was in Paris and Liz on her way to New York again; Yvonne was in London and might be available, but what was it coming down to—that I had to find a girl because I'd got nothing else to do? Better not tell her *that*.

I could go along to the dojo and hope to find Tanaka there and knock some of the rough edges off *Kanku Dai,* but even though I could use the exercise he'd see I was out of condition and that would embarrass me because he wouldn't say anything. I could go up to Norfolk and ask for a session at the long-distance night range and blast Loman's face all over the sandbags—they'd let me in, even if they knew I'd left the Bureau; the bastards would let me do anything I liked in the hope of getting me back. But there wasn't any point in going to Norfolk, as if nothing had changed.

Everything had changed.

I'd known it would feel like this in the first few weeks. I'd cut myself off from a way of life that had exposed me to the most deadly risks, time after time, and pushed me into that frightening, ethereal zone where I had to face those things in myself that in cold blood I'd never have the stomach for: weakness in one form or another, cowardice, a blind eye to the need for mercy, lack of grace. I'd expected, yes, to feel like an electric circus with the plug pulled out, the tension gone and the noise dying away and the dark coming down; but I wasn't ready for this sense of loss, of loneliness.

Bloody shame. Get used to it.

Some time after nine I made some toast and opened a tin of sardines and got out *The Tao of Physics* and wrestled with it, no sound in the room but the occasional muted horn of a taxi and the fretting of a casement as the night wind got up. The phone hadn't rung since I'd got back from the Brass Lamp, and at some time or other I went across and checked to see it was still working. Later I went to the safe behind the sliding Japanese-lacquered panel and took out the experimental cypher grid that Tilney had asked me to evaluate, and slipped it into its black self-destruct container and broke the seal and let the acid go to work. Then I found myself standing in the middle of the room with the book in my hand again, not knowing why I was trying to read it. The weight of the most appalling depression was pinning me down, so at last I forced myself to move, and it was then that I did what I must have known I would do, sooner or later, and dropped the book onto the sofa and picked up the phone and rang Floderus.

3

DUCKS

''Perfectly true. Absolutely.''

Floderus grabbed the strap as the cab lurched past a bus. He'd asked me for a mobile rendezvous with maximum security and I'd picked him up in Carlton Street. Last night on the telephone he'd kept the conversation down to careful monosyllables; now he was more relaxed, though not much.

''I offered it to him because this is something we can't possibly touch ourselves, since we're government. So is the Bureau, of course. What on earth made you—''

''The Bureau can't touch it either?''

''Absolutely not. But what made you leave?'' I went on looking out of the window. Floderus tugged a sleeve back, shooting cuff. ''Sorry. Not my business. Coming in with us?''

''Not bloody likely.''

A brief laugh. ''Things aren't *that* bad, you know. We leave the top-level people more or less alone, and you'd be one of them, naturally. I personally run Chepping and Shahan, among others. They're pretty wild.''

The cab slowed as a troop of the Household Cavalry rode past, plumes bobbing, sabres bared, breastplates flashing in the pale sunshine. In a moment I asked: ''Have you seen him recently?''

"Who?"

"Pepperidge."

"Not for a month or two. Why?" His horn-rimmed glasses caught the light as the cab swung into Piccadilly, and for a moment I couldn't see his eyes.

"He wants to give me the mission."

Floderus watched me thoughtfully. "You could do it, of course. It's rather"—head on one side—"exotic. But why not come in with us and do something we could help you with? I'd look after you personally."

"Nice of you." Floderus was the assistant chief of his department, and notoriously choosy about the people he ran. "But your operations don't go near enough to the brink."

"We try to please," he said drily.

"It's a different kind of field. I need"—I shrugged—"you know what I need."

"You'll get yourself killed, one day."

"I don't want to die in bed." I gave it a moment. "Which foreign power is involved?"

He clasped his thin pale hands and stared down at them, the shadows of leaves in the early light washing over them as we neared the park. Then his head came up suddenly. "Look, if you want to take this one on, you'll have to do it exclusively through Pepperidge. He's—"

"With your sanction?"

"Absolutely. It's there for anyone to pick up. Anyone of your capability. But we've got to keep right out of it. Our department. It's the kind of thing the UK daren't get involved in—or be *seen* to get involved in."

"What makes it so sensitive?" I wanted to get as much out of him as he'd let me. He was the source.

He glanced round to make sure the dividing window was shut, then leaned closer. "It's not only because there's an element of drug-running and the international armaments trade. South-east Asia is terribly complicated politically, and what you would be doing, Quiller, would be making an attempt to remove—or render neutral—certain elements threatening the balance of power in that region, including the potential risk of a confrontation between Western and Soviet forces in Thailand. We—"

"An *armed* confrontation?"

"In these days," he said bleakly, "*nothing* is impossible, after the disastrous failure of the summit conference. This isn't just the Cold War anymore: it's the freeze."

"Potent stuff. Where did this thing come from?"

"My department was approached by a foreign power in that region via the diplomatic bag. You would be working for that power, but the success of the mission would benefit the UK, and of course our ally the United States. Not to say world peace." He leaned back.

"It doesn't sound like my kind of operation. It's too geopolitical."

"The *background* is geopolitical, yes, but that wouldn't concern you operationally. In fact it's very much your kind of thing—the very careful, clandestine infiltration of a major opposition network." He tugged a sleeve back. "But why don't you go and talk to Pepperidge again before you decide? I'm due at the Travellers' in ten minutes, and you'll want to be on your way." He turned to the window to find out where we were, and slid the glass panel open. "Driver, you can put me down anywhere here." He turned back to me and said softly, "We haven't made contact, as I'm sure you understand."

"I've booked you out," Pepperidge said, "on Singapore Airlines Flight 297, change at Bombay, first class." He threw another crust for the ducks. "All expenses paid, though not by me. The hotel in Singapore isn't very posh, but there's a good reason. It's tucked away in one of the market streets, and you might want to make it your base."

Crouching beside him, I held the paper bag while he dug for another crust. A light wind came across the lake, ruffling the surface; in the distance the flags above St

James's Palace made patches of crimson and gold against the gunmetal clouds.

"Not that one, you silly little bugger, you'll choke yourself. Wait till it soaks a bit."

"What about cover?" I asked him. "Access, liaison, communications?" I was instantly sorry, but couldn't take it back. This wasn't the Bureau sending me out. This was just the remnant of a once-talented shadow executive, shrugging off a mission he couldn't handle himself. "Never mind—"

"I'm rather afraid," he said quietly, "you'll be pretty much on your own, old boy, this time."

"Of course."

"Take a little getting used to." A thin smile.

"Yes." I'd got a dozen passports and visas and border-franked papers in the safe and I could work out my own access once I was in the field, if I decided to take this thing on at all.

"The cover I'd suggest," Pepperidge was saying, "would be either import-export or some kind of weapons specialist. You'd get briefing on that, locally." He tossed the last crust at a pretty emerald-winged mallard and crushed the empty bag into a ball, stuffing it into his pocket. "As to access, they'll come to you, don't worry. It's all in there." He'd given me a sealed oblong envelope when we'd met. "As far as liaison goes, you'll have to pick a few people yourself, if you can find anyone you can trust."

He stood upright, and I noted the stiffness in his legs. He was out of training, an old man, for God's sake, and not yet forty . . . "I can't promise anything," I told him.

"Of course you can't. Just go and see them, and listen to what they have to say. If you don't like it, you're not committed—I gave them no guarantee." I caught a note of wistfulness. "You've nothing to lose: this trip's on them. Enjoy yourself."

I met him for the last time two days later, over a coffee in a Wimpeys along Edgware Road. As we came out to the street I told Pepperidge I'd drop him off on my way to the airport.

"Not to worry, old boy; I feel like a walk, do me good." He stood with his hands buried in the pockets of his mack as it flapped against his legs; a spring wind was buffeting through the streets, reeking of diesel fumes. "And listen, I"—his thin mouth tightened suddenly, then he made himself go on—"I haven't had a drink since the day before yesterday, and that's how I'm going to go on, if you take this thing over. I just"—a slack hand emerged, making a throw-away gesture—"just wanted you to know. And you'd better have this." He offered a card. "I'm renting a cottage in Cheltenham, not far from the GCHQ mast. The pubs around there are full of interesting info, of course, and if I pick anything up that might help you I'll pass it on. That'll be my number. Not my name, you see, it's the owner's, but just make a note of the number. I'll put in an answering-machine, all right? You can always leave a signal on it if I'm out sweeping for data in the pubs." One of his wintry smiles. "Tonic water and Angostura, that correct? God, not a festive prospect, I must say."

A double-decker swung past, blotting out the sky, its exhaust drumming against a dress-shop window. "I've got friends," Pepperidge said, "in Cheltenham, of course." A note of pride redeemed. "If necessary I could possibly get a signal to you over the mast itself, through the British High Commission in Singapore." He looked away for a moment, then his yellow eyes came back to rest on mine, squinting against the wind. "Not quite the service you're used to. Sorry."

An hour and fourteen minutes later, at 17:51, I got out of my cab at the Singapore Airlines departure point at Heathrow. Another one pulled in behind and I checked the single passenger as a matter of routine.

Flight 297 taxied to runway 9 half an hour later and then got held up while an executive jet came in. We were cleared by the tower at 18:24 and got airborne seven minutes after the scheduled departure time. The evening sky was almost clear, with a scattering of cumulus along the south horizon and the windsocks hanging limp.

Nine hours later in Bombay, waiting to change flights, I picked up a copy of the *Times* of Singapore and found a seat in the departure lounge. In Kuala Lumpur a top National Front leader had yesterday called for an end to unbalanced pro-Malay government policies and urged Prime Minister Datuk Seri Dr Mahathir Mohamad to crack down on corruption. In Bangkok, Thailand's new military commander, General Chaovalit, had ordered the army and its nationwide radio and television networks not to play politics in the coming general election. In Singapore, a government minister had accused police officers of being too strict, and suggested they should mix more freely with the public they served. Fights among teenagers in coffee-shops and at *wayangs* were becoming more violent, following the increasing practice of "staring down" in order to provoke attack, which had yesterday led to a twelve-year-old boy's ear being severed by a knife.

There was nothing in the paper to do with drug-running or the armaments trade. After twenty minutes I left my seat and picked up a copy of *Glitz* at the gift shop and went aboard Flight 232 for Singapore at 08:36. I was almost the last on.

During the flight I reread the instructions Pepperidge had given me, memorised their main points, and went forward to the toilet, tearing the three sheets of faint-ruled paper into small pieces and flushing them in the pan. As I went back to my seat a stewardess was pulling the curtain closed between the first-class and coach sections after pushing a drinks cart through. I notched my seat back a little and relaxed, slipping from beta to alpha waves.

There were a couple of moles, of course, digging away in SIS. It could be that.

"Would you like some champagne?"

Almond eyes, heavily shadowed; an exquisite silk kimono, ochre shot with emerald, a pattern of white cranes, a few stitches gone at the shoulder seam.

I shook my head. "Are we running on schedule?"

She glanced at her thin jade-faced watch. "Ten minutes early. We should land in Singapore in about three hours from now, at 1 P.M. local time. Is there anything I can bring you, sir?"

"Nothing." Patchouli on the air as she passed behind me.

It hadn't been Floderus who'd told me about the moles: everyone along the grapevine knew it and a lot of them couldn't sleep at night. They were having a swine of a time trying to find them, and until they found them they couldn't tell how much damage was being done. So it could be that. One of the moles had caught wind of the mission Floderus had been offered. Or Pepperidge had talked too loudly, in a pub or somewhere.

I wasn't totally surprised. Even at the clearance and briefing stage of any given mission there could be vibrations picked up and passed on for what it was worth, however tight the security. Last year they'd got on to me very fast indeed, moving in and having a go at me before I even left London, smashing my car against the Thames embankment and putting me into hospital. This time they'd picked me up almost as fast, but this was just low-key passive surveillance, one man with a black dress-bag for camouflage. I hadn't been looking for anyone; I'd just been checking the environment as a matter of routine, and the Asian with the bag—the one who'd got out of the cab behind mine at Heathrow—had turned away a couple of times in the departure lounge in Bombay, avoiding eye contact, and I'd followed up at once, heading for the men's toilet and fading before he got there. He'd panicked right away, checking the toilet *and coming straight out again,* not terribly professional.

At the moment he was somewhere back there in the coach section.

There was no actual problem. He wasn't strictly a tag: he wasn't trying to find out where I was going—you can't shadow someone and hope to get a seat on the same flight at the last minute if that's where he takes you. This man had just been told to make sure I got to Singapore without changing flights and finishing up somewhere else, where they'd never find me again. I couldn't shrug him off until we landed, and in any case I knew now that there'd be others, waiting at the baggage claim: they wouldn't leave it to one man to keep track of me through terrain as tricky as Singapore.

Action later.

Sticky heat against the face as we went through the walkway, then there was the cool of the air-conditioning again. I behaved precisely on cue at the baggage claim, checking no one, taking my time, chatting up a nice little American girl and helping her pull her two streamlined cases off the carousel.

In the cab outside I told the driver to take me to the Marina Bay area, and when we were moving along Fullerton Road I leaned forward on the seat.

"What's your name?"

"Ahmad." A big grin. "How are you?"

I passed him a US$50 bill. "Let me have your card. And head for Chinatown."

"This money not enough. Hundred dollar fare."

"Listen carefully, Ahmad. I'm going to leave my bags in your care. Drop them at your office and make sure they're kept safe. I'll pick them up there in an hour, and then you get another fifty."

"A hundred. I can't—"

"Ahmad. Look at my eyes in the mirror. Do I look like someone you can bullshit?"

His eyes met mine, then he looked away.

"What place you want to go?"

"Keong Siak Street."

"Okay."

When we got there the other cab was still close behind us but I hit the door open and dropped, pitching between two fish stalls and ducking under a bead curtain, scattering birds near a grain merchant's cart, the wet noon heat against my skin and the smell of sandalwood on the air, sandalwood and lamp oil and fish and curry and incense, a voice yelling out in Malaysian as I dodged past a medicine man and under a flower stall, finding an alley and lurching among bicycles and cane-work and dustbins, coming out into New Bridge Road and stopping the first cab.

"Chong Street, off Boat Quay." I slammed the door shut. "Not this way—through Cross Street. When's it going to rain, for Christ's sake?"

"Maybe tonight, cool things off."

"Jolly good show."

4

PARTY

The screams were coming from the room next door and I went into the passage. The door was locked so I shouldered it open and it swung back with a crash and I saw the woman standing on the windowsill, clutching the thin canvas curtain.

The window was open and she let go of the curtain and began tilting forward just as I got to her, pulling her back into the room. She started screaming again in Chinese, beating at me with small cold fists, her half-starved body naked under the cheap cotton wrapper, a huge mole standing out on her stomach.

"What's up?" Al said from the doorway.

"She was trying to jump out of the window."

"Ta-men sha-fsu le wo ti erh-pzu!"

"Take it easy now," Al said. "Six in the morning, for Christ's sake, you'll wake everybody up." He ran this place, the Red Orchid. "They hung her son," he told me, "over there, dawn this morning. Let's get her onto the bed."

She went on struggling for a minute and then suddenly went slack, and we laid her down, pulling a blanket over her thin ivory body as she went into a paroxysm of shivering. I went and shut the window, drawing the curtain to keep the brightness out.

"We were all praying for him," Al told her, "all of us. Take it easy now."

He sat on the edge of the bed and stroked the woman's thin untidy hair as the sobbing began, worse than the screaming had been, the quiet desolate sound of a breaking heart.

"What, then?"

One of the kitchen boys stood in the doorway, white slivers of wood from the smashed frame scattered around his feet.

"Get Lily up here," Al told him. "Lily Ling. *Now*-la!"

The boy flapped away in his rubber sandals.

"A fucking rope," I heard Al saying softly through his clenched teeth, "they gave him a fucking *rope*." He went on stroking the woman's hair, his face bunched and his eyes flickering. Voices began in the narrow street three floors below, the rattle of carts, a man's sudden laughter.

"You want me, boss?" Lily Ling.

"Yes," Al said. "Stay with her, okay?" He stopped stroking the woman's hair, looking relieved, a man awkward in the presence of suffering. "Stay with her the whole time, Lily. Don't leave her unless you get someone else in here to take over."

The Chinese girl came and sat on the bed, taking the woman's head in her hands, laying her face against the other's. "What happen?"

Quietly Al said, "She tried jumping out of the window. So watch her, okay?"

"She Mrs Seng. She say a man come to see her, maybe. Last night."

Al's mouth tightened. "And did a man come?"

"No."

"Good." He relaxed again, touching my arm. "Let's go, I feel like a drink."

In the bar he said, "They swung a few guys over there this morning. Like I said, he was one of them. Her son."

"And the man who said he'd come to see her?"

His eyes went hard. "Those bastards move in whenever there's trouble. He'd have told her he could pull strings, see, get him off, get him just a prison term. He'd have taken her life savings." He broke off to call to a boy going through the lobby. "Mahmood—there's a door needs fixing up there, number 37, okay? Go and check it out, need some tools." He poured himself another Scotch. "Three ounces of heroin and they get a life term over there. Four ounces and they swing. Malaysia's trying to beat the drug problem and I guess that's the way they do it. Month back they swung a couple Australians, you read about that? Everybody sent in an appeal—the Australian prime minister, Amnesty International, Margaret Thatcher. Those boys were caught with just six ounces of the stuff, they weren't trading a truckload, but they swung." He hit a mosquito that had settled on his arm, leaving a smear of blood. "They give it a lot of publicity, so people are going to get the message—they'll give these kids headlines in the evening papers over here." He took a swig at his drink. "Her son couldn't read."

The sound of boots came from the lobby.

"Police!"

"Shit," Al said under his breath, and went to stand in the archway. "So what's up?"

"Somebody reported a woman screaming."

"They're always screaming."

The young cop stood there hard-faced and angular, sharp creases in his uniform, the holster shining. "They said the sound came from this hotel."

"Sure. People laughing, it sounds the same. Always a party going on at the Red Orchid, right?" He shook his head. "Anything wrong, I'd know it, okay?"

The Chinese stood looking around the ceiling, waiting to hear if the screaming came again, and when nothing happened for a minute he gave Al a bright stare and then turned on his heel and went out through the swing door, his polished boots clumping and his leather belt creaking, his cap set dead flat on his head. Other sounds came in from the narrow street: cyclo bells, chickens, someone beating a gong. Then the door swung shut.

"Tell me about the drug scene," I said to Al, "in this region."

He swung his head. "All of it? Jesus, take some time."

Two days later the rain came pelting down out of a black sky with a noise like massed drums on the roof of the car. The windscreen wipers were only just clearing the glass enough for the driver to see through, and from the rear seat I watched the thick steel-grey haze on the bonnet as we crossed the river and headed for Orchard Road.

The Thai security man sitting next to the driver said something to him, a quick word or two, and the driver nodded without turning. They were professionals, these two: they'd come to the Red Orchid on foot to meet me because the market street was too cluttered for the embassy limousine to pass, and as soon as I'd come into the lobby they'd hijacked a cyclo and put me into it to keep me more or less dry, hurrying alongside like well-trained bodyguards to where the car was parked, checking the environment the whole time while the cyclo bell cleared the way.

It had been like that yesterday when the two embassy officials had come to find me—two, not just one, both stone-faced, asking me for my identity papers first and then presenting their own with a curt formality before they gave me the embossed card. *His Highness the Crown Prince Sonthee Sirindhorn requests the pleasure of your company at 8 P.M. on the evening of April 15th, 1987, at the Embassy of Thailand, on the occasion of his birthday.*

Obviously the man hadn't contrived to celebrate his birth precisely two days after this lone spook had landed in Singapore; the Thais had simply thought it a good opportunity to bring me into the centre of things and check me out from there. Pepperidge, tossing the last crust into the lake, had said, "As to access, they'll come to you, don't worry. Just go and see them, and listen to what they have to say. If you don't like it, you're not committed—I gave them no guarantee.''

Jesus Christ, he called that *access?* On the other hand there was no actual mission running yet. I'd done all I could do for now: I'd seen the shadow someone had thrown across me on the flight into Singapore and got rid of him, and since then I'd put the Red Orchid through routine analysis and found it safe—there was no covert or overt surveillance on the place, no bugs, no manned observation vectors, no one in the bar watching the fly-blown mirrors, no one cooling his heels in the street outside, nothing. I'd also got a lot of information on the South-east Asian drug scene from Al. From what he'd told me about his background he seemed a safe man to talk to, inside the parameters of my cover; otherwise Pepperidge wouldn't have sent me to the Red Orchid. *But how reliable was Pepperidge?* Good question. ''As far as liaison goes, you'll have to pick a few people yourself, if you can find anyone you can trust. Not quite the service you're used to. Sorry.''

The car slowed, passing a line of others and slotting in to a roped-off space outside No. 370 Orchard Street, the building ablaze with light, the Thai flag floodlit but hanging like a wrung-out dishcloth in the downpour. Umbrellas everywhere, bouncing off each other as the security man snapped open a big one above my head and steered me across the flooded pavement and up the steps, our shoes already waterlogged before we got inside, two white-haired diplomats tugging off their macks with the help of the embassy servants, peeling off their galoshes—''Hello, George, where did you moor your car?'' Gusty laughter, drinks in the offing, ''Where's Daphne, isn't she here?'' A gold cufflink came off with the mackintosh sleeve and someone dived for it. ''Her mother didn't feel like turning out on a night like this.'' A man with a mole, an Asian, suddenly close, watching. ''Then you're off the hook, old boy—make the most of it!''

An Asian with a small mole below the left ear, now speaking to one of the security men and then melting, not glancing at me, a bit embarrassed, probably, he should have kept up with his assignment a little more efficiently between the fish stalls and under the bead curtain and past the grain merchant's cart and through the alley full of bicycles and canework and dustbins into New Bridge Road. But it was reassuring to see him again: I knew now that it hadn't been some kind of opposition cell that had thrown him across me on the flight out; it must have been the Thais who'd sent him over to London to shepherd me across and make sure I wasn't got at. Civil of them.

The security man took me smoothly through the crowd of people under the dazzling chandeliers and edged me into the receiving line ahead of the rest, only three in front of me, the Crown Prince sporting a sash and cluster, his hand moist with sweat—

"How kind of you to come, Mr Jordan, and at such short notice!"

"A pleasure, Your Highness, and allow me to offer my congratulations."

The security man steered me deftly away and collared a flunkey with a tray of champagne.

"Something soft."

It took a bit of time and I eased my way to the silk-panelled wall and stood with my back to it, noting five or six more people from the Old Country, mildewed dinner-jackets and pinched-in satin, a shoulder-strap hanging down over a plump powdered arm; a small contingent of Japanese keeping close formation, beautifully tailored; a couple of Filipinos standing stiffly with set faces, not touching their drinks—Radio Singapore had put out a news flash just before I'd left the hotel: a major coup on the part of the military was in full swing in Manila; a group of Chinese, all smiles, and some Frenchmen arguing energetically about cheese—"*Pas possible dans ce climat, pas du tout possible de le garder en bonne condition!*" Four or five turbaned Pakistanis and a lone African in uniform and a rather tense-looking girl in a green button-through dress, her face pale under the chandeliers.

"Canada Dry, Mr Jordan."

"Thank you."

"This way, please."

He took me down a long corridor lined with portraits in gilt frames; a potted palm ten feet tall stood at the end under a domed ceiling; then we were in a small ornate anteroom with a circle of brocade chairs and a polished mahogany side-table with a copy of the *Times* lying on it, and someone's horn-rimmed glasses.

"Please wait here, Mr Jordan."

"All right."

Jordan had been the name on the papers I'd got from the safe in my flat in London; they'd offered the nearest cover to the one Pepperidge had suggested. Martin Jordan was an overseas representative for a small arms-manufacturing company in Birmingham: Laker Foundry.

The security man had left the door open and I could still hear the distant murmur of the reception, but it only accentuated the stillness in this small room, which I found encapsulating, unnerving. There was no mission running yet and there might never be, with me in it, if I felt like turning it down; but Pepperidge and Floderus knew the kind of thing I liked doing and they wouldn't have sent me out here to waste my time. At this day's end I could be moving into something dangerous, something terminal.

"Mr Jordan, I appreciate your coming to see me."

He was a small, bland, hesitant man, his eyes half-hidden behind tinted glasses, his hand outstretched, his body turning sideways a little to a limp as he approached. Two other men came into the room with him, aides, not bodyguards, and one of them said quickly—"His Highness Prince Kityakara, Minister of Defence."

"How do you do, sir."

"How do you do. Now let's sit down—there's no one with you, Mr Jordan?"

"I came alone."

"Excellent." He looked around quickly. "Let's shut the door, shall we?" He had a restrained Oxford accent and his speech was jerky, a little breathless. "This is Captain Krairiksh of Interior Security, and Major-General Vasuratna of Military Intelligence." He crossed his legs. "We shall understand perfectly, Mr Jordan, if your knowledge of the political scene in South-east Asia happens by chance to be slight. It's a small corner of the world, of course."

"I don't take long to learn." Pepperidge hadn't put any political briefing in the envelope and there was no point in taking a crash course because even that would need several weeks. Kityakara would have to pick the flesh off and give me the bare bones.

"Excellent." His hand dipped quickly to a pocket and tugged out a small inhaler, whisking it across his mouth and slipping it back. "I'll endeavour to give you the essence, then. Do you want to take notes?"

"No."

"Very well. We'll do what we can to put things into perspective."

He spoke for more than an hour, asking Krairiksh and Vasuratna to fill in the picture from their points of view and breaking for questions on the way. It didn't seem, I thought, to be much different in South-east Asia than anywhere else, a scenario of territorial fear at the brain-stem level and a general atmosphere of dog eat dog.

"Now let me try to put all *that* in a nutshell, Mr Jordan." Kityakara got up and limped across to the black marble fireplace, using sleight of hand again with the inhaler. "Soviet Russia is at present subsidising the Vietnamese armed forces in Laos and Cambodia to the tune of five *billion* US dollars a *year*. In return the Vietnamese permit the use of the naval bases in Da Nang and Cam Ranh Bay by the Soviet Pacific Fleet." He let a moment go by. "Those bases are vital to the Soviets. *Vital*."

I tilted my chair back until I was balanced comfortably, listening to Kityakara and at the same time wondering about the asthma and the limp and the tinted glasses. A lot of people of his age in this area had been lucky to come out of the Khmer Rouge holocaust alive, even those in power, *especially* those. He was one of them and he'd come through a nightmare, so how paranoid was he, about the Vietnamese, about the Soviets? I'd need to find out, because paranoia always distorted the facts.

"Now, since the Soviets took over those two former US bases in 1979, they've added five submarine dry docks and installed underground fuel-storage tanks and anti-aircraft batteries, so that in terms of its sophisticated electronic arrays the base at Cam Ranh Bay is one of the most important Soviet communication and intelligence-gathering facilities outside Russian territory. The aircraft carriers *Minsk* and *Novorossiysk* have made port calls, and those two bases alone offer the Soviets all the elements of a naval warfare strategy in South-east Asia—torpedo and cruise-missile strikes from aircraft, submarines and surface ships, linked by a land-based communications centre. Would you care for some tea?"

"Yes."

Vasuratna opened the door and spoke to the guard outside.

"The Soviets, then," the Prince said when the door was closed, "are holding a very strong position in Indo-China, bearing in mind the estimated number of 'advisers' here—seven thousand in Vietnam, three thousand in Cambodia, and two thousand in Laos. But the main concern of my government—given this background—is that by invading Cambodia, Vietnam has moved its borders west, right up to our doorstep." He whipped the inhaler across his mouth, and it confirmed what I'd noticed since he'd first come in here: that he used it whenever he was saying something that made him anxious. "That makes us nervous, Mr Jordan. Very nervous. The disastrous failure of the summit conference last month—with its critical heightening of international tension—and the increasing accord between the United States and China, where three US ships of the 7th Fleet actually made port calls last October, together with the first signs of nationalistic restlessness of the Vietnamese as erstwhile hosts to the Soviet fleet, *all* threaten the Soviet position in the Pacific."

He broke off as a white-jacketed steward brought in a massive silver tea-tray and put it down. Prince Kityakara lifted the lid of the heavily chased teapot and sniffed. "Lapsang Souchon—would that suit, gentlemen?"

I tilted my chair back again and watched the ceremony of pouring. A *Soviet* connection in Indo-China? I hadn't been ready for that.

"Lastly, Mr Jordan, there is this. Thanks to the increasing supply of arms reaching the rebel forces in Laos and Cambodia, those countries are approaching the brink of civil war. This of course would normally be seen as advantageous; we would hardly view the overturning of communist power as undesirable. But no one can predict the extent of the bloodshed that would ensue, or the critical increase of Soviet power in Indo-China. Milk? Sugar?"

"No."

"It's not unlikely, you see, that if the Soviets decided to support the Vietnamese in an invasion of Thailand, we might be forced to invoke the terms of the Rusk-Thanat Agreement of 1962, under which America is pledged to support us—militarily. The Agreement is an executive, not a treaty, but it is valid and extant. We have the option of invoking also the Manila Pact, which *is* a treaty, and extant." He sipped his tea, and I noted the slight shaking of his hand. "What we are talking about, Mr Jordan, is a possible military confrontation between Soviet and US forces. The first in history."

I stopped rocking on my chair.

By the window, Major-General Vasuratna uncrossed his legs, looking at no one. The other man, Captain Krairiksh, was watching the Prince, his hands locked tightly together on his lap. In the courtyard outside the rain fell steadily, ringing on something metal, perhaps the shade of an ornamental lamp. I remembered the quiet, urgent voice of Charles Floderus, inside that London cab. *The background is geopolitical, but that shouldn't concern you. This is in fact precisely your kind of operation—the very careful, clandestine infiltration of a major opposition network.*

The objective, then, didn't involve making a critical document snatch or bringing a hot spook across a frontier or digging out a mole. It involved defusing an East-West *military* confrontation in Thailand.

And Floderus had offered a job like this to Pepperidge? Something wrong.

"And such an event," Kityakara was saying quietly, "should, I feel, be energetically avoided."

I got up and paced, needing movement. Something wrong, yes, or maybe the people in London hadn't realized the size of this thing. Maybe Kityakara had played it close to the chest, and just asked them to send someone out. "But that couldn't actually happen," I told him. "I mean the actual engagement of Soviet and US *forces* on Thai soil."

"Not quite that, Mr Jordan." His cup rattled on the saucer as he put it down. "But *any* element of armed confrontation, with East-West tension as high as it is, could bring about a cataclysm."

"By escalation?"

"Yes. By a naval vessel's going off course at the wrong time and the precipitate order for a carrier to send up its aircraft and finally someone's finger on the button in a missile silo and the sheer lack of *time* to use the hotline and call a halt." Inhaler. "Once inertia has been overcome, Mr Jordan, in whatever field of experience, the momentum is difficult to stop. It has happened before, in two world wars, and it took everyone by surprise. Perhaps this time"—he shrugged uncertainly—"we can avert the third."

I waited, then said: "Does that complete the background, sir?"

"That completes the background. And it seems to me, and to my advisers, that the best way of preventing catastrophe is to re-stabilize the power structure in the region, to discourage the rebel anti-communist forces and render them incapable of overturning the present regimes in Laos and Cambodia. This can be done by cutting off their supply of arms and equipment.'' He picked up the teapot again, but got nothing more than a dribble. Captain Krairiksh got up at once and made for the door, but the Prince stopped him. ''It doesn't matter.'' He finished the dregs in his cup. ''Unfortunately the supply of arms and equipment has been increasing of late, and substantially. We've been allowing a steady trickle across Thai territory from China, of course, and that will now be stopped. But the greater part of the increasing supplies has been coming from five major international sources, funnelled through *one* distributor in South-east Asia. And that distributor is very powerful. So far, we've been quite unable to effect counter-measures.''

''What have you tried?''

''We've tried negotiation, by offering a high government post, with its attendant advantages. We've tried threats, including vigorous legal proceedings. We've tried massive police action in the hope of discovering drug shipments alongside the armaments, without success.'' He glanced to the door and away again. ''And we finally tried assassination.''

I moved my head. ''Who was the target?''

''The chief of the organisation.''

''How many attempts were made?''

''Three.''

''And?''

The Prince hesitated, then looked at his chief of military intelligence. ''You know the details better than I do. Would you—?''

Vasuratna sat to attention. ''Sir.'' He turned to me. ''We decided the only way was to make a personal attack on each occasion, but this organisation is extremely capable of defending itself. The first of our agents was dropped off the tailboard of a truck outside the gates of the presidential palace, full of bullets. The second was dumped outside Police Headquarters with signs of having been rigorously tortured. We have not found the body of the third agent, but his head was delivered to my office in a cardboard box.'' He looked down suddenly. "They were my best men, very experienced, very efficient. I have accepted the blame, of course."

I realised he was no longer speaking to me, but to Kityakara.

So here was the mission, if I wanted it.

"You're not expected to blame yourself," the Prince told Vasuratna. "We're up against someone exceptional this time."

"Who is it?" I asked him.

"A woman. Mariko Shoda."

5

YASMA

"Here for long?"

"I'm not sure yet."

"Come and see us at the Commission. Always something going on, lots of parties."

"How nice." I gave him a nod and turned away, finding a gap in the crowd and using it.

I'd left Kityakara half an hour ago and he'd wanted to give me an escort to take me back to the Red Orchid, but I'd said no. On the face of it the mission they had to offer looked feasible, and at this stage I didn't want to be seen around anymore with security men. In any case I wanted to stay on a bit here and check out the guests to see if I knew anyone. Pepperidge: *As far as liaison goes, you'll have to pick a few people yourself.*

I'd already noticed Mason, DI6, backed up into a corner with a glass of champagne; he'd been doing a little reconnaissance work from time to time, moving in to some Arabs in the thick of the crowd and standing with his back to them, tuning in. He hadn't picked up much, by the look of things. A stringer for the *Telegraph* was near the staircase and I would have gone over, because the man had done me a good turn a year or so ago in Hong Kong; but he was deep in chat with a stunning young Eurasian girl and I didn't want to spoil his fun. There wasn't, in any case, all that much chance of finding anyone at an embassy party who'd be any use to me in this kind of mission, if I took it on. I'd need people I could trust with my life.

I'd asked Kityakara: "What decided you to call on London?"

"It was a joint decision." The Prince had asked the other two men to leave him in private with Mr Jordan. "Major-General Vasuratna," he told me when they'd gone, "has run some very successful operations in the past, but those three agents are on his conscience. Last week one of his aides found him sitting at his desk with a gun to his head." He leaned forward on the edge of the brocade chair, his slight body at an angle. "I have no one else capable of undertaking a task so critical—and so dangerous. To attempt to get anywhere near Mariko Shoda is like walking through a minefield. I want you to understand that."

I gave it some thought. "Did you know I was coming here personally?"

"No. We simply asked for someone of the highest capability."

"How did you contact London, sir?"

"I approached the Foreign Office."

"Directly?"

"No, through your ambassador in Bangkok."

"In a personal meeting?"

"Yes."

"Was there anyone else present?"

"No one."

"Did he contact DI6?"

"I'm afraid I have no idea. I was told he would find someone if he could."

I got up and went to the window. The rain had almost stopped, and there was only the sound of dripping from the flooded gutters under the eaves outside. There were things I didn't like about this whole setup. I'd moved into the field across dead bodies before, though I'd always taken a lot of persuasion because they might have messed things up when they were alive—in this case the opposition had been alerted three times already. I was still prepared to go in, if I could find some kind of access, but it worried me that I'd been offered this mission by sheer chance, and by a burnt-out spook with a gutful of worms.

I didn't like it. I didn't like it to the extent that as I sat facing Prince Kityakara in the silence of the little room I could feel the hairs rising on the back of my hands and that sour, familiar chill along the nerves.

"Why did you contact London, sir, instead of Washington, considering the background you've given me?"

"Major-General Vasuratna is well versed in the international intelligence field." He left his chair and limped to join me at the window. "He told me that the CIA tends to work as a team, often with paramilitary support. He believes, despite our lack of success so far, that it's still a case for a single agent going in alone, without attracting attention. You people have a certain reputation for that approach." He used his inhaler. "Of course, that might not be accurate, and in any case I'm not pressing you for a decision immediately. Give it your consideration, Mr Jordan, for a day or two, and then let me know."

"All right."

"At this stage I'll simply tell you that since you would be working for the Thai government on private service, we would expect you to name your own fee. And of course you would have unquestioned access to personnel and facilities in our security and intelligence services."

I'd stayed another ten minutes to let him end the meeting with some diplomatic small-talk, then shook hands with him and left him standing there in the ornate little room with a courteous smile and his eyes still hidden by his tinted glasses.

"Thompson, isn't it?"

"What?"

"Bill Thompson?"

"No."

"Oh. Sorry."

He weaved away, a pink hand wiggling in apology. By

this time people were starting to bump into each other, spilling their drinks.

On my way through the marbled entrance hall I checked for company and saw none: I'd told Kityakara I didn't want any and he'd understood. He was obviously—

"Could you help me?"

The girl in the green silk dress, her eyes dark, angry.

I stopped. "How?"

"Just see me into a taxi, would you?" She was looking behind her, without turning her head.

"Of course."

She took my arm and we walked out between the two uniformed staff and down the steps. The street was running with iridescent water under the lamps, and a boy was sloshing through puddles. Our feet were soaked and as I opened the door of the taxi for her she slipped quickly inside and began tugging a bright green shoe off.

"You'll be all right now?" But she just pulled the door shut and I stood back from the storm drain as the taxi pulled away. A last glimpse of her pale face through the window.

"Please excuse—Mr Jordan?"

A chauffeur in navy-blue uniform with the Thai insignia.

"Yes?"

"I have a car here, sir. Please this way."

I followed him along the streaming pavement and got into the limousine. The driver closed the door and went round to the front.

Shoes off, yes, a good idea. They felt—

"Good evening, Mr Jordan."

She was in the shadows, half-lost in the opposite corner, small, Asian, her voice childlike. Now she sat forward at attention, legs together, hands clasped on her lap, giving me a little bow. "My name is Yasma."

Asian hospitality.

I couldn't see her in detail even now; there was just the impression of liquid eyes set in heavy kohl makeup, the glow of ivory skin, and the scent of jasmine.

"I'm happy to meet you, Yasma." I leaned forward to

tell the driver to pull up, because I didn't like women being used as toys; then I let it go. "Where would you like to have dinner?" She'd be interesting to talk to for a while: she'd be informative on the local scene; then I'd get her a cab.

"Wherever it would please you, Mr Jordan."

"Is the Siam Garden still going?"

"Yes."

I told the driver and sat back. "How pretty you are, Yasma. Were you born in Thailand?"

"Thank you. Yes, in Bangkok."

"I was there once." Hunched over a loaded Husqvarna with a man's head in the sights, showing faintly in the aureole of the temple across the square.

"My family is there," she said softly. "One of my sisters is a dancer, with the Royal Thai Junior Ballet."

"You must be very proud." An exchange of the niceties, while the car ploughed through the flooded streets. *How can I get close to Mariko Shoda, can you tell me that?* Not really.

"Yes," she was saying later, "but tomorrow we shall have sunshine again, though it will be humid, of course."

"Sticky."

She gave a little laugh, covering her mouth. "Sticky, yes!"

I leaned forward again. "Driver, the Siam Garden's in Mosque Street."

"Yes, sir, but the direct way is flooded tonight. Always problem with storm drains there."

We swung left, going south.

"You live in England, Mr Jordan?"

"In London, yes."

"I have seen picture-cards. I would very much like to visit London."

"You'd feel at home—it rains like this most of the time."

The streets were narrower here, and the car stopped for a cyclo blocking our way.

"You are here in Singapore for long time, Mr Jordan?"

"Just a few days. It's an interesting—"

I broke her wrist like a dry stick but the knife had come close, ripping into my jacket and shirt and cutting the flesh before I'd caught the glint of steel in the gloom. Both rear doors came open and I shifted to my left because I was right-handed and could bring the force of my hip and shoulder against the attack from that direction but a hand locked round my throat from behind and I used a four-finger eye-shot across my shoulder and connected and heard a squeal of pain. I couldn't see much detail but there was the figure of a boy or a woman silhouetted in the open doorway on the left side and I got purchase for my hands on the pile carpet and thrust upwards with my right leg, feeling resistance and then the release as the target fell away. Kaleidoscopic glimpses of the interior of the car flashed across my retinae—the face of the driver above the seat-squab and the play of light through the open door from a street-lamp and the eyes of the woman Yasma, as bright as the blade that was rising again, this time in her left hand. The only sounds were the voices of women, two of them in pain and another spitting out a vicious tirade in what sounded like Khmer as I blocked the knife and curled my wrist and got a grip on Yasma's hand and turned it, forcing the point of the blade into her small shadowed face and feeling it meet bone and then go through to the hilt as something flashed above me and I twisted on the floor and rammed my body against the rear seat and felt a slash of pain burning into my rib cage from the side.

The driver was angled across the front seat-squab and lunging down at me and I used a heel-palm with a lot of force and drove his nose-bone upwards into the brain and then twisted again and thrust my body through the doorway on the left side, hitting shallow water and stone and lurching clear of the car and starting to run, but they blocked me, two of them, their fine-boned faces etched against the lamplight as they came for me in their black track-suits, their hands bright with steel and their breath hissing, the bitter-sweet scent of blood on the air and a man standing a little way off, shouting something in English, the shuffling of feet as people hurried away, the slam of a door in the distance.

My hands were wet with blood, theirs and my own, theirs because I knew I'd killed, my own because the pain in my ribs was flaring as the air got to the wound. I had time to see a knife driving upwards at my face and time to block the woman's arm and force a strong flattened half-fist into the throat, seeing her pretty mouth come open and the lamp-light glistening for an instant on her bright curved tongue as her eyes opened very wide to stare into the face of death as she came down like a puppet with the strings cut.

The other woman had turned and was running and I staggered up, slipping and lurching forward against a soft wave of resistance like deep water, my eyes losing focus and finding it again, seeing the woman's shadow fluttering along the wall this side of the street-lamp as she moved through the pool of light and merged with the darkness beyond. I kept going, driving my legs against the rising tide of resistance, my ears filling slowly with the high single note of a violin string, kept on going because I wanted to know who she was, who they were, and if I could catch her I'd make her tell me, but it was no go because the rising wave and the endless singing of the string were bringing information to me, *blood loss,* information to me that faded from my brain as the dark wave leapt and brought me down.

"Phone for you," Lily said.

"I'll come down."

They don't have telephones in your room at the Red Orchid, nothing so fancy.

I picked up the receiver in the bar and said hello.

"What sort of condition are you in?"

I froze. *Pepperidge.*

In a moment I asked him: *"How did you know?"*

Some people came into the lobby and Al went to meet them. I checked them through the archway: two middle-aged Europeans with slept-in clothes and Air France tags on their luggage.

I checked *everyone* now. Things had changed.

"I told you," Pepperidge said, "I'd keep tabs on you from here. The thing is, are you—"

"What was your *source?*"

Paranoia, perhaps. So be it. They'd come close to wiping me out.

"The High Commission, of course." He sounded pained.

"The High Commission doesn't know a thing about it. Singapore put out immediate smoke—there was *nothing* in the press and *nothing* on the air."

Short silence, then: "You're not thinking, I'm afraid."

Perfectly right. The Thai Embassy and Singapore had got in touch very fast because of the dead driver's uniform, and there'd been a British national taken from the scene to the hospital so they'd automatically signalled the High Commission.

"The thing is," I heard Pepperidge saying, "what sort of condition are you in?"

Stink of antiseptics.

"I'll need a few days."

You had some luck. Dr. Robert Yeo, surgeon. *You had some luck, you know.*

Good or bad? Lost on him.

They reached the radial artery. It was a good thing you were found and put into an ambulance in time.

Otherwise she would have picked up the telephone when it rang and they would have told her: *It has been done.*

Shoda.

The worst thing was the self-anger. Thrown into a hospital for Christ's sake with half my blood left behind me in the gutter before I'd even accepted the mission. It was just because this wasn't a fully urgent five-star Bureau operation right off the planning table with all the pieces in place: access, communications, liaison, and a director in the field like Ferris. I'd have been on my toes if London had set it up, I'd have been locked in to the approach phase with my nerves already running at mission-pitch—*no, that was just an excuse and that was how far-gone I was, making excuses for the inexcusable.*

Anger seething in my blood. Major-General Vasuratna: *This organisation is extremely capable of defending itself. The first of our agents was dropped off the tailboard of a truck outside the gates of the presidential palace, full of bullets. The second was dumped outside Police Headquarters with signs of having been mercilessly tortured. We have not found the body of the third agent, but his head was delivered to my office in a cardboard box.*

But this time there'd been some luck, or the fourth man would have stayed there with the rest of his blood pumping into the storm-drain and the ambulance wouldn't have used its siren on the way to the hospital.

Shoda. An eligible antagonist, certainly, for someone Kityakara had called "of the highest capability," for someone who might one day get back on his feet and find enough savvy to give him a single chance in hell of getting anywhere near her, anywhere near Shoda, rocking a bit, I could tell by the way the ceiling was tilting, rocking a bit, *You must expect to feel a little weak for a while,* I could see his point, yes.

Lean against the bar.

"A few days?"

"What?"

"A few days to recuperate," Pepperidge said, "or to make up your mind?"

"I've made up my mind, but I've also had a bit of surgery."

"What did they do?"

"Sewed up an artery."

"Then you'll need more than a few days." He sounded worried.

"That's my problem."

There was a short silence. I watched the two Europeans giving their bags to a boy and trudging after him to the stairs.

"You said you've made up your mind." He sounded cautious. "You mean to do it?"

"If they'll still take me on."

"Why shouldn't they?"

"I haven't made a terribly good start."

"From what I was told, you did rather well. Four dead on the field, that right?"

"I walked straight into a fucking trap, don't you understand?"

In a moment, calmly, "Steady as you go."

I took the warning. Even anger could blow those delicate stitches around that tube.

I gave it a few seconds, trying to centre. "I need some information. All I know that means anything at the moment is my objective for the mission." A thought occurred to me. "Do *you* know what that is?"

Short silence. "Not objective. Target, actually. Yes, I do."

"Can you tell me anything about her?"

"Bit of a bitch, so they say."

"I think she's got someone inside the Thai Embassy."

I heard a grunt of amusement. "She's got people inside every embassy in South-east Asia, old boy."

"This one's in the Thai secret service." The man on the flight out, the one I'd had to get rid of. I knew now that on the night of the embassy party he hadn't looked embarrassed when he'd seen me again: he'd just wanted to avoid eye contact with a man he'd set up for the kill.

"Are you going to tell them?" Pepperidge asked.

"No. I'll leave him intact." If I blew the man he'd only go underground and work from there while the opposition sent in someone else whom I couldn't identify.

"Look," Pepperidge said hesitantly, "I *could* get you someone out there to protect the rear. I mean, she's going to try again, and next time she'll want to make sure. I don't like—"

"No shields." They could be dangerous unless they were

first-class material and I didn't imagine this burnt-out spook could find me anyone like that.

"I know someone who's *very* good."

He was catching my thoughts. "It's safer for me to work alone. But I can use some information."

"What sort?"

"Any kind of close-focus analysis of the Thai secret service. I think I know who set me up, but it could've been someone else in their ranks."

"Just takes one little mole, doesn't it? I'll work on it for you. Anything else?"

"Nothing I can't dig up here." I'd be doing a massive research job in the field as soon as I could find the right people to work with.

"Fair enough, old boy. Now take care, won't you? Take a *lot* of care."

An hour later I set up the night-defence system I'd worked out since I'd got back from the hospital, blocking one of the narrow beds against the door with the other one jammed sideways between it and the chest of drawers, clear of the only exposed vector through the window and across the alley where anyone could use a rifle from the rooftop.

It was too early to go to ground. Normally I would do that, drop into the shadows and operate from there, from safety. Pepperidge was right: they'd try again and the next time they'd want to make certain, driven by their pride and their Oriental fanaticism. I had a rough idea of what Mariko Shoda would expect of anyone who failed her—I'd heard in the hospital that a woman in a black track-suit had been brought in soon afterwards, found with a knife buried in the heart and her fingers still locked round the hilt. They'd come for me again, yes, but I'd still have to operate aboveground until I'd got the information I'd need to reach the target. Until then I'd have to move through the open, exposed.

I'd be as safe here at the Red Orchid as anywhere. I'd spent the whole day sniffing the place out like a fox in a badger's burrow, going from floor to floor and onto the roof and down the fire-escapes and into the basement, memorising distances, blind spots, alcoves, dead ends, doorways, until I could go through the building at a run and with five seconds' head start and get clear and survive, if they came for me here.

It was midnight before I slept, lying on my left side because of the long knife-wound that had slashed across my back from the right shoulder to the spine, the heel of the right hand swollen from the thrust to the driver's face, the other wrist throbbing under the dressings where the walls of the artery were slowly knitting, the blood pumping rhythmically through it to sustain the life in me that was already running out, if she had her way. Shoda.

A last thought before sleep, trying to betray me. Kityakara knew what had happened, and he wouldn't now expect me to take on the mission, so why not accept that, and go home, and live?

Because this was home, lying curled like a fox in the dark, unnerved and bloodied but with cunning still left for the morrow.

6

KATIE

"He was an absolute shit. Fantastic in bed, but that was all, and that was the trouble, I suppose"—she leaned across the little bamboo table, her thin shoulders moving forward, her eyes intense—"I mean sex isn't enough for a relationship, is it?" She forked some more satay off the skewer, dropping a piece of pork. "Do you think so?"

The girl in the green silk dress, today in khaki with a beaten gold necklace, her light hair swinging as she moved, moved constantly, restlessly, watching me hard, wanting to know what I thought. "Am I talking too much?"

I'd been coming out of the Thai Embassy an hour ago and she'd seen me and swung round—"Oh, hello, look, I'm sorry I was so—well, I don't know, *brusque* the other night." The night when she'd asked me to escort her to a taxi and then slammed the door on me without any thanks.

"I didn't notice." Then I'd suggested lunch because it looked as if she worked at the embassy or had some kind of connection with it, and that could be useful. I was parched for information and as soon as I could get what I needed I could go to ground, where it was safe.

"Love to." Her blue-grey eyes narrowed, focussing, taking me in. "What about Empress Place, on the river?"

Sitting next to me on the torn plastic seat of the cyclo she'd filled me in. "The divorce was only a couple of months ago and he still thinks I'm ready to hop into bed with him again—taking it in turns with his bloody *mistress,* thank you very much—and that night he was half-seas over and if you hadn't got me into that taxi he'd have pushed me into a corner and torn my clothes off—God, doesn't that sound sordid! But that's why"—twisting round on the seat and putting a thin ringless hand on my knee—"that's why I didn't even have the grace to thank you, because I was furious. Or scared, I'm not sure which." She took her hand away. "I'm Katie McCorkadale."

"Martin Jordan."

"Of course. Everyone's talking about you."

The nerves tightened. "Where?"

"At the British High Commission—that's where I work. You were almost killed, weren't you?"

"So they told me."

She stared into my eyes, beginning to say something and changing her mind and saying instead, "How did you manage not to be?"

"Bit of luck."

The cyclo lurched between a taxi and a standing bus and she grabbed the rail. "I was terribly upset when I heard the news."

I said carefully, "There wasn't any news."

"What? Oh. I know. I mean when I heard from my boss. There was nothing in the papers the next day, and that puzzled me. Who are you, actually?" Another level stare.

"I wondered, too," I said, "about the blackout."

"It came from the Thai Embassy, I know that. We traced it through. Their ambassador phoned the Singaporean minister for home affairs and asked him if he could hush the whole thing up."

"Well, this place has got a good reputation for safety in the streets, and tourists read newspapers."

"It could be that." Her eyes didn't leave mine. "But it wasn't. Was it?"

I didn't say anything.

"The Chief of Police was also requested to pursue his

enquiries with the utmost discretion, in the interests of the state. I quote."

Which explained why there weren't a whole drove of people from the Homicide Squad waiting round my bed at the hospital.

"I don't know how these things work," I said.

"No?" She blew out a gentle laugh. "There's something else that intrigues me. I'm pretty certain you're the first man I've ever met who can deal with five assailants armed with knives. And smartly."

"They weren't very good."

She laughed again and said, "Do you mind the Empress? It's only a food centre, but you can pick and choose among all the hawkers, absolutely anything—Chinese, Malaysian, Indian, whatever—and they bring it to you cooked. Or do you know all this—have you been here before?"

"Just passing through. The Empress sounds fine."

The place was crowded when we got there but some people were just leaving. It was a corner table not far from the river and I spent the first ten minutes sweeping the environment, simply as a matter of routine because there were upwards of a hundred people in this area and if any one of them wanted to do anything with a gun I couldn't stop him. But it was going to be safer for me in the open until I could go to ground. Shoda didn't want to make any fuss: the limousine thing had been set up carefully to provide discretion. My little Yasma had been meant to kill with the first thrust, and afterwards my body would have been buried deep in a rubbish dump and the car would have gone back to the hire company.

Shoda would have been very upset by the agitation at political level, in spite of the news blackout, and the next time she'd order the subtlest kill she could think of. But that was an assumption, and assumptions are dangerous. As I sat talking with this reasonably attractive but rather chatty girl at the rickety bamboo table my nerves were crawling, just below the skin.

"You take everything in, Martin, don't you?" She pulled

another kebab out of the basket and skinned the skewer. "I mean you actually listen."

"You're so interesting."

She gave me another stare, then looked down suddenly. "Not really. I talk like a bloody—" She shrugged, her thin shoulders coming forward. "I've made it a rule, you see, not to bore my friends—I mean about *him,* Stephen. And you turned up as an absolute stranger, and I suddenly felt like letting my hair down."

"It looks nice like that."

Two Asians watching me from the table twenty yards away, twenty-five yards, tough, track-suits, intent.

"Actually," Katie said, "the wounds are still raw. It hasn't been long. Do you remember that film? *A Married—* no—*An Unmarried Woman?*"

"I don't think I saw it."

They looked down, not away, when they saw I'd made contact. I didn't like that. But there were quite a few track-suits among the crowd; I'd seen joggers in the park on the way here.

"They were just walking in the street, in New York. She was Meryl Streep—no, Jill Clayburgh. She's asking him about where they ought to go for their holiday, and he suddenly tells her he's met someone else. And I mean it was a *long* marriage. And she doesn't say anything, or I don't think she does. All I remember is that she just goes across the pavement and throws up into a rubbish bin. God, what a script."

Perhaps I shouldn't be wary of *men* in any case, but of women—women in black jump-suits. She might use women exclusively in her death squads. But I glanced across the two men over there at short intervals. And others: the short Burmese standing with his back to the rail with the river behind him and his head turning in this direction every so often, and the two thick-necked Mongols on the far side of the flower stall: they weren't anything to do with it because they never spoke to the merchant; it was just good available cover.

The skin crept at the nape of the neck. Aftermath of the near-death experience. Discount. But don't discount *entirely*.

"Well that was how I felt, you see, when he told *me* the same thing—Stephen. Only I didn't throw up. I just turned and walked across the street and nearly got killed by a taxi, and do you know"—she was watching me hard with her eyes narrowed to make sure I was listening—"do you know the thought that flashed into my mind as the thing came hurtling so close to me that it tore my dress? I was hoping I was going to die because then he'd be tortured with guilt for the rest of his life." She shrugged, and her thin shoulders came forward. "So I suppose I must have loved him, to hate him that much."

"How long ago was it?"

"Three months. Three months and two days."

"And how d'you feel now?"

"Better for having got it off my chest for the thousandth time to a virtual stranger." She puffed out a laugh. "You're a patient man."

"I'm glad I could help."

"Can I have some more *sake?*"

I got her some from the stall. The two men in track-suits were leaving, not looking back. They could have been looking at Katie, fair-haired and slender.

When I sat down again she said, "The reason why I was so terribly upset that night, you know, the night when you helped me at the Thai Embassy, was because I realised later that when I slammed the door on you like that I was leaving you to go to your death, or damned nearly. I would've been almost the last person in this world you'd have spoken to. It gave me the willies—I didn't sleep much afterwards." She put her hand on mine for a moment. "I'm so glad you're all right. Who were they, anyhow?"

"I don't know. No one I recognised."

"So you don't know why they attacked you?"

"No."

The Burmese was a plain-clothes man. I'd got his

attitude down now, his movements. He was watching a group of Chinese at another table, not me.

"You must have some idea," Katie said quietly. "Was it to do with your Thai connection?"

She'd only seen me twice, but each time it had been at their embassy. "Possibly." It was time to see what she could give me, apart from the pain of a smashed marriage. "You asked me just now who I was. I'm a weapons specialist."

"I know. Representing Laker Foundry."

"You checked with Immigration?"

"We certainly did, after what happened to you."

She'd become quiet, attentive. Maybe this was her real self, intelligent, serious, now that she'd got the Stephen thing off her mind.

"So it could have been Shoda," I said. Either she'd pick it up or she wouldn't.

Her eyes were suddenly intense and she straightened on her chair. "Mariko Shoda?"

"Yes."

"Why should she want to kill you?"

"Have I got your confidence?"

"You can take my word, for what it's worth."

"How much is it worth?"

"It's priceless." She wasn't smiling.

"All right. We've found a leak at the factory. One of our ultra-special weapons has been reported missing. In fact, twenty or thirty prototype models. We put out immediate feelers, and our friends in the Thai government said they'd seen this particular weapon being used on a target range in Laos."

I waited. I'd given her enough to get a lot more back, if she wanted to talk.

"Whose target range? Which rebel group?"

"The Thais don't know, but they think it could be one of Shoda's." I was using some of the briefing Pepperidge had given me, and some of what I'd heard from Kityakara, but from now on I'd have to feel my way.

She sipped her *sake*. "Are you selling this weapon to the Thais?"

"We're negotiating terms, one of which is that we don't sell it to anyone else in South-east Asia." Whatever I said, Kityakara would back it up if necessary: that had been agreed.

"If it's so special, Mariko Shoda would certainly want to get at it." She toyed with her heavy gold chain. "The people who attacked you were women, weren't they?"

"Except for the driver."

"She uses women for her bodyguards, I know that."

"What else do you know?"

"About Mariko Shoda?"

"Yes."

"Not a great deal. But I might be able to find someone who does. I mean"—she levelled her blue-grey eyes at me with that characteristic stillness—"you're going to need all the help you can get, aren't you? She won't just leave it at that."

I was watching a short, compact woman now, not in a jump-suit but a chongsam. She looked too athletic to be wearing silk, too butch. She'd glanced across me two or three times from fifty feet away, near the sushi bar. But it was just my nerves: if there were any kind of surveillance on me it'd be from behind.

"The kind of help I need," I told Katie, "is information."

She turned her head to watch a Greek freighter moving past the docks on the river, her eyes narrowed in thought. "What I know most about is the drug trade. It's part of my job to keep tabs on it for London—we're trying to help cut off the supplies. But look, if you think your special weapon—what's it called, or is it classified?"

"The Slingshot."

Pepperidge had said it was already in the press.

"All right, if you think it's reached Laos illegally, what are you doing in Singapore?"

"They wanted to meet me here."

"The Thais?"

"Yes."

The woman in the chongsam was making distance-contact with someone else, someone I couldn't see, lifting her head slightly, her gaze oblique, oblique in this direction. In the language of the trade it could mean several things, but one of them was, *He's over there.*

The Greek ship gave a blast and the sound brought sweat out on me.

"Are you all right, Martin?"

"Relatively." Katie didn't miss much.

"You must still be a bit sore. You smell like an operating theatre."

"Doesn't turn you on?"

"No. But everything else does." Her thin shoulders came forward again as she folded her arms on the table, looking down for a moment, thinking, then raising her head to look at me. "Aren't you absolutely scared out of your mind?"

"Fraction edgy."

"God, I've never been so close to so much *drama.*"

I said quickly, "I don't think you're in any danger, Katie. I'm the one they want."

"I don't really think I care." She was looking over my shoulder now. "In my job, life is so bloody—"

I waited, but she left it, looking down again. "You really ought not to have any more *sake,*" I said.

She blew out a soft laugh. "It's always my undoing at lunchtime. But it never makes me say things I don't mean. Now look, if you want to know about the weapons trade out here you'll have to know about the drug scene too. They're sort of interlocked. The game's the same in South America and Turkey and everywhere else—drugs for money for guns. Only here, of course, it's on a massive scale. Do you want this now, or some other time?"

"When d'you have to be back?"

"This is my day off—I was just delivering a note to the embassy. So, to put the whole thing into a nutshell, the power of the drug traders is just too big for anyone to break them. We're talking about half a trillion US dollars in annual sales—I said *trillion*. And the alliances between the dealers and the drug-producing countries are equally unbreakable. The dealers—the big ones—have got more money than most of the governments in the world, and they've got their own shipping fleets, air transports, and even their own armies. And the *governments* of the drug-producing countries can't be got at either. I can give you a whole file on this from my office, if you like—I mean Xeroxed, but I'm just trying to—"

"This is exactly what I need. The nutshell." I had to take shortcuts wherever I could find them, on my way to ground. I was living on borrowed time.

"All right." She wiped the tip of her finger round the sake cup and licked it. "I mean, Reagan and Thatcher and other world leaders have to give the people circuses—you know, the war-on-drugs bullshit—but what else can they do? They can't arrest foreign governments for producing drugs when they've got political treaties and trade agreements with them." She was looking behind me again, her eyes ranging. "Thailand and Burma are the big centres here, as I'm sure you know. I mean there are some very ritzy clubs around in the major capitals where most of the members are growers, refiners, couriers, dealers, middlemen, pilots, you name it. But what interests you is the arms connection. I'll—"

I was standing over him and he looked frightened to death, his eyes very wide and his mouth open, and it took a second before I could cancel out the whole operation and get things back to normal, though I knew it'd take much longer than that for the adrenaline to shut off and the nerves to come down from their high. It had just been the noise, that was all—he'd dropped a metal tray and it had touched my left shoulder, just lightly but enough to trigger me, and then the organism itself took over and I had a sensation of flowing light and a series of stop-action photographs—the background swinging down as I was suddenly on my feet and then his face and body superimposed in close-up—the ear, temple, neck, the vital targets—while my right hand was moving so fast that I felt the air-rush even on its way up. The reflex was still building up its force but the left brain had started doing some very urgent work and the motor nerves of my right arm got the signal just in time and the braced half-fist stopped an inch short of his neck, even though the necessary imagery was still flickering in my mind: the knuckles moving through the sinews and crushing the carotid artery against the spinal column.

Everything had slowed down and for a while we just stood there in a clumsy tableau, the Chinese in a half-crouch with his eyes staring up into my face, my arm fixed at an angle and my body leaning over as the force died away and the first breath came and sounds filtered into the consciousness and movement started up again.

Faces in the background, watching. Other still figures, people poised in whatever act they'd been performing, a hawker with a basket, three women caught in mid-stride with their mouths open, a small child staring upwards with a doll in its hand.

"I'm sorry," I said.

He was relaxing and straightening but not trusting me yet. I picked up his tray and got my wallet out. There was a whole spill of mangoes and papayas and oranges on the ground and my small bamboo chair was quite a long way off. "Sorry—I made a mistake." I gave him a S$50 note and he stared at it for a moment before he took it, gingerly. "A mistake," I told him, "all right?"

Katie was standing up too and I took her arm and she went with me between the little tables and the hawkers' stalls and the trunks of the trees, neither of us saying anything. Of course I was making a big deal of it in my mind because of the security situation but in point of fact the whole thing had happened so fast that no one had actually seen the details; all they'd seen was a man standing up from his chair and accidentally knocking some fruit out of a hawker's hands. But the rule is to get away, fade, leave as little as possible in people's memory. Creating a scene is not terribly good cover.

We stopped to talk for a moment under a magnolia tree at the edge of the park.

"Is that the most help I can be?" Katie asked me. "Just to get information?"

"Yes."

Her eyes didn't leave my face. I had the thought that she wanted to catch the memory of what I looked like in case she never saw me again.

"I was watching the crowd," she said, "behind you."

"I know."

"I don't want them to find you again."

"Maybe they won't."

The woman in the chongsam was just at the edge of my field of vision, a blob of colour in the distance.

"A good source of information," Katie said in a moment, "would be Johnny Chen."

"How much can I trust him?"

"All the way." She wrote on a slip of paper and gave it to me. "You can find him there. And take this." She wrote on an official card. "That's my flat, in Victoria Street. I'll be home all evening."

I got her a cyclo.

"You're not coming with me?"

"I'll walk. It's the other way."

She touched my arm. "Martin, you already know how dangerous Mariko Shoda is, so shouldn't you just call it a day?"

"I'm committed."

She compressed her lips. "I see."

When the cyclo started off she looked back once, but didn't wave.

I began walking, and after ten minutes the woman in the

chongsam was still with me, and after an hour there were two of them and I used right angles, windows, crowds, cabs, and any kind of cover that would give me five seconds and a vanishing point, but I couldn't lose them, and at the end of another hour there were three, so it hadn't just been nerves, not just nerves.

7

JOHNNY CHEN

"Who are you?"

I didn't move.

"My name's Jordan."

Lamplight fell slanting across the rough timber wall.

"What do you want here?"

I couldn't see him. He was behind me.

"Some information."

"But why come *here?*" He dug into the psoas muscle.

"Katie sent me."

"*Sent* you?"

"She told me where to find you."

The balcony was thirty feet up and there was nothing I could do anyway. By his tone he wasn't playing.

"What name did she tell you?"

"Johnny Chen."

He began whistling softly, no actual tune.

My face was still bleeding from the flying glass.

"Open the door."

I turned the loose brass handle.

There was low light in the room, and a smell I couldn't identify, a chemical smell.

He patted me down. "Get over there, face to the wall."

Crates everywhere, crates and rope and a cluster of jade

vases, a Buddha. The light brightened as he switched another lamp on. Pictures of aeroplanes on the wall, photos of crashes.

He was dialling.

Perhaps I'd got it wrong, or she'd got it wrong, and I wouldn't be able to trust him, or trust her. This wasn't Bureau. Feeling my way through the dark.

The blood itched on my face. It had taken me another two hours, nearly till sundown, to shake the tags, and even then it had needed luck: I'd gone into an office block and gained enough time to get round a corner and wait. It had worried him, this particular tag, and he was running flat out, his rubber-soled track-shoes squeaking on the marble floor like a bird chirping, and when I tripped him he spun in a twisting arc and smashed through the glass door like a bomb, fragments flying. It was luck because they hadn't had time to cover the rear entrance.

"Johnny. Look, there's a guy here says his name is Jordan."

American accent, Oriental tonation.

"So why didn't you call me to say?"

Someone gave a sigh, or a yawn, not Chen. I wanted to stop the itching but he wouldn't like it if I moved. He wouldn't have put the gun down yet.

"I was in Laos." He raised his voice. "Okay, turn around."

He was sitting in a bamboo chair with his flying-boots crossed on a table, half desk, half table, the gun on his lap. "What's he look like?"

I took in what I could, a low divan with rumpled clothes in the shadowed corner, more crates, bamboo furniture, mostly chairs, some cheap handmade rugs. It was a cavernous place, a warehouse, only two doors, no windows.

"Let's have a snort!"

It was by the river, with the river smell mingling with the chemicals. Unrefined opium, as a guess.

"Okay. But Katie, don't ever send anybody here without *talking* to me first. But you're beautiful." He put the gun onto the table and sat upright. "Sure, see you around."

He rang off and threw me a packet of cigarettes and I caught it and threw it back. "Trying to kick it? Sit down, Jordan."

I took a chair near him. He was a full Chinese, scarecrow-thin, close-cropped hair beginning to gray at the temples, a weathered face, something wrong with one ear. *"Tsou-K'ai. Pieh ch'ao wo."*

The blankets on the divan moved and a naked woman rolled over and then stood up in the lamplight, ivory-skinned, tiny breasts, jet black pubic hair, walking to the inner door with her knees uncertain, like a young colt taking its first steps. She closed the door.

"She was starving," Chen said. "Pick 'em up for nothing." He lit a black cigarette with a gold tip from the packet. "So what's the story, Jordan?"

I told him I was with Laker Foundry, and about the leak.

"Let's have a snort!"

Parrot.

"So what precise information do you want?"

"I need to know as much as possible about Mariko Shoda."

He gave me a dead stare. "Mariko *Shoda* . . ." Smoke drifted under the lamp. "Jesus Christ."

A cistern flushed behind the wall. "Katie said you could tell me something about her."

"Mari-ko *Shoda* . . ." He got out of the chair, tall for a Chinese, walking like a cat, crouched a little, eyes on the floor, thinking. "What did Katie tell you about me, Jordan?"

"That you run a small freighter service and know your way around the South-east."

He nodded, straightening up, looking around the walls. "Sure. I fly everywhere. I flew with the Yanks in 'Nam, made good money—this is me here, come and have a look, my whole life history.'' He went on talking while he showed me the photographs, four of them of light-plane wrecks with Chen standing on the top with a big grin and his arm in a sling or a pair of crutches under him. ''What I'm doing now is kinda worse than those days in 'Nam, because you're strictly on your own and the name of the game is Russian roulette, you're due in at an illegal airstrip somewhere up there in Burma or maybe Laos and it's night and all they can give you is a couple of flares this end of the strip and it's thick jungle, Jesus, and maybe you're down to the last sniff of gas, even in the auxiliary tank, which is often just a waterbed inside the cabin with you, a potential fireball if you crash—and sometimes you're not sure the strip is still in friendly hands and you can go down into machine-gun crossfire, that's happened to me twice, look at this old crate, see the holes? But even if the strip is still friendly you can hit bumps or misjudge the flares or whatever, and there's a gentlemen's agreement—you're a helluva long way from any kind of medical aid out there so if you're trapped in the wreckage or it's on fire they just put a bullet in your head, like you do with horses.''

He led me back to the desk and we sat down. ''You use a drink?''

''Not just now.''

''So what happened to your face?''

''New blade.''

He laughed in his throat. ''You want to go clean up?''

''In a minute.''

''She's not still in the bathroom. So you want some information on—''

The telephone rang and he picked it up. ''At first light. Sure, if you can. What's going to be the ceiling over the coast?'' He listened and then said, ''Hell, no, I'm not putting down anywhere, they just hung another bunch of guys over there, did you hear about that?'' He listened again and asked for an updated met report and rang off. ''I don't ever do any trading, see, I'm just a transporter, I never take possession—that stuff over there is waiting for shipment, and anyway most of the freight I hump isn't drugs, it's arms.'' He got out of the chair. ''C'mon and take a look.'' A nail screamed as he levered one of the crates open and showed me neat rows of ammunition, perfectly stacked, the steel and copper glowing in the light. ''.223, 7.62, 9mm. Nothing to write home about in this batch; the more interesting stuff's in the other crates but I don't want to break the seals. Semi-automatics and some fully auto calibre .50's, mostly Belgian, and some very nice rifle-scopes from Hungary. And some inserts''—he kicked a crate with his ripped leather flying-boot—''put them in a shotgun and you can feed it with 9mm or .223 ammo, just the trick for your trigger-happy anti-communist citizens up north around Phnom Penh or Saravane. You want any stuff like that for trading on the side, you know where to find it.'' He went back to the desk again. ''Then there's other stuff that's worth shipping around, bit of gold, gems, things like that, cut a small profit when you can. You want some coffee, Jordan?''

''No, thanks.''

''Jesus, you must have some very interesting secret vices.'' He lit another cigarette. ''So you want some information on Little Kiss-of-Steel. Well I guess I don't have much but maybe it's more than most people do.'' He blew out smoke. ''She's still twenty-one, Cambodian, no bigger than this kid in here you saw just now, lives very simply and controls maybe forty, fifty million US dollars' worth of business every year, half in drugs, half in armaments. People who regard her as a friend give her presents—an apartment in London or Paris or New York or Tokyo or a palace in Rangoon, or maybe a yacht off Khiri Khan or a shipment of diamonds from South Africa. People who regard her as an enemy also give her presents, to calm her down—a permanent suite at the Manila Mandarin, gold ingots from Pakistan with her name carved on them, or a fleet of limousines. She moves around in privacy, using her own 727 and going through the VIP lounge with dark glasses on and a dozen bodyguards to keep people away, because she doesn't like being photographed.''

He got up again and unlocked the drawer of a massive Japanese lacquered cabinet across the room and came back with an eight-by-ten photograph and gave it to me. ''Rather a lot of grain, but the best I could do.''

I turned it in the light. ''This is Mariko Shoda?''

''That is Mariko Shoda.'' He sat down, leaning his arms on his knees, dropping ash. ''I was in transit in Saigon and I happened to know she was coming in, so I took a chance and hung around while my crate was being refuelled, and I was lucky, if that's what we're going to call it. She came out of her 727 without her dark glasses on and I had a zoom lens ready and bingo, isn't she pretty?''

The grain was so bad that I had to hold the picture at arm's length to smooth out the dots. It was a pretty face, yes, delicate cheekbones and large eyes, black hair cut like a boy's, a kitten's nose and small pointed chin. Her head was half-turned as if she suspected someone was watching.

''What was the distance, Johnny?''

''Two or three hundred yards. But whenever she lands anywhere, see, she not only has a whole bunch of bodyguards close around her—they're all women, by the way—but she has a whole lot more waiting around in the area, placed there before she arrives. One of them saw me take the picture. I didn't know that, but I wasn't taking any chances either so I mailed the film for processing right there at the airport.'' He shrugged. ''They got me that night, on the street. I still had the camera and they pulled it open and took the film that was in it—no problem, it was a new one, blank—and smashed the camera and then worked me over.'' He tugged one of his earlobes. ''This is my own, but the left one's a prosthesis they stuck on for me at the hospital. I hear Shoda very clearly with it—*no photographs, please.*'' He took the picture and said on his way to the cabinet, ''I can let you have another print, Jordan, if you want one. Nice pinup." He locked the drawer again and came back. "But tell me something—are you going to try getting *near* that gal?"

"Possibly."

He pursed his mouth. "That could be difficult. She'd have to want a meeting, and even then you should maybe think twice. She has all these bodyguards, but she does her own thing a lot of the time. People always tell me the same thing about Little Kiss-of-Steel—don't stand too close, and above all don't touch. They say you never feel it because the blade's so sharp. And she's very spiritual—she always prays for you before she kills. Of course, she may take a shine to you, but even then I'd be careful. She has a keen sense of the priorities, like the praying mantis."

The phone was ringing and he picked it up and spoke in Hokkein, which I didn't understand. I got up and went to look at the stuff on the wall—photographs, pinups, philosophical maxims—*There are old pilots and there are bold pilots, but there are no old bold pilots*—some faded lading bills with customs franking, a woman's black lace glove and a dried monkey's head and Player's cigarette packet with what looked like a bullet-hole through it and a lock of black hair in a blue ribbon. I wanted to know as much about him as possible, and particularly why he'd met me with a gun in my back and ten minutes later had shown me around the place without even telling me to keep my mouth shut. Did he trust Katie *that* much?

"The way Shoda works," he was saying, putting the phone down and coming over, "is something quite remarkable. She never goes out to public places like restaurants, and when she has to visit somebody like in downtown the most anyone sees of her is between the limo and the building, dark glasses and bodyguards and the whole bit—and those bodyguards are kind of cute too; have you heard of the Kunoichi?"

I said I hadn't.

"It's the deadly sisterhood of the Ninja, originally

Japanese. Like the geishas, they were trained in singing and entertaining, see, so they could get access into the household of an enemy warlord, and just when he'd gotten her nice and cosy in his arms he'd end up with an icepick through his ear into the brain—one of their favourite tricks, in my language the *ssu chieh wen*—the kiss of death. You know something? I was in Phnom Penh maybe around six months—"

A beeper sounded and he broke off at once and went to the desk and picked up his gun. "You just stay there, Jordan, I'll be right back."

He went out through the door where the girl had gone, not the one where he'd brought me in at gunpoint. So this was the alarm I'd tripped on my way up the outside staircase, and there must be another one covering the entrance he was going to check on now. I was tempted to get out of my chair and take a look at the crates and the other two desks and the Japanese cabinet but I stayed where I was because I didn't know this man yet, and I didn't know if he'd simply asked the girl beforehand to trigger the beeper and give him an excuse to get him out of the room so that he could see what I did while he was gone. I hadn't got access yet, the most vital phase of the mission, *access to Shoda,* and maybe he could give it to me.

He came back through the same door and went to the desk and dropped a small chamois bag onto it, using a key on the padlock. "Chu-chu!" The key stuck and he had to worry it. "Chu-chu, c'mon in here!"

She was wearing a cheap cotton shift now, and looked younger than ever, glancing at me and standing awkwardly in the middle of the room, watching Chen.

"Hold out your hand, sweetheart." He opened his own, palm upwards. "*Hand*—this thing, right?"

She obeyed him hesitantly, and he fished in the leather bag and dropped a ruby onto her palm. "A present, okay? Worth a thousand dollars, maybe more." He stood over her, pleased with himself, with her, with his gift. "You're my thousand-dollar baby.'' She gazed steadily at the gem; it was cut, polished, and glimmering on her palm, and I sensed the uncertainty in Johnny Chen now: he'd ''picked her up for peanuts,'' probably from a refugee camp on the Cambodian border or from parents who needed food for themselves more than their daughter's mouth to feed, and now she was his, Johnny Chen's, but he didn't know how to get through to her, and not just because of the language. Perhaps on an impulse he'd taken over a life, and wasn't sure what to do with it.

''Present, Chu-chu. Present.'' He circled his hands, awkwardly. ''Means I love you.'' He kissed her on the brow and touched her cheek and came away. ''You can stay here now,'' gesturing to the divan. ''Chu-chu stay, okay?''

She walked away with the gem held out in front of her, gazing down at its colour; I was aware of the softness of the nape of her neck, the back of her knees.

''Okay, she's just a kid,'' Chen said defensively. ''But kids like her get raped every day over there, up at the borders, in the villages. She doesn't get raped, she gets loved, okay?''

''I can see that.''

''Okay. So what's the deal, Jordan? You want to know if Little Kiss-of-Steel has this weapon you're talking about?''

''Very much.''

''If she doesn't have it, she'd sure as hell *want* it.''

''Have you ever seen one?''

''No.'' He toyed with the chamois bag. ''But I've seen some of the specs. I'd say if that thing got into the wrong hands in South-east Asia we could see the whole damn place go up. It can knock choppers out of the sky, right?''

''Any aircraft up to thirty thousand feet.''

The bag hit the desk with a soft thump. ''Thirty *thousand,* Jesus Christ. And hand-held? That's more than the Stinger can do.''

''By a factor of three.''

He thought for a while, his eyes down; then he pulled

another black cigarette out of the packet and lit up and looked at me through the smoke. "How long have you known Katie McCorkadale?"

"We've had lunch."

"You must have impressed her."

"Perhaps she's just a good judge of character."

"I guess. I mean, when Katie tells me I can trust somebody, it's for real. She's never been wrong."

"That's why you had a gun in my back."

"I didn't know you were from Katie." He picked some tobacco from his lip. "So I've told you what kind of woman this Mariko Shoda is. You still want to meet her?"

"It's why I came."

"Thing is," he said, watching me obliquely, "she doesn't want to meet you, right? Weren't you the guy in the limo, few nights ago? There wasn't anything in the news, but there's a whole bunch of grapevines in Singapore."

"She's got the wrong impression," I said. "I don't mean her any harm." That too was for the grapevine.

"Then you're pretty unusual." He straightened on the bamboo chair and picked up the phone, dialling. "Couple of months back," he told me, "someone dive-bombed a monastery where she stays sometimes, blew it apart. She wasn't home." On the phone he asked for Sam. "That gal has so many people who want her dead, she's kind of jumpy. I guess that's why she gave you the grief in the limo. Sam? How's things? Listen, do something for me. I believe there's a guy named Lafarge in town from Bangkok. He's due out of the airport some time in the next few days but I don't know which flight. I know he's made a reservation because I picked it up when I was coming through Anna Siang's office. Can you hit the computer for me?" He dropped ash into the jade bowl on his desk. "Okay, get back to me, Sam."

He put the phone down and crossed his spider-thin legs. "Like I was starting to say, I was up in Phnom Penh a while back and took a chance and checked out an illegal airstrip out of the city. We have to do that, the flyers. We need to know where the strips are and how to get in there if ever we have to—and you never know when. There's hundreds, see—make that thousands. Anyway, I happened to see some troops drawn up in some kind of a training camp, place was thick with barbed wire but you could catch a glimpse of what was going on. The guys were being reviewed by their colonel, as best I could see, a tiny little guy but absolutely impeccable, like they all were. Even from that distance I could see they were all officer rank, by the uniform. Then I kind of put a few things together—the location of the camp and the obviously elite performance going on, see, and then I got it. That tiny little guy was Mariko Shoda, because, believe me, there isn't another female colonel around in *this* neck of the woods. I mean, just to see the salute she snapped up—even at that distance I knew I was in the presence of real *style*. So that's Shoda too, she's—"

The phone rang and he picked it up. "Yes? Sure." He pulled a scratch pad towards him and got a pen from a drawer. "Okay. I have that, Sam. And listen, I never asked you about this guy, okay? I didn't even call you up. With the you-know-what connection, if there's any trouble it's going to be my ass. Or *head.*"

He asked about someone called Lee and said give him my best and rang off, tearing the top sheet from the pad and giving it to me. "Okay, Dominique Lafarge is a French-born naturalised Thai subject and he's booked out on that flight in the morning. He got himself naturalised because he works for Shoda and she calls the shots. From the grapevine *I* use, Lafarge has lived in Thailand for the past ten or eleven years and at present he's the major source of the weaponry flowing into Shoda's hands and out again to the rebel forces in Indo-China." He pressed his cigarette butt into the bowl. "I don't know what he's doing in Singapore and I don't know why he's flying to Bangkok in the morning, but if you asked me to make a bet I'd say he's very likely visiting his boss, because that's where she is right now." He got a fresh cigarette. "Make any sense?"

"This grapevine. How reliable is it?"

I hadn't expected this amount of luck, so early. I was desperate for access, because once I found a way in to Shoda and her organisation I could leave the deadly environment of open ground and go clandestine and that would give me a tenfold chance of survival. And it would give me the mission.

"The grapevine I use," Chen said, "is better than most. What I've just told you about Lafarge is true, vouched for. I'm in the arms trade, okay? I therefore make it my business to know the others. So if you aim to tag on to this guy tomorrow you'll at least know he's the right guy. But what's going to happen to you at the other end of that flight, God knows—and don't hold me responsible. You'll be moving into Shoda's territory."

I got up and walked around and looked at the photographs and the black lace glove and the dried monkey's head and the cigarette packet with the bullet-holes in it and then came back to talk to Johnny Chen and took a risk so big that my skin crawled.

"If I took that flight, I wouldn't want you to tell anyone."

He got up and crushed out a butt and stuck his thin hands into his hip pockets and shrugged. "It's your ass, Jordan, if anything goes wrong. But if anyone finds out you've got plans to take that flight, it won't be from me. I don't want your death on my hands."

I cleaned my face up in the small sandalwood-scented bathroom before he showed me out through the back way, down some stairs and across a freight-storage hangar and through a door leading into an alleyway stacked with emptied crates and rubbish bins and oil drums, with only one high yellow lamp at the corner of the warehouse.

"Happy landings," he said, and went back inside.

I spent thirty minutes checking the riverside environment

before I walked into the open street and kept to whatever cover I could find, trying to talk my way out of the half-knowledge that I was driving myself into a trap and talk myself into believing that I'd got access—access to Shoda, and that tonight the mission had started running.

8

FLIGHT 306

"Will Mr Martin Jordan please pick up the nearest paging phone?"

I didn't move.

It could only be Chen.

If I took that flight, I wouldn't want you to tell anyone. I don't want your death on my hands.

So it could only be Chen because only Chen knew I was here, except for the airline staff, and they wouldn't have me paged: they'd phone the gate desk. It could only be Chen, but the sweat had started running because I'd spent the last two hours securing the *whole* of the environment here—the check-in counters and the telephones and the snack bar and the gate area—because Gate 10 could be my way out of continuous and hazardous exposure aboveground and my way into the safety of clandestine operation, and I *had* to go through it clean.

All I could do now was use the soft-eyes technique and let the immediate scene come into the brain unfocussed and ask the memory to alert me to any change. There aren't many situations worse than finding yourself ten paces away from the break-off point between overt and clandestine and then have your cover name called out over a public-address system. I took my time, half a minute, but couldn't pick up any significant change in the movement around me: no one had turned on their heel within seconds of the PA call; no one had started to move towards me; no one was going to a telephone.

So I moved now because if I didn't they'd repeat the call and I didn't want that. I picked up the phone.

"Yes?"

"Is that Mr Jordan?"

Ice along the nerves. It wasn't Chen. It was a woman's voice. And that was impossible. Correction: not impossible, no.

He'd blown me.

"Please, is that Mr Jordan?"

A young woman's voice, Asiatic, Japanese inflection.

I was still watching the environment but with hard eyes now, focussing, remembering. They were my friends here in this small comfortable area, my good friends. The three Australians over there were booked to play in Bangkok in the international semi-finals sponsored by the Royal Thai Tennis Championships; one of them had just had a row with his wife and wished he'd had time to make it up before he flew: he didn't like flying. The party of four people near the snack bar were from Milwaukee; they'd done Hong Kong and they'd done Tokyo and now they were going to do Bangkok, including the Phrakaeo Wat and the Royal Palace and the Reclining Buddha, and Elmer had said if they didn't take home a half-ton of souvenirs he'd never let them set foot in the Kiwanis Club again. The two nuns by the gate desk were almost enveloping the teenage French girl in their black habits and she was no longer crying quietly as she'd been doing when I'd passed close to them twenty minutes ago; *Maman* had died at a hospital in Singapore yesterday and they were escorting her to Bangkok, where *Papa* was waiting for her; the body had been flown out last evening.

I knew a great deal about the rest of the passengers gathered here in the small comfortable area at Gate 10, enough to know that they were my friends, my good friends, if only because none of them was here to trap me into a shut-ended situation and set me up for the kill. The only one here who wasn't my friend was the voice on the paging phone.

"It is very urgent, please. Are you Mr Jordan?"

I didn't answer. I needed time. If I said no, or just hung up, I wouldn't learn anything, and what I might learn could save me. If I said yes they'd get here as fast as they could and might not be far away.

"We are now boarding passengers on Flight 306 for Bangkok. Will passengers for Bangkok please board at Gate 10."

Things I didn't understand. The woman was phoning because she believed, *they* believed, I was here. Then why didn't they come here for me physically? Because they weren't certain, or there hadn't been time. Time since when? Since Chen had blown me. *As far as liaison goes, you'll have to pick a few people yourself, if you can find anyone you can trust.*

Chen. Katie McCorkadale.

But I'd known yesterday the risk I was taking when I'd asked Chen to keep total security on my taking this flight, and here was the moment of truth. There wasn't a lot of choice. If I dropped the phone and got out of the airport I might not be in time before they came in, and I wouldn't learn anything, anything this soft Asiatic voice on the telephone might tell me. If I stayed here and said yes, this is Mr Jordan, I could be doing precisely what they wanted me to do: let her keep on talking to give them time to close in.

But this was a public place.

"It is very urgent, please. *Are you Mr Jordan?"*

This was a public place and there wouldn't be anything they could do until I tried to get clear at the periphery and there was a chance, a thin chance.

"Yes."

There was an echo, but not on the line, in the psyche.

"Mr Martin Jordan?"

"Yes."

I began watching the walkway area, where they would have to come.

"Will passengers on Flight 306 please board at Gate 10. We are boarding now for Bangkok."

I saw Lafarge going through with his two bodyguards. I'd seen them when they'd come into the gate area: Lafarge, dark, elegant, his initials on his pigskin briefcase, the case chained to his left wrist; his guards, unobtrusive, shut-faced, tough, trained. Others followed: the two nuns with the little girl; the Americans.

Watching the walkway, not taking my eyes away for an instant. They would not be my friends, when they came.

"Mr Jordan, you must not board that plane."

A man came running, a man in a track-suit with a flight bag, running towards me along the walkway, and I felt my nerves set, ready for preservation.

"Mr Jordan, do you understand? You must not take Flight 306."

Running hard but not towards me now, veering for the group at the gate—*"Hey Charlie, tell 'em to wait!"* Or they'll start the international semi-finals without you, my son.

So I mustn't take this flight. Why not, you little bitch? Sweat running.

"All passengers must now board Flight 306 for Bangkok at Gate 10. We are leaving in five minutes."

It tallied with the figures on the departure screen.

"Mr Jordan." She didn't sound impatient. She sounded concerned, emphatic. "Please tell me that you understand what I am saying. It is very urgent."

Not very. I've got five minutes.

I asked her: "Who are you?"

"It is not important, Mr Jordan. I have information that concerns your welfare. There will be an accident, do you understand?"

"What kind of accident?"

"To the plane. To Flight 306."

"Then you'd better tell someone. The pilot might be interested."

The timing was becoming critical, and I began watching the walkway half the time and the departure gate half the time. I didn't know if I could learn anything more from the soft, urgent little voice on the line, or whether this was all: that someone—Shoda?—was trying to stop me boarding the flight for Bangkok. The time gap was narrowing quite fast now and the best way I could use it would be to stay here on the line in the hope of learning something more, and wait until the girl at the gate began closing it—then get there, get on the plane. If anyone came along the walkway who looked dangerous I could go through the gate anyway and they wouldn't be able to follow: if they came here for me at all they'd be in a hurry, getting here while the woman kept me on the line; they wouldn't have time to buy a ticket.

"This is the final call for passengers on Flight 306 for Bangkok."

Two more people went through and the girl looked around the gate area for stragglers, checking her passenger list and finding one missing. There was nothing she could do about it. All she could see was a man using a paging phone.

"Are you still there, Mr Jordan?"

"Yes. What is the source of your information?"

"It is reliable. I am your friend, Mr Jordan. Please listen to me. There will be no survivors on Flight 306. You must not take it."

"All right, I'll go and warn the crew."

"They would not believe you."

"Any more than I believe you."

For the first time her voice had a note of impatience, the hint of a sigh. Not impatience, exactly. Resignation. "If you wish to live, Mr Jordan, you must not take the plane. That is all I can do for you."

Maybe if I told the girl at the gate I was officially working for the Thai government and showed the *laissez-passer* that Prince Kityakara had given me she'd at least tell the captain, but I still had no source to offer except a voice on a telephone.

"What kind of accident will it be? Is there a bomb on board?"

If I could give them any details they might listen.

"I must go now, Mr Jordan. I am sorry. *There will be no survivors.*"

The girl at the gate was giving herself a manicure, one panty-hosed leg crooked, her head tilted in concentration.

"I am going now," the voice on the line told me.

There was something getting through to me but I didn't know what it was; it was simply a feeling. There wasn't time to work out the dozen or so explanations for this call on the paging phone. A decision had to be made and it had to be made now and there was absolutely no reason to think that this wasn't a crude last-minute attempt to keep me here in Singapore and on treacherous open ground instead of going to the gate and apologizing to the girl and slipping through to the safety of clandestine operations, but I listened to the voice—not hers, not the voice on the line, but the one in my head, in the primitive brain-stem, the seat of intuition.

"I'm taking the flight," I said, on the principle that if you change direction you must cover your tracks. Then I put the phone down and went over to the gate and showed my Thai Government credentials and told the girl that I'd learned from an unidentifiable source that Flight 306 to Bangkok was compromised.

She phoned the agent at the other end of the tunnel and I was put on to the captain direct as I watched the starboard wing moving slowly past the window; the 727 was backing under tow and over the phone I could catch the copilot going through the routine checks with the tower. The captain asked me the expected questions and I hadn't got any answers. I told him that to satisfy myself I wanted him to know that an unidentified woman's voice on a paging phone had told me that his aircraft would "have an accident."

Two of the airline's officials came along to the gate and talked to me but there wasn't anything I could add and they finally told me that the security checks at this airport were the most sophisticated in the world and that I'd probably been the victim of a hoax. My name was noted and I was thanked for my concern.

Eleven minutes later I watched Flight 306 turn heavily at the end of the taxying road and line up with the runway and wait for the green and then gun up and start rolling. It was airborne at 10:17, on schedule.

It was then that I knew that because of touchy nerves I'd let Shoda set me up, and that my chances of seeing nightfall would have been infinitely greater on Flight 306 than here on the ground in Singapore where she knew how to find me.

She swung round on the staircase.

"Martin!"

Framed by the light from a high window, her hair still moving, her lips parted, her eyes wide, shadowed.

I said hello.

She came down slowly, not looking away from me, one foot faltering in its high-heeled sandal, her thin hand sliding down the banister-rail as if she were feeling her way. When she came down the last step she was still watching me, mesmerised; then she just took a pace and leaned against me with her head on my shoulder and stayed perfectly still. In a whisper, "Oh, thank *God.*"

I held her until in a minute she straightened up; her eyes were wet and she lifted a cupped hand, tilting her head. "Oh bugger, can you help me? Bloody contacts, they always float loose when I cry."

We found it in the palm of her hand and she got it back deftly on the tip of her finger, and I wondered how much practise she'd had, how often she'd cried, because of Stephen. She looked at me steadily again.

"Why weren't you on board?"

I didn't answer. There was a lot to work out.

"You *do* know it crashed, I suppose?"

"Yes."

It had been on the radio an hour ago. No survivors.

"My God, it's a miracle. I mean"—she brushed the air helplessly—"I was sitting there in my office today for about half an hour—for *exactly* half an hour, because I remember looking at the clock, sitting there *knowing* you were dead."

I didn't know if the timing was accurate, because I didn't know when she'd heard the news of the crash. But I wanted to.

"When did you hear about it?"

"About an hour ago. They said you'd phoned—"

"No. When did you hear it had crashed?"

She looked confused. "About—I'm not sure—soon after noon, I think."

"And when did you hear I was still alive?"

"I told you—an hour ago. Why?"

"And how did you know that?"

She was watching me with her eyes narrowing. "They phoned me. The people here."

One of the staff came down the stairs, a Thai girl, loaded with files, dropping a pencil. I picked it up.

"Thank you. Are you being helped?"

"Yes," Katie said. "I'm from the British High Commission." When the girl had gone she said, "There's a little office here where we can talk."

"No, let's go up there," I told her. There was a gallery on the floor above, overlooking the entrance and the staircase. Rooms, even small rooms, in embassies—even the embassies on friendly territory—are notorious for being bugged. We went up the stairs together.

Her timing was probably accurate, then, because as soon as I'd heard the news of the crash I'd phoned the Thai Embassy, because Lafarge was dead and my access was cut off, but there was a chance I could rescue just a thread.

"Why did the people here phone you?" I asked her.

She looked surprised. "Because you were on the passenger list."

There were windows along the gallery, facing the buildings on the other side of the street. The strong afternoon light streamed in, throwing thick shadows across the carpeting, glowing on some crimson leather-bound books. I sat clear of the window.

"How did you know I was on the passenger list?"

She pulled her soft briefcase closer to her on her lap, hesitating before she spoke, but not because she didn't know what to say, I sensed, but half-deciding not to answer at all. "Whenever there's a transport accident," she said deliberately, "we always check on the passengers, in case there's a British national involved, so that we can help relatives. I think we do quite a good job, at the High Commission, looking after our people."

It was very quiet here, and motes of dust floated in the sunshine; there were the distant sounds of a telephone in someone's office; Thai voices, muted; quick footsteps across marble. I supposed most people were at lunch at this hour.

"Why did this embassy call the High Commission to say I wasn't on Flight 306?"

She said carefully, "They're friendly to us. Thailand is an ally of the West." Her eyes were still narrowed, and I didn't think it was anything to do with the contact lenses.

"How did they know I hadn't gone on board?"

I knew, but I wanted to know if she did.

"They said you'd phoned them, to—"

"When?"

"A few minutes after the news came on the radio."

"Did they tell you why I phoned them?"

"They said you were going to be here."

"Who spoke to you on the phone?"

"I don't know. Or I'd tell you. It's odd," she said, looking away, "it's the first time someone hasn't trusted me. It makes me feel rather . . . sordid."

I realised I was aware of totally irrelevant things, the soft arch of her neck as she sat with her head down, the sharp outline of her nipples under the tan cotton shirt, her stillness.

"How long," I asked her, "have you known Chen?"

She looked up. "Who?"

"Johnny Chen."

"Oh. I don't know. I think about three years. Three or four years. Why? Didn't you find him helpful?"

"Not terribly. He suggested I should take Flight 306."

There'd been footsteps and they were coming closer along the gallery. It was one of the staff, all white blouse and navy blue skirt and heavy glasses. "Mr Jordan? Excuse me for disturbing you. It's Thai International Airlines on the telephone."

"Tell them I'll ring them back."

"They said it was urgent, Mr Jordan."

I'd been expecting a call. I said to Katie: "D'you mind?"

"You want me to wait for you?"

"If you've the time."

"All right."

In the girl's office I told the man on the phone that I'd nothing to add; I'd done all I could to warn the captain, and all I knew about the voice on the paging-phone was that it had been a young Asian woman's, possibly Japanese.

"Did she mention what *kind* of accident might happen, Mr Jordan?"

"Would happen. *Would.* As I told the captain and your airport officers."

"You must understand, Mr Jordan, that we have to do everything possible to trace that caller. We need to establish responsibility. This is a major disaster for us."

So forth, and understandable. But it brought back the scalding onrush of guilt I'd felt when I'd listened to the radio in Al's bar, knowing then that I should have *forced* them to hold that plane and search it.

I told the man, yes, he could send someone round here to talk to me, but I might be leaving soon. No, I didn't know if I'd be available as a witness at the enquiry.

Katie was sitting just where I'd left her, but hunched on the cushioned window-seat, her long legs drawn up and her arms round her knees.

"Thank you for waiting."

She didn't answer, glancing across my eyes, that was all.

"They don't know anything new," I said, and took one of the Louis chairs.

"Johnny Chen," she said in a moment, "is a drug transporter. Not a drug-*runner*. There's a difference. But even so, I can imagine how you're feeling. It's the second time you've escaped death in a matter of days, so you can't trust anyone. I can vouch for Chen, but what's the good of my word, if you don't trust me?"

"It's nothing personal."

She swung her head and looked at me. "Isn't it? Martin, you can't be DI6, or we'd have been asked to help you. But what—?" And she stopped right there, looking away again.

"Did Chen tell you I might take that flight?"

"No. Why should he?" She came unhunched and put her feet on the floor and sat hugging her briefcase, her shoulders forward, protecting herself. "Martin, do you think they were trying to kill you again?"

"No. They wouldn't need to blow up a planeload of people just to get at me. They'll come for me on the street."

She leaned nearer me, prepared to meet my eyes again after the anger. "I wish you weren't so bloody matter-of-fact about it. I also wish—" But she had the habit of leaving things unsaid.

Footsteps again, and I looked across at the staircase. This time it was Rattakul, the Thai security officer I'd been here to see.

"Mr Jordan." He stopped short, and I went over to him. "Your request has been approved."

"When can I leave?"

"Immediately."

"Give me two minutes."

"I'll be down there in the hall."

I went back to Katie, and found her with the briefcase open. "This came for you, Martin. From Cheltenham."

Long manila envelope, thick; diplomatic bag frankings. The only thing I could imagine Pepperidge sending me was a breakdown on the Thai security personnel, which was why he'd sent it to the High Commission instead of here.

He trusted her *that* much?

I took it from her. "I'm not sure," I said, "when I'll be back."

"Where are you—" she left it, looking down, zipping her briefcase shut.

I went down and found Rattakul waiting for me.

9

ASH

It was difficult to see clearly, with the gas mask on.

Who would warn me?

Voices were muted: there were no echoes here.

Most of them spoke in Thai, a few in American English.

A man was coughing somewhere, or crying.

Who would warn me?

It kept repeating itself in my mind, but there was no answer yet. It was important for me to know, simply as vital information; but apart from that, it was now being brought home to me what I'd missed.

Another yellow plastic bag was zipped shut and taken away.

We were north of Chathaburi, in deep jungle. A light breeze was blowing, taking the fumes away to the east. Upwind we could take our masks off and exchange information, but they had to be worn in the vicinity of the wreckage itself. Rattakul, the Thai intelligence officer who'd brought me out here, said it was raw opium burning, though God knew what opium was doing on a flight from Singapore to Bangkok.

There was mess wherever I looked: smashed bulkheads, seats, torn panels, windows, and lengths of white wire, thousands of lengths, miles of it, buried or half-buried in the churned, scorched earth of the jungle. Some of the bits and pieces were painted with yellow-green inhibitor that the fire hadn't reached, and had serial numbers on them; when you pulled just one piece of wire you'd unearth a tiny electronic component, a miniature junction or relay or fuse. I didn't pull at any wire, I'd just seen one of the wreckage analysis team doing it. I was here to hunt inside the unburnt forward section.

Flight 306 had come down windmilling, someone told me, cutting a swathe through the heads of the palm trees and the tropical undergrowth like a spinning scythe, and then the rear section had broken away and taken fire and was still smouldering, sending a whitish stream of smoke into the emerald green undergrowth, eastwards on the breeze. The choppers had come down in the clearing to the west, upwind of the wreck; there'd been five of them here already when our own had brought us in more than an hour ago—two Red Cross, a military, and two civilian machines. Work had been delayed because of the fumes: they'd sent one of the military aircraft up again to fetch the gas masks.

A young rescue worker, with no one to rescue, said there was a tiger half a mile to the east: he'd seen it as the chopper had come down. "If there's a tiger there," the American analyst had said, "then he's stoned out of his mind."

Another yellow bag was zipped shut and lifted by two men; one of them let his end slip from his hands and drop; he got it up again and they trudged off through the mess of torn earth and leaves and ash and soot, their boots tripping on the webs of white wire everywhere.

Who would warn me? I should have been in one of these yellow plastic bags now, but for the voice on the paging-phone this morning. *Who was she?* As a guess, she must belong to whatever group had brought down Flight 306. It had been a strictly clandestine action, and anyone outside the group wouldn't have known what they were going to do.

There will be no survivors.

Even with the gas masks we couldn't shut out the bittersweet smell of cremated flesh; it was heavy on the air before we put the masks on, and got trapped inside. Sweat was running on me, stinging and itching under the hospital dressings, and my left wrist burned. I didn't know if there were anyone here, among these twenty or thirty men, who'd been sent to finish me off somehow; I wasn't in good shape and it worried me. But I couldn't have stayed away: the death of Lafarge had cut off the access I'd hoped to gain, and if there were a new thread to follow I'd find it here.

At the end of an hour I'd covered the first row of seats in the forward section, picking carefully at the debris for the body I was looking for. It was going to take time because the explosion—the American analyst had said yes, there'd been an explosion first—and the windmilling action and the final impact had turned the inside of the plane into a maelstrom, and the fire had smothered everything in ash and silver-grey soot. You didn't expect to find people still sitting in orderly rows: the cabin was tilted almost upside down in the thick vegetation. It was worse in the rear section, where they were hunting for the black box, because of the fire.

Rattakul had presented his credentials to the chief of security here and got me cleared, and now he was covering me, watching everything as the rescue team worked alongside, their movements slow and their gloved hands gentle. There was no hurry now, and this was sacred ground.

I took a break. "Find out, will you," I asked Rattakul, "who everyone is. I'd like to know."

It was partly to get rid of him for a bit; he haunted me. But it would also be useful to know if there were anyone here who couldn't be accounted for; he'd have the authority to question them.

A chopper was taking off from the clearing, and the turbulence from its rotors stirred the smoke, swirling it in a vortex, and we put our masks on again. Silence came back when the machine had gone, an eerie silence disturbed by sounds muted by the echoless jungle: men coughing inside their masks; the clink of metal as someone used a fire-axe to clear the debris; the cackling of a monkey high in the tropical vines.

Rattakul came back in half an hour. "The Minister of Civil Aviation is here, and the chief of the National Transportation Safety Board, also the president of the airline. The rest are their staffs, the Red Cross workers, the rescue teams, and the wreckage analysts." He watched me wiping out the inside of the mask. "I've asked all of them for their identity cards, *all* of them."

"Thank you." He was short, compact, impeccably dressed in the ubiquitous khaki tunic and slacks, and had the eyes of a man I'd rather count a friend than an enemy. "Whenever a chopper arrives, check it out too, will you?"

I went back into the wreckage, helping one of the rescue team clear the debris from the seat area. At some time after the jet had come down the wind must have changed, because the whole of the front section was smothered under a pall of ash and soot, and as we picked gently at the shapes still hanging from the seat-belts or lying huddled or spreadeagled among the jungle leaves, we unearthed bright colours suddenly, the red of a child's T-shirt, the brash gilded cover of a paperback, the stripes of a silk tie. Sometimes—often, during the next hour—the rescue workers would stop and put their gloved hands together in brief prayer; one of them, working alongside me, just stopped moving and crouched there in the mess of soot and began shaking, and when I touched him he broke down completely and I led him away and left him with someone.

Then Rattakul came over, masked and beckoning, and I followed him through the swathe of vines, where men were working with machetes to clear them. When we could take off our masks Rattakul took me to talk to the American analyst, who was crouched over some kind of mess: that was all there was here, an asssortment of different kinds of mess.

"Hi. It was a bomb." He prodded fragments and pointed to things, one of them a man's head. "He blew himself apart with it, look at this, here's the central source of the blast, see these panels? His body's over there, no clothes on it, blew them away. No identification."

I was tidal-breathing; we all were; in the past hours the reek of death had been growing stronger. "What nationality would you say he was?"

"For me that's not so easy." He looked up at Rattakul. "I guess you'd have a closer idea."

"I would say Burmese." He crouched with us, narrowing his eyes as he looked at the head, the face; then he looked away and stood up.

"Why's it so undamaged?" I asked the American.

"It was the way the blast went, mostly into his body before it took off through those panels. His head was forced upwards and back from under the chin—see here, and this flap of skin."

"Why would a Burmese want to blow up this plane?"

"Be a drug connection, I guess, not political. The opium should've been unshipped in Singapore, but maybe there was a check in progress, so they had to ferry it back." He gave a shrug. "Listen, *most* major crime in this area is drug-connected, and there's intense rivalry."

I went back to the forward section and started work again. The thing was, how had anyone got a *bomb* past one of "the most sophisticated security systems in the world"? It could have been sheet plastic, pressure-detonated.

In the heat of midafternoon the mosquitoes came in, and the Red Cross people handed out citronella. Later they brought sandwiches and coffee, and we sat on the cool fibrous earth clear of the wreckage to take a break. A light plane was circling, with big red letters on it: *TV-2 Bangkok,* banking sharply to get the camera angles it wanted. Choppers were leaving regularly now, returning regularly, taking the bodies out and bringing in supplies—parka jackets, torches, tools. Every time a machine landed, Rattakul went across to it as soon as the rotor began slowing; then he came back to tell me who had arrived. Four priests were now among us, a Catholic and three Buddhists in saffron robes. Incense blended with the other smell, the thick, overall, inescapable smell; the wind had died and the freight had burned out under the fire foam; the air was still and sounds seemed louder, and we spoke even more quietly.

Towards dusk they found the black box and brought it clear of the mess, bright orange under the soot, and looking intact: it had been in the tail section but was fireproof. The American carried it to his chopper, tenderly; later he'd listen to the voices that had been silenced here among the trees as the big jet had come whirling through them from the sky, mortally crippled and carrying only the dying. It was easy to believe, as dusk turned to dark, that the spirits of the departed were stealing through the shadows thrown by the floodlights the rescue team had rigged—because we were tired now, and the stress of what we were doing had soaked us in our sweat; we itched all over because of that and the mosquitoes. Things had got worse, progressively, because the more ash and soot and debris we removed from the mess, the more we discovered of people, their faces, hands, feet, the colours of their clothes, the things that had belonged to them that had been so important, a nun's rosary, jade Buddhas with the price still on, a tennis racket—*Kangaroo King*.

Later the moon rose and the jungle held back a little, the shadows shifting as more lamps were rigged; the throb of the generator motors was constant, punctuated by the cries of birds and monkeys, restless and uneasy among the trees.

By midnight we were shivering, and the jackets were passed round. The night had taken on the semblance of a slide-lecture without sound as consciousness took pictures, sometimes out of sequence: a man flicking away a half-dead snake with a bamboo stick; a Red Cross worker standing perfectly still with tears streaking the soot-film on his face; a panel breaking away and a body falling to the jungle floor, groaning as the air was forced from its lungs—to be surrounded at once by a dozen of us, but that, yes, was all it was, just the air in its lungs.

By three in the morning we were working without any more pauses for breaks, because every time we took a rest we knew what we had to go back to, and it was easier to stay with it and get it over, though by now it seemed we'd been here all our lives, been born here just to do this, and would go on doing it, and never be done. Our eyes, fatigued and losing focus, had to keep on adjusting as someone moved a floodlight on its stand and the moon brightened and the landing lights of another helicopter flooded the scene and froze us in a silver-gray wash.

Then I found Lafarge.

He was flattened against a bulkhead that had been thrown thirty feet from the cabin section; his seat-belt had snapped and he'd been catapulted forward. It had taken an hour to clear the debris away from him and get a look at his face. I'd seen him at the airport and he was still recognizable, though his face was now ashen and his scalp had been ripped away. The briefcase was still chained to his wrist, and when I wiped the soot away I could see the initials D.J.L., heavily embossed in gold. His keys were in his pocket, and I tried the smallest of them first, opening the chain-lock and bringing the case away, the chain with it.

Rattakul took me across to the chief of the Thai police unit and I signed the necessary form, undertaking to return the under-mentioned passenger's personal effects, these being one leather briefcase and contents not herein identified.

Then we picked our way, Rattakul and I, across the web of white wires and the lamp-cables and the torn tree-roots to where our small military helicopter was standing.

"This is what you came for?" he asked me.

"Yes."

It was all he said, and all I said. We were dog-tired, dirty and depressed, and my mind kept shifting focus—from the comfortable air-conditioned gate area where the nuns had gathered the young girl to them, her pale face upturned, and the Australian had gone running past me—*Hey, Charlie, tell 'em to wait!*—shifting focus to the grey and shapeless grave that we were leaving behind us in the jungle night.

As the machine lifted and the pilot opened his set and

reported departure at 04:03, two thoughts came together in my mind. One was that Mariko Shoda hadn't ordered Flight 306 destroyed, because Lafarge, the chief source of her arms supplies, had been on board. So it had been someone else, and they might have ordered the bomber to carry out his mission for the same reason: that Lafarge had been on board, and on his way to meet Shoda.

So what worried me, as we headed south for Chathaburi, was that the briefcase that had been chained to Lafarge's wrist was now chained to my own.

10

VOICES

''This side's the Flight Data Recorder, which does pretty well what you'd think.'' The American wiped the bright orange casing with his soot-smudged handkerchief. His name was Bob Ryan. ''It records the time, speed, heading, and altitude of the airplane and every movement it makes—climb, descent, turns, gravitational forces, acceleration, stuff like that. This side's the CVR—Cockpit Voice Recorder. It picks up from a mike in the flight-deck ceiling—every sound there is, radio speech and ordinary conversation between the crew.'' He glanced at me with his red-rimmed eyes; it was now gone six in the morning and we still hadn't slept. Rattakul had talked to the chief analyst, a Thai, when we landed in Chathaburi, and arranged the meeting.

I wanted to know whether the crash of Flight 306 had in fact been ''drug-related,'' as the analyst had said, or not. It wasn't anything I could find out from the black box directly but it might give me a lead.

''The tapes run for thirty minutes,'' Ryan said, ''and then erase themselves. That's considered long enough to give us all we need to know about an accident situation. Often it's much less, maybe a couple of minutes or even a couple of seconds, like when they hit a mountain in the fog.'' Sitting slumped in the tubular-frame chair, he reached for the box again. "Okay, we'll just give it a whirl."

While we were listening I peeled off the Red Cross parka; there was no air-conditioning in the small cluttered office. Rattakul sat upright near the window with his hands on his lap, his eyes uneasy; on our way out of the jungle he'd told me he'd survived a major crash three years ago, and still had nightmares.

Altitude 24,000. Airspeed 250 knots.

Then there was some conversation in Thai, and I asked Ryan to give me anything important; he was fluent.

We heard some laughter, and I looked at the American, but his eyes were closed; his head was forward and I thought he might be dozing off.

Heading 347. Medium aircraft at nine o'clock, four miles, five to six thousand feet below.

I looked at the map on the wall. Flight 306 was at that time fifty miles or so north-west of Chathaburi, on an almost direct course for Bangkok.

Airspeed 250. We're descending to—

There wasn't a crump or anything but Ryan's eyes came open. It had sounded more like a break in the transmission, but now there was muffled noise coming in and he started translating from the Thai as speech broke out.

"That's the captain, telling everyone to stay calm. Says there's been an explosion and he's going to try putting the ship down at the nearest alternate."

There was a jumble of sounds and then the flight-deck door clicked open and a woman's voice came clearly.

"She says there's a hole blown in the cabin, oxygen masks are mostly in place, there's not too much panic."

But we were listening to screams now, one of them a child's. Then in accented English—*There has been some kind of explosion in the rear section of the cabin. We are losing height, airspeed, and directional capability. Please have Chathaburi give me a runway and—*

There was a break, then more voices in Thai, quick and

urgent. The door was still open to the sounds coming from the main cabin. I glanced at Rattakul; he had his eyes shut now, squeezed shut.

Eleven minutes after the explosion the jet's altitude was only two thousand feet and Ryan was sitting upright, peeling the silver paper off a packet of chewing-gum, his eyes on the box.

We are now out of control and starting to spin, a left spin—

A lot of noise came in and the loudest was the screaming, and I heard Ryan say *fuck* under his breath before he prodded the stick of gum between his teeth, his eyes never leaving the box.

It is reported that fire has broken out in the rear section and we are sending extinguishers back there, but we—

Sound of buffeting now, and a steady roaring in the background, probably the air-rush past the hole in the cabin wall. The screams went on and I thought of the little girl and the nuns and the Australian while the captain started talking again but now in his own tongue.

"Says there isn't anything more he can do," Ryan told us. There was sweat on his face, on all our faces. "Says they're just going to—" he broke off and stared at the box in silence for a while.

I told Rattakul he could go outside if he wanted to, but he didn't answer, maybe didn't take it in.

"Okay, he's—they're praying now, just praying and—" Ryan got out of his chair and stood with his hands dug into his belt, his body in a crouch. "Just doing that and asking to have messages sent to their mothers, Jesus Christ, it's always—"

Then a lot of sound like drumming, drumming and creaking and buffeting, and a man's voice in Thai.

"He's saying—Jesus, can you beat these guys—he's telling the captain it's been an honour to serve with him . . ."

A lot of sound now and I got up too and stood with my

back to the box and began counting for some reason and got to nine before there was a break in the transmission and silence, total silence.

It went on for a bit and then Ryan said in frustration, "I mean I just don't know how many times I've had to listen to that bullshit but it's never any different, it still gets to you." He went across to the coffee percolator and busied himself, making a noise. "You guys ready for your caffeine shot?"

Rattakul went out now, his face pale, and closed the door quietly, circumspectly.

"The rest of it is," Ryan said, "we've started getting some stuff from the aviation toxicology lab." He looked for some papers on the desk near the silent box. "Case No. 5023, received by J. Mathieson from Dr Lee Yu, samples, one bag of human bone, one container each of skeletal muscle and hair—I'll have them give you copies of all this stuff as it comes in, okay?" He dropped the sheet onto the desk and paced around the office, a cup in his hand. "Some of it's always misleading, like we get a whole lot of heart-failures on this kind of trip, but often they're not actual failures or even heart-*attacks*. When people know they don't have a chance any more they produce tremendous tensions, and it just rips at the heart muscle and breaks it down. What I'm saying is, you shoot a guy in the back of the head and the autopsy doesn't show any heart-failure, but these guys on the flight-deck can see it coming and they'll build up so much tension in them that it kills. We've had control columns torn clean out by the roots, and captains with their arms broken by the force they used trying to get the nose of the ship up—it isn't the contraction of the muscles that does that; it's the amount of pre-tension in them. But I'm not an expert on this stuff—they could give you a more accurate picture at the tox lab. But I doubt you'll find that bomber died of what looked like heart-failure. Jesus, anyone who can board a plane and sit there waiting to get blown up with it has to have pretty good nerves." He drained his cup and took it over to the sink.

"Do you think his motives were drug-related?"

He swung his head up to look at me. "I'd say the only thing that isn't drug-related in this whole area is the Salvation Army. And you know what that jet was carrying, don't you? There'd been a slip-up somewhere along the line—no one ships poppy-milk from Singapore to Thailand—that's the wrong way around."

"The name on the passenger list was Burmese."

"Doesn't have to mean anything. In this area you get people who are Chinese-French-Cambodian, British-Malaysian-Indian, you name it. Shifting populations, adopted refugees, mixed blood from colonial times, that kind of thing, then there's Singapore." He picked up his flight-bag, cupping a yawn. "I don't know about you but I'm ready to crash. Jesus, what am I saying . . ."

"Where are you?"

"Chathaburi Air Force Base, Thailand."

A tall steel mast flexing in the night-wind, 4 A.M., Cheltenham, six thousand miles away. I'd slept until noon.

"Why did you miss the flight?"

"I was warned off it."

"Who by?"

"I don't know." I told him about the voice on the paging-phone.

"It could only have been the Thais."

"No. They'd have stopped the flight and made a search."

A young lieutenant came into the office, whistling. "Oh. Excuse me." He went out again.

"What?" I asked Pepperidge.

"Then you've got friends out there."

"Not the kind I like."

"You mean the woman on the phone was involved?"

"It points to it."

"What are you doing to find out who they are?"

"Everything I can, but that's not much. That stuff you sent," I said, "looks clean enough, but you wouldn't be able to pick out a mole. I can't trust them totally. Or anyone. Why did you send it to me through the McCorkadale woman?''

''Because she's impeccable.''

''Spell it out for me.''

''Her father's Sir George McCorkadale, the M.P. She was at the Foreign Office for five years and she's been in Singapore for three. The British High Commissioner speaks highly of her. Otherwise,'' he said tartly, ''I wouldn't have used her to pass the material.''

''She sent me to a man called Chen, and he tipped me off to take that flight.''

''I've done some homework on him, too. At the moment he's in shock—the copilot on that plane was his best friend.''

I didn't say anything. I was thinking.

''Does that help?'' he asked me.

''Yes. Quite a lot. I thought he was all right, and maybe he is.'' If Chen were totally secure I could use him again if things got tricky.

''Did you find out anything from the wreck?''

''Hold it a minute.'' There was an F-11 taking off outside and the office became a membrane, filled with its power-scream. When quiet came back I told Pepperidge, ''Quite a bit.''

''What was in the briefcase?''

''That's not bad,'' I said.

He sounded indignant again. ''I don't sleep when there's work to do. I've been in Signals with the Thais most of the night.''

''No offence.''

''None taken. So what was in it?''

''Copies of the blueprints for the Slingshot, including specifications, modifications, computerised performance figures, and component manifest.''

There was a short silence.

''Good God.''

''Dominique Lafarge was the Shoda organisation's main armament source.''

"I know," he said. "But why—"

"Who is General Dharmnoon?"

There was another silence. He was doing a lot of thinking, which didn't surprise me.

"He's Shoda's chief army commander, in charge of all her splinter groups."

"There was a copy of a letter in the briefcase, written to Mariko Shoda. It said that Lafarge was 'at present furthering arrangements for the acquisition of one hundred Slingshots, as outlined to General Dharmnoon.' That's a quote."

I waited for him to do some more thinking. Data input came to the surface: the sharp smell of antiseptics, an itching under the left wrist, hunger. They'd changed the dressing for me at the base hospital and I hadn't eaten since the Red Cross had brought us the sandwiches at three o'clock this morning. Faint voices from outside, one of them an American's.

"They can't *buy* them," Pepperidge said.

"For acquisition read steal."

"Absolutely. I'll tell Laker Foundry to double the guard at the factory. And I don't know why you're so wary of Johnny Chen. This is a major breakthrough."

"Just that it crashed. I'll get over it." The memory wasn't ready to let go yet, that was all, the memory of the two voices, the one on the paging-phone—*There will be an accident, do you understand?*—and the one on the radio three hours later—*It has just been reported that a Thai International Airlines plane has come down in deep jungle north of Chathaburi. The names of the crew and passengers are being withheld until more information is available.* One of the names on the passenger manifest had been Martin Jordan.

"Yes," I heard Pepperidge saying, "I know how you must have felt." With hesitation he said, "They kept me up to date, you see, the Thais, so I knew you were down to take that flight, and when they signalled me that it had crashed I broke the rules and hit the scotch for a while. All right now, stone cold sober. You understand, I suppose, that a hundred of those things would give Mariko Shoda complete control of all air movement up to thirty thousand feet, wherever she chose to deploy them? Just a hundred launchers, plus, say, ten missiles to each."

He was right. Major breakthrough.

"It's coming together," I said.

"Indeed. And too bloody fast. I've got to go and get a few people out of bed, do some phoning round London. Look, can you send me copies of that stuff in the brief-case?"

"They're on their way."

"Where to?"

"The Thai Embassy in London. I did it from the air base here through Bangkok."

"First rate. I need to check them with Laker for authenticity. Have you got anything else for me?"

"No."

"Well, this is more than enough to get on with. Listen, old boy"—hesitating again—"I ran into Fletcher yesterday." I waited. The only Fletcher he could mean was a high-echelon control at the Bureau. "I didn't say where you were, of course, or what you're doing. But they'd take you back, you know. Any time."

"No."

Once you've gone, we can never ask you back. That bastard Loman. Changed his tune.

"They'd be pretty accommodating. They'd send you a director in the field, right away. Anyone you asked for. Even Ferris."

My God, what wouldn't I give for Ferris . . .

"They can't touch it," I said. "You know that. They haven't got—"

"Strictly under the table, of course."

"That's where they put that fucking bomb."

In a moment he said ruefully, "Message understood. But I want to ask you something. When can you go to ground?"

"As soon as I can."

"You're not going to survive, otherwise. They won't just leave it like that." He meant the clowning around in the limousine.

"I know. As soon as I can."

"I've got someone standing by," he said, "out there."

"Listen, if you—"

"Now don't fidget. All I've told him is that I *might* want to call on him at any given moment. He's *very* good, and—"

"I've told you I don't—"

"I simply want you to know," he said with studied patience, "that if you ever need support, you've got it, instantly. If, for instance, you decided you can't trust Thai Intelligence." I didn't say anything; he waited and then asked, "Have you ever heard of a man in that region named Colonel Cho?"

"How do you spell it?"

"C-H-O."

"No."

"If you do, tell me. He's someone I'm working on. And listen, signal me at any time on any subject, and I'll get to work immediately." With a kind of weary persuasion, "I really am on the ball, you know."

I told him I understood that.

Then I rang off and wondered if I should have told him that I'd just made up my mind to do the most dangerous thing I'd ever done in any mission up to now. Better to have left it; he'd only have hit the bloody scotch again.

11

SHODA

Dusk was falling.

It lowered among the cypresses, softening the edges of the shadows as the day's light died, covering them minute by minute until the lawns and the pathways began losing substance, leaving only the slender trees to stand on their own, holding the sky aloft on their dark columns. The air, even at this hour, was not still; it was filled with the gong's vibration.

The gong was huge, hanging between the beams of its timber frame, and the striker itself was massive, ten feet long and hewn from a single tree trunk, its end capped with cowhide to muffle the sound, its cords passing through a pulley as big as a man's head. A monk in a yellow robe dragged on the end of the main rope, timing the strokes at long intervals, so that the gong's sound was a continuous vibration, booming and fading but never becoming silent. It seemed to possess the power of something palpable, as if without its presence filling the air the whole temple would fall down.

I had come alone.

The catafalque was ornate, red and gold and encrusted with carvings, and six men were bearing it step by step across the ancient stones; four monks paced beside it, intoning the prayer for the dead.

Khor hai khwarm song cham Khong thun dai rap karn way phorn . . . Khor hai phraphuttha-ong rap than wai nai phra-maha-karunathikhun talord karn . . .

Dominique Edouard Lafarge.

Inside the temple the light was low, coming mainly from the lanterns hanging from the arched ceiling but also from the rows of candles burning beneath the many Buddhas; as the guests came in, more were lighted, and more prayers said.

Khun yang khong pen thi rak lach yang khong yu nai khwarm song cham khong thuk khon. Khwarm khit khamnueng khong rao thueng than ca tham hai vinyarn khong than pay su sukhati talord karn.

In here the air was heavy with incense. There was no music, but the cavernous space made an echo chamber for the booming of the great gong outside. The guests were either in black or white, many of them robed. As the catafalque was lifted to the raised platform, two men opened the top, and the right hand of Dominique Lafarge was exposed, palm upwards with its fingers curled. The mourners had already formed a line, and one after another poured the holy water into his hand, above a chased-silver bowl.

Than priap samuean phi khong rao sueng sathit yu bon suang sawan.

I'd come alone because I didn't want the responsibility of anyone else's life. I hadn't even told Rattakul where I was going, because where I was going was into hazard, taking a calculated risk. This was hostile ground, and my only chance was that it was also sacred.

There weren't many guests, but I sensed that it wasn't because Lafarge lacked status but because Mariko Shoda's organisation practised privacy. Most of the people here would be the elite of her entourage, including, I hoped, General Dharmnoon. I supposed the chances of talking to him in any safety were less than a hundred to one, but if I could talk to him, knowing what I did, I could accelerate the mission and get close to the objective and find out what I had to do then, how to destroy Shoda without killing her. This much had been understood by Pepperidge and was understood by Prince Kityakara and his intelligence services: the only time I've ever killed except to save my life was to avenge a woman's death. It's never, in any case, an elegant solution; to take a life shows a lack of style.

Chivit than nai lok manut dai rap tae kwarm chok-di laeh chivit khong than bon sawian kor jah pen chen dio-kan.

There were several round-eyes among the guests, as I knew there would be from what Chen had told me: Shoda employed Europeans. Otherwise I couldn't have come. As it was, I stayed at the back of the congregation, near the massive decorated doors. There was constant movement; the mourners were now approaching the catafalque again, to light candles and leave them on the dais below it, with posies of canework flowers smoking with incense.

One of the mourners was in uniform, but not of the Thai Army. Two aides flanked him: perhaps General Dharmnoon. I began watching him, wherever he moved.

I was also watching the environment as more people came in. Along the gallery that circled the temple there was movement sometimes, or it seemed like it: I couldn't be sure. The lamplight threw shadows there, and there seemed to be patches of reflected light, the size of a human face. Aware of them, I began thinking for the first time that coming here had not been a calculated risk, but a fatal error.

Nerves. The ritual of death in here was subtly playing on them.

Five monks in saffron robes took their place near the catafalque, bare-headed but holding ornate fans to hide their faces as they chanted their prayers.

Rao ɔhu sueng mai dap rap khwarm karuna hai tarm thau pai jah raluek thueng chivit khong than duai khwarm thert-thun talord karn.

Then it began, and I wasn't ready for it.

One of the women, only half-seen in her black robes, was moving down the aisle towards the catafalque, and several others were going with her, but at a slight distance, falling away in a soft wave of silk and giving her room; their robes too were black. Their sandals would be making a susurration on the marble floor, but because of the monks' chanting they seemed to move in perfect silence, spreading out as they reached the wide space before the dais, like the petals of a black tulip opening. At the same time there was movement among the rest of the throng, though hardly even that; a stirring, an expression of sudden attention, as if their breath was now held as they waited. I could have been wrong, but I thought that the chanting of the five monks had become softer behind their spread fans, more resonant, like the vibration of the gong outside whose waves of sound had floated endlessly on the air.

This had been the risk, and I'd taken it, and it was too late now.

The woman was kneeling, her hands together and her head lowered, facing the red and gold catafalque. The others followed, and now I could see them clearly enough to know that there were eight of them, four on each side and forming a double arc with the single woman at the centre. I could have believed they'd rehearsed their tableau for hours a day, and knew that they hadn't.

No one, anywhere, was moving now, and in the great stillness my mind slowed to the rhythm of alpha waves, and three-dimensional reality began losing its definition, drawn into the shadows by the vast stillness here, by the heady fumes of the incense, the mesmerising glimmer of a hundred candle-flames, and above all the presence of death.

Too late, yes, but already I could believe that it wasn't simply a calculated risk I'd taken, but that she'd somehow drawn me here to the temple, the woman who kneeled alone, Mariko Shoda, drawn me here by the ethereal force of whatever demonic spirit burned in her, and burned those who touched.

People always tell me the same thing about Little Kiss-of-Steel—don't stand too close, and above all don't touch.

There was still no movement anywhere. The sense of

time was slipping away, because time, too, was an illusion, a part of the three-dimensional reality that no longer held any meaning in this place. The monks' rhythmic chanting never ceased; it had become the sound of endlessness, the continuum of the universe. The smoke of the incense was the essence of Nirvana, distilled from the scents of life's experience long forgotten until now. My eyes, focussed on the slender neck of the woman who knelt there, Shoda, the woman who prayed there, Mariko Shoda, could look nowhere else, because there was nowhere else.

Danger. This mood is lethal.

Yes, but I would have thought of that a long time ago, if it hadn't already been my karma to come here. The left brain can be very tiresome at a time when—

You mean you're ready to give up life?

I wouldn't say that.

Then what else can you be saying?

I think I moved, then, feeling the return of beta consciousness, raising my head and looking along the shadowed gallery. Yes, there were faces there in the gloom between the lamps, faces looking down.

So be it.

You'll go as easily as that?

Leave me alone.

It had been a try, I suppose. I'd slipped back into reality enough to check the environment, and wished I hadn't. Serves you right, so forth.

My eyes went back to the kneeling woman.

She's very spiritual—Chen—*she always prays for you before she kills.*

So be it.

A cold draught somewhere, though it didn't worry me; a movement of the air, its chill coming against me but not touching my skin, waking me a little, bringing enough reality back to let me know what it was: the creeping of the sense of death along the nerves.

Then there was nothing, for a time, for whatever period

of timelessness it was that seemed like time. We were held, all of us, in the cosmic thrall that had its centre in the woman there, Shoda, the woman praying. There was nothing. Nihil. It had stilled us forever, and we no longer breathed because there was no need to breathe, no need to experience anything but Nirvana, the stillness of perfect love.

Shock came and I flinched, unprepared for it as she began moving, the woman there, lifting her head and letting her arms fall beside her as she rose to her feet and stood for a moment facing the catafalque. I'd felt the shock go through the others here; some of them had caught their breath. The incense smelt acrid suddenly and the monks' chanting took on monotony, became obtrusive. One of the children I'd seen earlier had started crying, unable to deal with the sudden change of dimension.

Do what you can.

Yes, I know what you mean. But there's nothing. Nihil.

She turned, Shoda, and began walking back towards us, and the other women held for a moment where they were and then closed in a little, following, their steps in unison with hers, Shoda's. Their eyes were soft, in the way that can be seen when *karatekas* are joined in *kumite,* in contest, or when Olympic athletes are performing "in the zone." The eyes are not focussed, but simply allow vision to come in from the entire field, so that you look at nothing but see everything.

I saw only her face.

It was long, noble, the cheekbones rising to wide, luminous eyes, her brow clear, ivorine under her night-black hair; but that's just a description and there is no way of telling you how the face of Shoda appeared to me in the temple on that evening, because it was more than the face of a woman—it was also the face of death, fashioned in beauty. My own death, of course, no question of that.

So easily?

I know what you mean but when there's no question you

don't question it, do you, surely that's reasonable?

You haven't got very long now. What are you going to do?

The cold draught came again and this time my skin crawled and I went straight into left brain and the shock went through to the bone because it was true: I'd been insane to come here even though I'd believed there was a chance of getting away with it and accelerating the mission and somehow surviving.

Sheer bloody pride—I hadn't got a chance in hell.

You're just going to let it happen?

Oh, I wouldn't quite say that, no. When it comes, I'll go down fighting, never say die, lads, so forth, *nerves like ice while I whistled in the dark* because it wouldn't be very long now. This time they'd make certain.

There were some other things done, though I'm not sure I can remember exactly what; I think they took the wooden coffin out of the catafalque and carried it into the ornamented hearth where the flames were to be lit. People came and went, and some kind of reed instrument began playing.

You could leave now, while there's time.

I looked upwards again, but the faces along the gallery weren't any clearer, even when I centred and relaxed to stimulate the retinae and the optic nerve, though I detected a slight movement by one of them and this told me at least that they were, yes, faces, watching. Well of course they'd be there: they'd be everywhere. *She not only has a whole bunch of bodyguards around her*—Chen—*but she has a whole lot more waiting around in the area.*

I turned and looked towards the big entrance doors; they were wide open still, and people came and went bringing candles and wicker-work posies, some of them crying as they left the temple, one of them a boy of six or seven—*"C'est pas vrai, Maman, c'est pas vrai . . ."* The woman with him, then, was the widow, leaving before the anguish of the condolences could begin.

The bodyguards on each side of the doorway didn't move, a dozen of them, women in black silk robes because jump-suits of course wouldn't be appropriate, have to watch the proprieties, but there wouldn't be one of them without a blade on them, sheathed under the silk.

So there we are.

Make your run. Make it now.

Don't be so bloody silly.

Sweat on my sides; I could smell it, the raw emanation of fear, and that familiar bitter taste in the mouth as the adrenaline began flowing into the blood. *C'est pas vrai . . . Mais oui, c'est vrai: la mort m'attend, m'attend.*

Flamelight strengthened against the walls as the fire beneath the coffin burned brighter. Mourners were gathered there in a circle, and the voices of the monks rose more strongly from behind their fans; the piper's notes became infinitely sad.

She hadn't moved, Shoda. She was in her own space, isolated by her women, standing with a stillness that hypnotised, the stillness of a reptile, of a creature totally in command of its environment.

Just turn and walk through the doors. They can't do anything here.

No, not here. They'll wait till I'm outside—they'll need the dark for this.

The flamelight grew, fanning across the coloured walls, deepening the scarlets and turning the greens to ochre. It was all rather beautiful, as it was meant to be, and I suppose you could say there were worse preludes to the act of extinction; what I mean is we don't often get this kind of luck, the shadow executives, the busy little ferrets in the field, we usually finish up spreadeagled in the dust at a checkpoint with the guns suddenly silent, or smeared under a truck or shoved in an unmarked grave because otherwise we'd stink and there are the local health laws, so forth; I mean we don't expect this kind of thing, a temple indeed, with candles and prayers and everything, the impressive trappings of ritual—*because that's what she's doing now, you know, she's said her prayers for Dominique Edouard Lafarge and now she's praying for you, hasn't that occurred to you for Christ's sake, she prays before she kills, didn't you hear what Chen said*—sweat running, stinking the place out, the mouth like a husk, so come on, let's get it over with, let's make—

Shoda moved. Moved with that extraordinary suddenness that brought a shock to the senses, because now it seemed she'd never been still. She was turning and walking this way as her women fell aside a little and then closed in, beautifully done, absolutely first-class choreography, a part of my mind standing off from the reality of what was going to happen very soon now and indulging itself in an appreciation of the fine arts while the brain-stem was producing a stream of desperate last-ditch schemes for snatching some kind of survival from the obvious certainty of death.

She was close to me now, Shoda, and her head turned on its slender neck and she looked at me, stopping and standing there a few yards away, and I was staring into the eyes of the angel of death, the luminous night-deep eyes of the woman who was to be my executioner; and I knew now without any doubt that she'd been praying for me, because I felt, in these last moments of my life, raised to a state of grace.

You mean you won't even—

Oh, I'm not hanging around, don't worry, I'm going out there now and let them get it over with, too many of them this time, but fight like a tiger, yes, of course, as a gesture at least, to let everyone know I was capable of doing more than just stand there and bare my chest for butchery.

So I turned and went out of the temple, dodging between people but not running, not even hurrying, one has to be seemly in a sacred place, just making my way out, knowing she was following me now, Shoda, knowing also that as I went through the enormous doorway the others were following too, the women I'd seen standing there guarding the doors, and when I reached the temple gardens I crossed the grass towards the black columns of the cypresses so that we could play out the matter in privacy, and with the cool night air on my face and my shadow moving ahead of me in the moonlight I heard them coming for me with a rushing of silk and I turned to face them and saw the shimmer of drawn blades.

12

SLINGSHOT

"Don't come any closer."

No one moved.

I could hear the plane levelling flight now.

"When you're ready, Lee."

The soldier hefted the launcher and set up the aim on the drone.

"Don't inhale the smoke. It's hydrogen chloride gas."

"I'm ready," the soldier said and pressed the trigger.

I was watching the plane towing the drone. "What altitude's that thing?"

"Three thousand feet."

The missile left the canister and lifted fast but was slowing; then it accelerated again.

"That's the main booster coming in," Hickson told us. "It's to protect the firer—there's too much noise and fumes going on when she cuts in, so we made it two-stage. The Yanks have done the same thing with their Stinger."

The missile reached the drone and there was a bright orange flash and then bits of debris started flowering from the centre of the explosion.

"Thanks, Lee."

Hickson shoved his hands in his pockets. We knew each other's names but that was all. Instructions from Pepperidge had been to that effect: Hickson wasn't to know any more than that I was a civilian guest of the Thai government.

"I asked for that altitude because with a towline as short as that one there'd be a very definite risk of hitting the plane instead of the drone." Thin, terrier-faced, earnest, he swept a look around us. "That isn't because we can't aim the Slingshot accurately even at thirty thousand feet; it's just the nature of the beast—she seeks the most heat she can find, and after all you're not going to be towing drones around in a war."

I'd phoned Pepperidge earlier today and asked him to set up a demonstration for me. My cover was that of a rep for Laker Foundry and I needed to know as much about the Slingshot as possible.

I hadn't told him about the temple thing.

"How much does it cost?" I asked Hickson.

"Six thousand pounds per missile. Considering you can take down a twenty-million-pound aircraft with it, I wouldn't say it's all that expensive, would you?"

I didn't know whether he was being defensive because of the price or because he was uneasy having me here, an unknown. This was his toy and he liked to know who watched him play with it. Or he could simply be worried because of the leak in Birmingham.

Prince Kityakara came over to me. "Would you like to see another firing, Mr Jordan?"

"Not unless you would, sir."

He turned to Hickson. "I think we might send another one up."

There was something very attractive about the Slingshot—the size of the thing, only five feet long, and its devastating potential—and I had the impression that Kityakara and his army chiefs here were as pleased as Hickson with it. They had fifty of them, stored under the heaviest security I'd ever seen.

One of the aides switched on his radio and asked for another drone.

It would only have worried Pepperidge if I'd told him.

There are phases in every mission where you decide to push things right to the brink, not because of the exciting way it tickles but because you've weighed the odds and calculated the risk and looked at all the data again and then gone for it, shit or bust, and that's what I'd done when I'd decided to go to Lafarge's funeral. I'd known that Mariko Shoda might be there but it wasn't certain, and that had given me enough margin of safety to make the decision. After that point I'd relied on what Johnny Chen had said.

She's very spiritual. She prays before she kills.

But she hadn't been able to kill on sacred ground.

"—Mr Jordan?"

"I'm sorry?"

He whipped the little inhaler across his mouth. "You haven't seen the Slingshot in action before, in England?"

"No, sir."

"Are you impressed?"

"Very."

We began walking about to relieve the tension. You had to stand perfectly still when that thing was being fired; it was like watching those people at St Andrews.

She'd wanted to scare me, of course. Maybe not scare, but get the message across: she'd one day be my death. That was why she'd let them get their knives out before she'd called them off. Then all I'd heard in the shadows of the cypresses was her quiet voice—"*Dio korn! Ploi man wai korn!*" It could only have meant *No, not now,* or *Leave him,* something like that. Not a pardon, though. Just a reprieve.

"It's mounted with these control surfaces in the nose," Hickson said. "They produce roll and lateral shift." He was holding the thing like a baby, cradling it. Pepperidge had told me that Hickson had been in on the actual design.

I could hear the aircraft climbing again.

"Fire-and-forget," Kityakara said. He was looking at the specifications. "What does that mean, Mr Hickson?"

"Pretty well what it says, sir. Once she's fired and on her way, the soldier can move off to a new position if he wants to, or get under cover if there's the need. The Slingshot's computerised, fully automatic. She *thinks* for you.'' A definite note of pride.

It had been nerves, that was all. I'd been in the wrong mood for pushing myself into hazard. I was already morbid after the long night in the jungle, picking over those tortured bodies, and the ritual in the temple had made things worse, and what the boy had said, that it wasn't true, his *papa* couldn't be dead. And finally of course there'd been Shoda, and the almost mystic power coming from her, and her eyes when she'd looked into mine, with the need for my death in them.

I can put a car through a checkpoint and take the barrier with me and I can undo a bomb in a barn and take the fuse out and I can go through implemented interrogation inside Lubyanka and come out sane, but Shoda was different, operating on a psychically different wavelength, with a force in her that chilled you to the bone when she came near.

I didn't just walk away two nights ago, don't think that; I didn't just walk out of the cypresses and get into the car and drive off. I'd come away shivering, with my feet unsteady and my eyes flickering, the closest thing to what I've read about shell-shock. And I knew this feeling wouldn't leave me, not entirely. If I could get through this mission it was going to be with the constant fear of death inside me, like a haunting.

''Stand away, please,'' Hickson said.

The Thai soldier plugged in the cable from the battery strapped to his waist and got the pistol grip into his right hand and heaved the canister onto his shoulder and took a sighting; then he flicked some switches and swung the missile to the right, angling it to something like fifty degrees; then he began tracking as the military jet trailing the drone began its pass across the airfield. Kityakara was using his inhaler every half-minute or so now, becoming very tense; the others weren't moving or saying anything—three full generals and a small crowd of colonels and lower brass, all immaculate, strictly on parade and not only because Kityakara was here but because of the Slingshot. With its cunning, sinister potency it outranked them all.

"When you're ready," Hickson said.

The soldier nodded and went on tracking the drone.

"Watch out for the gas cloud, gentlemen. Don't breathe any in."

Tracking.

The man squeezed the trigger and there was something like a second's delay while the pressure from the initial charge built up in the tube and then the missile was forced out and began climbing, twisting to the left and correcting its course before the main booster came on and kicked the thing higher, leaving a plume of white smoke that drifted on the breeze. I was counting, and got to ten seconds before the Slingshot nosed into the drone and made the hit and left an orange fireball hanging in the sky.

Silence on the ground; then the sound-wave reached us, nothing more than a soft "woof" because of the distance and the fact that the drone carried no fuel.

When I looked down, the soldier had moved almost fifty yards away, demonstrating the Slingshot's "fire-and-forget" capability.

"Of course," Hickson said—and I thought his tone was deliberately conversational for the sake of effect—"with a rocket-powered drone you can shoot at thirty thousand feet. They're on their way."

Prince Kityakara gave a brief nod. "Thank you, Mr Hickson. An impressive demonstration. Are there any questions, gentlemen?"

It took half an hour, with two interpreters picking up when the non-English-speaking people wanted to know things; then Kityakara took me across to his staff-car and we got in.

"I'm sure I don't need to emphasise, Mr Jordan, the devastation that weapon could cause, in the wrong hands."

"Or the right."

He tilted his head. "I am not talking of war, but of

full-scale revolution, initiated by someone like Mariko Shoda and her organisation. It's not just the technical capability of the Slingshot that makes it so deadly. In jungle terrain, one man could use it at five-minute intervals and continue to move around so that he could never be flushed out. *One man* could bring down half a squadron of bombers, and of course any given number of helicopters moving in at a low level.'' Inhaler. ''It means that any armed revolution could proceed with its enterprise in the certainty that it was completely safe from the air.'' He laid a hand on my knee, became suddenly aware of protocol and removed it at once. ''It means, Mr Jordan, that if the Shoda organisation acquired this weapon, it could set Indo-China aflame within a week. And that, of course, is its intention.''

''Noted.''

''I'm kept fully informed of your reports. Can you give me any hope that you can move into Mariko Shoda's operation before too long?''

''I met her yesterday.''

He stiffened. *''Shoda?''*

''Yes.''

His head was turned to watch me from behind his tinted glasses. ''I don't understand. She lets no one near her.''

''I didn't talk to her.''

''But how—?'' He left it hanging.

''I took a chance, in the hope of getting some information. It didn't come off. Or maybe it did. I know more about her now, what kind of adversary she is. It's not always,'' I told him, ''the angle of the shot, or the distance from the target, or the timing. Sometimes you just need to know how to get under their skin, and work from there.''

''I see.'' His voice was hushed. ''I shall pray for you, Mr Jordan.''

Rattakul flew me in a Thai military staff aircraft to Singapore and their embassy had a rented plain van waiting for us on the tarmac and I climbed into the rear, which was facing away from the terminal buildings.

I was given an envelope with the insignia of the British High Commission in the top left-hand corner and I slit it open.

I've been doing a bit of homework for you that I think might help. Why not let me cook some spaghetti for you this evening if you're not doing anything? You know my address.

It was now 15:31 and I thought about it. She wouldn't be fooling: underneath the ingenue breathlessness she had a good mind, and she knew what sort of information I wanted.

"Drop me here, will you?"

South Canal Road, with some of the best cover in the area and close enough to Boat Quay to clean out the Red Orchid. Al said there were no messages but in any case they could only be from the Thai Embassy, because this was my safe-house and security hadn't been breached, but just before five o'clock Lily Ling told me there was a phone call and I went down to the bar.

"I am glad you did not take plane."

A soft woman's voice, but it sounded like an explosion because security had been blown away.

"What plane?"

"Flight 306."

Smells came into the lobby from the street: fruit, spices, chickens. It had rained again, and the air was sticky, even in here.

I didn't ask her how she'd found this number—it was better to let her think it wasn't important. Instead I said, "I owe you my thanks."

"You are welcome, Mr Jordan."

"May I know your name?"

"It is Sayako."

"Sayako-san, how did you know that plane was going to crash?"

Silence, then: "Someone tell me."

"Who gave the order?"

"Enemy of Shoda."

Target: Dominique Lafarge. I said, "Which enemy?"

"Is not important. Was important to warn you."

"Why are you telephoning me now, Sayako-san?"

"To warn you again."

"About what?"

"Shoda has ordered you killed."

"Quite probably." I didn't like the way she was using short sentences, which was the classic method of drawing people out.

"She is furious with you."

I knew that. I didn't say anything.

Lily Ling came slipping from the kitchen to the desk in the lobby, walking like a flame in her red shift. Al had fired her twice since I'd arrived here; the humidity was getting people down.

"Do you know why?"

Why Shoda was furious with me. "She lost face, I suppose."

"Yes. You went to temple knowing she could not attack you there. It was insult, as if you say, you wish to kill me, so here I am, yet you cannot. You understand, Mr Jordan? This is very important."

"I understand."

Lily Ling was still at the desk and I could ask her to get Al very fast and ask him to phone the special number I had at the Thai Embassy and tell Rattakul to see if he could get her number traced, Sayako's, through the Singapore police; but at best it would take twenty minutes and I wouldn't be able to keep her talking that long.

"Shoda has ordered one man to kill you, Mr Jordan. His name is Manif Kishnar. He has never failed to kill. He will leave Bangkok soon now."

"What does he look like?" All Indians didn't wear turbans. But the real experts favoured piano-wire.

"I do not know. Of course, you must now leave your hotel. But he will find you, unless I can warn you in time where he will be, and what he will be doing."

Longer sentences, which made me feel better. There was

also a timbre in this woman's voice that attracted me, in terms of trust.

Don't trust *anyone*.

Quite, but she'd saved my life, and even though she'd done it for her own purposes it meant she was a friend, not an enemy, and might remain one. A friend in Shoda's camp was worth having. But I'd better check that out.

"Sayako-san, are you in Shoda's organisation?"

In a moment she said, "I have access to information."

I watched a cockroach skirting the base of the bar, darting around a bottle-top and a half-burnt match. I knew what Ferris would have done with that.

"Why are you helping me, Sayako-san?"

"You are here on mission to destroy Mariko Shoda. I wish for that."

The *only* way this woman could have got my number was from the Thai Embassy. They didn't have it officially even though I was working for them but they'd come here to take me to the birthday party. They could be working, then, through this woman, to help me.

I didn't think so. She sounded like a lone wolverine.

"You wish for Shoda's destruction," I said carefully. "Why?"

Shoda had deadly enemies but I wanted to know if there were something personal.

In a moment: "It is not important." Her voice was like ice suddenly. "But you know that others have tried, and not succeed. It is because no one can kill Shoda with a gun, or a way like that. You make the right way, I think. You know how to do this thing, by knowledge of woman."

I didn't ask her, but was Shoda a woman? The divine face, the slender body, yes, but what I'd seen in her eyes was the evil of Diabolus. And it was attracting me, and I knew it, and knew its dangers. This was going to end when one of us brought death to the other.

"If we could meet, Sayako-san, you could tell me more about her."

She hesitated so long that I began listening for background sounds, other voices, the turning of a tape. "No, we cannot meet. It is too dangerous for me. I will help you as much as I can, by telephone."

That could be true. Anyone informing on Mariko Shoda was in deadly peril.

"All right," I said.

"I will need to know where to telephone to you, when you will leave your hotel."

I was going to ground now as soon as I could but it wouldn't be to any kind of safe-house because I didn't know of one, and in any case you don't give away the phone-number of your safe-house even to someone who's just saved your life. But a temporary number would work.

"How do I contact you?" I asked her.

"Write your new number down and place into an envelope with name Sayako on. Deposit in night safe at Bank of Singapore, in Empress Place." She added quietly, "I will not visit there for it. I will call."

She knew some of the rules. "I'll do that," I told her.

"Very well. Now please listen to me, Mr Jordan. Manif Kishnar is to leave Bangkok by air, at some time on day after tomorrow, which is Thursday. I will find out his movements for you, and tell you what I can. But please believe me that you must do everything possible to protect your life. This man succeed to kill always. *Always.*"

Noted.

13

ZABAGLIONE

Bolognaise.

"Too much garlic?"

"Not for me. It's excellent."

"I didn't think you'd come."

"Why not?"

She spilled some spaghetti from her fork. "God, I've always been a messy eater. Because you put me through the third degree the other day at the embassy."

"That day I wouldn't have trusted my own mother."

Day of the plane crash.

"Yes, I understand that now, but it took a bit of time. I was furious when I left there."

"Then it didn't show."

"That's not bad, for me. Have you still got a mother?"

"What? Oh. No."

"Father?"

"No."

"I thought not." She gave me her level stare, her blue-grey eyes narrowing as they focused. "You come across like an orphan."

What can you say to a thing like that?

The shutters were still open to the last of the daylight; if I asked her to close them now it'd be too early. She was looking particularly sensual this evening, not exactly looking but behaving, with slight body movements, bringing her thin shoulders forward in that familiar way, her head tilting in brief gestures as she left things unsaid, her hand brushing the air when she couldn't find the word she wanted. Sensual because intimate, knowing I trusted her again.

"Did you lose them when you were young?"

Mother, father. "I don't remember."

She puffed out a little laugh. "Or anything about your past at all. Sorry."

A shutter or something banged on the other side of the street and she caught my reaction and said quietly, "Martin, do you *enjoy* living like that?"

"It's not that I'm paranoid, it's just that everybody's trying to get at me." But she didn't think it was funny.

I poured her some more wine.

"You sure you won't have any?"

"Not just now."

"You're safe here, darling." Then she said, "Or are you?" She turned to glance across the windows.

"I wouldn't have come near you if I weren't."

"I don't mind catching some flak."

"I'd rather you didn't."

I'd given it a whole hour before I'd rung the bell downstairs, taking it street by street, house by house, melting and emerging and melting from cover to cover, drawn blank. It had surprised me; I'd thought I'd pick up ticks and have to get clear and call her with an excuse. It told me a lot about Shoda: all she could think about was killing off any kind of opposition. The women she used for tagging were good, once they'd seen the target, but there was no real field work. They should have tagged Katie too, the day we'd had lunch at Empress Place, and seen where she worked and put a peep on her night and day on the assumption that she'd meet me again. That was basic surveillance work.

Sayako was different.

"You go to the Thai Embassy quite a bit, don't you?"

She looked at me steadily. "We liaise with them. Why?"

"Do you talk about me there?"

"I'm not exactly a gossip."

"I know. But don't assume that because I'm in with them they can be totally trusted to look after me."

It was the closest I could go to the truth.

Her glass remained poised halfway to her mouth. "This is important, isn't it?"

"Fairly."

"All right." She put down her wine and put a thin ringless hand on the table for me to take. "So you really do trust me now."

Was that true? I wasn't sure.

"I don't think you'd do me any intentional damage."

She took her hand away and I saw that her eyes were moist. "You really are a bastard," she said lightly. "I'd do bloody well anything for you."

"I can't think why."

"Because of what you are." She pushed her plate away and wouldn't look at me for a moment, furious, I thought.

Probably hard up for a man. Four months into the divorce and he'd been "fantastic in bed," so forth, too much of a lady to take the first man she could find, too much pride or just too hurt, bugger them, I hate them all.

The phone rang and she got up to answer it. The flat was small, understated, a few bamboo chairs and a chaise-longue, stereo, poinsettias in a Chinese vase, worn silk rugs, half a wall full of books, mostly paperbacks, a lot of them reread, ragged.

"I can't do it now," on the phone, her slender body arched backwards against the wall, leaning, examining the nails of her right hand in the light from the windows. "Look, ring up Holli and ask her if she can pop round there—she's always terribly willing to help. I'll ask her about it in the morning."

I finished my tomato-juice and left the table and went across to the alcove to look at the water-colours—*Romney Marsh—The Shore at Rye—Lewes Crescent, Brighton.* Delicate, wistful, blues and greys.

"I'm awfully sorry, Martin. Had you finished?"

"Yes. Did you do these?"

"All my own work." She stood beside me, faintly scented, but it was more her skin.

"They're charming."

"Honestly? There's some zabaglione." She took my hand.

"Are you having some?"

"I don't know. Perhaps later. You'll be wanting to know about the homework I did for you." She turned and went across to finish her wine, and then curled up on the floor with one arm on the chaise-longue. "I've written it out for you and you can take it when you go. Don't you want a chair?"

"I like it here."

"It's something I learned as a child, or taught myself, found out, I don't know which. When you're on the floor, you can't fall any farther. Anyway, it's about Mariko Shoda. I—don't want that bitch to hurt you, so I dug up everything I could."

"You do a lot for me."

"I told you, I'd do anything."

"Because of what I am. What's that, exactly?" I didn't know if she meant because of what I did, how much they'd told her at the Thai Embassy. But of course she was a woman, and I'd missed the point.

"Tough as hell on the outside, but vulnerable, endangered, hence dramatic, hence sexy." She brushed the air, feeling for the words she wanted. "Pushing yourself to some kind of brink all the time. And therefore"—she looked away—"doomed, I suppose. So I just want to help you"—her fair hair swung as she looked back at me, her eyes resting on mine, gravely—"while there's time."

Piano wire.

Random image, unimportant.

This man succeed to kill, always.

Ignore.

"Anyway," Katie said, "this is roughly the picture. Her

father was Prince Shoda Phomvihane of Cambodia, and in 1975 the Khmer Rouge stormed his palace—that was when they were sweeping across the whole country, as you know. She was eight years old at that time, and when the Communists attacked the palace her father tried to get her to safety. She was in her father's arms, coming down the steps of the palace, when a sabre cut his head in two and Shoda fell, with his blood all over her. I got this from an eyewitness, an old woman in one of the refugee camps we help to look after. A man picked her up and ran with her through the melee and got her clear—but then lost track of her the same night in the jungle. This I got from someone who used to know her, *after* she reached safety.'' She stretched out a stockinged leg, smoothing it. ''Sometimes we don't know the half of what other people go through, do we?''

Her face was losing definition—dusk was down, with equatorial suddenness.

''Do you mind pulling the shutters across?''

''What? All right.'' She turned, halfway across the room. ''But you said—''

''Just routine.''

She came back, switching on the big oil-jar lamp in the corner, turning down the rheostat. ''Is that too dim?''

''No.''

I like dim light, shadows, darkness, night, invisibility. Going to ground soon, have to, because of Manif Kishnar.

''Are you all right?''

''Yes.'' There'd been nothing in my face, in my eyes; she was picking up vibrations again. That'd be so dangerous in an enemy.

''Well''—curling up on the floor again—''she was seven months in the jungle, alone.''

''At the age of eight.''

''Yes.'' Her shoulders lifted an inch—''I don't think it's just legend, although there are plenty of legends about her. I mean it's feasible, plausible, that a woman like Mariko Shoda, vicious and powerful and so on, could easily have been that kind of child—resourceful, adaptable, savage, especially after losing her father like that in a literally bloody rite of passage. Wouldn't you think?"

I said I would.

"Or to put it the other way round—that a resourceful, savage child could have become what Shoda is now. Someone asked her how she could possibly have managed to survive seven months in the jungle, and apparently she said it was easy, once you became an animal. She watched the monkeys, and ate only the berries and things they ate, so as not to get poisoned. She killed a tiger."

"How?"

"When she found out which berries *were* poisonous, she stuffed a half-dead marmoset with them and dropped it from a tree near the tiger's beat." She pulled her hair back. "That sort of thing. Is this of any use, Martin? I mean—"

"It's vital to me."

"Oh." She touched my arm. "That makes me feel"—leaving it, looking away—"Johnny Chen didn't give you any of this?"

"No."

"He's terribly cut up, you know, about losing his best friend. That pilot." Her eyes levelled, focussing. "He's genuine, Martin. You can trust him. And I wouldn't say that unless I were a million times certain. I wouldn't want to do or say anything that might hurt you. I'm beginning to wish I'd never met you, as a matter of fact. It's such a responsibility." She leaned and tugged at a loose thread at the fringe of the rug, her fair hair falling across her face. Quietly—"Just joking. Well anyway, when she got out of the jungle she fell foul of the Pol Pot forces again, and went through five years of torture, starvation, terror, repeated rape, and an epidemic of cholera. Hundreds of thousands like her didn't survive. She was at the infamous execution centre at Tuol Sleng, but got away. When—"

The telephone began ringing and she looked around. "That'll be the office again. Unless it's for you?"

"No one knows I'm here."

"Then it can go on ringing. When she reached a refugee camp on the Thai border she looked like a skeleton and couldn't even speak—it took a year to get her back to something like normal. I got this from the actual camp administration. There were thousands there—still are—but she gradually began standing out from the crowd, helping with the work and the organisation—she was about fourteen by then, and she'd already had something of an education as a princess of the royal house, up to the age of eight." She swung her head—"That *bloody* phone"—then it stopped ringing. "There's a gap after that, but someone else said that by the time she was seventeen she was helping them to administrate the whole camp. That was when she killed one of the officers for trying to mess about one night in the sleeping quarters. There was an enquiry, but nothing was proved against her, not enough even to have her charged. The woman I spoke to was a witness, but refused to give evidence—like Shoda, she'd been through absolute hell and felt that any man who started any funny business ought to be shot. Then a year later there was a camp guard found knifed, and very expertly. The next day Shoda was missing. So are you getting the picture, and would you like some zabaglione now?"

We went back to the table and she brought it in and talked some more about Mariko Shoda. "A Thai police inspector told me that so far she's killed off fifteen of her top competitors in the drug trade, taking care of six of them personally and using her crack hit man for the others—he's from Calcutta and his name's Kishnar." She went to put on some music, kicking off her snakeskin shoes. "Any questions?"

I asked her for the Thai police inspector's name and phone number, and she gave them to me.

"Anything else?"

"Yes. Have you heard of a woman, probably Japanese, named Sayako, who could be in the Shoda organisation?"

"How do you spell it?"

I told her.

"No. Where does she come in?"

"It was just something I picked up."

"I'll keep my ears open." She came over to me slowly in her stockinged feet, and it struck me that the effect made by a woman taking her shoes off has been underrated. "We'll go on talking about Shoda," she said, "for as long as you want to, Martin; I asked you here to give you all the information I can. But do you feel like a brief interlude? *Un petit après-zabaglione?*"

"My God, I've never seen so many scars on a man's body. All I've got is this little one."

"Caesarian?"

"Yes." She looked away. "But he died. One of those bloody crib deaths. The thing is, he might have kept the marriage together, and that would have been awful. Do you believe things like that work themselves out in life?"

"I believe we create our own reality."

"You mean we *decide* to mess everything up?" She lay against me again, one leg dangling off the divan onto the cushions she'd thrown down. "How did you know I like it very slowly?"

"I didn't."

"But I mean, I never knew foreplay could be so absolutely mind-blowing." She began moving her hands again, stroking the sweat on the skin. "I felt like a goddess or something. Do you always—" She left it.

The light was soft in the room; the record-player had shut itself off, hours ago. The phone had rung twice and she'd let it go on ringing. The overhead fan was turning slowly in the middle of the room, spreading the humid air. I hadn't meant to stay; looking back, I thought it was probably because I didn't want to return to the reality I'd created for myself outside. *He's from Calcutta, and his name's Kishnar . . .*

"I wish," she said slowly, "we could've met before." I began playing with her again, very gently: she liked *karezza*. "But I suppose it wouldn't have worked out, I mean our—'' She left it, then said, ''Oh my God . . . do you know what that does to me?''

Through the kitchen doorway I could hear the fridge cutting on and off; the only other sounds were the sounds we made. She used *pompoir,* and delightfully, which I hadn't expected from her.

''Martin, will you stay the night? There's not much of it left anyway.''

''I'd like to.''

''Keep back the dawn. Wasn't that the title of something?''

Sometimes we slept a little, and then there was a flush of rose light between the slats of the shutters, and she made coffee and we sat facing each other on the floor, sharing the discovery we'd made.

''I was absolutely wrong,'' she said, ''he wasn't fantastic in bed after all—he hadn't got a bloody clue.'' A sleepy laugh. ''Was I all right, a bit?''

''Exquisite.''

Then the shutters brightened, throwing silvered light across the ceiling where the fan still turned, and Katie made eggs and toast for us, not smiling very often now, not even talking much.

''I suppose what you need most,'' she said at one time, ''is to know what her Achilles' heel is. Shoda's.''

''That would be useful.''

The cushions were still all over the floor when I left, and Katie was in a thin kind of nightie, looking like a child, barefooted and soft.

''Martin, I'm a bit telepathic sometimes, have you noticed? I pick up vibes.'' She came as far as the door with me, lifting her thin arms to hold me and kiss. At last she said, ''It's going to be so bloody dangerous out there for you, isn't it?''

I don't remember quite what I said, something about my luck lasting, I think.

''Do something for me, will you?'' Her eyes were very steady now, and dark. ''For God's sake, if and when you can, pick up a phone and call me, so that I'll know things are still all right.''

Then it was too late to go to ground because an hour after I got back to the Red Orchid I saw they'd thrown surveillance around the hotel and knew I was trapped.

14

COUNTDOWN

I phoned Pepperidge but he wasn't there.

Just the answering-machine. I left a message.

I'm in a red sector. Phone me.

This was at 10:03.

The first thing you do when you find a trap closing on you is to note the time because later it can save your life.

At 10:03 there were five of them outside the hotel and I checked them again, using shutters, the mirror in the bathroom of the vacant room at the end of the third-floor corridor, and the angle of vision across the courtyard at the rear between the edge of the roof and the vent-pipe from the kitchen, leaving myself only enough of a gap to sight without exposing more than the width of one eye. It took more than an hour.

11:14.

I wished Pepperidge would telephone.

That'll be my number. I'll put in an answering-machine, all right? You can always leave a signal on it if I'm out sweeping for data in the pubs.

He wouldn't be in a pub at three in the morning.

Then where was he?

Not quite the service you're used to. Sorry.

There was a chance of getting clear of the trap if I could

talk to Pepperidge and set up a last-ditch thing before nightfall, but in any case I'd have to assume that Kishnar would get here before I could use it.

They'd send for him, of course.

Sayako had said he'd be leaving Bangkok the day after tomorrow, taking his time, making his plans while Shoda's people here in the city did a square search for me in the streets until they found me and cornered me and had me waiting for him. They'd had some luck and they'd done that and I was set up for the kill and they'd send for him now—*had sent for him*—and he wouldn't waste any time. Shoda would put him in one of her private jets and it was only a three-hour flight.

At noon I telephoned Thongswasdi, the Thai inspector of police Katie had talked to. Pepperidge had checked out their Intelligence ranks for me and hadn't found anyone doubtful, but that didn't mean there wasn't a Shoda agent in their embassy here. If I asked them for information on Manif Kishnar it could warn him that I knew he was coming and I didn't want that.

"How can I help you?"

Thongswasdi.

"You were talking to Miss McCorkadale recently about Manif Kishnar."

"That is so."

The smells came in from the street as a man went through the swing-doors into the morning sunshine where I couldn't go, where I might, by nightfall, be carried.

"Can you describe him for me?"

It wasn't useful: a characteristic Hindu, five feet nine inches, ten stone, black hair, brown eyes, no scars, no other distinguishing features.

"What are his methods?"

"Excuse me?"

The line wasn't very clear.

"How does he kill?"

"With the garrotte, exclusively."

Thuggee.

"Does he use assistants?"

"No. He has always worked alone. He is a man of great pride in his efficiency."

"Does he prefer daylight or darkness?"

"He kills only by night. That is understandable, since he must approach from behind the victim. It was Kishnar who dealt with one of the agents mobilised by Thai Intelligence against Mariko Shoda."

Two men came in from the street and I watched them through the archway.

"Is there anything else you can think of, Inspector, that might help me?"

There was a short silence. "Miss McCorkadale mentioned that you might at some time find yourself in danger from this man. Is that correct?"

"Yes."

"I could send you a copy of his dossier, if you like."

"That's not necessary. I think you've given me all I need."

They were at the desk now, talking to Lily Ling; I caught snatches of Italian. Neither of them had been part of the surveillance team I'd seen outside.

"If you would like my advice," Thongswasdi said, "you should take the utmost care to avoid Manif Kishnar."

"I'll do that."

I thanked him and rang off and went out to the lobby and listened for a minute or two while the Italians were booked in, representatives of a minor shoe company in Naples. Then I went upstairs and made routine sightings again.

One of them was a woman who'd worked with the team that had got onto me when I'd been on my way to see Johnny Chen; I recognised her because it had taken me two hours to get clear of them. Another was the young Chinese standing near the salted-fish stall fifty yards from the hotel entrance, lifting on his toes all the time, flexing his ankles; he'd been in the previous team and had the walk of a *karateka*. At the back of the hotel there were two more men and a woman, one of them on the balcony of a shop-house backing onto the river, two of them in the street and keeping on the move the whole time, blending into the crowd on the narrow pavement as far as the intersections and then coming past again, not looking upwards because my room was on the other side, looking only at the gate of the little courtyard and along the low whitewashed wall.

13:15.

No call from Pepperidge. At intervals I centered on the area at the top of the stairs where Al or Lily Ling would pass if they wanted me to go down to the telephone. Then as the long afternoon began I went through the whole building as I'd done as soon as I'd got here, but now more critically.

He would come for me barefoot. The nerves and muscles in the sole of the foot are infinitely sensitive, controlling and balancing and refining all the movements made by the upper body as well as the legs and hips. To put shoes on is to deaden the information received by the naked foot from the terrain, so that all the body has to work on is the crude fact that it's more or less upright, the inner ear alone controlling balance. Shoes also create noise, and he would need to come for me in total silence.

If he came into the hotel he would look for me in my room first, and I ignored it, because I wouldn't be there. I concentrated on the only areas where he could come at me from behind: the corridors, the landings, and the stairs. I started from the roof and worked downwards, noting whatever looked useful. The roof was dangerous for three reasons: access was difficult, with small skylights and only one trap door. I used the trap door because the skylights were jammed with paint and I might break the glass. On the roof itself there was almost no cover and even at night I'd show a partial silhouette against the city-lit haze. Thirdly the drops were mostly sheer, except where the rusted fire-escape ran down on the north side; but I noted that a jump could be made from the roof to the first landing of the fire-escape seven or eight feet below, providing the tiles at the edge of the roof didn't break or shift and send me wide of the landing and into the courtyard five storeys down—a killing drop.

At intervals I had to stop work and wait until one of the guests or a whole party of them had left the corridors and gone into a room or down the stairs. I saw Lily Ling twice and she didn't say there'd been a call for me.

14:10.

I would have liked, I would have liked very much, to hear the voice of Pepperidge this afternoon. He was a burnt-out spook with no network behind him but in the last couple of conversations with him over the phone I'd begun sensing a calmness in the man that had come from experience in the field. He knew more than most what I was up against, how lonely I was out here, how afraid. He understood my paranoia, almost as well as Ferris had when he was running me. And Pepperidge had pride: *I don't sleep when there's work to do, you know. I've been in Signals with the Thais most of the night.*

But I didn't just want to hear his voice on the telephone. I wanted to set up the last-chance thing in case nothing else would work.

The hours were going by, and the stress of a trapped animal mounts progressively. The work I was doing now was essential, vital, and could save my life, but it was an intellectual exercise, and in the brain-stem there was a primitive creature shaking the bars of its cage.

If I went out of the hotel I'd still be in a trap: they'd move with me through the streets and wherever I went they would go, and this time they wouldn't let me get clear, because Kishnar was coming and their orders were to hold me ready for him.

I was beginning to know Shoda. *You know how to do this thing, by knowledge of woman.* Sayako. I knew there were enough of them out there to make a concerted kill by sheer weight of numbers, but they'd tried it before, five of them in the limousine, and this time Shoda had known that the only way to make *certain* was to send Kishnar. To let these minions attempt a kill would be like asking the *peons* in the *plaza de toros* to go for the bull instead of leaving it for the matador.

She had style, Shoda. This time she wanted the act accomplished with certainty, discretion, and grace. She would be praying for me, I knew, at some time in the hours of this night.

14:25.

Most of the vacant rooms were on the fifth floor because there wasn't a lift and the stairs were steep; they were also ancient, and creaked. That would be the terrain of my main defence: the staircase. It would send me immediate and accurate signals if anyone set foot on it, even bare. Kishnar would know that. He was a professional. He would look at this building and know by its age and construction that the stairs would creak. He would therefore try to bring me out to the street, and lead me to dark places. I didn't know how he would do this, but with the passing of these uneasy hours I might come to know, or catch a gleam of intuition. My mind was already engaged with his, as the distance closed between us.

At three o'clock I went downstairs and asked the kitchen boy to bring me some food in the bar, a two-egg omelette and whole-wheat toast, fat, protein, and carbohydrate. I sat with the long window at my right side, the window overlooking the street, where they could see me and be reassured that I knew nothing, felt myself to be in no danger.

"We're here for the gee-gee's." A sly laugh.

Al was booking them in, wouldn't know what gee-gee's were, unless he was versed in the vernacular of the suburban Londoner.

"It's always too bloody wet at Epsom." Rueful chuckle.

Have a nice stay, Al told them, not knowing what Epsom was, or where, it's good to have you folks at the Red

Orchid, so forth, while this compatriot of theirs, this undistinguished spook, sat eating his eggs and toast and tried to keep his mind off the fact that there was a narrow-angled vector running from this window to the roof on the other side of the street, from this head to the muzzle of a .22 single-shot rim-fire Remington 40XB with Redfield Olympic sights, one quick squeeze and the glass of the window flying inwards and the little grey cylinder meeting the skin and then the bone and then the brain and nuzzling into the consciousness at two thousand revolutions a second and blowing the world away, morbid, yes, just a touch melodramatic but the fact remained, the fact *remained,* damn you, that a calculated risk is still a risk and this was going to be a long day and it wasn't over yet.

"Hell's Epsom?"

"What?"

Al looking down at me, a toothpick in his mouth, his lazy, cynical smile covering his habitual apprehension.

"Oh. A race-track near London."

Just a thought, that was all. They wouldn't use a gun.

"And the gee-jaws?"

"Al, you slay me." Now *what* a turn of phrase. "Gee-gee's, horses, don't ask me why."

"I get it. Penang. People think we speak the same language, you know that? They okay?" Looking at the eggs.

"Excellent." Penang was the race-track just across the border.

"You want anything, you name it."

He went away on his small, careful feet, his shoulders a little hunched against the rains of Providence. There's nothing, my good friend, that I want, though it's kind of you to ask, unless perhaps you can by some ethereal magic erase the beginning of this day and run reality through once more and render the street out there innocent of the death-bringers, so that I might stroll through the doors and wander among the stalls and the handcarts and the colourful canvas awnings and pick perhaps at a ripe guava, paying too much for it and loving the merchant for his greed, which would equal mine, though mine would be the greed for life itself.

Someone shouted and the skin crawled suddenly, tightening across the skull, a man protesting that a cyclo had nearly knocked him down. I'll have to do better than this, my masters, better than this if I'm going to outdo Manif Kishnar when he comes for me.

"You want coffee?"

Said no, because I couldn't judge the timing yet, didn't know precisely when I would need the stimulus of the caffeine before its effects died away and left a treacherous dip in the energy-wave.

"No time in the day when breakfast doesn't go down just right, what? You from the Old Country?"

Red face, clipped white moustache, club tie, a jolly laugh.

"Excusez-moi, m'sieur, mais je ne parle pas l'anglais."

"Ah. Sorry, my mistake. Er—par-*dong*." Hurried away, waving.

Think nothing of it, old boy, and good luck with the gee-gee's, I'd try a little flutter on Kinross Lad in the fifth race, I think Ismail's riding and it'll be soft going after the rain.

15:34 and Pepperidge hadn't phoned so I went upstairs and got on with the good work and put him out of my mind because I didn't know what time it would be when it would become, across the span of a single second, too late for him to phone, too late for me to set up the last-chance thing.

I took sightings again and saw that two of them had gone, to be replaced by a slight woman in a track-suit with International Fitness Clubs printed across the front and a male European, Teutonic, very cool, adept at the sweeping glance that took in everything.

Still only five. They thought that was enough, and of course it was, because there'd be a dozen more in the background waiting to move in and man the mobile trap if I tried to leave the hotel.

This time you will please ensure that he does not survive.

Shoda.

I mean it's feasible, plausible, that a woman like that, vicious and powerful and so on, could easily have been that kind of child—resourceful and adaptable and savage. Wouldn't you think?

There was nothing in my room or any of the vacant rooms that would make any kind of weapon better than my hands, but what made me nervous was the idea of looking for weapons at all: I couldn't remember doing it before, even when things were touching the brink of extinction. My hands were lethal and I knew that.

It was the first hint that in the late afternoon my nerve had started to go.

It wasn't the waiting. I'd waited before, in Moscow and Bangkok and Tangier, waited for hours, for days, and kept the nerves intact, operational. It was Shoda. She kept coming into my thoughts, the memory of her face with its high cheekbones and its wide, luminous eyes, the clear brow under the night-black hair, the face of the angel of death.

Someone asked her how she could have possibly managed to survive seven months in the jungle at that age, and she said it was easy, once you became an animal.

Voodoo is real. It exerts its influence all over the world, not just in places like Tahiti. It is the stage, insidiously reached, where fear becomes belief.

What the hell is that bastard Pepperidge doing?

Where fear begins to ask questions like that, questions that shoot into the mind through the defences you thought were impregnable.

Why hadn't he phoned?

Like bullets coming into the brain, already there before you even heard the shot.

Because if he didn't phone before nightfall I knew there wasn't a chance left for me—I *knew* that now.

She watched the monkeys, and ate only the berries and things they ate, so as not to get poisoned. She killed a tiger.

Shoda.

Her name was voodoo.

So all right the nerve was going and something would have to be done about it and I set up a whole tactical scenario from one end of the building to the other and from top to bottom, creating a dozen situations where he could come for me, Kishnar, and I could get clear and survive or engage with him and kill him and survive, but it was an intellectual exercise to keep panic away because I knew what the deadline was now, the deadline for Pepperidge to call before it was too late for me to set up the last-chance thing: it was the time, the hour, the minute, when Manif Kishnar landed in Singapore.

Unless of course for some reason unknown to me he hadn't been sent for yet. That had been an assumption on my part and assumptions are always dangerous and sometimes lethal. He could still be taking his time, leaving Bangkok the day after tomorrow, not hurrying, confident, perfectly confident, knowing I was in a trap and held ready for him.

That would mean I'd have two more nights and a day to work something out and surely to God I wouldn't need more than *thirty-six hours* to set something up that could get me away from this bloody place with its doors and passages and windows and stairs and skylights and blind spots and escape routes spinning around in my mind with the nerves rubbing raw while I soaked in my sweat and listened, listened the whole time for the sound of the phone down there.

"Mr Jordan?"

Lily Ling.

I went to the staircase.

"I'm here."

"Telephone, please."

"Thank you."

16:21.

Pepperidge. I went down the stairs, the nerves going slack like the cut string of a cello, the legs without any strength in them, *where the hell had he been all this time?*

I picked up the phone and said hello.

"Mr Jordan?"

"Yes."

"This is Sayako. Kishnar has just left Bangkok."

Three hours' flight.

Countdown.

15

WHISTLING

Tequila Sunrise. Tote, Penang: $43, $19, $13.
Fruit smells from the street.
"How do you know?"
"I know."
In the third race, Saracen, Chacha Mambo, Honest Injun.
"Is he alone?"
Tote, Penang: $12, $5, $26. The winner—
"He always alone."
I took a slow breath, centering.
The trainer was Lim Hock Chan.
Radio.
"Sayako-san, you may be mistaken."
It was an attempt to draw her out, that was all.
Tote, Singapore: $23, $14, $22.
Red plastic radio at the end of the bar.
"Not mistaken."
Stink of sweat but the nerves steadying now.
In the fifth race, Mudlark II, Chankara, Bumble Bee.
I mentally tuned the thing out. The nerves were steadying because now it was certain, and all assumptions were blown away. Certain that he was coming.
"Mr Jordan?"

"Yes."

"Also, your hotel is being watched."

"I know."

"Ah, so. It is then very difficult for you. In some way you must leave hotel."

Trying to flush you from cover.

No. She saved my life, remember?

I said, "All right." No point telling her there wasn't a chance.

Be very careful.

Oh, shut up. She warned me he'd been ordered to make the kill. Wasn't that in my interests?

"Listen, please, Mr Jordan. I will do what I can for you. But there are many watching."

"Yes."

I could see one of them through the window, the Chinese *karateka*.

"I wish for you"—there was a break on the line, or she'd hesitated—"good fortune."

Click, went dead.

Make a decision, then.

"How's about a drink?"

Al.

"Not just now."

Not really in the mood.

Make a decision, yes. If we were going to do it here, here at the Red Orchid, I was ready. The kaleidoscope of images—staircase, skylights, roof-drops, escape routes—had coalesced, presenting me with a complete architectural blueprint for survival. There was nothing more for me to do here.

So I came round from behind the bar and walked through the archway and through the doors and out into the street.

"How much?"

"One dollar."

Greedy bugger.

"Give me one of those plastic spoons."

Messy to eat, but a guava, like life, is sweet.

They'd reacted fast—you should have seen them. Hadn't expected the little ferret to walk out of its trap and start stuffing guavas. The *karaketa* had turned his head immediately and signalled the woman in the track-suit and she'd swung away from the corner and started down the street on the other side, leaving another one to move in and cover while she walked past the doorway of the herb shop, glancing in and moving on. Pawn to K4, so forth, they'd got it worked out.

But they knew I wasn't a bloody amateur either so I spent almost an hour going through the motions of spotting and evading and closing circuits and breaking out and doubling tracks, using three taxis and the alleyway giving onto New Bridge Road I'd used the night I'd arrived here.

I've got out of mobile surveillance traps in Moscow and Berlin and Warsaw but it was the first time I'd had to *simulate* getting clear. There was no chance, absolutely *no* chance of getting out of this one because it was massive—I'd counted fourteen of them at the end of the first half-hour. They weren't just trying to establish my travel pattern or see if I made a contact or dropped a signal for someone; they had to make sure I was set up for Kishnar when he came, because if they failed they were finished, a sabre blade across the first vertebra—they were responsible to Mariko Shoda.

What I had to do was establish the fact that I had a purpose in leaving the hotel—that I wasn't just making an attempt at getting clear and going to ground. They knew I was professional enough to have seen them in the street, and knew I hadn't a chance of getting clear with so many of them manning the trap, so I had to make them believe I was flawed, and thought I could work miracles. So when I walked into the Hertz office in South Bridge Road I didn't even glance behind me.

"What model do you prefer, sir?"

"Compact."

Smaller windows.

Toyota Corolla.

Driving-licence, Amex, so forth. And this pretty smile, these almond eyes, the slight lift of the breasts beneath the silk blouse, are they the last I shall see?

"Will you please sign here, Mr Jordan?"

And the last signature?

With a flourish, then.

Outside in the car park I walked round the Toyota once to check the bodywork and then got in and started up and clipped the belt on without taking in the environment. In the first three blocks I picked out the taxi, a yellow and black Streamline three vehicles behind. There would be others closing in; I didn't look for them. It was tempting to try driving clear but it would mean risking lives—not theirs, I'd settle for that, but the lives of the innocent on their way home in the evening rush-hour. So I drove carefully, with due circumspection.

Countdown.

18:00.

He would be here in two hours.

There was an alley with a dead-end alongside the Red Orchid, where there would be deep shadow by eight o'clock. Al's Chevrolet was farther down and I'd be blocking him, but he never left the bar at this time in the evening. I parked the Toyota and locked the doors and went into the hotel by the front entrance, not looking back.

The last-chance thing.

But only if Pepperidge telephoned.

"Hi! Set it up?"

"Yes."

Six drops.

"You invent this one?"

"Flash of genius." *Ask him.* "No calls for me?"

"Guess not."

I took my drink across to the corner where I could sit with my back to the television screen: the optic nerve would have to adjust to the periodicy and tonight I wanted eyes like a cat's.

Do something for me, will you?

I could see part of the street from here but it didn't interest me now. They were out there, and I knew that.

For God's sake, if and when you can, pick up a phone and call me, so that I'll know things are still all right.

That was tempting too, to go across to the phone and hear her voice as she swung her long hair back from her eyes, *Oh Martin, where are you calling from?* But no, we couldn't meet, tonight or ever again, unless he telephoned, Pepperidge, and even then it was a thousand-to-one shot.

18:31.

Rain began soon afterwards.

"Here we go!" Al said from the bar.

The stalls and barrows had been cleared from the narrow street an hour ago, and the stones began taking on a sheen as the rain fell harder. People out there were hurrying, some of them with newspapers over their heads.

It wouldn't change anything.

19:00.

An hour to go. He would land in an hour.

The adrenaline began; I could feel it like a subtle vibration in the bloodstream, in the nerves. I centered at intervals of a minute, hearing the leather of the chair creak faintly as the tension came out of the muscles and the body sank lower. I would need the adrenaline later, but not now: it was too soon.

The rain steadied in the street, on the rooftops, closing us in, sequestering us in this small seedy hotel in Singapore as if we'd been washed up in an ark. They would be standing in doorways now, taking shelter from the rain, not from the inexorable tolling of the minutes, as I was, the inescapable measurement of time moving towards the deadline an hour from now.

Not that it's a foregone conclusion, my friends—don't think that. I've slipped the executioner a dozen times and he's brought the axe down on the bloody block with an oath I didn't stay to listen to. I'm strong; I'm trained; I'm ready for the moment of truth.

Do you hear the sound of whistling in the dark?

I do.

Because it wasn't going to be one against one. Even if I pulled off an overkill with Manif Kishnar they'd finish me off, the *peons,* if they had to. Those would be the orders from Shoda: *this time it is to be certain.*

The smell of the rain came through the doors as someone opened them, the smell of the rain, of the fruit lying squashed in the gutters, and on a different level of consciousness the smell of the world outside, of the death-bringer.

Telephone.

I didn't move.

"Red Orchid Hotel."

The man who'd come in stood dripping by the desk on the other side of the archway, a shapeless bag by his feet.

"Oh, hi! You bet. How are things with you?"

I checked my watch at 19:34 and thought that would be unfortunate, wouldn't it, if Pepperidge finally called me and heard only the engaged tone while Al was asking about his girl-friend's health or his aunt's or whoever the hell it was on the other end, my chest's easier but there's still this cough, and the doctor says *I do not care what the doctor says, just get off the line.*

"Look, Betsy, I have to go now, there's a guy at the desk, okay?"

Works like magic: you just go into zen and concentrate and create your own reality, get people off the telephone, get people to call you no matter how great the distance—*Pepperidge, are you listening, damn your eyes?*

Watch it.

Centre, yes. Centre again.

The chair-leather creaked. Felt better, much better. If he came in now with his bloody cheese-wire I would rip the heart out of his body and throw it to the dogs.

"Sure, I'll see you get some extra towels, guess it caught you when you weren't ready." Noting the time in the register, 7:35 P.M. "Happens all the time like that—one minute there's a clear sky and the next minute you're trying to find a canoe.''

Or in the terminology of international chronometers 19:35, now 36 because time, like life, has its rendezvous to meet.

As do I.

The adrenaline was still seeping into the bloodstream even though I was spending most of the time in alpha now and coasting along in the philosophical dimension below full consciousness, and I tried to go lower still because the conclusion wouldn't be made in thirty-five minutes from now, that was when he would arrive, and he'd have to take me into the dark to do what he wanted and that could happen at any time, at midnight or beyond.

''You bet.''

His footsteps came through the archway and across to the bar behind me; I knew Al's footsteps.

Well if Mary was so upset about it why didn't she call me?

Maybe she just didn't want to bother you.

Look, she knows I'm always ready to help, Cindy.

''You don't ever watch this stuff?''

Turned my head. ''I like watching the rain.''

''Makes a whole lot more sense, I guess. You okay there, you need another of those specials?''

Said not just now.

For fifteen minutes I brought the waves back into beta and went through the building again, reinforcing the memory and testing out some of the options; there was one that worried me: the drop from the roof to the top platform of the fire-escape at the rear. It was chancy enough in dry conditions, seven or eight feet and at an angle, but tonight the tiles would be wet and so would the fire-escape and it was a killing drop, five floors and a stone courtyard below and in any case they'd cover that area and even if I did the drop and hit it right they'd be waiting for me below, on any of the four landings below. Cancel that one, then, yes, cancel it. If I was forced onto the roof I'd stay there till they came for me.

Not they. Him. Kishnar. On the dark rooftop.

Early this morning the body of a man was found lying at the rear of the Red Orchid, a hotel in the Chinese quarter. His identity is being withheld until relatives have been informed.

19:59.

Sweat starting on the flanks, and the adrenaline pumping—the very lack of control was frightening and I asked questions. I'd been in a red sector before and I'd always been able to hold back the defence mode until it was needed, minutes or even seconds before the attack, but tonight I was ready too soon, much too soon—I felt primed, galvanised, invincible. I think it was because of the timing, the gradual nearing of the deadline, the need to wait, and do nothing, to wait in a trap for the hunter to come in his own good time with his bright skinning-knife. And there was something else.

Shoda.

Shoda, my deadly succuba.

I could smell the fear on my skin.

Because she had a long reach, sending her finely tuned vibrations across time and space, to stroke insidiously the tender membrane of the psyche, soft as the searching touch of the black widow as she seeks the area where her bite will most easily penetrate and her poison most quickly kill.

He'd be at my throat but Shoda was already in my soul.

In Kuala Lumpur today, a top National Front leader, addressing his party's annual convention, demanded that the ugly encroachment of corruption at high levels be halted as soon as possible.

Eight o'clock news.

Datuk Dr Lim Keng Yaik also referred to the matter of Malaysia's threatened economy, stressing the—

—Sex symbol of the fifties. She was fifty-seven.

Al didn't go for politics.

Touching down now, with plumes of smoke curling back from the landing-wheels, and I got up quickly because the only way to get rid of the excess adrenaline was to exercise the body and there was a staircase out there with four flights I could use. If I—

Telephone and Al took it and said yes he's here and then called out to me and I went over to the bar and took the phone from him, hello?

"Mr Jordan?"

"Yes."

"He has landed in Singapore."

Sayako.

"What is he wearing?"

"He is wearing dark business-suit, head is bare."

"He'll need a raincoat. Is he carrying one?"

"He carry only a briefcase."

What had they asked him, at the security check in Bangkok, about the coil of piano-wire on the X-ray screen?

"Is there anything else you can tell me, Sayako-san?"

It might not have shown up; it would be very thin.

"There is nothing else, Mr Jordan. But I will help if I can. You must be very careful, and leave hotel if is possible. I pray for you now."

Line went dead.

Pray for me, yes, Sayako-san, as Shoda is praying for me now.

She prays before she kills.

I put the receiver back.

Steady rain in the street and Al sitting hunched on his stool behind the bar and three men coming in from the stairs, Asians, I'd seen them before in here and heard them talking, they were waiting for a shipment of silk to come in from Laos, important to them but not important to me because Kishnar was here in the city and the deadline for Pepperidge to call was past and the last-chance thing was blown away and what I must do now was try to contain the body's preparedness, try to damp down the effusions of life-preserving hormones as the glands obeyed the panic mode of the mind.

Start with the stairs, then, bring the muscles into play.

"Mr Jordan!" Al caught me on the first landing and I looked down. "You got another call."

Impossible.

Kishnar would never phone me.

But he'd just landed and was coming through the terminal building in a dark business-suit, not some hessian rag with a headband and a knife in his teeth—*he would have style:* Shoda would expect style in a man close to her in her organisation, a man who had despatched nine of her top competitors in the drug trade, her *top* competitors, warlords like Khun Sa whose income was in the billions of dollars, so that each time he'd hit one of them it would have increased Shoda's own fortune by the same figure. He'd be a millionaire, then, himself, Manif Kishnar, the executioner, one of the elite, stepping off one of his employer's private executive jets and walking through the airport past all the telephones—yes he *might* call me.

Mr Jordan, my name is Manif Kishnar, and I believe you have heard of me, knowing as I do the extensive sources of information at your disposal as a preeminent intelligence agent.

Letting my mind run wild but that was understandable because of the woman I was up against, the mystic and psychotic Mariko Shoda, and because of Sayako, with her uncanny knowledge of the environment I was moving through, shadowed, tortuous and cryptic—these weren't the KGB with their orderly and predictable methodology; these weren't the paramilitary executives of the state machine; they were shadows, voices in the night.

The skillful practitioners of voodoo.

You will therefore surmise my reason for coming to Singapore tonight, and since there is no question of my failing to accomplish my mission for my employer, may I suggest with all respect that we meet somewhere removed from public gaze, and deal with the matter circumspectly. I feel that might be your wish.

Don't make the mistake of thinking that Manif Kishnar

wasn't a man like that, with a mind like that. I've met them before, intellectual, supremely competent, even though their work is deadly. They are the elite, and they can operate on a level of sophistication you won't find in the lesser breeds.

Removed from the public gaze.

The dark.

And this would be his reason: to draw me into the dark.

The circumstances, Mr Jordan, are well defined. If you choose to remain in your hotel, then I must come for you there. But will that not be a little . . . unseemly? The owner is trying to run an honest business, after all, and we would embarrass him, and jeopardise the reputation of his establishment, do you not agree?

Sirens in the night.

The flash of blue and red and white across the walls in the street outside, diffused by the downpour; the faint squawk of the zip-fastener as they closed the black plastic bag before they lifted me; Al's white face on the stairs, Lily, for Christ's sake get a mop and hot water.

He had a point, Kishnar, had a point.

If you agreed to meet me on what we might call neutral ground, Mr Jordan, I would offer you all due ceremony. Men of your calling seldom die with dignity, but for you I would vouchsafe it.

With the rain falling steadily on our heads, its drops silvering the dark. The exchange of courtesies and then the quick movement and then nothing, *finis*.

Not while there's life, my friend.

But Mr Jordan, it is a foregone conclusion. You know that. I shall not fail—indeed I dare not. I am simply attempting to bring this matter to an end in a rational and civilised manner.

Do you see his point? A desperate stalking operation through the building here, waking the guests however quietly we moved, however secretly, each seeking the other's death until the end-game and the last hot deed enacted in the close confinement of the flesh or a missed foothold and the hideous drop to the stones below or a lost chance and the wire's bite and the blood spilling and the cry cut off, and then the mess, the messiness of a violent death—or alternatively his offer of due ceremony, out there somewhere in the privacy of the rain and the dark with no one near and no sound but the intoning of my executioner's prayer.

If this was in his mind you couldn't say he wasn't civilised. Better, surely, than baring one's neck to a brute.

I went down to the bar and picked up the phone.

16

TOYOTA

"What kind of red sector?"

Pepperidge.

His tone was sharp, brief.

"I think it's too late," I told him.

"Sorry, I had to go up to London, then your phone's been engaged. What can I do?"

"I'm in a massive surveillance trap and Shoda's sent a hit man here."

"Who?"

"Kishnar."

"Manif Kishnar, yes, he works for her exclusively. What are your chances?"

"About nil." The clock on the wall said three minutes past eight.

"Why not signal the Thai Embassy?"

"There's no point. I—"

"Police, then, get them to send a gun team—"

"No, it's—"

"I can phone the High Commission. They'd—"

"It wouldn't work."

"Fuck."

It was a shut-ended situation and he didn't like it. We never do.

The reason why it wouldn't work was because Shoda was running things and this time she wouldn't let me get clear; this time she'd ordered a sure hit and even if I could persuade Rattakul to risk a diplomatic showdown against every known principle of intelligence policy or persuade the Singapore police to send in a gun team it'd be the same thing in the end—these people would bring me down, if necessary with a rush attack, if necessary with a suicide run, if necessary with an exchange of gunfire with the police team despite Shoda's wish for a discreet kill that would cause no fuss and leave no trace.

Three minutes past eight but that wasn't significant. What could conceivably make any difference was that it would take Kishnar twenty minutes to reach here from the airport. There'd be a car to meet him and the driver would know the way, would know this city intimately, but in this rain and with the cabs in demand and cluttering the streets it would take twenty minutes at least. The earliest he could arrive here would be at eight twenty-three.

Then give it a go.

"I can send you some shields," Pepperidge was saying. "I could raise three or four, if—"

"No. But I want a contact to make a letter-drop. One man."

"Look, you can have more than—"

"One. One man."

Hesitation, then, "All right. Got a pencil?"

"Yes." I reached for the phone pad.

"His name's Westerby. He's at 734.49206."

"Description?"

"Thirty, five-eleven, thirteen stone, dark brown hair, brown eyes."

"I've got that. Give me a backup."

"Lee Yeo. Asian. He's at—"

"No. Caucasian."

"All right." Short pause, the scuffing of paper. "Veneker, at 734.289039. Thirty-five, five-ten, eleven stone, black hair, dark blue eyes, a *san-dan* in *Shotokan*."

"That's all I need," I told him.

"Look, I'll man this phone non-stop. You've got immediate access."

"Don't lose any sleep." Because I knew how he felt: he'd handed me a mission and after twelve days I was trapped and set up for the kill and although it wasn't his fault he knew the situation, knew it of old. It's the time when the laughter stops.

I pressed the contact and dialled for Westerby and got the ringing tone and waited.

Clock. Nineteen minutes to go.

Went on ringing, wasn't there.

Jesus Christ this wouldn't have done for the Bureau.

I dialled for Veneker and got the ringing tone again and waited again, Al talking to the three Asians, they were showing him a swatch of raw silk, the TV flickering above the bar, *Mary came straight round here the minute she heard, but Cindy was over at the ball-game with Bob and we couldn't give her the news,* they'd never get their fucking lives worked out, went on ringing—

"Hello?"

"Veneker?"

"Yes."

"Jordan."

"Yes, sir."

"I want you to come to the Red Orchid Hotel in Chong Street, just off Boat Quay in Chinatown. It's in a—"

"I know where it is."

"All right, how soon can you be here?"

"Ten minutes."

"That'll leave us nine for a critical deadline, can you make it?"

Running it bloody close, wished I hadn't said it, wished I'd called it off—

"Oh, yes—"

"In this rain?"

"Yes, sir. Ten minutes it is."

"Bring a suitcase or something, look like a tourist and

register at the desk—I'll make contact immediately afterwards."

"Got it."

"Synchronise watches at 20:05 hours."

"20:05."

"Now listen, *your* deadline for getting here is 20:21, which will leave you exactly two minutes to spare. If you can't make it by then, *stay away*. You'll be coming through heavy surveillance."

"Understood, sir. But I'll be there."

I put the receiver down and asked Al for some paper and an envelope; then I centred for a moment to slow the adrenaline but the nerves were humming with it and I walked out of the bar and through the lobby and up the stairs, climbing them slowly, steadily, counting them as a mental exercise to keep the left brain occupied while I went through the next sixteen minutes, checking to see if there were anything else that should be done and coming up blank—everything was done, the fuse had been lit and it was burning.

Fifteen stairs and a Chinese woman on the second floor, carrying a child, Lily coming along from my room on the third—

"You eat here tonight, Mr Jordan?"

"I don't know," I told her, didn't know what was going to happen tonight, could be anything, life, death, the wire biting deep or the courtyard coming up, spinning slowly, they say you never cry out, maybe the air rush, or of course the dawn and no conclusion—he'd take his time, make certain of me, no hurry.

Negative thinking, yes, all right, try it this way, with a bit of luck I might turn it into an overkill, catch him off balance and use a sweep or get to his throat, whatever, blow his world away instead of mine.

Whistling.

Fifth floor and the rain drumming on the roof, a crack of yellow sky through a window, a freak sunset over the sea, down again and up the stairs again like a rat on a treadmill until it was nineteen minutes past the hour and then I went down to the lobby and walked past the man registering at the desk without looking at him, going into the short passage that led to the courtyard at the rear, turning, waiting.

Al was writing in the big book with its worn soiled cover and its oxidised gold tassel, a gesture to elegance, a suggestion that this was in fact the Mandarin Oriental and not a sleazy doss-house on the waterfront, writing in the book, dear Christ we haven't got time for that but then it has to be done because the shutters don't fit exactly across the windows and they're watching him now, the man at the desk, just as they've been watching me for the last hour from the doorways opposite.

Two minutes to go. *Two.* Not long but within the critical time-frame, centre and relax.

The doors banged open and someone came into the lobby from the street and I froze and waited for them to move into sight, a woman with a dog in her arms, middle-aged, Caucasian, discount.

"Okay," Al said to the man at the desk, "you need a hand with the bag?"

"No."

Early thirties, five-ten, twelve or thirteen stone, black hair, dark blue eyes, his raincoat soaked, he'd walked here, quicker, no cabs available but got here in time, good as his word, a *san-dan* in *Shotokan,* to be expected.

He picked up his bag and turned and saw me and I made a signal and he came into the passage, an easy stride, confident—

"Veneker."

"Jordan."

"Nice weather for ducks."

I gave him the envelope. "Take this to the airport and leave it at the Hertz counter, to be picked up by this man, who's flying in tonight."

"That's all?"

"Yes." I gave him the keys of the car. "Toyota, parked in shadow. Don't be seen getting into it, and in this rain you'll keep the windows shut anyway. If you're followed, try and lose them, but don't try too hard: they won't let you."

He stood with his feet apart, balanced, tapping the envelope on the knuckle of his thumb, some of the tension in him coming off because he'd expected something a lot more dangerous than this.

"Roger. Once out of the car, sir, do I try and lose them? Going through the terminal?" A beat. "I'm quick off the mark."

"Again, *try* to lose them but don't."

"And once I've done the drop?"

"Fade. They won't be interested in you after that."

I sensed his hesitation as he stared at the name on the envelope, Harrison J. MacKenzie. He was wondering why I was doing a drop in a public place and involving other people, and what would happen when the surveillance team asked for the envelope.

But they wouldn't.

"Okay, sir. Do I report back to Cheltenham?"

"I'll do that." I checked my watch. "You've got less than two minutes. Leave the bag here."

He put it down. "Do I go out by—"

"No, this way."

I took him past the kitchen and into the courtyard at the rear. Rain in the lamplight, falling straight down, smelling of steel.

"Use that door in the wall across there. The car's on the other side."

"Toyota."

"Right."

He slipped the envelope into his mack and gave me a sudden straight look. "You be all right, will you?"

"Never say die."

He nodded and ducked through the rain towards the door.
I turned back into the hotel and went along the passage, picking up his bag and putting it behind the desk, and that was when the heavy booming sound came and the slats in the shutters were lit with a white flash and I stood with my eyes squeezed shut—*no, oh no, Mother of God forgive me.*

17

CRUCIFIX

Rain on the roof.

Underneath its sound I listened to the silence, tuning the rain out, listening to the silence. But even then I was picking up small sounds that came into the silence and faded: a distant voice on another floor of the hotel; a door shutting; the far faint note of a ship's siren from the river.

It was necessary, vital, to keep the steady drumming of the rain tuned out and to identify every small sound in the undertow of the silence, because he would come for me barefoot, and my only chance, here on the fifth floor, would be the ability to catch any slight sound he might make: the creak of a floorboard, the rustle of his sleeves as he brought his arms up in the final instant, the jerk of his breath.

Dark—pitch dark.

The lights had been burning when I'd reached here, halfway along the corridor, a minute ago, four dim bulbs under dusty silk shades with burn-marks on them. Now they were dark. The switch was not in the corridor, but round the corner by the stairwell. That was how I knew he was there: he needed the dark.

Dead man's shoes.

In the last few seconds I suppose he'd make a rush and all I'd know about it would be the sudden change in the air pressure and the breath blocking in his throat and the hot sharp bite of the wire before I could—

She moved.

The rain drumming, louder here than in the other place, would Al find the bag behind the desk?

In a dead man's shoes, dear Mother of God.

Stirred beside me.

He came at me in a flash and I screamed—

The hands of a child, still.

"Fuckee, fuckee?"

Her small pointed breasts against me, the smell of her as she moved close and held on to me, not held me, held on to me, there's a difference.

"No," I said and drew a long breath and lay still, listening to the only sound that had crossed the bridge of nightmare into reality: the rain on the roof, louder here because it was falling on corrugated iron, and maybe that was why she was frightened, and would also be frightened of thunder.

So I put my arms round her, bring her child's body curving into the arch of my own. She mistook me and opened her legs and began moving, and I whispered, "No, Chu-chu, no fuckee."

"No?"

"You must sleep," I said. She stopped moving and held me now in a different way, not dutifully like a prostitute but almost tenderly, for her: there'd been no tenderness for her to receive or express for a long time, I suppose, in the refugee camp, unless Chen had thought it necessary to teach her again, in between the fuckee.

At some time in the next few minutes she fell asleep, her head in the hollow of my shoulder, and I forgot about her and the rage came back, the self-rage, scalding, because when I'd walked out of the Red Orchid it had been in a dead man's shoes: Veneker's.

I hadn't been thinking.

It was like a dog-pack tearing at my throat, the guilt, I

couldn't shake it off. Sleep was the only anodyne, and even then I saw it again, the white flash in the slats of the shutters, heard it again, the dull booming, and Al's voice, startled, *what was that for Christ's sake?*

Veneker.

You be all right, will you?

He'd been thinking of me, of my welfare, knowing that I was in the middle of massive surveillance and knowing from Pepperidge that I was up against Shoda—he'd hesitated, hadn't liked leaving me there on my own, Veneker, a man used to helping people out, getting them through if he could, I'd known men like that and he was one of them and it was my honour, my everlasting privilege, *and all I'd done for him was send him straight into a booby-trap and let him get blown apart, oh Mother of God have mercy on my soul.*

Chen had seen the rage, felt it—"So what happened?"

"Wheel came off."

He'd told me to come in, shut the metal door, and reset the alarm. "A *wheel* came off?"

Bureau idiom. "Someone got killed." Very intense and he stared at me with his lidless eyes and decided not to say anything more. He was tense himself, shut-faced, and I said, "Sorry about your friend." The co-pilot of Flight 306.

"You went out there, didn't you?"

"Yes."

"What was—I mean did he look—" and I waited, then he said, "What the fuck difference does it make, come on upstairs."

In the huge cluttered room he asked me: "What did you come here for, Jordan?"

"Shelter."

"From the rain?"

"From people."

"Shoda's people?"

"Yes."

"You mean you want a safe-house?"

"Call it that. For a few days."

He angled his narrow head, thinking, watching me. "I'm due out on a flight in an hour, but you can stay if you want. Guess you could use a shower. Hang your things over there—they'll be dry by morning; this place is watertight."

When I came back he gave me a worn silk robe; it smelt of opium. "Some things you'll have to do for me while you're here, okay?"

"Whatever you say."

He was still watching me, considering. "When that flight went down, you must have thought I was in on it, right?"

"It occurred to me."

"I'll bet. Now you know different, or you wouldn't be here."

"Katie told me about your friend." Pepperidge had also cleared him: *I've done the necessary homework.*

Chen looked at the aircraft chronometer on the desk. "Sure." Head on one side. "You're putting a whole lot of trust in me, right?"

"I don't think it's misplaced."

"But if it is, you're dead."

"Correct."

"There's no particular reason," he said casually, "why I should drop you in the shit, but if I find a reason that's what I'm going to do. You don't have anything to worry over so long as what you've told me about you is true. You're also okay by Katie." He got one of his black cigarettes and lit up. "Just spelling it out for you, because I have to trust you too, if you're staying here in my absence." Blew out smoke, watching it. "I'm not talking about little Chu-chu, so long as you're gentle with her—she's only a kid. But feel free. I'm talking—"

"She'd have stayed here alone, if I hadn't come?"

"She's learned life the hard way. She can take care of herself."

"Is anyone likely to come here?"

"Nope. If anyone rings the bell—that's just figurative—she'll deal with the situation. You won't be disturbed. What

I was saying was, I'm going to trust you with one or two things you can do for me that wouldn't get done if you weren't here, because she doesn't speak English, maybe a couple of words.'' We were sitting on two of the leather-covered tabourets, and a coin fell out of his pocket as he reached for a notebook; he picked it up and wrote in the book and tore out the page and gave it to me. ''That's where you can call me, in Laos. There's an answering-machine over there, and I want you to monitor calls, okay?''

''Okay.''

''There won't be too many, nothing social—this place is a kind of safe-house for me too, as I guess you know. But if there's anything that sounds urgent, call me.''

''Will do.''

He nodded. ''When did you eat?''

''God knows.''

Let's have a snort!

''They been giving you a hard time?''

''Not as hard as it could've been.'' Another wave of guilt, hot and overpowering. The hard time had been for Veneker.

Chen left another telephone number with me; it was punched out on an embossed strip and stuck to the side of the Autocall machine.

''I should be back in a couple of days, Tuesday sometime. If I don't show up by Wednesday, or haven't contacted you here, call this number and tell them I'm overdue, okay?'' He was stuffing a Walther P38 into his airline bag. ''This trip I'm not sure what's going to happen.'' He zipped the bag shut. ''If you want to leave here before then, that's okay. And she'll be fine on her own. Take care.''

That had been hours ago and now she rested like the child she was, curved against me with one thin arm around me, her breathing as soft as a young animal's. I slept again, and the next time I woke it was because of the silence. The rain had stopped and it was almost first light.

She stirred.

"Johnny?"

"No. He'll be back soon."

She drew herself up against the pillows, and when it was light enough to see her face I said, "Can you smell smoke, Chu-chu?"

She watched me quietly, that was all.

"I can smell smoke," I told her. "I think this place is on fire."

She didn't turn her head to look anywhere.

"Are there any extinguishers here, Chu-chu? We don't want to be burned alive."

She gazed at me with soft and uncomprehending eyes, and I knew it was all right to call Pepperidge.

"Veneker's dead."

Short silence, and I heard something being knocked over, alarm clock or something. Over there it was eleven o'clock last night and maybe he was trying to conserve sleep in case I needed him.

"What happened?"

"They rigged a bomb. I should have thought of that."

"Can't think of everything. You—"

"Then I bloody well should have."

In a moment he said quietly, "You've got a war on. We have to expect casualties."

I got control again. "He didn't know a thing, of course." Desperate for consolation.

"Best way to go. But I don't understand. That doesn't sound like Kishnar."

"No. It must have been one of the surveillance people. I'd left a car standing outside, and they assumed I'd use it again."

"And he got in."

"Yes."

It had been a thin chance but any chance had been worth taking, so I'd worked it out: Veneker would get into the car without being seen and drive to the airport. They'd tag him there and when he was under the bright lights they'd see it wasn't me, but by that time it would be too late because they'd have been drawn away from the Red Orchid and I could have walked out when I wanted to, and that's what I'd done, but in a dead man's shoes.

"It was obviously a temptation for them," Pepperidge said.

"They must have been mad." Shoda had wanted absolute discretion and had sent a soft-hit agent to take care of me with no fuss and no trace and she'd have that man's life when she heard about this, have his neck under a sword, because this time it wasn't going to be kept out of the papers and Veneker would be identified and she'd know I'd got clear and gone to ground, *have his neck,* another little shred of consolation, an eye for an eye, so forth.

"True," Pepperidge said. "She won't like it. Where are you?"

"At Chen's." I gave him the number.

"What sort of condition?"

"I wasn't anywhere near."

Should have been. Jesus Christ, a simple letter drop and bang and he was dead.

"You'll be all right," Pepperidge was saying, "at Chen's. I'll vouch for him personally. But you'll have to be careful from now on. Kishnar won't be called off."

"Nothing's changed, except that I'm now clandestine." Wouldn't be going to the Thai Embassy or the Red Orchid or anywhere else above ground, wouldn't be meeting anyone, my only exposure the need for transport, a plain van, a risk that had to be taken.

"Can I do anything for you?" Pepperidge asked.

"No. You can turn in now."

"Pissing down, here." He was trying to make light of the Veneker thing for my sake, but he'd be taking it hard: I knew a first-class man when I saw one and Veneker had measured up—bright, brief, reliable, and concerned.

"How long had you known him?"

"Who?"

"Veneker."

"Oh." Couple of beats. "Did a job with him once. H

wouldn't have wanted to die in bed.'' Another pause. ''Don't worry, old boy.''

''I'd give anything.''

''I understand.'' He cleared his throat. ''You still haven't come across a Colonel Cho out there?''

''No. That's C-H-O?''

''Yes. I've been doing some work on him, but it's not easy at this distance. It'd be an idea for you to ask Johnny Chen. He might know about him. I'll talk to him myself, if you like.''

''He's not here.''

''When you see him, then. Cho could be *very* important.''

''Alright.''

''What we need to find,'' Pepperidge said, ''is her exposed flank. I mean Shoda's. And Cho might tell us.''

Katie had said much the same thing: *I suppose what you need most is to know her Achilles' heel.*

''It'd show me the way in,'' I told him. ''And if I don't find it soon I think we've had it.''

There were two dangers but I didn't spell it out for him. Shoda's fury would now be intensified and she'd make my death an ambition—the very powerful were like that: any show of opposition came as a personal affront and they couldn't rest until it was destroyed. The second danger was that I was now in a rage of my own and ready to take uncalculated risks to get at her because I didn't like being stalked through the bloody streets and forced into a foxhole and I didn't like the way they'd wiped out Veneker, a man who'd saved my life with his own.

And there was the voodoo factor and I didn't know how long I could stand up to it because at the Red Orchid last night I'd felt a degree of vulnerability I'd never known before and it had worried me in the background of my mind—I'd almost accepted the foregone conclusion that Kishnar would make his kill, inevitably, and all I'd been doing was running around the place like a rat in a trap, working out the escape mechanisms I couldn't have hoped to trigger once he was inside the building. It had been unnerving and it was still on my mind, the sense of oncoming doom.

"Say again?" Pepperidge.

"If we don't find a way in, I think we've had it."

"Any specific reason? I mean apart from Kishnar."

"I just think I'm outnumbered. Outgunned."

"I'm sure you do." A different tone, sharper. "And I'm sure you're not. Take any mission and there's a time when you can't see the light at the end of the tunnel. It gets dark in there—I've been down it a good few times. You need to rest up for a bit, that's all, restore the nerves. If it's any help, old boy, I'm working hard at this end and I'm in constant signals with people in London and the field." The sharp tone had faded, taking on a hint of false comfort. But what else could the poor bastard do but try to rally the ferret he was running?

"Yes," I told him, "that's a help. It's all I've got."

"Jolly good show. Keep in touch."

She pulled the gun out of the drawer and checked the safety catch with the movements of a trained marksman and I wondered whether she'd picked it up in the refugee camps or from Johnny Chen. She went to the door and down the open-slatted wooden steps and stopped on the landing halfway down and waited, watching the iron door in the side of the wharf.

The beeper had sounded a minute ago and she was quick to react but not flustered. I watched her from the top of the steps and the minutes went by and Chu-chu turned and came up again and put the gun away and looked at me and made a figure on the top of the desk with her hand, three fingers and thumb down and a finger sticking out in front, an animal walking along.

"Dog?" I said.

She walked her hand close to the jade paperweight and lifted her thumb, dog, yes, peeing. The alarm was triggered by infra-red ray and angled too low, or of course it could be Kishnar down there or any one of the surveillance team but I'd have to watch thoughts like that because I'd taken infinite care to get here clean and there was no way they could find me.

They found you at the Red Orchid.

Because I'd been walking in and out of the place, that was why—I hadn't been clandestine.

"Dog," I nodded to the girl, but she didn't repeat it.

She spent the morning cooking some food and washing the bare wooden floor while I rested on the divan between phone-calls, drifting into alpha and working a few things out. One of them worried me: I didn't know how long it would be before Shoda found out I was still alive. The Toyota had been totally burned out when I'd left the hotel an hour later, going over the wall at the other side where it was dark, though the surveillance team had broken up and moved away by then, assuming I was dead. Veneker might have been carrying papers but they could have been under a cover name; in any case they were now probably ash. The metal figures of the number plate would have been decipherable and the police would have run them through their computer and gone to the Hertz office. I'd used my cover name and address, and that would have sent them to the hotel. But—

A bitter smell had come into the air and I opened my eyes. Chu-chu was sitting at the small rickety table by the lamp with the dragon shade; the ruby Chen had given her was on it, glowing in the light like a drop of blood. She was gazing at it, her eyes lost in its colour as she inhaled the tendril of smoke rising from the tin ashtray in front of her, where she'd lit a slug of opium.

I closed my eyes again. At the hotel, then, the police would have checked the register and Al would have said yes, a Martin Jordan was staying there, but he hadn't seen him since a few minutes before the explosion had sounded. He would have said this because the instant I'd realised what had happened I'd kept strictly out of sight. So I would be down as a suspected victim, but they'd also go on checking, trying to find out where the man named Veneker was, and why he'd registered and left a bag behind the desk and disappeared.

But had Veneker used his own name when he'd registered? Pepperidge might know. I didn't have enough data to give me a fix on the deadline—the time when Shoda would find out I was still alive. But it would be some days at least before they could identify Veneker's body through the dental records—if any existed in Singapore.

Gimme a kiss, honey.

Some days. Perhaps that was all I would need.

In the afternoon there were some phone-calls and I made notes for Chen. Three of them were from people who didn't leave their names, or use his.

We didn't make it. The strip was waterlogged after the rain and we put down in Chiang Mai. You better tell them over there—you know?—we'll try again in a few days.

Two calls in Chinese, the Hokkein dialect, which I didn't understand. Then another American-accented Asian.

The price is right, but they want guarantees. Can we make them? Get back to me as soon as you can—Blue Zero.

In the evening I phoned Chen in Laos, using the number he'd given me. A woman answered in a tongue I didn't understand, but I kept on repeating his name and she got him for me.

"How's it going?"

"I've got some messages for you. Do you want them now?"

"Sure."

I read from the notes. "The rest I didn't understand. There were four."

"Okay, what else?"

"Nothing by phone. The alarm sounded about midday, but Chu-chu said it must have been a dog."

"That thing's too low. I'll fix it when I get back."

"Is this girl safe with a gun?"

"What's she doing?"

"She went to the stairs with it, when the alarm beeper sounded—"

"Oh, sure, yeah. She's trained."

"All right. She's also using opium."

"So what else is new?"

"Different viewpoints."

"She doesn't have long, Jordan. She's been on coke for two years. Thing is to show her some kindness while she has the time left, okay? That's why I took her in."

"Understood."

I could smell cooking. Housekeeper, concubine, gun-handler, drug addict, and soon to die. Chu-chu, fourteen.

"Signing off," I told Chen.

"Sure. Take care."

The phone rang again in twenty minutes and I went for the note pad.

This is Katie. Do you know where Martin Jordan is? If he contacts you, let me know, will you? I'm worried about him. Look after yourself too. 'Bye.

To avoid it seeming like a coincidence I didn't do anything for an hour, not because I didn't trust her but because this was a safe-house and I didn't want her involved: I didn't want her to get in too deep, where the waters were dangerous. Then I took the parrot cage off its hook and took it into the bathroom and shut the door and came back and phoned her.

"Martin?"

"Yes."

I heard her let out a breath. "You sound all right."

"I'm fine."

"Where are you?" Then she said, "Sorry. As long as you're all right."

"Yes. How are you?"

Her fair hair swinging as her shoulders came forward; the fan turning slowly under the ceiling; cushions all over the floor; the taste of zabaglione.

"I'm all right too," she said. "And I've been working hard for you. Is it safe to talk?"

"Yes."

"All right, well listen, darling, there's a man you ought to see if you possibly can, although I'm told it's difficult. But he could be terribly important to you. His name is Colonel Cho."

I didn't say anything.

"Martin?"

"Listening."

"I thought you'd gone."

"I was thinking. The spelling is C-H-O?"

"Yes."

"Is he in Singapore?"

"No. I don't exactly know where he is, but Johnny Chen does. So will you phone him, and talk about it?"

"Yes."

"All right. Well that's—all. God, I wish I could see you, darling."

"Soon."

"Yes. Please."

Later I shared the food that Chu-Chu put on the table, rubbing my stomach to tell her it was good, and pointing to things and naming them for her, as if she had time left to learn a new language. Then, when she lit another slug of opium I found a couple of wooden slats from where the crates were stored, and got some string and made a rough cross, propping it against the wall while she watched me. I bent over the little tin ashtray and made a gesture of inhaling, then went and lay down with the cross above my head, doing it three or four times and pointing to Chu-Chu, knowing she'd seen enough of Western customs to know what a cross meant.

She got it at last, and just nodded, knowing that too; then her eyes opened wide and she pointed at me, saying something quickly, a question, and its meaning came to me—she was asking me if I meant that *I* were going to die under a wooden cross; and the atmosphere in the room, the vibrations, the malevolent scent of the opium, and the eyes of this doomed child that had already seen too much of life brought a sudden tremor and tightened my scalp, and I picked up the cross and broke the string and threw the bloody thing into the corner.

18

MOON DROP

Dropping through the dark.

"He's half-crazy," Chen had said.

"Have you met him?"

We were talking about Colonel Cho.

Pepperidge: *He could be very important. What we need to find is her exposed flank. I mean Shoda's. And Cho might tell us.*

"I haven't *met* him," Johnny Chen told me, "no." He'd got back late on Tuesday night. "Nobody ever *meets* that guy. He's holed up in a burnt-out rebel radio station in the jungle in Laos and like I say, he's half-crazy. There were two guys who tried to get near the place earlier this year, and the dogs got them. He has killer-dogs around."

Let's have a snort!

Dropping through the dark.

Chen was sitting on the floor with his back against the wall and one thin leg drawn up, his arm hooked across his knee; he looked tired, drained, the fine lines in his face deepened by the light and shadow, his almond eyes strained, looking beyond their focus, seeing, I thought, his dead friend.

"So I'd forget it," he said, and swung his head to watch Chu-chu, a spark of light coming into his eyes now. She was kneeling in front of a garishly costumed *Xieng* doll that he'd brought back for her; she seemed to be greeting it, formally, according to some kind of custom, giving it hardly perceptible bows, her hands—not much bigger than the doll's—placed together, steepled.

I didn't like disturbing the silence, their thoughts.

"It's necessary," as quietly as I could, "for me to see him."

In a moment Chen swung his head in my direction. "Then you're half-crazy too."

"How was your trip?"

"My trip? Okay, I guess." He seemed to be coming back to some kind of present. "She look after you?"

"Yes, very well. She's an accomplished lady."

"Cooks good. *Thai Suki*. I taught her that. She give you *Thai Suki?*"

"Yes." I didn't know what it was called.

He lit a black cigarette, squinting through the smoke. "She likes you. Said you think you're going to die, is that right, made some kind of a crucifix?"

"I was just doing some mime for her. Trying to tell her *she's* going to die if she keeps on with that stuff."

"She knows that." He shrugged. "We all know where death is, out here. It's all in the same place, in the poppy fields. Why's it so goddamned necessary for you to see this goon?"

"I've been told he might have some information I need."

"You have any connection? Some kind of introduction?"

"No."

He blew out a stream of smoke with a whistling sound. "Jesus, have you ever seen the front end of a war-trained Doberman that never gets anything to eat?"

"There are ways of handling dogs."

"Oh, sure. You shoot their ass off and the next thing you know is your own's gone up in smoke. Cho is real *mean*, but you don't seem to be getting the message."

Dropping through the dark, the lines hissing.

"What else do you know about him, Johnny?"

"Not much." He was watching the child again. "You look cute, sweetheart. *Cute.*"

She looked up, knowing the word *sweetheart*. It wasn't quite a smile that came into her eyes, but a lessening of melancholy, the most, I knew now, that she'd ever be able to give him.

"He was chief of intelligence"—to me now—"of an insurgent group affiliated with Shoda's organisation. He was clever, but he wanted to handle things his way, and she didn't like that. She had him arrested and slated for execution, but he got away with it somehow, with a head wound you'd never believe."

A current of air drew the smoke beneath the dragon lamp and upwards through the shade, quickening as it reached the heat of the bulb, making me think of ectoplasm, of ghosts, hers, mine, his.

"Who's with him there?" I asked Chen in a moment.

"At the radio station? He's on his own. Been there a couple of years, maybe more, I doubt anyone really knows—he's become a kind of legend, I guess. But if you want cold facts, the cold facts are that he doesn't like anyone going near him, which is why, understandably, he's holed up in a remote place like that in the jungle, thirty or forty kilometres from the nearest village, which is a narcotics center anyway, buried out of sight. I've made a few runs in there; otherwise I wouldn't have picked anything up on the guy. Ask me to guess, I'd say there's damn few people in the whole of Indo-China who know about him, just the villagers and flyers like me who go there."

"Does Shoda know where he is?"

"I doubt that too. She'd have the place dive-bombed if she did. Well"—he tilted his emaciated hand, rotating it in the French manner—"maybe that's not true. He can't do her any harm, for Christ's sake, the way he is now. That's how he knew about the place himself—he ordered it dive-bombed for his group, to wipe out some rival operations."

"Does he use the transmitter?"

"There'd be nothing left of it, and nobody's ever picked up his signals, or they'd have said." He plucked some tobacco from his lip, studying it. "Who the hell told you he has any kind of information for *anybody?"*

"I got it on the grapevine."

He shrugged. "D'you trust it?"

"Yes."

"Well, okay. But I mean if you want to go see the guy, I guess it's as good a death as any. But what am I saying? You'd have to shoot every goddamned dog first, to get yourself your own bullet. There's better ways."

In the poppy fields.

"Would you drop me there, Johnny?"

Impatiently—"He watches the track, see. There's a track from the village, where they ran the stuff to build the station with. You can still get a vehicle through, but weren't you listening? You try—"

"I mean by night. A moon drop."

"By *parachute?"*

"Yes."

He shifted his position, letting his long thin legs rest on the floor, his flying-boots angled. "Fuck, I just don't know why you won't listen."

It was dark inside the van, almost dark. Chen had hired it for the day and bought some gear for me, a back-pack with things I might need: sleeping-bag, torches, flares, first-aid, insect-repellent, snake-bite kit, a machete.

"Look," he'd said, "you're going to have to walk up to the goddamned place even if I drop you from the air, so why not walk up to it by the track? He can't see in the dark."

"He won't expect anyone to approach from the other side. Nor will the dogs."

He'd settled for a thousand US dollars.

We parked the van on the tarmac near his Windecker AC-7 and checked out at the crew station. He'd found me a pilot's uniform and sunglasses, but I wasn't worried about the environment; the van hadn't picked anyone up, and the only people we went anywhere near were the airport officials. And I was here in my dead man's shoes.

"You been in deep jungle before, Jordan?"

"In training."

"Training. How real?"

"Real."

"Commando type?"

"Yes."

He'd been putting questions like that all the way to the airport, a man with a sense of responsibility. "I don't need a thousand lousy bucks that bad, and what I don't like about this whole thing is I'm offering myself as a party to suicide before the fact."

Dropping through the dark.

The lines hissed in the air-rush, and somewhere high in the canopy a tag of fabric fluttered, sometimes so fast that it produced a musical note, a low whining. The canopy was grey, because the moon was almost full; otherwise we couldn't have done it. The sky was clear of cloud or haze, the colour of white eggshell, with the moon's brightness blanking out most of the stars. He'd dropped me from three thousand feet and there was no wind; his computer had done a fairly accurate job: I could see the shape of the radio station almost directly below, and I still had a minimal drift from the aircraft's one hundred knots at the dropping-point.

The lines hissed.

There'd been doubts and I'd expected them. I still didn't know what resources Pepperidge could tap, what kind of information he could get at that distance. He could pick things up in the pubs and they'd be from the communications mast; but the raw intelligence going through it non-stop was massive before it hit the computers and was broken into streams for analysis. But he'd just got back from London, and that was probably where he'd been working on the Colonel Cho lead. The only thing I had to rely on was that he knew that whatever move I made would be dangerous, and he wouldn't willingly expose me without good reason.

Signal me at any time on any subject and I'll get to work immediately. I really am on the ball, you know.

Or I wouldn't be here now.

The jungle was coming up. Moonlight, shadow, a spread of dense leaves like a dark sea rising.

I'd told Chen that if Katie asked about me he wasn't to tell her how difficult it would be to talk to Cho.

The sound of his plane faded to silence, southwards in the direction of the village. "Cho won't take any notice if he hears us at the drop altitude; planes run in to the strip most nights." He'd told me I was crazy not to bring a gun, and offered me his. "Or are you one of those nuts that get their kicks making things tough for themselves?"

"The last thing I want to do is make a noise."

"Shit, even if it's to save your life?"

"The first shot would bring the dogs, Johnny."

He had certain blind spots. The night-glasses, for instance. He'd finally put a pair in the bag for me but I wouldn't be using them, even though it was a strong temptation. They'd reflect.

Dark sea rising, the light and shadow of the leaves taking on the semblance of waves running below me. All I could see was the rough shape of a building half-buried in the undergrowth, with a thin stem of a mast leaning at an angle. There was no flat ground, no clearing; the place looked like a wrecked ship lying on the sea-bed, smothered in weeds.

Stink of the insect-repellent on my face and hands. I wore no gloves; I wanted to feel things, the lines, the handle of the machete, a dog's throat perhaps, I didn't know, it could go any way, an easy fall among the leaves or an errant movement in the air and my legs smashed against the mast or a hot death with my own throat ripped by their teeth.

I never have liked dogs.

Though they weren't the worst. "I guess you've got

everything, Jordan.'' Stuffing the gear into the bag for me. ''Couple of things I should tell you. If you sleep on the ground, check for ants; they're *this* size. And in that region there are black mambas and they hunt by night; if you get unlucky, don't bother with the snake-bite kit: their venom takes less than a minute to knock out the heart muscles.'' Zipped the bag shut. ''Have fun.''

Dark sea rising fast now with the mast leaning away from me, its shadow lying across the broad leaves, silver under the moon. I held the machete behind me, its bright blade hidden from the light. I couldn't hear any dogs, but it didn't mean they were sleeping. If they'd been well trained they wouldn't bark, even when they attacked; but they could be jungle-happy by now, undisciplined, half-starved, voracious.

Air spilled from the canopy on the left side and I tensioned a line and straightened the drop, watching the spread of leaves and their shadowed gaps. The radio station was half a mile away and the distance was closing but I was almost down and I drew my legs up and brought them together and became aware of the real speed of the drop as the jungle rose fast and the shadow of the canopy spread suddenly black on silver to my right and grew in size and swept in a dark wave as the leaves leapt to meet me and I was among them with the machete out of its sheath and its thong tight round my wrist and we were down and I shielded my face with the other arm and felt the tugging of the lines and the whiplash effect of stems straightening as I plunged between them and found nothing under my feet, nothing but the air and then the rush of undergrowth and then the ground, impact, my legs doubling as I leaned into a roll and dragged on the lines and started work with the machete at once because I might need the ability to move at any given second, move fast.

Cut myself free and waited.

Damp smell rising; my flying-boots had churned the fibre of the jungle floor; a smell of fungus. Silence overall, with small sounds coming into it and breaking off, fading. I stood still, waiting for the retinae to accommodate. Vines hung overhead, festooning the patch of sky, lacework against the moon's light; something was moving not far away, making a rhythmic whispering, sometimes fading, coming back—then a sudden rush of sound as a bent stem freed itself and straightened like a whip, tearing leaves away.

It wasn't dark here; it was worse than darkness: the moonlight spilled through the gaps overhead and dappled the undergrowth, creating a mosaic of black and white with nothing defined except the edges of shadow. I knew where the building was, and that was all; if there were trip-wires I wouldn't see them; if the dogs came I would only hear them.

The rhythmic whispering had stopped, not far away. A snake wouldn't attack unless I seemed threatening or was near its nest; if that sound had been a snake it would have come for me by now. But the thought of it persisted, its sinuous length contracting, forming coils, the flat head held still as it heat-sensed me. A trickle of sweat gathered and ran; I breathed tidally, the better to listen. There were no distant sounds, only nearer ones, small and subtle and once a creature voicing, a swift kill in progress, it sounded like, because of a cry cut off and then scuffling.

I waited another few minutes and then unbuckled the harness and lowered it to the ground, stepping away, tripping on a tendril and getting my balance again. There was no accurate measurement possible, but if the jungle were this dense as far as the building it could take me the rest of the night to go half a mile, given the need for silence. It was now 01:09, and in four hours the moon would be down and there'd be total darkness here under the leaves, with only the glow from Sirius through the gaps overhead. I could stay here and sleep and acclimatise during the coming day, but there'd be heat, moist and enervating; and by daylight the dogs might roam, hunting, and if a wind rose in the wrong direction they'd pick up my scent at once. Or I could move now, and try to reach the building before first light, and deal with whatever I had to deal with in the dark. I thought that was the best way.

It was just before three o'clock when I saw the top of the radio mast leaning across the gaps in the leaves, and I put the distance now at three or four hundred yards. The silence was still not absolute, though there was no sound from inside the building; all I could hear was the nocturnal life of the jungle around me. Some kind of big cat had voiced an hour ago, perhaps a tiger, a low wickering in the distance, two miles away, maybe three. I'd heard a dozen more kills, one close, the scream of fright piercing the night and bringing the sweat out on my sides; there'd come the smell of blood, raw and intimate, then the swishing of leaves as the predator had carried the prey into the deeper reaches.

And then towards dawn there was another sound, of a snout rooting, scenting, and in the mottled light I caught the shape of the dog as it froze for an instant and then came leaping for me with its ears flattened and its jaws bright.

19

COLONEL CHO

Bassai.

The jungle was in here, creeping through cracks.

Migi gedan barai and then *hidari,* the triple blocks, very fast.

A rat ran along the far wall in perfect silence.

I was kneeling.

Migi shuto chudan uke, a whipping sword-hand.

His breathing was steady, then explosive.

The final sword-hand, *hidari*.

Kiai.

He bowed, and in bowing, saw me.

Stillness.

From my kneeling position I returned the *rei,* not only out of respect for his obvious rank but also to emulate the male wolf that arches its neck to the side, offering its death to the adversary in the hope of life.

"*Os*."

When I looked up again he hadn't moved.

He was in the centre of the room, a big room, almost bare, its floor earthen, its walls fissured, with leaves and whole branches of the undergrowth thrusting inside; the jungle was slowly devouring the place, though I could see where he'd been hacking at it regularly, working his way round.

He was above average height but not tall; his *gi* was worn, patched, but clean; his feet of course were bare. His one eye watched me. The other eye had been buried in the hideous cleft, made by a blade of some sort, that crossed his face diagonally, cruelly distorting it. His mouth had escaped the blow, but it was no more than a thin line, set in an expression of total cynicism—or hatred or hostility: the mouth can only express so much, unlike the eyes.

His eye watched me with the look of a wild creature assessing the presence of another, of a smaller creature who could offer no threat but might be considered prey. The ice along my spine was because of this look he was giving me, robbing me of my identity. I was nothing, his look told me, human. There was also the similarity between this man's head and the dog's, because as the dog had leapt for me I had buried the machete into it, splitting open the skull.

Sunlight, pale and slanting, was coming through one of the gaps in the wall, and around the man's feet were motes of fibre drifting, still airborne from the final movements of the *kata,* of *Bassai.* The place smelled of damp, of fungus, of the jungle, a raw blend of animal droppings, fresh blood and chlorophyl. The shadow of Colonel Cho leaned right across the earthen floor, thrown by the low-angled light, its head against the whitewashed wall.

I waited, still in the kneeling position. There was nothing else I could do.

The bombs must have blown the rest of the building down, and there'd been fire afterwards. One wall was missing altogether, and on that side the room was criss-crossed with fallen girders, plaster and timber-work, festooned with creeper. The flooring in here must have been burned away, and he'd cleared the ashes, dumping them into the jungle, taking great care: there was no trace of them. He'd also found some whitewash, and covered most of the blackening the fire had left on the walls. The roof was still in place, a tilted expanse of corrugated iron, almost intact. The door I'd entered by was behind me; it had been open, and—

"Qui êtes-vous?"

Flicker along the nerves.

"Un ami, Sempai."

Acknowledging his rank. I would have said *go-dan*.

"Vous êtes arrivé comment?"

"By air," I told him.

"En français."

So I went back to French; it was the tongue we were going to use, obviously. "We made a moon drop," I added.

"When?"

"Just before midnight, Colonel."

He hadn't moved yet. I wasn't looking forward to that. His movements in the *kata* had been swift and powerful, and underneath his chilling calm he must have been enraged to find me here. This place was more than just his territory; it was his refuge, his only haven in a world where he was an outcast, because out there he would have had to see people flinch when they looked at him. In coming here I had violated his very soul.

"How did you get past the dogs?"

His French had the formality, the over-correctness in those who speak a foreign language learned by education and not usage.

I could have lied, but he would have known. And on the wall was a faded picture of Funakoshi, and there was the ingrained principle in me that disallowed my lying to a *sempai*. But by God it was a risk.

"I had to kill one of them."

He was silent for so long that I didn't think that any kind of change was taking place; he was standing perfectly still, as before. Then I saw that something was happening to his face; it was altering its shape, moment after moment, in a way I didn't immediately understand, until I saw that his eye was now almost hidden by his nose and the raised flesh of the scar. He'd been turning his head, and by such infinitesimal degrees that I hadn't noticed. He was now sighting me, rather than watching me, and the impression I had was that he'd withdrawn behind himself, to observe me from concealment.

This was my first intimation.

"Why?"

It was a whisper.

"It would have killed me."

Silence. At the edge of my vision I saw another rat on the move, and heard its faint squeaking.

"Then I shall throw you to the others. But not yet."

There was something coming into his voice, too, a different tone that I couldn't quite identify; but it reminded me of the way Fosdick had spoken to us when he'd got back from Marx-Stadt.

One of the dogs barked outside, the sound coming from a deep chest, resonating; others took it up, excited by something, an animal they'd sighted. I showed nothing.

"Who is your *sensei?*"

"Yamada."

"In London."

"Yes, *Sempai.*"

He was still sighting me in that strange way, as if hiding behind himself—this impression was quite clear; it wasn't my imagination. It was bringing a chill to the nerves: they were vulnerable at the moment because I hadn't known whether I was going to come down the wrong way and smash my legs on the building and then there'd been the Doberman with its jaws wide open and then the sickening business of stopping the thing short and now there was Cho standing there and I was perfectly sure he meant what he'd said about throwing me to those bloody hounds.

"You may rise."

"Os." I made the *rei* and got to my feet, and then something screamed outside and the sound of the dogs took on a different note: it was a kill. He was listening to it, Cho, his maimed head lifting a fraction. But his eye was still sighting me.

"How many are there?"

I hesitated. "Dogs?"

"No. There are seven dogs." His eye disappeared as his head was turned, and then sighted me again with an expression of exaggerated cunning, aided by the set of his mouth. "Six, now." A flash of revelation came to me, then vanished before I could grasp it. "How many *men?*"

"Where, Colonel?"

"Out *there*. How big an army?"

Mother of God.

Yes, the same tone that had been in Fosdick's voice when he'd got back from Marx-Stadt with the burns from the electrodes still on him and that strange light in his eyes—the East Germans had put him through implemented interrogation for three weeks and it had driven him mad.

"I don't know," I said carefully.

Because what could I say?

I didn't know what they'd done to this man before they'd tried to kill him but it could have been that massive head injury alone that had affected his brain. He was probably as big a danger to me as anything out there in the jungle and if his mind was damaged he could blow up at any minute and come for me or call the dogs in. The only chance I might have could be in humouring him.

"But you must have seen it," he said.

The army.

"I came down in moonlight, Colonel. All I could see was jungle."

His face was changing again as he brought his head back by infinite degrees, and I noted this. The movement could be significant: his way of "sighting," of seeming to hide behind himself, might indicate the times when his brain went out of phase. He was facing me now and asking normal questions again.

"Why did you come here by air?"

"I was told you like your privacy."

"Yet you still came."

"Yes. I—"

"Why?"

"I think we can help each other."

His head began turning again, and the hairs on my neck rose in reaction. He said nothing, and I waited. This time the phase didn't last long, and his head moved back.

"To do what?"

"To destroy Shoda."

You must have seen a cat facing a dog—the eyes narrowing and the ears flattening and a hiss coming from the open jaws. It was like that. It's not enough to say that he recoiled. He tensed, drew back, threw up his guard, all those things, without making much movement or much sound, and somehow it looked worse for that: it was an expression of total hate, total menace, contained within a bare degree of detonation. If Shoda had been here now she would have been ripped into pieces. This man didn't need those dogs.

It took time for him to recover, and the aftermath was a grimace of pain, not of physical pain now but the pain he had felt when that monstrous blow was struck, cleaving his face, and the pain he'd been feeling ever since, day after day, remembering what he looked like and what people—especially women—would think if they ever looked on him again. He was still young, say forty, and that must be his photograph I'd seen on the wall near Funakoshi's, the picture of a handsome Asian, high cheekboned in the Yul Brynner mould, large-eyed, sensual. Colonel Cho would have loved many women; now he was a creature, a Caliban, self-imprisoned in a hermit's cave.

A whisper came. "*Shoda . . .*"

Something was moving in the background behind him, and I noted it, even though it wasn't defined. Cho was watching me intently, as if I'd offered some kind of revelation. His expression was perfectly sane now, and it occurred to me that in simply mentioning Shoda's name I'd recalled memories he'd been keeping forced down under his need to forget; but I couldn't tell what this would do to him, bring him increased sanity through release, or drive him deeper into madness. I had the feeling of stepping through a minefield in the dark.

Snake.

That was the movement behind him, high among the creeper that itself was winding its way through the beams and girders of the fourth wall. The bloody thing was hanging from the leaves by the tail, its head down and moving from side to side, heat-sensing the earthen floor.

Still in a whisper: "You said, *destroy?*"

"Yes. The whole of her organisation."

He was chief of intelligence in an insurgent group, Chen had told me, *affiliated with Shoda's organisation. He was clever, but he wanted to handle things his way, and she didn't like that. She had him arrested and slated for execution, but he got away with it somehow, with a head wound you'd never believe.*

"Come."

He led me across to a corner, and that was when the snake dropped and the rat squealed and my skin crawled, though he took not the slightest notice. He shared the life of the jungle here and was used to it; but it came to my mind that if he was ever struck down with a fever or couldn't move around he'd die with the jungle too, or the dogs would scent easy meat and pick him clean.

"Tell me," he said, "why you wish to destroy Shoda."

I was his guest at table, towards noon; we sat on the floor, Japanese-style, on each side of a slab of redwood with a great crack in it; he'd lashed thin cord across and across to keep it together.

"You know of course that there have been many attempts to kill her?"

"Yes."

We ate some kind of root, peeled and sliced, with dried fruit and a bowl of mashed turnip, by its taste.

"And you are confident that you can achieve what so many others have failed to achieve?"

"No. But I shall try. It's a matter of intelligence,

Colonel—the *gathering* of intelligence. Information. That was your own field, I believe.''

He didn't answer that. ''Who told you that I might have such information?''

''One of the pilots who fly into the village here told me you'd once been involved with Mariko Shoda's military forces.''

He didn't ask Chen's name. I wouldn't have given it.

God knew how many rats were in this place. One of them was moving close to the table, smelling the food.

''I doubt,'' Cho said carefully, ''if I would have any information that would be useful to you.'' But the problem was that his head was moving again, turning, his one eye sighting me. It was like having to learn a language: he was distrusting me, so whatever he said could be almost the opposite of the truth. I knew perfectly well that he'd got information for me, or Pepperidge and Katie wouldn't have told me to see him.

''Then I was misinformed,'' I told him. Go with whatever he said, don't contradict.

The sleek brown rat jumped onto the table; not much of a feat; it was only about a foot and a half from the ground. It looked rather pretty, but presumably had rabies.

Colonel Cho's eye was still sighting; I didn't look at him directly, but watched him at the edge of my vision.

''What else have you heard about me?'' The tone silky.

''Very little, Colonel. Only that you were an exceptionally gifted intelligence chief and a loss to the rebel forces.''

He didn't answer for so long that I looked at him directly. The mood-phase was over: his head was turning back and now he was looking at the rat.

''But how flattering. And of course true.''

His movements in the *kata* had been very swift and it was over before I actually saw what was happening—he brought a sword-hand down with great speed and perfect control and the neck of the rat gave a delicate sound as it snapped.

''So we have meat today,'' Cho said and took his knife

and skinned the rat and sliced into the small bright body and worked there, bringing out the liver, offering it to me.

There's always some kind of joke we can take back to London if we get through the mission, and pass around in the Caff.

"Thank you, Colonel, but I'm a vegetarian."

They'd love that one.

"Then I shall profit from your preferences." He put the tiny liver into his mouth and broke one of the delicate bones in the rat's neck, slicing it into short lengths and eating it slowly. "I feed as the tiger feeds, first the vitamin A and then some calcium. They are synergistic."

I don't know why the hell I wasn't sick. The thing's skin looked strange, lying there empty on the table.

"And how am I to know," he asked me, "that you are not here in order to spy on me for Mariko Shoda?"

"Should I lie to my *sempai?*"

That got through. He looked down, considering, wiping the rat's blood from the corner of his mouth. I followed up without waiting. "I've told you the name of the company I represent in England, and you could verify that." I left it to him to find out how, from the depths of the jungle. "Shoda has already tried to have me killed—she set some of her women on me in Singapore, with their knives."

He watched me closely, his eye calm now, intelligent. "And who came to your aid?"

"No one. I killed four of them."

"Indeed. You did well."

"Shoda didn't think so."

He was watching me intently. "I can well imagine. Such a thing would have incensed her, as a personal affront. What action did she take?"

"She put her top hit-man onto me."

He put his bloodied knife onto the table, carefully, without taking his eyes off me. "Kishnar?"

"Yes."

''When?''

''Three or four days ago.''

Short silence. ''Yet you are still alive. Do you know that is remarkable?''

''He didn't get a chance to close in.''

''But he will.''

''He'll try.''

He looked away at last and slipped into one of his contemplative phases; I was beginning to know him. We had some fruit and he cleared the table and told me to sit with him in the corner where the rugs were, and some half-wrecked chairs.

''I begin to see why you expect to succeed in your mission,'' he said quietly, ''where others have failed. A mission of this order is not new to you.''

''Not really.''

''You make a formidable antagonist.''

''I've upset a few people in my time.''

''And you would make a formidable ally, if I decided to take you into my confidence. An ally against Shoda.''

''As I told you, Colonel, that's why I came.''

''Quite so.''

Making a bit of progress, but oh Christ I wasn't at all sure of that because his head was turning again and all I could see was that one eye sighting me from behind what he believed was cover, and I thought I knew what was happening: these relapses of his into psychosis weren't haphazard; they happened when he was suddenly afraid he'd made himself vulnerable. It didn't seem to make sense that he'd just offered, virtually, to let me become an ally, and then suddenly retreated; but in fact it did. He felt he'd put too much trust in me, and it could be dangerous.

I waited, because I couldn't do anything else. If I said a wrong word it could make him enraged, violent, and in this place I wouldn't stand a chance.

His head came back to face me, and my nerves felt a

chill. He was two people, this man, and one of them potentially deadly.

"We shall see," he said, and got up from the frayed rug where he'd been sitting and left me, his bare feet padding across the earth.

He didn't talk to me for the rest of the day, except for an occasional word in passing. He spent his time hacking at the creepers that were threatening to smother the doorways and a window, and I helped him, getting the machete that I'd left outside with the gear I'd dropped with. In the late afternoon he wrote at the long redwood table; it looked like a journal: the book was as big as a telephone directory and leather-bound. Two or three times I turned to find him sighting me, even though we hadn't been speaking; it was obvious that he was giving me a lot of thought, and that some of his thoughts led him to distrust me. I didn't find it easy to turn my back on him; his bare feet wouldn't make a sound on the earth.

What I had to think about before anything else wasn't to find a way of getting information out of him, information on Shoda, but to find a way of leaving this place alive. I had absolutely no protection here. Cho had kept himself in regular training and from the *kata* I'd seen was totally capable of killing me, and not by stealth; and even if I managed to placate him the whole time and not let a wrong word slip out, the dark side of his personality could suddenly decide that I was here to betray him, and then he'd come for me. And even if I could kill him in self-defence, if he came for me, there were the dogs: they'd smell death, and seek the carrion, and find me here.

When night came he lit oil lamps and we had supper, but he said nothing about Shoda. It was as if she'd never been mentioned, and it occurred to me that as well as his intense bouts of paranoia he might experience lapses in memory, and lose its content, wholly or partially. I wanted to test this out, but it was too dangerous. The first time I'd spoken Shoda's name he'd reacted violently. For all I knew, he might have completely lost the conversation we'd had earlier in the day.

In the end I decided to sleep on it. He was behaving now as a dutiful host, showing me where the running water was to be had, and explaining the system he had of catching it from the heavy rains and directing it into a reservoir. There was no bed here, he apologised, but he himself slept on a straw mattress, and gave me one to use. When he doused the lamps I curled up in a corner of the room with the machete underneath the edge of a rug and within easy reach.

"We shall talk tomorrow," was all he said, and this confirmed my assumption that he'd spent a lot of his time thinking about me and what I'd told him. He'd got the data, and needed time to assess it.

That was fair enough, but I had *no* way of knowing that he might not decide at some time in the dark hours that I was too much of a danger to him and slaughter me out of hand, as he'd done with the rat.

Not easy to lie there, uncertain; not easy to sleep. It was the same out there in the jungle; its creatures slept always at the brink of death, and knew it, and knew what it meant when a scream came suddenly, close or distant: the remorseless cycle of life was going on, red in tooth and claw under the rising moon.

I didn't know what time it was when I woke, disturbed by sounds. I'd chosen this corner of the enormous room because it was on the opposite side from the wall of creepers where the snake had hung, and dropped. A rat had moved across my legs, earlier, and I'd jerked them and it had gone. There'd been the cry of a night bird soon afterwards, and I'd been brought awake with my skin crawling, coming out of a dream that I didn't remember except for a lingering visual trace of coils and shadows. Now it was different, the sounds coming to me from across the room; they were human.

Voices, I believed. They were faint, but I could hear their

rhythm changing, and their tone. There was more than one person speaking; it had the sound of dialogue.

Or it was a dream and I waited for some kind of data to come in, lying so still that my own breathing was inaudible. Moonlight was striking softly across the earth floor; it came in rays, filtering through the creepers on the far wall; in it I saw something on the move, small, longer than a rat, some sort of stoat, a predator, its thin tail held stiffly behind as it darted suddenly and made its kill, with nothing more this time than a scuffling, the teeth going into the throat before the cry could come.

The voices didn't stop, and for a time I lay listening to them and at last surfaced through the twilight zone and knew for certain I was now awake and that the voices were still going on.

Cho had lain down in the corner where he slept, beneath the picture of Funakoshi; he wasn't there now. I got up and moved to the centre of the room and turned slowly until I got the direction of the sound; then I went over there, to the door in the south wall that I'd never seen open. The voices were louder here, and the words audible.

Radio.

No. There was no consistency: it wasn't a programme.

. . . *But I told him there was absolutely no certainty of that. So what was his reaction? He simply said we would be going ahead in any case, since the ambassador wanted to.*

Yes, radio, then, but taped. These were tapes I was listening to, being played over to check the contents.

—But I'm damned if I'm going to give in to him. The Prime Minister's quite adamant on that score—we dig our heels in, she told me, and tell them we're not going to budge. All right, sir, what do I tell Blakeney? Tell him to go to hell. The real issue—

—Et je vous assure, M'sieur le Consul, que nous allons faire tout le nécéssaire pour produire le résultat que nous cherchons. C'est tout à fait impossible de faire

autrement, en considération des nouvelles de Paris, surtout—

—As I guess you know. But if there's anything that sounds urgent, call me. Will do. When did you eat? God knows. Let's have a snort!

20

THE RAT

This time it was a woman's voice on the tape.

Colonel Cho was watching me intently. "Do you know who is speaking?"

"No."

"It is the voice of Shoda."

The sibilants were silky and drawn out, emphasising certain words, but the tone of her voice was harsher than I'd imagined, carrying a deep energy, filling the small studio, commanding, authoritative.

There was a break in transmission, and Cho stopped the recorder.

"Do you understand Cambodian, Mr Jordan?"

"No. What was she saying?"

"She was ordering one of her army chiefs to hold back the mobilisation of his forces until the shipment arrives. She also told him that it was essential for him to remain in close liaison with her other forces, to avoid a precipitate action."

They were right—Pepperidge, Katie. This was a major breakthrough. My target for the mission was Mariko Shoda and in the temple in Thailand I'd been close to her physically for the first time and now I was listening to her voice—and as it issued orders to one of her army commanders.

There was massive data coming in for questioning and analysis and I'd have to take it in stages.

One: *Johnny Chen's place was bugged.*

But I'd have to get the answers from Cho with infinite care because he'd come close to killing me five minutes ago when he'd opened the door and found me outside. God knew how he'd sensed me there, but he lived in the wild and was jungle-sensitive. He hadn't been startled, simply informed, and his head had turned slowly to sight me, and in his one eye there was the light of rage. His body was also moving, subtly, his breath drawing deeply from his abdomen as he gathered force, his right shoulder lifting by degrees as he brought the arm back, preparing the vector that would bring the edge of his sword-hand slicing against the carotid artery in my neck. I'd initiated this blow often enough to recognize its preparation.

He was ready now and when I spoke I think it was within a half-second of my death.

"*Sempai,* Funakoshi watches you."

I waited.

I'd run through the whole gamut of options open to me and none of them would have worked: I knew that. But I'd remembered something that had got through to him when he'd seen me here for the first time and was ready to attack me for my flagrant intrusion: I'd addressed him punctiliously as my *sempai,* my respected superior in the sacred tradition of *Shotokan,* and it had given him pause.

I went on waiting. Movement in him had ceased, and his mind alone was active, its dark side, ravaged and traumatised and vengeful, willing his body to destroy this creature, this threat to his sacrosanct privacy, while the light of reason flickered also within him, a candle's flame beset by the wind. Then it was over, and his head turned to face me.

"Come in. I want you to see my communications centre."

The tension went out of me and as the left brain began functioning again I noted that whenever this man's mind returned to reason, he had no memory of his lapse into psychosis.

The room was small but walled on three sides with dials, signal-strength meters, switches, charts, and time-schedules. It must have been the original receiving-transmitting studio, and it had escaped the worst of the bombing. Cho went to the ripped vinyl chair on the dais in front of the main panel and began running the tapes, ignoring me as the signals came through again. There were cassettes everywhere, stacked on the shelves and along the console, with boxes of blanks bearing the Sanyo shipping label.

Then the voice of Shoda came again, its sibilants lingering, the consonants frank and articulated.

Cho turned his head. "That was monitored some days ago. She was giving instructions for the British agent named Jordan to be brought to his death."

"Really."

"You are a fortunate man."

He went back to his editing, and when signals came in English, French, or Russian I listened to them; when they were in a language unknown to me I worked on the data that was still coming in.

Two: *Chen's place was bugged. By whom?*

Not by Cho. I'd noticed that whenever an English signal came through he stopped it short, even though one of the dialogues had been on a high level politically, mentioning the British Prime Minister.

Chen's place could have been bugged by one of his competitors in the drug trade but I doubted it: he wasn't big-time, running a whole network. Leave it for now.

Three: *Who had bugged Shoda's communications?*

Sayako?

"Sayako-san," I'd asked her over the telephone at the

Red Orchid, "are you in Shoda's organisation?"

"I have access to information."

Sayako, then, yes, it was logical. This could have been the signal she'd picked up just before she'd warned me—the one I'd just heard, "giving instructions for the British agent named Jordan to be brought to his death."

Another signal was coming through in English, and I listened to it before Cho cut it short. It was from the flight deck of a Northwest Orient jet, the accent Japanese.

Not a bug.

I began listening the whole time now as Cho made notes and fast-forwarded some of the signals, running others back to monitor again. I'd have said at this stage that he was searching for specified transmissions and I could have been right, but I was beginning to realise that there was no order in this material, no sequence. He was picking up bugs in four languages but among a whole range of random signals, a lot of them aircraft, some of them hams, two of them radio-taxis in Singapore. What worried me was that he didn't edit out the garbage.

He should be doing that.

And wasn't.

He looked up suddenly, fixing me with his eye. "He is always late, that one."

Taxi-driver.

Oh Jesus Christ.

"Late?" I asked him.

"Yes. They will fire him soon, you mark my words."

He turned back to the console and listened to a signal in French, Chinese accent, aircraft to base, while I tried to think how to get out of him what I had to get, *because he was just listening at random,* picking up whatever signals he could find as he turned the dials—and he was just as interested in what some bloody taxi-driver was talking about in Singapore as he was in what Shoda was giving him.

Check that.

"Where is the bug, Colonel, on Mariko Shoda?"

He flinched at the name and I expected him to react as he had before, but it was all right this time: we could talk about her now. "I am not sure. I think in one of her limousines, or perhaps an aircraft. The wavelength tells me nothing." There was some speech in what sounded like Laotian in the background and in a moment he said without changing his tone, "This man is drug-running, but he is an amateur. It is a bug placed by the narcotics branch. It will be amusing, won't it, when they catch him? The spider and the fly?"

No. Not in the least amusing. This poor bastard's mind was like the console here, filled with random signals that had no pattern. When that sabre had swung down and cleft his face it had turned his brain into a mental kaleidoscope.

All I could do was put questions.

"Have you any idea, Colonel, who placed the bug in Shoda's communications system?"

"No." But I didn't think he'd heard that, or understood.

"Do you think it could have been a woman named Sayako?"

His hand stopped moving the dial and his body became totally still.

He didn't turn his head, didn't look at me, just sat there. I didn't know what I'd started in him; I was ready for anything. No movement in him for what seemed minutes, then his head lowered and something fell onto the chipped, grimed shelf of the console, glinting in the light. It was something so extraordinary to issue from such a man that I felt the strangeness of compassion, the stirring of a mood in me that I believed was long ago buried within the shell of indifference demanded by the life I'd chosen. And so we sat there in the cramped, cluttered room in the Laotian jungle, a foreign agent and a former chief of intelligence, while on the console the human tear made a dark patch that had already begun drying.

Colonel Cho turned his head at last and looked across at me, his riven cheek glistening.

"No," he whispered, "it was not Sayako."

At first light I woke with a jerk of the nerves but there was no threat that I could see. It was simply that I'd slept with the subconscious awareness that my host might at any time go pitching over the edge of his fragile sanity and come for me.

In the hours of the morning he spent his time hacking at the creeper and writing in his journal, and towards noon he went into the radio room and talked into one of the microphones at the transmitter console, speaking sometimes in his own tongue, Laotian, and sometimes in one of the Chinese dialects. I stayed near the open door, and once went in, to ask him if I could take a message with me when I left here.

It was the first time I'd mentioned it, and I watched him carefully. He'd been lucid for the past hour, except for that fact that the mike he was using was dead: none of the transmission dials were registering.

"When you leave here?"

"Yes. I need to go on with my work."

He sat looking in front of him, not up at me.

"Your work?"

"My plans to destroy Shoda."

He turned now and faced me, his eye rational.

"So."

I couldn't tell if he'd remembered what I'd said when I'd first come here, or whether it was something new to consider. I thought I'd follow up, with the big question.

"If you agree to let me have the wavelength of the Shoda bug, I can use it very effectively, Colonel."

He gazed at me for a time and then looked away. "We shall see. We shall talk of that."

So I had to wait, and in the afternoon he took off his kimono and put on his *gi*, moving to face the portrait of Funakoshi and giving the *rei*, the punctilious bow with the head lowered and the eyes down, expressing trust in an opponent.

He then worked out for an hour and went through *Kanku* and *Jion,* allowing me the privilege of watching. For a time there was no sound but the movement of his feet through the stances, and his deep, guttural *kiai*. The powdered earth, churned by the kicks and turns, floated above the surface of the floor. Again I noted his great speed and strength. It didn't reassure me.

Later he motioned me to sit with him on the rugs in the corner. His eye was calm, but his head turned a little sometimes, and I sat facing him with a kind of prayer running through my head. It was the first time in any mission I'd had to deal with a deranged mind, and in a man capable of overwhelming me with his bare hands.

"You wish to leave," he said.

"Yes."

"Why should I trust you?"

"With what?"

He moved a hand. "With my presence here. I have enemies who would like to find me."

"I understand that. But you can trust me because I am your *cohei, Sempai.*"

His subordinate in *Shotokan.*

"Is that sufficient?"

"Funakoshi would think so."

His eye flicked to the portrait on the wall.

"Even so, you would be carrying my life in your hands, if I let you leave here."

"I understand that too. It would be an honour, *Sempai,* that I would respect even at the cost of my own."

It would have sounded less formal in English but the meaning was there. What had happened, after all? I'd come here by stealth, a stranger, killed one of his dogs and entered the privacy of his dwelling uninvited; yet he'd offered me food, which is basically an offer of life itself. He had also forgiven me for looking upon his maimed, grotesque countenance that he'd hoped to keep hidden from the world for the rest of his life. That was the least I owed him: his life.

"You are persuasive," he said.

"It's not my intention. I hope simply to reassure."

His head began moving and I held my breath and centred. He'd been slipping into the psychotic phase less often than yesterday, perhaps because he'd learned to trust me a little; but he was now having to make up his mind to trust me totally, and his brain was in overload. I sat perfectly still and faced him, as I'd learned to do, faced his one eye as it sighted from the edge of his riven cheekbone. I still found the effect chilling, transfixing; he was so certain that he was now in hiding and watching me from behind cover that there was a degree of transference: I half-believed that this wasn't his body, but some object that concealed him.

A rat squeaked in the silence, even this slight sound bringing shock. Cho hadn't heard it, deep in his meditation; his eye didn't change expression, which was one of fierce enquiry; I could have imagined a ray of light playing on my face, searching it.

I wanted to move but couldn't, daren't.

Wait.

All I could do.

Wait.

And then I heard his breath come, releasing. The turning of his head was so gradual that for a moment I didn't catch it. After a while he was facing me again, his eye calm.

"Very well, *Cohei*."

I left the next morning.

Cho gave me the wavelength of the Shoda bug, but none of the tapes. They were "his voices," as he put it, though I wasn't quite sure what he meant, unless they peopled his self-made prison. If he'd been normal it would have been easier for me: he would have given me the Shoda tapes for editing and analysis in Singapore; they offered the kind of information that an intelligence agent would give his soul for. But there was nothing I could do about it. They were his, and I couldn't steal them or force them out of him; they were his "voices" and his obsession, and he couldn't see the logic of letting me have them to use as a weapon for Shoda's destruction.

But the wavelength alone was a breakthrough and I'd have to settle for that.

I asked him about the reference to the arrival of a "consignment" on the Shoda tapes, but he said he didn't know what she meant. I asked him if she'd mentioned a missile, but drew blank again. I didn't want to press it, because he'd agreed to let me leave and I wasn't keen to have him change his mind.

He took me to the door that I'd never yet seen open. Outside were the dogs.

"Don't move," he told me.

Six of the bastards. The seventh was lying at the edge of the jungle, a skeleton; they'd found it and dragged it here and picked it clean. This was their stamping-ground, the jungle floor beaten down and littered; they'd brought other carcasses here, half of them rotting.

When they saw me they went into the attack posture at once, ears flattening and the neck-muscle rising, the dry, mangey fur bristling. They had teeth like bright knives.

Colonel Cho was talking to them in a Chinese dialect: he'd had them brought here from the village, probably. But I didn't know whether he could control them or only believed he could; he lived half his life in fantasy, and this could be part of it. He was less predictable in a way than a raving lunatic; you couldn't tell reality from the dream, the nightmare.

"Ta shih shou jen! Pieh yao t'a!"

Telling them I was a friend, presumably. Yes—he was putting his arm round my shoulders to show them, and I had an instant's mad idea that in this pose we should be asked to smile.

The bastards didn't look too impressed. They backed off a little but moved in restless circles, their heads hung low and their eyes up to watch me, a concerted snarling deep in their throats; didn't care for it, I tell you I did *not* fucking well *care* for it, in a pack this size they were sudden death and the only man in control was stark raving bonkers, sweat running on me, only two options left, go back and stay with him until he had a brainstorm and did me in or walk out there through the dogs and let them do it.

"They will not attack you," Cho said, and took his arm away.

Didn't ask him if he were sure, too much bloody pride.

"Thank you, *Sempai.*" Took six paces, turned, gave him the *rei* and turned again, not looking at the dogs because that's the first rule—if you look into their eyes they'll take it as a challenge and that's all the excuse they want, kept on walking, looking straight ahead and listening to the snarls they were making, getting louder because they'd stopped circling and started to follow, closing on my heels, look straight ahead, it's a pretty view, everything green and moist with a blue haze above the trees, something to remember but not for long if they get their bloody way, it'd be like sharks in a feeding frenzy, the first taste of blood sends them crazy, and what was *he* doing, Cho, turning his head like that, perhaps, turning it very slowly, sighting me from behind himself, deciding once and for all that I was going to give him away the minute I reached civilisation—

"Ta shih shou jen! Pieh yao t'a!"

Jesus Christ what's he telling them now but it's too late anyway because I'm past the point of no return and in the end it's going to depend on karma, kismet, whatever the hell you want to call it, running with sweat, the bastards are coming after me, I can hear them, keep on walking and *don't look back,* look straight ahead, it's such a pretty view—

21

WATER-BED

"Are you all right?"

"Yes."

"Where—" She left it.

Hot as hell, and humid. Phone sticky in my hand.

"Listen, there's something you might be able to do for me."

"Anything," she said.

"What's your signals staff like at the High Commission?"

"Pretty keen types. They're friends of mine."

Slapped my left arm, left a streak of blood.

"Ask them if they can monitor a signal on Megahertz 416, short wave. They'll need to understand Cambodian."

"I'll try. Who's sending the signals?"

"Shoda."

"Who?"

Line rather dodgy, wonder it worked at all in this beaten-up hole.

"Mariko Shoda."

Silence, then: "My *God* . . . But why should she—*oh,* you mean she's being *bugged?*"

"Yes. Strictly under your hat, Katie."

"Of *course*. I'll start action on it right away. Is that everything?"

"For now."

"You mean we need a round-the-clock monitor, don't you?"

"Yes." I should have thought of that, walked forty kilometres through the heat of the day, no bloody excuse. "Yes, non-stop."

"All right. Martin, this is *very* good, isn't it? How did—" Left it. "*Very* important, isn't it?"

"Yes. I've got to go now."

"All right. When can I see—" Hesitated, left it again. "Take care."

Rang off.

How many degrees was it in here? It was a wonder the bloody mosquitoes could even fly, the fan didn't work—the last time it was switched on it left the ceiling charred, a close thing in a place like this.

I got the operator again and asked for the number and waited.

View through the filthy window-pane of the street, the only one they had here, no cars on it, just mules and cyclos and people walking, a lot of them bent double under yoked baskets full of poppy seeds, this whole place reeked of wet sacking and something else, something bittersweet; there was a refinery across there by the look of it, a ramshackle corrugated-iron hangar like a lab, long windows, daylight tubing; it was getting near sundown.

The thumping from the next room got faster, then some moaning; the bed was against the wall and kept on hitting it. Girls everywhere when I'd checked in, *Wanna girl? No, but have you got anything for mosquito bites?* Gave me a bottle, kept a whole supply on the front desk.

Chinese, one word.

"Chen?"

"Who are you?" In English.

"Jordan."

Short silence. "Jesus, you're still alive?"

"Listen, Johnny. Your place is bugged."

"Say again?"

"There's some kind of electronic surveillance on your place. A *bug*."

Just crackling on the line for a bit.

"No way. It's never left empty." But he sounded shaken.

"Then it could be somewhere in the telephone circuit outside, or on a wall. You need to have a good look."

Silence again, then: "Are you sure?"

"Yes."

"How—" He left it, just like Katie, because he'd realised that if I were right, we were being bugged *now*. "Okay. Over and out."

I rang off. Priorities first. The most urgent thing had been to man the monitor on Shoda and start logging her signals. The next had been to warn Chen and I'd done that. What I hadn't done was to ask him if he could fly me out of here, but I wasn't putting that on the bug. I'd give Katie an hour and phone her again.

My aircrew uniform was pretty well in shreds after the drop and the trek through the jungle and I went into the street and found a shop-house festooned with jeans and jackets and kimonos and bush-shirts and spent some time there and then took the clothes I needed back to the hotel and had a shower and changed, smearing the mosquito stuff on my face and hands again as the sun went down across the jungle. I shut the window and pulled the thin faded blind down and put on the only light, a bulb in the ceiling.

Katie wasn't at her flat so I tried the High Commission and got her.

"We're running," she said.

"You mean that?"

"I'm quite good, when there's something important to do." Sounded pleased, not piqued. She'd worked damned fast.

"I didn't have any doubts."

"That makes me very happy. Why are you calling again? Are you all right?"

"Yes, but there's something else you could do for me.

Call Johnny Chen and ask him to meet you inside the High Commission building. *Inside it*. When he comes, ask him if he can fly me out."

"Where from?"

"He knows."

I didn't want her to be seen with Chen in the open and I didn't want her to know where I was. Whoever was bugging Chen could be tailing him too and I didn't want her exposed.

"All right," she said.

"Tell him to see if he's being watched. Tailed. If he is, tell him to lose them before he goes to your building. If he can't lose them, he doesn't go there."

In a moment: "Is he in danger?"

"No." Chen could handle whatever came up; that was the way he lived. "Finally, tell him that when he's found the bug, I want it."

"The bug."

"When he finds it, let me have it."

"All right."

Sound of a shot and I reacted. Somewhere on the far side of the street but quite loud, a heavy calibre.

I said: "That's it for—"

"What was the bang?"

"Car backfired."

Short silence, then, "Shit." Didn't believe me. "Look after yourself, Martin."

I rang off at once in case there was more shooting. Someone out there was yelling his head off and there was another shot and he stopped. I'd have said it was just the life-style in this place; when I'd got here along the half-obliterated jungle track the first thing I'd seen were three burnt-out aircraft near the airstrip and a troop of Laotian soldiers guarding the mule-train coming in from the mountains and half a dozen ranking police officers and an army colonel, guns on their hips. In the street there'd been people with attaché-cases chained to their wrists on their way to the refinery and more soldiers guarding a flat-bed cart leaving the refinery for the airstrip. Everyone looked tense except the local workers, and a lot of those were stoned out of their minds. In this heat I wouldn't have thought it needed much to provoke some gunplay.

I'd been surprised at first to find a phone in the room here because it didn't go with the rusty wash-basin and the burnt-out fan and the caked fly-papers and the peeling walls, but this was the only hotel I'd seen and this was where a lot of the business must be done, so they'd need telephones.

I tried calling Cheltenham but the girl at the switchboard told me it couldn't be done, so I stripped off and lay on the bed under the mosquito net reeking of citronella and waited for Chen to call and tried not to think that he might not do that. I didn't know how long that bug had been there—it could have been for months, a routine narcotics operation by the Singapore police, or it could have been put there recently by people who'd decided to move in on Chen, and it'd be logical for them to stake out his place with surveillance. On the other hand we'd got into the van perfectly clean the night he'd taken me to the airport and flown me out, so it could be just the narcs.

They couldn't have done the same thing at Cho's place, but it was too late anyway because I was past the point of no return and in the end it was going to depend on karma, kismet, whatever the hell you wanted to call it, running with sweat, the bastards were after me, I could hear them, teeth like knives—

Phone ringing.

Woke me, I'd drifted off, yes, nightmare, are you surprised for Christ's sake, you didn't see those dogs, thought they'd got me.

"Yes?"

"Jordan?"

"Yes."

"Chen."

18:00 on my watch; I'd slept for two hours after that bloody trek.

"Where are you calling from?"

"The British High Commission."

"You weren't tailed there."

"No." By the way he said it, he was sure.

"Did you find the bug?"

"I haven't had time to look. What do you want it for?"

"In case I want to talk to Colonel Cho. Johnny, can you fly me out of here?"

Silence, thinking.

"No. But hold it a minute." I heard the sound of paper scuffing on the line. The bed was hitting the wall again; one of the girls' rooms, then, poor little bitch; one of them told me once that boredom's the worst thing about it. "You there?"

"Yes."

"There's a guy named Tex Miller, a Yankee. He's putting a Partenavia P.68 Victor down on that strip some time around midnight. You got a pencil?"

"Yes."

"The ID number's NK6-75832. Tex is okay, talks a lot but he'll do whatever I want. He'll get you as far as Nah Trang on the Vietnamese coast—they're shipping his goods from the seaport. It's a civil airfield and you can get a scheduled flight from there to Singapore, if that's where you're aiming for. Got that?"

Said yes.

"If you don't have the right papers, ask Tex to get you through—he can do that, they earn big from him. Okay?"

"I'm grateful."

"Think nothing. Telling me about that fucking bug, you don't know what you might be saving me from."

I thought of asking him to tell Katie I'd be back in Singapore soon but didn't. Never chance fate.

The whole village was blacked out except for a few chinks of light where the blinds didn't meet. All I could see from the edge of the airstrip was the glint of metal as the soldiers moved in the moonlight, some of them carrying rifles. Cigarette smoke hung on the still night air, laced with marihuana.

I thought he was running late but that was because I hadn't picked him out from among the stars: he was coming in with no lights on; there was just the sound of his twin engines gunning up for the approach and then a generator tripping in from somewhere near; then the strip lamps came on, only six of them, and half-hooded. His landing lights blazed suddenly a thousand feet from the ground and the plane's shape began blotting out the stars as it passed against them. The wings yawed as he corrected the angle and he gunned up some more and then settled, throttling back, and as his lights threw a pathway down the strip I could see how rough it was, pitted and undulating. As the edge of the jungle was lit beyond it there were cries of alarm; it sounded like monkeys and parrakeets, some night birds.

By the time the P.68 had come to a halt it was surrounded by troops, and as Miller dropped to the ground a police captain flashed a light on him briefly and then asked for his papers. I waited for him in the half-dark, then stopped him as he came through the group.

"Jordan."

"Who?" He peered at me. "Oh. Yeah. C'mon over here, okay?"

Metal attaché-case chained to his wrist, cold cash. He peered at me again as light from a window passed over us, and stopped suddenly. "Jordan, okay. You got some ID?"

I showed him my Thai papers and he held them to the thin ray of light, squinting, a short man, pot-bellied, red-haired, a pilot's cap stuck on his head at an angle, a gun outlined under his bush shirt, his left hand loaded with rings: diamond, ruby, emerald, one with a snake sculpted from gold and topaz.

"Okay, yeah. Johnny briefed me." He lit a cigarette and drew the smoke deep, "Jesus, that's better, you can't smoke up there.'' Gave me my papers back. ''Let's go in here, I got a little business to do first.''

Under the tube lights of the refinery he looked ready to drop, red-eyed, pouchy, his skin sallow, his hands shaky as he unlocked the wrist-chain and pushed it into his pocket.

''Pakdee here?'' he called out.

''He's on his way, Tex.''

''Well Christ, I hope so. I'm down on time.''

Stink of ammonia in here. It was a small hangar, tin-roofed, with twenty or thirty girls working at the lab benches, five or six supervisors walking constantly down the aisles, two offices at the end, their doors closed.

''You been in places like this?''

''No.''

''They stink, right?'' Put a hand out. ''I'm Tex Miller, I guess you know that. What's your first name, Jordan?''

''Martin. It's good of you to offer to take me out.''

''My pleasure, I guess I owe Johnny the ride.'' He was watching the girls. ''This is Kuhn's operation, the whole village, I mean it's just one of them. He'll pay around a couple of thousand bucks for a batch of raw opium out of the fields up there in the mountains and then they do the refining in this place and a good few others like it, spread around the Triangle. Jesus, look at those tits, big for a coolie girl.'' He dragged on his cigarette.

She looked about sixteen. They all did. Sixteen and dull-eyed and half-dead.

''Then they ship the pure heroin out in kilo bags to Bangkok, where it'll retail at around fourteen thousand, maybe around that figure, then it'll go direct by air to the States or through the Mafia labs in Sicily and it'll wholesale in the Big Apple and L.A. at around eighteen thousand, maybe twenty thousand before it's cut with lactose, quinine, baby powder, strychnine, brickdust, you name it, going through a whole chain of dealers before it hits the street, where that original two thousand bucks' worth of opium brings in around two *million* bucks as street scag.''

He turned as a man went past him—"Hey, where's Pakdee for Christ's sake? I'm due out in three hours, goddamn it, and I need some sleep."

He turned back. "Course in Laos they have their local trade going too. They run a cigarette factory lab, turns out No. 4 heroin and sells under the brand name Double U-O Globe, hundred percent pure, guaranteed, and you know what the logo is? Couple of fucking lions roaring at each other over a globe, kind of appropriate considering the competition around here. You wanna smoke, Marty? These are straight Camels."

"Not just now. Is that why the village is blacked out? The competition?"

"Partly that, partly the way things are run. Sure, you could have some competitor—Vang Heng or Tricky Lee or Mariko Shoda, people like that—you could have them send a couple of dive-bombers in here and wipe everything out, so they just don't make things easy for them. Then there's the official side, see, the Laotian army general running this operation for Kuhn greases the narcs division in the government to let the place alone, but just for the look of things they pretend it isn't here, then the government can say they never knew what was going on. It's big money, okay? Maybe three or four million bucks runs through this place every day, and that's—hey, Pakdee, for Christ's sake! Take a minute, Marty, I'll be right back."

He was fifteen minutes and brought his attaché-case back but didn't bother to chain it to his wrist again. "Okay, they'll be loading the stuff on right away."

At the hotel he signed his name in the register, all his movements quick in spite of his fatigue. I had the feeling his time was short and he knew it.

The Asian at the desk spun the book around. "You wanna girl, Tex?"

"You bet, make it a couple, is Kim here?"

"I'll have to see."

"Tell 'em to hurry, I gotta get some sleep too. Okay,

Marty, can you be down here again at three? That's in''—he checked his heavy gold watch—''two and a half hours, can you make it?''

Said I could.

We sat at the end of the strip and waited, nothing but moonlight.

''So you ain't in the trade, Marty?''

''No.''

''So what're you doing in a place like this?''

''I'm an agent.''

''Shipping?''

''Narcotics.''

If he'd been drinking he'd have choked.

''You gotta be kidding.'' But he was close to reaching for his gun.

''Just joking, yes.''

''Well Jesus Kee-rist, that isn't the kinda joke you make around here, you know that?''

''British sense of humour.''

''No wonder you lost the fuckin' empire.''

A green light flashed a couple of times and the strip lamps came on and he gunned up and got the brakes off and the pressure came against the spine and we were airborne and the lamps went out below us.

''Sorry, Tex.''

''Huh? Oh. That's okay. You just don't understand the situation. You comfortable? Be there in a couple hours.''

''Nah Trang.''

''Right. In South 'Nam.''

We went into a tight bank and the compass settled at sixty-seven degrees. ''What were those burnt-out planes doing down there, Tex?''

''It's a tricky strip, and some flyers are better than others. It doesn't take much to burn us out if we get the touch-down wrong—if the trip needs extra fuel we shove a water-bed on board full of gasoline.''

''That's what this thing is?''

"Right. You wanna smoke, you better go out there on the wing and do it."

"American sense of humour."

"Too-*shay.*"

"I heard some shots down there, earlier. What was happening?"

"Well, sometimes one o' the coolies or the freight-handlers or the mule-drivers gets on a bummer—you know, has a bad trip?—and they can just take off and go crazy all over everybody, so the troops or the cops shoot 'em down, because we can't have that kinda thing around a place like that, you know, everyone's so nervous and it could start something. Or I guess it could've been some dealer on the cheat and the supplier wouldn't stand for it or the buyer got pissed off, you know—it isn't too different from the Wild West with the gold rush on, except the money that changes hands in the Triangle is about a thousand—make that a million—times as much on any given day. It's a jungle, see. You think that's a jungle down there? It's just a daisy-field."

We levelled off at ten thousand feet with the heading south-east.

"How long do you plan to stay in the trade?"

I was talking partly to keep him awake. He'd looked dog-tired when he'd brought this plane in three hours ago and he couldn't have had more than two hours' sleep, given thirty minutes to bring the wall down, three in a bed. We were flying a petrol tank and the fumes were no help.

"How long do I what?"

"Plan to keep working?"

"Give it another couple o' years, maybe around that. By then I'll have stacked up three or four million bucks an' I guess I'll be ready for Acapulco or Monte Carlo for a while, ease off a little."

"Is there much rivalry between you actual pilots?"

"Not usually. Get personal feuds sometimes, but we don't often try and cheat each other out of trips."

"You wouldn't bug each other, say."

"How's that again?"

"You wouldn't slip a bug into a rival's communications."

"Guess not. We all kinda know who's goin' where, an' we keep our asses clean. Bugs? Nope, I never heard o' that."

Noted.

We came down from our ceiling at 05:14 over South Vietnam and called up the tower in Nah Trang. There was cloud cover across the coast, topped with a gilding of light from the east, and we dropped through it into the dark again.

"Johnny said you'd get me through the barriers, is that right?"

"Sure. Don't show your Thai papers, okay? Gets too political."

He left me on the terminal side of the tarmac at 05:52 with a wind rattling the shutters on the cafeteria and the heads of the palm trees rustling, shining under the floodlights.

"You want another ride, Marty, check with Chen. I'm always around."

"I'm much obliged. And I hope you make it."

"Make what?"

"Two more years."

He gave a shrug and a wave and left me, a cloud of smoke across his shoulder as he walked away.

I'd need some secure transport when I landed in Singapore so I went to the line of telephones and called the British High Commission but she wasn't there, Katie. Then I gave the operator the routing code for Cheltenham but the phone went on ringing and I hung up at twenty.

If it's any help, old boy, I'm working hard at this end and I'm in constant signals with people in London and the field.

All right but who the hell were the "people in London" and who were his contacts in the field and why couldn't he get that bloody phone manned near the mast in Cheltenham for God's sake, because I needed *direction* and I needed it *now*—as well as a safe-house in Singapore because there was nowhere else I could use as a base that'd let me keep the mission running, and the police could have identified Veneker by this time and if it went into the news media the Shoda team would be on the watch for me again and Kishnar would close in. Chen's place was hazardous now because we weren't certain that Sayako had bugged it and if it were someone else they could have mounted surveillance on it as soon as they'd found out the bug had died.

There was a Malaysian Airline flight out of Nah Trang at 16:58 and I booked on it and tried Cheltenham five times while I was waiting and drew blank again. That *bloody* man was as much use to me as a dead duck.

We were ten minutes late on takeoff but landed early on a tail wind at 19:47, the moon behind clouds and puddles on the tarmac after rain, the air humid and scented with blossoms. I used my Thai papers and they didn't hold me up with any questions and I used a side exit marked AIRPORT PERSONNEL ONLY and found myself in an alleyway and came round to the rear of the taxi station and began looking for cover, man in a raincoat stepping from a doorway—

"Excuse me."

Not quite sure of me in the pilot's cap and sunglasses. Then he nodded.

"Good flight?"

Pepperidge.

"Yes. What—"

"First thing is to get you off the street, come on."

He took me to a car with smoked windows and diplomatic plates, Katie at the wheel.

Style, give him that.

22

THE CLINIC

"What did *you* try?"

"Carbon monoxide," I told him. "What about you?"

"I tried to overdose on Valium." Thin, pale, hollow-eyed, still young, thirty-odd. "But you can take a whole bottle of that stuff and it won't work for you."

"That was the last time?"

Two male nurses zeroed in on a man going towards the door and got hold of him gently.

"Yes."

"How long ago?" I asked him.

"A week. That's why they sent me here."

Wife and two kids killed in a car smash. He'd just picked up the phone and the police clerk had said, "Is that Mr David Thomas, please?"

How do people stand it?

"Feel any better?" I asked him. "Any different?"

"I suppose so. Thing is, when I get out of here, and go back to the house where we all—" He couldn't go on.

"Let it all come out, David."

"There's nothing left in there."

"Hit the wall, then."

"It wouldn't bring them back, you see."

Nancy Chong was waiting for him and he looked up. "Excuse me," he said and followed her.

I was down as *Paranoid, suicidal tendencies, nonviolent, general health good but traumatised following airline accident. Voluntary patient, agreed readily to curfew and confinement to clinic limits pending initial psychiatric evaluation.*

"The advantages," Pepperidge had told me in the car, "are manifold. Everything's found for you there as a patient, so you won't have to go into the open. You can also make and receive unlimited phone-calls, so that you'll be in close and constant touch with me, either directly or through someone manning the phone, night and day."

"How did you get me in there?"

He was different, sharper than when I'd last seen him in London. Perhaps it was just that he'd knocked off the booze.

"The clinic is British-managed, and I talked to the resident doc at the High Commission. Your cover will be simply that you've been through a tricky time and need to rest. They won't ask any questions and you won't be evaluated or given counselling or anything. Understood?"

"Yes." Was it just the lack of booze? There was something else. He'd turned professional and was doing a good job, had got Katie out of her office and a car with CD plates: he would have needed first-class credentials for that.

"So *this* little problem's taken care of," he said, and pulled a copy of the *Times* out of his raincoat and slapped it onto my knees.

Front page: photograph of Veneker.

Following the car-bomb incident of last Tuesday night the police had identified the victim as James Edward Veneker, a British national. Enquiries being pursued with utmost rigour, so forth. It was the photograph that clinched it: the Shoda hit team wouldn't think I'd just changed my cover name.

I gave him back the paper. "Do you know where Kishnar is?"

"No. But you'll be safe at the clinic." His yellow eyes

watched me, clearer than they'd been before in London, his gaze direct. "Trust in me."

"I'm beginning to." He took it well, didn't look down. "What brought you out here?"

"We'll come to that later."

The Radison Clinic was in Pekin Street and Katie got us there without losing her way. As Pepperidge got out she looked back at me once.

"You all right, Martin?"

"Yes. You?"

"I am now."

Pepperidge was scanning the street and I waited.

"All right," he said and I touched Katie's hand and got out and crossed the pavement with him.

When I'd signed in he took me to the small rectangle of lawn in the centre of the building and we sat in shadow on garden chairs still damp from the rain, the grass soggy underfoot. There were lamps along the verandahs, and people moved there, some in white coats. The air was steamy, oppressive.

"What brought me out here," Pepperidge told me, "was partly that McCorkadale phoned me in Cheltenham and said she thought you'd hit on something important. She said you'd got access to some kind of electronic surveillance on Mariko Shoda. That right?"

"Yes. She had your number in Cheltenham?"

"I gave it to her a few days ago, the last time I phoned her at the High Commission. For an amateur, she's extremely bright—I'm sure you've noticed."

"Yes. But I don't want her to get too involved, now that Kishnar's back in the picture. I don't want her at risk."

He thought for a moment, then said quietly, "She can look after herself, you know. Pretty accomplished."

"Just keep her well in the background, Pepperidge."

"Message understood."

He was sitting more or less sideways on to me and I watched his profile, angular against the distant lights, pensive as he worked something out; then he faced me suddenly.

"Look, we need to put this whole thing on the line. As I've told you, I've been doing a great deal of work in London, and a great deal more out here, through unimpeachable sources—particularly on Mariko Shoda and her background."

He waited.

"Are you here to brief me?"

"No. I'm here to tell you that I've compiled a massive amount of raw intelligence right across the board, and I'm in the process of analysing it. When anything comes up that I decide you should know, I'll tell you."

He waited again but I let the silence go on, because I knew now what his drift was and I needed time to think about it.

"Your mission, Quiller, is now at the stage where you can break right through and go for the objective. But you can't do that without a director in the field."

"I know."

"Of course you do." He angled his head. "I'm putting myself up for the job. *That's* why I came out here."

I'd already had enough time. In London he'd looked like just another burnt-out spook and all he'd had were a few connections in the trade he was hanging on to, people like Floderus and a few chums down at Cheltenham with an ear at the mast, and if I'd known what it was going to be like to work in a distant overseas field without a director there I wouldn't have touched the mission he'd offered me, I'd have turned it down flat; but I'd been smarting from the meeting I'd had with that bastard Loman at the Bureau and I was scared to death that I'd been out for the last time and was going to finish up training recruits or helping Costain with the industrial counter-espionage network he was trying to set up—*industrial,* Jesus, an armchair operation, the end of the bloody line and no future, no brink; so I'd done it without thinking, taken this one on and wished to Christ on half a dozen occasions that I'd left it alone.

But it was different now. Pepperidge had changed. He'd straightened himself out and got off the booze and established his credibility at the British High Commission and found me a safe-house at a time when I couldn't have survived in the field without one and now he was sitting here in the shadows watching me and waiting, and I knew he wouldn't say another word until I'd made up my mind and told him yes or no. And the reason why it wasn't an easy choice was that the relationship between a director in the field and his shadow executive is close, circumscribed and demanding. If I said yes then I was going to put my life in his hands, my life and the whole of the mission, and he was going to have to move heaven and earth if necessary to safeguard them both. He'd have to feed me with info and provide for my welfare and get me contacts if I needed them, couriers, drops, signals facilities, and local liaison, whatever I asked him for. He would also have to deal with my nerves, the accelerating risk of paranoia that always gets into the ferret when he's down there in the dark and starts smelling blood—his own or someone else's, *theirs* by the grace of God or the luck of the Devil according to how you look at things.

Above all I knew that if I were going to take him on it wouldn't have to be simply because there was nobody else—you can get killed that way. I'd have to do it because I wanted him, trusted him.

"Have you ever directed in the field before?"

"No." He didn't look away.

"I suppose there's a first time for everything."

He let out a breath.

"Be a privilege," he said.

"Mutual."

He got up and took a pace or two, watching the lighted windows, the people moving along the verandahs, not seeing them, I knew that. I also knew that it had suddenly hit him that he was taking something on that even a seasoned director like Ferris would have shied at, without the Bureau behind him.

Then he turned and took a slip of paper from his pocket and gave it to me. "My number. Round the clock."

I memorised it and gave the slip back to him.

"You've got your Thai papers?"

"Yes."

"Any others?"

"No."

"If you need any we can get them done here, overnight. You know Mayo Street?"

"No."

"Reliable."

He'd been out here two years ago on *Flamingo,* with Croder running him. That was a help: he knew the field.

He came and sat down again, sitting sideways to face me. "Debrief?"

"All right. Thai Intelligence—did you do any more on that?"

"Yes, but I didn't get anywhere. If there's a mole, he's down deep."

"At the embassy itself?"

"You know what you're asking."

"Of course." It was next to impossible to check out a government intelligence agency without months of work, and in place. "I'm still not easy on that score, so I'm not reporting to Prince Kityakara or anyone else for the moment, and they're not pressing me."

"That's fair enough. They gave you the job and you said you'd do it and you've only been out here for how long? Fifteen days. They've already been months trying to bring Shoda down and they couldn't do it."

"That's how I see it and that's why I phoned Katie to ask her to get the Shoda bug monitored. It's running now."

He nodded quickly. "Incredible. It might give us all we need. Now what about the bug on Johnny Chen?"

"It could have been put there by Sayako."

"The woman who's been trying to protect you?"

"Yes. It could have been the Singapore narcotics people who bugged Chen but I think they'd have dropped on him by now. It wasn't the Shoda hit team because they'd have heard me asking Chen to fly me out to the jungle and they'd have brought Kishnar in for the kill. But it could have been Sayako—and this is just an idea—because there's a connection between her and Colonel Cho.'' I told him about Cho's extraordinary reaction when I'd mentioned her name.

''What is she? Wife, mistress?''

''Or possibly his daughter.''

''Married to a Japanese?''

''Not necessarily. A lot of the Chinese girls here have taken English names.''

''What's the connection—'' He looked up.

''Mr Jordan, please?''

Lee Siang, one of the doctors: I'd been introduced to him when I'd signed in.

''Ah, right.'' Pepperidge got up and spoke close. ''Dr Siang, why not go and see Admin. about our friend here? Ask Mrs Yih—she'll explain.''

''Need to make examination.'' He tilted his clipboard to catch the light. ''Mr Martin Jordan, yes?''

''She'll tell you all you need to know, Doctor. Mrs Yih, all right?''

''Oh. Very well.'' Big grin. ''Not know about this. Excuse me.''

I got up too and we made the round of the lawn under the frangipani trees, the scent of their blossom heavy on the air.

''They'll take a bit of time,'' Pepperidge said. ''So what's the connection, with the Chen bug?''

''It could be anything, but he flies into that airstrip regularly and it's within forty kilometres of Cho's radio station.''

''We'll see if we can get her to talk a bit more.'' He put a hand into his pocket again. ''For you.''

He dropped it into my palm: a small, round plastic component like a black pillbox. The Chen bug.

''Thank you.''

''Chen gave it to McCorkadale and she gave it to me. What do you want it for?''

''I might need to talk to Colonel Cho some time, and this is the only way.''

''Does he speak English?''

''French.''

''He was monitoring Chen?''

''Not specifically. He was picking it up by chance across the wavelengths; he's got a whole range of stuff going into those tapes, totally at random.''

I reported at length on Cho and it took half an hour; Pepperidge got out a mini-recorder and put it on the cassette. ''The only two transmissions I heard in Shoda's voice were in Cambodian, and Cho translated for me, so I got this bit at second hand—she was telling one of her army commanders to hold back on mobilising his forces until the arrival of a consignment of some sort. She said it was vital for him to stay in liaison with her other forces, to avoid precipitate action.''

''Oh really.'' His voice was quiet. ''A consignment of what?''

''Cho didn't know. I asked him that one, of course.''

He stood thinking. ''We'll be picking up some more about it as the material comes through; I'll analyse it myself and give you the essence. At the moment it looks as if she was talking about the Slingshot, and I'll pass that straight on to my people in London, see if they're willing to do a little research for me. Go on, will you?''

I finished the debriefing and filled him in on the village out there in the jungle and the way it was run. Then I went over the whole of the material and found something I'd missed.

''On the Chen bug, there's something else that points to Sayako. I was at his place when he said I should take Flight 306, and the next day she got me paged at the airport to stop me going. At the time I couldn't understand how she'd known.''

''And now perhaps we do. I wonder,'' he said, ''just *how* useful Sayako could be to us, if we really explored the question? We've got her phone number now, by the way.''

Got my attention very fast.

"How?"

"She gave it to us." He pulled out the little recorder again and changed the tapes. "She phoned Chen today and gave him the number and asked him to pass it on to you. He didn't know where you were, so he phoned McCorkadale with it and she contacted me. I phoned Sayako and taped it for you."

He switched the thing on.

Yes?

My name is Pepperidge. Mr Chen passed on your number to me, since I'm a close friend of Mr Jordan's. Can I give him any message?

Where is he now, please?

I'm not quite sure, but I shall be seeing him soon.

A break as she hesitated.

Very well. I wish to talk to him, if he wishes also. It is very important to me personally. Also he should know that Mariko Shoda is very angry because of car bomb happening, which allow Mr Jordan to escape Kishnar. She order execution of person who placed bomb. I will tell him more, if he wish to talk to me by telephone. Please tell.

I will. But he has my confidence, Miss Sayako, so you can tell me anything that—

Please? Confidence?

I mean you can tell me anything that you can tell him. It is safe to do that.

She hesitated again, this time for longer.

I very much wish to talk to him. Please tell.

Click on the line.

"She rang off," I asked him, "not you?"

"Right. She's protective."

"D'you think I should phone her?"

"Yes. Unless she's got some kind of official status she can't have your number traced."

There was the sound of shoes on the wet grass, then a woman's voice.

"I'm sorry, but it's nine o'clock."

Curfew.

"Thank you," Pepperidge told her.

The rectangle of lawn went dark before we reached the verandah; they'd switched off the main lights and now there were only pilot lamps going.

"Can we go along to your room?"

"Yes."

"They don't allow visitors after curfew, but I'll fix that if necessary. The thing *is,* what Sayako said on the phone means quite a bit more, maybe, than you realise." The corridors were quiet, and he brought his voice down. "We've been hoping to find Shoda's Achilles' heel, and I think we've done that. And I think it can give us the mission."

"It's the bug?"

"No. It's you."

23
OBSESSION

I want his head.

The smoke from Dr Israel's thin cheroot hung on the humid air, floating in the glow of the pilot lamp in soft grey skeins.

You have exactly twenty-four hours. I want his head, do you understand that?

Mine. My head.

"Tell me," I asked Dr Israel, "about obsession."

He was quiet for a while. He'd had a busy day. There'd been two more suicide attempts during the evening and I'd seen three male nurses at a steady jog-trot along the north verandah twenty minutes ago, heading for the room where a woman was screaming.

"This isn't a rest home," Pepperidge had told me earlier, "it's in the front line. Try not to let it worry you."

The place was quiet now, and Israel sat with his short legs crossed and his white jacket hanging open and the end of his little cigar glowing in the half-light. In front of us the expanse of lawn was dark.

"Obsession . . ." he said, and smiled. "What can I tell you about it? Well, it's real. I mean"—he waved a thin, angular hand—"people say their husband's got an obsession about golf, you know? Or they say their wife's got an obsession about her diet, something like that.'' He shook his head. ''That is not obsession.''

Wanted to ask: what about heads? My head?

Didn't ask.

''It has an infinite number of presentations, you see. One can be obsessed about so many *things,* but the real obsessions are focused on *abstracts*. Hate. Revenge. Life. Death. Sex. Sickness. Health.'' He shrugged. ''There was a man who was convinced he had cancer of the stomach, you see, and they gave him all the tests and they were negative. But he wasn't satisfied! He was sure he had cancer of the stomach. Why? Probably—we never found out—probably because his father had died of cancer of the stomach and this man had been unkind to his father so when the old man died the son felt so much remorse that he wanted to suffer the same fate, you see—not on a *conscious* level, of course, not at all.'' Another weary smile. ''Not much of what we do is ever done on the *conscious* level. So''—another shrug—''he walked into a telephone kiosk and called the hospital and pulled out a gun and shot himself in the stomach and told them to come and get him. They'd told him, you see, that he didn't need to undergo exploratory surgery, which he'd asked them for. So now he *had* to have surgery, and he knew they'd find the cancer.''

Soft shoes. ''Dr Israel?''

''Yes?''

''Is Mary all right?''

He didn't look round. ''Yes. Until she tries again. Don't let her try again.''

Rustle of a skirt as the girl moved away.

''Did they find cancer?'' I asked Israel.

''All they found was a bullet. *That* is obsession.''

''A killing disease.''

''Sometimes, yes. Often. A patient of mine was obsessed with his lack of attractiveness to women. He wasn't bad-looking and he was gentle with them and he was *rich,* yoy, isn't that attractive to women? But no, someone had said in his childhood that he was a little runt, something like that, it happens all the time—kids are cruel, brutal, to each other, sometimes. So this man spent all his money on screwing one woman after another to prove how attractive he was and finally he got AIDS and hung himself. *That* is obsession."

The movement of a white coat in the gloom on the far side, a woman's soft laughter. Christ, how could anyone laugh in a place like this?

"It's something you can't stop," I said.

"Yes." He uncrossed his legs and crossed them the other way. "It starts at ten miles an hour and gets to fifty and then to ninety and you can't stop it. You crash."

Twenty-four hours. Her voice had gone onto the tape three hours ago. Twenty-one.

"But someone very powerful," I said, "someone clever, intelligent, authoritative, say, given an obsession, what you call the real thing—they can finally lose control, and crash?"

He blew out a curl of smoke. "You have heard of Adolf Hitler?"

The smoke straightened into a long skein under the lamp.

Has Gunther been dealt with?

Not her actual voice: a translation, accented English.

"There was a man on the hit team," I'd told Pepperidge, "watching the Red Orchid, a European, Teutonic. He could have been the one who rigged the bomb. Gunther."

Pepperidge had nodded, concentrating again, releasing the pause button.

Where is Kishnar? I want your report on him. Tell him I will give him twenty-four hours. I want that man's head.

The translator put emphasis on the last word.

We have not found the body of the third agent, but his head was delivered to my office in a cardboard box.

Major-General Vasuratna, Thai Military Intelligence.

"Part of their culture," Pepperidge told me, trying, I suppose, to make light of it.

"Once you're snuffed, you won't care where the bloody thing is."

He switched off the recorder and ran the tape back. "Bit poky, this room, isn't it?" Looking around, bed, chest of drawers, upright chairs, rush mat, lamp, small mirror, and that was it. "You want me to get it changed?"

"I shan't be spending any time in here."

His yellow eyes brooded on me. "So what I mean is, I think we've found her Achilles' heel, and it's you. Agree?"

"You mean she's obsessed?"

"Yes. That is exactly the word."

"It's beginning to sound like it."

This was why I'd got hold of Dr Israel later, to gen up a bit.

"As I told you," Pepperidge said, "I've been doing quite a lot of homework, some of it with Kityakara—personally, in view of a possible mole. He agreed that there was absolutely no need for Shoda to order the bodies of those agents sent back to the palace and the police headquarters and so on. She took it *personally*. He says it's because of her childhood experiences—she's intensely vulnerable to challenge."

Also a clock, a tin clock by the bed, a loud tick, getting on my nerves. I tried to tune it out.

"She was absolutely incensed, you know, by your going into that temple to face her out." Head tilted—"Why did you do that, exactly?"

"I thought it'd be useful to—" Then I stopped because I'd caught what I was saying and we don't always do that; we trot out a convenient rationalisation and leave it at that, a stand-in for the truth we'd rather not talk about. I started again. "I thought it'd be useful to try talking to General Dharmnoon, because he was the man Lafarge wrote to about the Slingshot, but that was just a reason I'd cooked up."

After a bit I realised I hadn't finished, still didn't want to talk. Pepperidge was waiting patiently. "I wanted to see Shoda," I said at last.

Silence again.

"To 'see' her."

I started walking about, feeling trapped. "I think it's becoming a bit obsessive on my side, too. Becoming personal. And I think it's because she scares the shit out of me, so I want to confront her, face the bitch."

In a moment: "I see."

He didn't.

"I've been scared plenty of times. Life on the brink's like that—you know what I'm talking about; you've been there too. And I've been pretty certain I've had it, too, often enough. But this is the first time I've felt"—I couldn't find the right word, so I threw in something close, though it was appallingly melodramatic—"the first time I've felt *doomed.*"

Pepperidge said nothing. The word hung around like a whiff of cheap scent. I began wishing to Christ he'd break the silence, say anything he liked to cover the ticking of the tin clock.

Finally I stopped pacing and stood looking down at him; he was sitting on one of the upright chairs with his feet together and the tape-recorder on his knees and his head tilted as he watched me, and I was suddenly looking at a new dimension in the man, and it shook me. It was as if the Pepperidge of the Brass Lamp in London had been an act.

"Doomed," he said, because he knew what I'd seen and he wanted to cover it, not give it any attention.

I took a step away, a step back, touched by anger. "I suppose you're playing straight with me, are you?"

"Yes," at once and with emphasis. "You and your mission are my total concern."

He wasn't lying. I would have known.

"I've no choice," I said. "I've got to believe you."

"Oh, you've got a choice, old boy. You could just tell me to fuck off, couldn't you?"

Deadly serious.

"I suppose I could."

"But you're not going to, and of course you're perfectly right." Tilted his head straight—"Doomed, you were saying."

I let out the tension on a breath. "Yes, I mean we've faced situations, you and I, in whatever mission, and we've had to deal with them and get them behind us and go on, since we're still alive. We've had periods of relief, in between, when we can breathe again." I leaned my back against the wall, feeling its cool in the warm room. "It's different, Pepperidge, this time. For the last week I've begun to feel I've walked into a shut-ended operation that's going to be the death of me *whatever* I do."

In a moment he said, "I've never felt that, but I know what you mean."

"Do you?"

Even his understanding would be something to grab and hold on to—but even that thought was a warning of how far gone I was. The room grew even smaller suddenly, the walls pressing in. It could just be this bloody place, all these poor bastards cutting their wrists and swallowing Valium, could just be the atmosphere here, the vibes.

It wasn't.

"I understand very well," he said, "what you're feeling. It's the effect Mariko Shoda has on people, particularly people she doesn't like. I've talked to a couple of them. They told me the same thing as you, in their different idiom—she scares the shit out of them."

Cho was suddenly in my mind, the way he'd reacted when I'd spoken her name, Shoda's: he'd looked like a cat facing a dog.

"So it's not just my . . . nerves," I said.

"No." He shoved the recorder into his side pocket and got up, going from wall to wall. "I'll really have to get you a bigger room, you know. You need *space*. But we're doing some good work here, and I think you know that. Let me tell you"—stopping and standing in front of me, very direct—"that I've been getting a very distinct picture of what this mission really is. I didn't see it at first, nor did you. This is a very different sort of job from the ones we've been used to doing—getting someone across, digging out papers or tapes or hot product, cutting down an assassin, the usual things. This has turned into a *duel*. You agree?"

"On a psychological level."

His eyes narrowed. "You could even have said psychic. Because that's what she's like, and I know that now. And so, quite clearly, do you. Which is exactly why I asked you why you felt *compelled* to go into that temple and confront her, though I must say I didn't know you were going to take half the night to come out with it." He looked at his watch. "So how do you feel about the future?"

I took a minute to think.

"Bit keyed up."

He was doing an extraordinarily good job as a local director, considering he'd spent most of his career life as a ferret in the field. He was critically concerned with what was going on in my mind, in my nerves, and this could be because he'd got some briefing set up for me that would push me right to the brink, but I didn't think so. He'd come out here because he'd sensed that if he'd stayed in Cheltenham I would have lost direction and run the whole of the mission into the ground, and now that he'd got here he was testing the ropes for slack and getting down to business, conning a safe-house for me and tapping the High Commission for resources and debriefing me within hours of his landing in Singapore.

But now he wanted to know what condition the ferret was in, and how far I was prepared to go. And I didn't know. I hadn't had time to think. But I'd have to, and soon, because Shoda was putting a *lot* of pressure on and we'd have to react, push it back, before it became overwhelming.

"Keyed up," Pepperidge nodded. "That's understandable. But I mean how do you feel about Mariko Shoda herself, as an adversary?"

"Do I think she's too powerful for me to break?"

"Sort of."

"It'll take a bit of doing, but I suppose anything can be done." Didn't sound too sanguine, no. "All right, then, yes, I know I can bring her down."

"Given," he said, "a secure base and a director and immediate access to support, the whole works. I want you to think about that. You're not alone anymore; you're not hunted, as long as you stay inside these walls. The thing is"—he checked his watch again—"I think you're absolutely right: you *can* bring the Shoda organisation down, given enough support and briefing, and I'll get that for you."

I could feel the nerves steadying.

"When?"

"At any next minute, because it'll have to come from the tapes—from the Shoda bug. We've got a window on her now and all we've got to do is watch. The critical factor is the Slingshot, as you know, because the minute she gets her hands on it then God help us all. Now I'm meeting the Thai ambassador in half an hour, so why don't you phone Sayako before I leave here?"

He gave me the number and stuck a suction pad onto the side of the phone and plugged the lead into his recorder and I dialled.

Ringing tone.

"She said she wanted to talk to you," Pepperidge murmured, "about something personal, remember? She might have meant Colonel Cho, and that could be interesting."

I nodded.

Ringing tone.

"If you can, persuade her to let you meet her. I'd like to know what other bugs she might have been putting around."

Nodded.

Ringing.

"She's not there."

"Then try again later, and put it on tape for me." He dropped the recorder onto the night table. "Anything interesting, give me a signal."

I went into the main hall with him and he got me a *laissez-passer* from the night-staff desk, so that I wouldn't have to keep to my quarters after curfew.

"Questions?"

"Yes."

He knew very well I'd got a question and he'd been waiting for me to come out with it and I hadn't done that until now because it was so very important and I think I was scared of the implications.

He watched me steadily, his yellow eyes narrowed.

"If *all* further briefing," I told him, "depends on the Shoda bug and what it gives us, I might never be able to move out of this place. If the bug stops transmitting—if it's found and destroyed—we'll be working on a very thin chance."

"True."

He waited.

"And there's also Kishnar."

Tilted his head. "True indeed."

This time I waited but nothing happened, and it was then that I knew what he was doing, and it was going to change the whole of the mission from this point onwards.

"How much discretion are you giving me, Pepperidge?"

He looked down, then away. In a moment: "Let me put it like this. The Shoda bug and the other data we've got on her is in fact all we have to work with, and that could be compromised if someone finds the bug. And there's Kishnar. But for the moment we'll have to let these things take their course, however long it needs." Now his eyes came back to mine. "Unless you can think of a quicker way."

I could. But I didn't tell him that. He knew.

"Keep in touch, old boy."

When I was back in my room I tried Sayako's number

twice in the next thirty minutes and got no answer but she was there the third time at 20:35 and among other things she told me that Mariko Shoda had just landed unexpectedly in Singapore.

24

THE BIRDBATH

"He is my father."

Cho.

The recorder was running.

"I see."

Silence for a while. I think she took a quick breath to say something, then stopped herself. Then decided.

"He speak of me?"

In a way, though he'd said nothing, he'd spoken volumes, spoken of love.

"When I mentioned your name, Sayako-san, he was very moved."

"Move?"

"He showed that he has great love for you."

Silence again, for longer this time. I waited. She'd heard me talking to Johnny Chen on the bug, making our plans to see her father.

"He say he has love for me?"

"Yes."

If his love for her had not been in that single bright tear, what else had it meant?

"I want to ask," she said, as I knew she would, and with painful hesitation, "how is he now?"

That last word told me a lot. She hadn't see him since that

vicious blade had struck and left him . . . how he was now. She had only heard.

"He can only ever be," I said, "as you remember him."

"People say—" And then quietness again, not quite silence.

"He is very strong, Sayako. He trains every day in *Shotokan*. And he listens to the voices coming to him by radio. He is not alone."

After a long time: "So." And she was over the worst. "You ask him for wavelength of Shoda bug?"

"Yes, and he gave it to me."

"I am very glad. I could not give it to you, because I did not place it. My brother place it. But after, he"—three seconds, four—"she find him and execute."

Dear God, what star had she been born under?

I said nothing.

"He give wavelength to my father. He listen to Shoda?"

"Yes."

"He hate her."

"Yes."

"I hate her also."

"Of course."

It was then that she said that Shoda had landed in Singapore.

"What is she here for, Sayako-san?"

"Is extremely angry because of you. Angry with Kishnar. So you must be very careful, Mr Jordan. If possible, you must leave Singapore."

"Perhaps. But I would like to meet you, first."

"Not possible. Too much danger."

I didn't press it because if she agreed to a rendezvous it'd have to be arranged with so much security that it'd hardly be worth it. I didn't know if the hit team was aware that she'd been in contact with me, and if they tagged her to this clinic it'd blow the safe-house and leave me exposed, *finis*.

"How did you learn to use bugs, Sayako-san?"

"I work in factory, assembly line. Sanyo."

"I see. And why did you place a bug on Johnny Chen?"

Hesitation, then: "Somebody say he fly to village, often. Village near my father. I hope to learn about my father perhaps."

"Chen would have flown you there, if you'd asked."

"Yes, but friends of my father tell me he not wish to see me again, ever, and I might meet with him in village, without meaning. He—"

"You mean your father didn't want you to see *him*."

She thought about that. "Yes."

I wondered which would break her heart the more effectively: for her not to see him, ever, or to see him, as he was now.

"Sayako-san, do you know where Mariko Shoda is staying, in the city?"

"Yes. She has house in Saiboo Street."

I asked for the number and noted it. "We will keep in touch," I said.

"Touch?"

"We will talk again on the telephone."

"Yes. But you must leave Singapore now, Mr Jordan. Kishnar not play games."

"Thank you for your warning. I will phone you again, Sayako-san."

Tick of the tin clock.

Sweat running on me; midnight and the sweat running as the ceiling fan stirred the warm air.

I could put the clock outside the door or throw it out of the window; I didn't necessarily have to listen to the bloody thing but what would that prove, it'd only prove my nerves wouldn't stand it anymore and they were going to have to stand a lot more than a clock in the next twenty-four hours.

You have exactly twenty-four hours. I want his head, do you understand that?

Shoda.

Bitch!

Do you know what she's come here for, to Singapore? For my bloody *head,* you know that?

The *impudence* of the bitch!

I think that was what had made up my mind. But the nerves were rioting in this small quiet room at midnight because I couldn't be sure whether I was going to do what I was going to do on the impetus of sheer rage or the dictates of a sound mind. Pepperidge would have said no, if I'd put it to him; he'd have finished with me, walked out of the mission, I knew that. It is *not* secure behaviour on the part of a shadow executive in a red sector to break out of his briefing and commit himself to an act that his own director in the field would *forbid.* But that was what I was going to do and the thought of it was firing the nerves and costing me the sleep I'd need later, costing me the strength.

Did she know what my contacts were, Shoda, what my communications were; did she know that as soon as she landed in Singapore I'd be informed? Probably. And that was probably why she'd come, to visit me in the dark of night, to creep under my skin with the stealth of a succubus and there spread her venom in the veins as I lay with a dry mouth and my hands cold, freezing in the heat of the room, my breath quickened and urgent as if each were to be the last as she came close to me now, her head turned on her slender neck as she looked at me, stopping a few yards away in the cavernous silence of the temple, until I was staring into the eyes of the angel of death, the luminous night-deep eyes of the creature that was to be my executioner, cup of tea, yes, *would you like a nice cup of tea?*

"What?"

"I've brought you some tea."

Thanked her, yes, bright morning light, they looked after you well in this place, cleared up the mess when you cut your wrists, so forth, brought you a nice cup of tea.

And a different view of things, of course, much more confident, not a mistake, no, it hadn't been a mistake to make up my mind to do it, because the thing *was,* it would have to be done before we could move on to the objective. Needed a shower, stank like a polecat, shave, a slow and careful shave with only one bright bead of blood from the right cheek because I'd held the blade a degree or two from a right-angle, drawing blood before the day's had a chance to get into gear, now don't start *that*.

At 08:17 I left my room and talked to the girl at the nurses' station on B Block, Jasmine, Jasmine Yee with quick eyes and the knack that most of them had of looking into your head and deciding what condition you were in while they were saying yes, but it'll rain before the afternoon, smiling, having to be observant because they might be asked later to report precisely how this patient appeared to them, had he shown any signs of depression, so forth.

Pepperidge would worry if he phoned here for me during the next hour and they told him I couldn't be located, but Jasmine would at least assure him that I'd been in B Block at 08:17 and had looked perfectly normal.

The doors weren't locked during daylight hours, only at curfew, and I used the one at the end of the corridor near the kitchens and walked into the street and blew the safe-house from under me.

"British High Commission."

A twenty-minute run, and at the halfway point I went through the whole thing again and tested the logic. The street had been absolutely clear when I'd left the clinic and I could still ask the driver to turn back and put me down where we'd started—it was like paying out a lifeline and it was getting the nerves on edge because I knew that when we reached the High Commission the line would break. But that was all it was, nerves, and I sat watching the street, noting the people.

Eight forty-five and the cab pulled in to the kerb and I got out and paid the man through the window and turned and crossed the pavement and walked into the building, one of them, yes, at least one of them on the other side of the street, and I could almost hear the whip of the lifeline as it broke.

At the main desk I didn't do more than ask if they had an airline time-table; the girl pulled one out of a cubby-hole and gave it to me; a new girl, one I hadn't seen before, fair head bent over her nail-varnish while I flipped through the pages of the time-table, a couple of minutes were enough, and gave it back to her.

Counted five of them while I waited for the taxi; three women in European clothes, two men, one of them blond but not Gunther: he'd been outside the Red Orchid.

I don't like this.

Like dropping into ice-cold water isn't it, I know what you mean, but you can shut up all the same.

This is a hell of a fucking risk.

Not really, no, not in daylight.

But what about tonight? Jesus Christ, you're—

Bloody well shut up.

There was of course the very reasonable thought that it was her influence that was making me do this, pushing me to the brink. Voodoo can turn a man's mind. But it was impossible to get any perspective: yes, it could be her influence, and yes, there was a calculated chance that tonight I could push the mission into its final phase and reach the objective and destroy it. But there was this to be said: I knew how to do what I hoped to do; there wasn't going to be any luck thrown in, except conceivably the slip of a foot on damp ground or an instant's loss of balance.

Ignore the effects of luck and concentrate on the demand for excellence in application.

Another taxi had stopped at the corner as we pulled in, and a blue Toyota cruised past and then accelerated. I went into the clinic by the side door and got to my room without seeing anyone I knew, two Chinese in white coats, a woman walking with one hand sliding along the wall, a man talking to her, carrying her bag.

I phoned the number Pepperidge had given me but it was someone else who answered and I asked him for the parole and got it and responded and said: "Tell him that I'm not absolutely sure, but there might be some surveillance on this place. Tell him to keep away."

"You want any action?" A thin voice, rather quiet, unsurprisable.

"No. I'll keep you posted."

Over and out.

Then the waiting began.

"I killed him," she said.

"I see."

They'd been wrong: it hadn't rained this afternoon; the lawn where we sat had lost the glow we'd seen last night under the lamps, Dr Israel and I. If the rain kept off, the grass would be almost dry tonight, and not slippery underfoot.

"I got off," she said, Thelma Someone, I hadn't caught her last name, "but I've got to undergo treatment for six months." Not a big woman, and not aggressive; just withdrawn, until I'd shown I was ready to listen. In her thirties.

"Why?" I asked her.

"I told you, because I killed him."

The lawn was a hundred and twenty feet square; I'd paced it. There was a birdbath in the centre, cast out of concrete and leaning slightly. The shallow basin on top of the pedestal didn't move if you tried to lift it; I suppose it was bolted down.

"But you told me he'd been beating you up for seven years."

"That's right."

"Drunk every night, and violent."

"Yes." No particular tone in her voice; it was as if she were talking about a play she'd seen, not a good one.

"So you shot him."

"That's right."

She needs to talk about it, one of the Indian nurses had said, if you don't mind listening.

"Well for God's sake, Thelma, what's wrong with that?"

"They call it pathological loss of control."

It was just gone five o'clock; it would be dark in two hours, and the night would come down suddenly. I missed the English twilights out here.

"Pathological bullshit," I said—"if you'll excuse my French. You *kept* control for seven years, didn't you? That wasn't enough?"

She was watching me, her eyes puffy, her hair a mess, not unattractive though, just unkempt, undone by life, unwanted, and do you take this woman, not bloody likely, she shot the last one dead, didn't she?

"You're doing me good," she said, and as her pasty face cleared there came a certain beauty. "Not many men would agree with you."

"That's their problem."

The last of the daylight was leaving the gardens and the lawn, well, not gardens quite, a few bushes and flowering plants, a glorious magnolia tree with blooms like water-lilies; and as the light lost its brightness the shadows softened, the shadows of the trees and the shrubs and the birdbath in the centre.

"Where were you?" Pepperidge had asked. He'd phoned while I was at the British High Commission this morning.

"Working out in the physical therapy room."

"Tell me about the surveillance."

"I'm still not sure. I thought I saw one of the hit team that were round the hotel. Touch of paranoia, possibly, but all the same I'd be rather careful."

His silence meant worry. God knew what he'd have said if I'd told him where I'd been.

"Let me know," he'd said, "if you see them again."

Said I would. He'd taken a lot of care finding me the

safe-house and couldn't really believe it had attracted ticks so soon. I felt for him.

"Keep away," I told him, "just in case. I mean that." It wasn't a safe-house anymore because I'd blown it across the street but that was going to work itself out. I didn't want Pepperidge walking into a surveillance net the first day he'd taken over the mission in the field. If I ever left here with vital signs I'd need him again. "By the way," I told him, "Shoda's in Singapore."

"Sayako told you?"

"Yes." He hadn't sounded surprised, so I said, "Did the bug stop producing?"

"Yes. But it told us that much—I think it might be on her private jet." As lightly as he could, "Don't worry about it." I knew now that he hadn't been going to tell me she was here. I liked that: it was good handling of the ferret, protecting him from unnecessary worry.

"What are you doing here?" Thelma asked me.

"I'm paranoid."

The light grew less, and sharp edges softened. People had started filling the verandahs on their way to the cafeteria for the evening meal.

"What form does it take?" she asked me.

"I think someone's stalking me. But only when it's dark."

Had some Pork Pad Kee Mao, but didn't eat the meat, just the vegetables. The protein I'd eaten middle day was into the sinews by now, and all I needed was something light, with the chili paste as a stimulant for the blood.

David Thomas sat next to me in the cafeteria, call me Dave, all right, but don't you dare call me Marty, I can't stand that, made him laugh a bit, he was the man who'd lost his wife and children, shut himself in the garage with the engine running.

"Boy," he said, "this stuff's red hot."

"Good for the circulation."

According to the pathologist's report, the contents of the stomach was corn, bamboo shoots, green beans, onion and chili. Pork Pad Kee Mao.

Oh, balls.

"Who?"

"He said his name was Singh."

A couple of the doctors had been talking in the hall, earlier today, when I'd gone through there.

"I've never heard of him."

"He's new here. Calcutta University."

"They should have told us at Admin."

Coconut ice-cream.

"How was your day?" he asked me, Dave.

"Can't complain. What about yours?"

"Okay." He held his fork still. "There's a chap here whose wife jumped out of a window, *because they'd been rowing*. How about that?"

"You can make a start with that, Dave. Find someone worse off even than you, and you can take another look."

"That's what Israel said."

"Terrific. You're on your way."

Then I went along to the games room and played some snooker, or made an attempt, hitting the balls all over the place regardless, taking the tension down a degree. There wasn't anything worth looking at on the box, so I worked out again, this time with the weights to tune up the red muscle; I'd worked on the white muscle earlier with some speed punching at the bag.

Watching the time, of course, watching the people, the doctors in their white coats, most of them English because the place was run by them, but quite a few Chinese and Malaysian and one or two Indians.

"Going to bed?"

Thelma. We were in one of the corridors and it was a few minutes to nine, curfew time.

"On my way," I said.

"Don't let it worry you. It's all in the mind."

"That's right."

I went out through the swing-door and crossed the

verandah onto the lawn, the scent of the frangipani blossom sweet on the air, and sat on one of the wrought iron seats, where Thelma and I had been sitting earlier, and now it was nine o'clock and the main lights went off, leaving only the pilot lamps burning and the lawn dark, so that from here I couldn't even make out the birdbath.

25

SILENCE

There was no moon: it hadn't risen yet above the east wing. But Sirius was bright, its colours changing like a prism in the heat-waves over the city.

People went along the verandahs now and then, a door swinging shut behind them, their footsteps quiet, rubber soles on the wood planking. Silhouettes passed across my line of sight, becoming fleshed out as they neared a pilot lamp. They couldn't see me here at the edge of the darkness.

Wrong.

"Who's that?"

White coat.

I got up, not quickly but resting my right hand on the back of the iron seat: it would make a good pivoting point, or I could push back from it, gaining speed.

"Jordan."

He came closer. Stethoscope, clipboard, one of the meds, as distinct from one of the psychs, clinic patois.

"Oh, hello. Taking the air?"

"That's right." He knew about me, that I didn't have to be in my room at curfew.

"Wonderful scent, isn't it?" He looked up at the trees; he was half in silhouette against a lit window beyond, and half-illumined by the nearest pilot lamp. He was all right, name was Hawkins, I was just taking the opportunity of using him as a model. "Trouble is, the pollen's giving a lot of people hay fever. Let me know if it bothers you—we've got plenty of antihistamine."

He wandered off, and I noted that his shoes made only the slightest sound on the grass.

Peggy was working the evening shift, Peggy Mitchell, at Reception; I could see her through the window on the west side of the building, and the less distinct figure of the security guard by the doors. In fact security wasn't all that strict; I'd been in the front lobby a couple of times when there was no one at the desk, and the doors weren't locked in the daytime. And anyone could use the little door by the kitchens, as I'd done myself. I suppose it wasn't surprising —all the patients here had come in on voluntary admission.

Sirius had neared the roof of the psychiatric block in the east wing, changing from blue to green to ruby as I watched, listening with my head turned to the right so that sounds coming from the verandah in that direction would reach the right ear full on, for analysis by the left hemisphere; it had been a voice, that was all, a long way off or half-muted by the walls. The doors on that side had all been shut a minute ago and there'd been nobody on the verandah, and what I wanted the left brain to work out as fast as it could was the oddness of the voice; it wouldn't be audible through the closed doors or the walls or windows: I'd been aware of that since I'd come out here; but it had been audible just now, and no one had opened a door, unless they'd done it very quietly for some reason.

Tidal breathing, the better to listen.

There was a sound from behind me, distant, from the verandah, a shoe, I thought, catching on something; anyway it was enough, and I looked away from Sirius and began walking, tired of standing still, needing a little exercise. I walked towards the centre of the lawn, and my shadow thrown by the lamp behind me soon faded out, because here the dark began. I believe—

Analyse *fast*—close, was it close, feet, bare feet?

Went on walking, dark now intense, walking, not hurrying, the nape creeping—

Bang of a door, unmistakable, Jesus *Christ* can't you relax, you know what it was now, went on walking, lifting my feet to quieten them so that I could hear other things.

"Caroline? Are you out here?"

Shut the door again. Putting the whole thing together, she'd opened a door *quietly,* not for any particular reason, and the voice in the corridor had become audible until she'd let the door bang shut: it was the *swing*-door. Then she'd gone in again, did that work, make sense?

God it was dark here, it was enveloping, like a shroud, and as I walked—

Watch it!

Bumped the right thigh, the birdbath, I'd thought it was farther to the left. Went on walking because there was still a chance I'd been wrong and from behind me I'd now be silhouetted against that lamp over there, the moths spiralling round it, gold in the glow.

Reached the iron seat on the far side and turned and looked back, nothing but the dark between the distant lamps, my God the *adrenaline,* I could have jumped clean over the roof, strength of ten men, so forth, well that's the idea, that's what the stuff is for.

Have a seat, take it easy, the whole thing felt like a firework show, my body I mean, the nerves flaring and the blood on fire, well, no harm really, we just have to be patient.

Because this was the *only* way.

It was the only way for several good reasons and I'd given it a great deal of thought and I knew I was right. You don't take *major* action unbriefed by your director in the field and blow your safe-house and put the mission in gross hazard unless you can justify it later, assuming you survive.

There was of course an added factor, not a reason but the necessary impetus: that *bitch* had become too bloody impudent, coming here to claim my *head.*

That's really very personal, you know.

Bitch!

Steady, lad, don't take on so, there's a job to do.

Of course it might not work at all, my little master plan, make me look a bloody lemon, especially in front of poor old Pepperidge, *you mean you blew the safe-house just on the fucking off-chance,* so forth, every right to be pissed off about it, yes, but it might not come to that so let's take another little stroll shall we, it's such a lovely night.

In the course of the next hour I put in some more ground-work and chatted up Peggy Mitchell in Reception, standing at the desk under the bright lights, who's come in tonight, anyone interesting, we never talk about the patients, she said, but not unkindly.

I couldn't talk to David or Thelma because they were in their rooms, but there were a couple of night-nurses snatching a quick cup in the cafeteria, male nurses, these, some good muscle under their green cotton jackets—sometimes one of the patients would go over the edge and try and do something and the male nurses were here for that.

I did the whole square, walking steadily under the lamps along the verandahs, checked my watch two or three times because you wouldn't come out here for a two-hour stroll just for the exercise, have to be waiting for someone, perhaps a new patient due to check in.

Jumpy now, very on edge because of the adrenaline: I could have tossed a caber right out of the field or outrun a train, a taste in the mouth, familiar, the taste of cold steel, all the glands working overtime, triggered by the alarm that had hit the organism, calm down, there's a chance yet, the night is young.

"Is that George?"

"No," I said, and he peered at me in the half-dark at the edge of the lawn, one of the doctors, moving off again, some kind of panic—he'd come at a trot from the psych-section, fumbling for something in his jacket, I assumed a syringe, rotten life when you come to think of it. He made haste along the verandah and said something to a man coming the other way, white coat again, dark skin, what had the first one told him, anything?

I turned my back on him and started walking into the darkness, making for the centre of the lawn, listening to his footsteps along the verandah, hearing them stop.

Not exactly: he hadn't *stopped*. He'd moved onto the grass, and I held my head to the right, lifting my feet and breathing tidally; silence, a pool of silence inside the four walls, cutting us off from the city outside, a pool of stillness cold enough to chill the nerves, deep enough to drown in.

I thought I caught the movement of a shadow thrown by one of the lamps, some way off to my right where the darkness bled away to a field of illumination towards the verandah; I wasn't sure; I kept on walking slowly, floating feet down through the pool of silence, the ears straining, the hairs lifted on the skin, the organism brought to that pitch of alertness that will make the difference between life and death, between—

"*Dr Hawkins! She's up here!*"

I spun and saw them under the lamps, a nurse and the dark-skinned doctor and now the other one, coming back along the verandah with his white coat flapping—

"She's all right, Doctor, but I think you should come."

"Is she conscious?"

"Yes, she's sitting up."

"Don't worry, then."

Voices fading out and the slam of a door in the distance.

Sweat running as I came off the high, the organism lurching, trying to find its balance again, the onset of raging thirst. I walked quite fast to the verandah, my legs thrusting me forward, the whole of the musculature avid for movement. The nearest water was in the toilet in C Block and I headed that way, going through the swing-door and down the passage, MEN. They normally left the lights on all night in the toilets but this one—*oh my God*—

26

KISHNAR

We didn't move.
We waited.
When I'd gone in and found it was dark I turned to switch on the light and had my back to him and I heard a faint rustle of fabric as his arms came up and across my head and started down again past my face with his hands bunched and the wire between them and it was then that everything slowed down and as I brought my right arm rising in a *jodan uchi uke* it felt as if I were moving it through water, through quiet water, the forearm bone meeting the wire and my fist snapping back against the front of my skull as his two-handed force pressed it there and we began waiting.
The initial half-second of his attack was over and we needed time, a few tenths of a second, in which to make decisions. He was pulling back on the piano wire very hard, and if it had been brought across my throat it would have breached the skin and cut through the thyroid cartilage and the jugular vein and the carotid artery and he could have simply stepped back to avoid the blood and walked away, as I suppose he'd done so many times.
He succeed to kill always. Always.
Sayako.
It was very quiet, and a tap dripping in one of the

hand-basins made a kind of music, bringing us solace. It hadn't gone well for either of us. I'd made it too obvious, perhaps, waiting for him out there on the darkened lawn. He would have been confident, yes, arrogant even, certain of the kill because he'd never failed; but Mariko Shoda had singled me out as a special assignment, and a full hit-team had been ordered in to prepare me for him, to find and fix so that he could strike. It would have told him that I wasn't just another agent, untrained in close-range issues, and so he'd decided to let me go through my charade and wait for me to develop a thirst in the warm night air. If I hadn't come in here he would have dogged me through the hours of darkness with the patience of the instinctive stalker who knows that time is not important, given the certitude of the kill.

He moved and I reacted.

I'd made it too obvious, then, and let him trap me; but so far I had survived. It hadn't gone well for him either, on this count, and it was possible that it was the first time he'd ever swung the wire across the victim's head and failed to bury it in the throat. That would have dismayed him, and changed his attitude a little, his attitude towards himself, his omnipotence, the natural order of things wherein he was preeminent, unsurpassed. The solace of the musical tap was not misplaced.

He moved and I reacted and a grunt came out of him because what he'd tried to do was drop the front of his knee into the back of mine and bring me down and it didn't work because I'd been expecting it: I'd have tried the same thing if I'd been where he was. The grunt came because I'd used his own force through his arms and the wire to let my head snap back against his face. I couldn't tell how much damage I'd done: the back of the head's insensitive.

I'd seen two iguanas once in Bali, their jaws locked together, their size equal, and for minutes on end they'd waited with the perfect stillness of the reptile, and then one or the other had brought its sinews to the point of explosion-

and the tails had thrashed and the great heads swung and shaken from side to side until their force was for a while exhausted.

He wasn't a big man, Kishnar; I hadn't expected it; but he was strong and fast, understandably. He smelled of something, of some kind of oil; either it was on his hair or he'd anointed himself in ritual before the act he was embarked on; it was a little like almonds, the faint smell on him. It wasn't gun-oil: he wouldn't carry a gun.

The tap dripped, and I was aware of the thirst that had brought me here.

I let another second or two go by and then I twisted and brought the edge of my shoe down his shin but he stepped back so I brought my heel upwards, going for the groin but not connecting, and now we were on the move and the waiting was over for a time—I used an elbow strike and found muscle and brought a hiss of pain from him and he slackened the wire and then dragged on it with a strength that bit through the flesh of my arm and into the bone and sent a flash of nerve-light blinding me for an instant, though it wasn't critical: there was nothing to see in here, the vague outlines and reflecting surfaces of the cubicles and basins and tiling and that was all; the door had swung shut and the only light was filtering through a small window somewhere.

I felt the need for a better stance to preserve balance so I shifted my weight and my foot moved something on the floor, small and light, one of his shoes I suppose: he would have taken them off before I'd come in here because ritual would have demanded it, and the need for silence. I found my balance again but he tensed and swung his body in a feint move and then swung the other way and I had to shift my stance again and we were both in motion suddenly, spinning together in a dance of death, faster now, the momentum taking us to the point where balance became critical. Both his hands were still on the ends of the wire and he daren't let it go; my right arm was useless, still thrust between the wire and my throat and with the ulnar nerve paralysed: it was keeping death away but couldn't move to make a strike, so as we went on spinning I used my left elbow again in a series of fast jabs, connecting and then losing him as he arched away.

We were relying on our feet to give us some kind of decision but the *danse macabre* went on and we spun together until I tried the first throw and timed it right and he lurched and pitched sideways and took me with him, a shoulder smashing against something and my right foot finding an instant's purchase and letting me thrust hard away from him but the wire was there and it didn't slacken and what happened was that his body was flung out feet-first with my trapped forearm as the pivot and a screaming began and glass smashed, the mirror, the fragments cascading to the floor as we lay there still locked by the wire.

Fatigue setting in now and I didn't like the noise, didn't know what it was because conscious thought had blanked out and there was a dangerous degree of disorientation clouding the mind as the screaming went on and the dragon's breath blew hot against my face, imagination bringing me a flash from a fable. We lay on the floor among the shards of mirror-glass like drunks, or lovers, each of us just this side of death and each knowing it, while the screaming—

Stopped. Hand-drier, yes, I'd hit something with my shoulder as we'd gone pitching down.

I didn't know what he was thinking. Our heads were close together but that was all: there was no transference, no communication. The infinitely complex process of conscious thought was going on inside the skull, brilliant with the flash of synaptic interchange, presenting images, projections, options, and alternatives while far distant in the organism was the grosser interplay of emotions, the urge to survive overriding the contemplation of extinction.

Who are you, Kishnar, where were you born, how old are you, my brother under the skin, being of this earthly clime and of similar mould with a head and a face and hands and feet, and how was it that through the course of our complicated lives we came finally to lie here on the floor of a lavatory whose doorway would allow only one of us exit?

I suppose he didn't want to let go of the wire because it was the weapon he was used to. That was a weakness in him; it's the same thing when a man carries a gun: he begins to rely on it and feels naked without it, lost, vulnerable; it's why I prefer my hands: you can't forget them or leave them somewhere, and at close quarters they can be just as deadly. If this man, Kishnar, let go of the wire he'd have both hands free and that would give him a critical advantage because I could use only one: the nerve in the right arm was paralysed and I couldn't feel my fingers on that side; the fist was bunched against my forehead and that was all I knew.

But he wouldn't let go. I wasn't going to persuade him.

The fatigue was setting in because we couldn't take this appalling tension off: there was no respite. We weren't like boxers who could punch and relax, punch and relax; we were locked together like those two iguanas in a monumental exercise in isometrics, the muscles beginning to tremble now and the sweat trickling, while the left brain went through a thousand potential moves and the right brain drifted into the imagery of potential death, the passing over of one of these two souls to a new dimension, and the overall sense of loss, of having failed the challenge and been found wanting.

Voices.

Oh Christ I wasn't ready for that—he'd jerked the wire upwards and down again in the hope of my arm falling away and leaving the throat exposed but it didn't work and I felt an explosion of rage and used my free hand, driving an eye-gouge against his face again and again and he jerked his head away every time, no go; so I drove a half-fist against him, lower, targeting the neck, the carotid artery, but he twisted clear and light flashed under my eyelids, the first warning of exhaustion, listen, something will have to be done, and soon, because if he brings his cultural mysticism into play, shifting into the zone where fatigue is controlled and overcome for as long as life demands, I shan't have an answer, well yes, but not as arcane as his, not as practised, and not enough to tip the balance.

Voices outside, one of them saying they thought they'd heard glass breaking somewhere.

He moved again and I reacted and the tails thrashed and the heads swung, shaking, the scales flashing in the hot sun as I sat watching from the rock, my interest caught because it was a contest to the death, and if they—

Watch it, you're on the edge of hallucinating, watch it for Christ's sake.

Dehydration taking its toll, a progressive lack of electrolytes—I'd been thirsty before I'd even got here and now it was fire in the mouth.

They were outside now, talking about the glass breaking, might come in here but what could they do, throw water over us?

He'd kill ten men, Kishnar, if they got in his way.

We were lying on our sides and my free hand moved over the shards of mirror glass, feeling them for size, for sharpness, as careful as the hand of a jeweller assessing the angularity of a diamond's facets, for there were gems here more priceless, offering more than profit or loss in the marketplace or the envy of a duchess at the opera, feeling them tenderly, the fingertips appraising while under the eyelids the light flashed to the pulsing of my blood.

His knee came up and I blocked it with my thigh and the pain burst, swelled and diminished to numbness: he was very strong, well trained, not your thug from the dusty streets with throats to cut for a penny.

I want his head, do you understand?

Bitch! I used my own knee and insisted, presenting strike after strike and going beyond the matter of physical force and adding the strength of zen and two or three times his breath was caught in his throat and I knew I'd given pain and perhaps with any luck had found a nerve, the femoral or the rectus femoris, inducing paralysis, but the effort had been appalling because of the tension already there in the muscles and I brought it down, dangerously, to the point where I could recover a small measure of the strength I'd need when the final effort had to be made, a half-second or a minute from now, no later than a minute because fatigue moves into a steepening curve towards the point of total exhaustion.

The voices had gone away; there was just the music of the dripping tap, each drop worth a diamond in my mouth but each one wasted.

I listened for sounds from him, from Kishnar, for a loss of controlled breathing, for a slackening of the muscles, however slight, that would tell me that if I could exert and endure this amount of tension I might yet prevail. But there was no sign from him that he was weakening. I would have said at this stage that his game plan was simply to wear me out, to tire me to the point where I could no longer parry a blow from the knee, where pain so ferocious could be induced that the whole organism would be paralysed if only for a second, giving him time to lift the wire and smash my arm aside and come in again to the throat.

I think that was his game-plan, and the decision was close now.

A longing for water, for peace, for the sinews to grow slack and lie quiet, a longing for cessation, for a conclusion, one way or another, even for death, and a rose for Moira.

Then he brought his knee up and smashed it into the thigh-bone and the light burst in the dark and I twisted to avoid a second strike but he connected again and the breath blocked in my throat and something drove through my spirit like a cold wind and that frightened me because I wasn't ready yet to go but he *struck* again and I twisted again but this was as far as I could move, *struck* again and I rolled, sliding my leg downwards and trying to find his neck in the half-light, his throat, but I was losing strength and he sensed it and came in for the kill, hurling away the wire and rearing for an instant and then plunging with both hands for my neck as I turned just enough to do the only thing I could do while everything slowed down again and I saw my left hand moving an inch, two inches until the shard of mirror glass was correctly placed so that as he came down against me it went into his throat, and for a moment it seemed that nothing was happening, until his hands began closing on my neck, strong hands reaching confidently for my death, and they would have found it but for the sliver of glass—it had pierced his windpipe and begun to weaken him as he sucked in air, once, twice, before he began sucking on blood, his hands leaving me and reaching up to try to do something; but there is nothing to be done when the breath of life itself is compromised, and I lay waiting, just this side of consciousness, as his blood began trickling onto me, onto my face, its hot touch bringing me back to full awareness and reminding me that it was now honoured, the unspoken pact between us that one or the other should come to see his life vouchsafed or vanquished, so be it, let it now abide.

I twisted from under him and lurched to the line of handbasins and spun a tap, wrenching at it until it gushed, then bowed my head and drank like a beast at a waterhole.

27

PINK PANTIES

A lot of noise.

"Keep them away."

Not loud noise, but a lot, voices, feet shuffling, the ring of metal.

"But I have to know—"

"Keep everyone else *away,* for your own sake."

Sounded like Pepperidge.

They'd put the lights on, too bright, half-blinding me, I was lying on my back.

"All right," someone said, "you can dress it."

My hand was burning. She was a Chinese, the nurse, her eyes intent.

"Just take my word for it. I know what I'm doing and I know what's best for you, for the clinic, believe me."

Pepperidge, yes. Someone had come in while I was still at the waterhole and I'd told him to phone this number, *nothing* is the matter, just go and phone him *now* and tell him to come here, my name is Jordan, for Christ's sake don't just *stand* there, go and phone.

"Don't move, please," the nurse said. Her young face was puckered, queasy, and I turned my head, remembering, and saw him lying there, Kishnar, my brother in blood, in blood indeed, it was everywhere.

"But we've *got* to call the police, don't you understand? There's been—"

"Call them by all means, then, and you'll see the whole story spread all over the front page of the *Times* in the morning. Or *don't* call the police and I can guarantee you a complete coverup. Your choice."

I could see the face of the clinic's chief of administration, Culver, met him when I signed in. Looking a bit upset, understandably: they were used to the odd suicide here, but this was different.

"If you could convince me of your authority—"

"Look, go and ring the British High Commissioner—he'll give you the score. But meanwhile *don't* let anyone into this area."

Head ached a bit. I'd hit it on something when we'd been jigging around.

"What's this?" someone said.

"Let me have it." Pepperidge, sharply.

The piano wire, covered at each end with rubber tubing. He coiled it and put it into his pocket.

"Is painful?"

"What?"

"Is hand painful?" The nurse.

"No."

"Pain anywhere?"

"No. You're very pretty."

"Oh." Surprise, her mouth rounded, then a smile that shone right into my soul. It'd been a nervy twenty-four hours, from the time last night when I'd known what I would have to do. Then there was all this mess in here, most unpleasant.

"You all right?"

Pepperidge, stooping suddenly over me.

"Yes."

"Won't be long now. There's an ambulance on its way."

"I don't need one. I can—"

"Yes you do." He straightened up again. "Keep that door *shut!*"

Throbbing going on: there was some feeling coming back into the right forearm where he'd held the wire; the left thigh felt twice the size because he'd driven his knee into it just before we'd got it over with; left hand sliced somewhat from gripping the shard of glass: the medic had put some stitches in. There was a residue of shock in the system but I could probably walk all right and Pepperidge knew that; the ambulance was for security. The hit team knew that Kishnar had come into the clinic for me and they'd expect me to go out on a stretcher and that was what Pepperidge had arranged: he didn't want the team to take up station; we needed a new safe-house and we had to reach there clean.

Someone knocking.

Pepperidge opened the door an inch and looked through the gap and then pulled it wide open.

"All right—this man here."

On the way to the street I had a sheet over me, face as well. Lights glowed through it, coming and going.

"Hot under there, old boy, but it won't be long. You all right?"

Said yes.

In the ambulance he pulled the sheet away, hunched alongside on the tip-up seat. There wasn't anyone else in here. Under the dim pilot light he looked strained, his yellow eyes flickering sometimes.

"Thirsty?"

"Yes."

He gave me a plastic cup of chilled water.

"I couldn't stand the waiting," I said when I'd finished it.

"The what?"

"The waiting."

He thought about it. "Oh. For Kishnar."

"Yes. It was a question of time before he found me, so I thought the best thing to do was to get it over."

"Was that your only reason?"

"No. I thought it'd get Shoda to the edge."

"Hit her again on her weak point."

"Yes."

"You're right, of course. It could bring us the whole mission. This was *major*. You didn't only get Kishnar out of the way as a constant threat, but you actually turned him to good use as a tool. As a weapon. Could be the turning point."

I started to pull my shoulders higher against the pillows but he stopped me.

"Relax. You're going to need your strength later."

He didn't say why and I didn't think to ask.

"The thing is," I told him, "I had to bring him into the clinic."

"I know."

Of course he knew. If I'd gone into the streets at night and waited for Kishnar and taken him on and killed him the hit team would have closed in at once, *finis*.

"I owe you an apology," I told him.

"For what?"

"Blowing the safe-house, keeping you in the dark."

"Ah." He looked away and I couldn't see his eyes, their expression; then he swung his head back and put his hand on my shoulder. "Don't worry, old boy. I knew you were going to do exactly that."

"Bit fancy," he said, "I'm afraid."

We were in the main room, a big one, Victorian decor, faded red plush and gilt candlesticks, tapestries, a couple of dozen small round ironwork tables and chairs, bit of a stage or a dance-floor, the light coming from rose-shaded lamps, a smell of stale scent.

"This?" I said.

"Don't worry, old boy. Everything's taken care of. Why don't we sit down for a bit?"

"What is it, a nightclub?"

"It was. The owner couldn't afford to do it up to conform with the new fire laws, put a sprinkler system in and so on, so it's temporarily closed." A faint smile, "We're renting it. How d'you feel?"

"Bit depressed." I dropped onto a red velvet couch.

"Kishnar?"

"Yes."

He nodded, clasping his thin hands together, looking down. *"Post mortem animal triste est."*

I didn't think it was funny. I *know* the bastard had been after my blood and I *know* his orders were to sever my head and take it to Shoda—*do you know we found an empty cardboard box in that toilet, did I tell you, with a plastic bag inside?*—and I *know* he wouldn't have given it another thought, I'd have been just another job done, another stiff shoved under the rug, but all the same I'd killed a man and it always slowed me up, made me wonder what kind of life I'd got into.

"When did you fix this up?" I asked Pepperidge.

"This place?"

I didn't answer; he knew I meant this place, he was giving himself time. He'd been a bit odd since the lav thing, looking down sometimes, looking away, clasping his hands for something to focus on. It wasn't because of what I'd done to Kishnar, I knew that—he was too seasoned, he'd worked in the field for years.

"I fixed this place up," he said carefully, "at the same time as I fixed the other place up, the clinic."

When we'd been in the ambulance he'd said he'd known I was going to blow the safe-house—*I knew you were going to do exactly that*—and it'd shaken me, but when I asked him how he'd known he'd just said we could talk about it later. I think if I'd been feeling less switched-off about Kishnar I'd have caught the drift.

"D'you want to brief me?" I asked him. Because he'd also told me to relax, I'd need my strength.

"No." He swung his head to look at me, his eyes critical. "You're probably ready for a bit of shut-eye, aren't you?"

"No." I didn't know what time it was: my watch had been sprung off my wrist in the toilet and I hadn't missed it until we'd come in here, but in any case I wouldn't sleep even if I lay down somewhere; the nerves weren't off their high yet; they'd been tightening all the time since last night when I'd known what I was going to do, and it had been a long day, waiting.

"Going to stay up for a bit?" Pepperidge said, still watching me. "Girls have all gone, I'm afraid, but we could talk a bit, I suppose."

"Girls? Oh." Nightclub, stale scent, so forth.

Then he put his hand on my arm and said, "Look, old boy, you're not going to like me for this, but don't take it too hard. It's just business, after all." Gave me a rather strained smile and got off the couch and walked between the tables to the doors on the other side of the room and went out and spoke to someone: I could hear their voices. I think I heard someone say, *I'll get him,* or it sounded like that, and through the doorway I saw Pepperidge give a nod and then he started back, not hurrying, hands dug into his pockets and his head down, not looking at me. He was about halfway across the room when another man came through the doors on the far side, and for a moment I didn't recognise him, and then I saw it was Loman.

He came on steadily, picking his way between the tables, short, dapper, his arms held behind him, passing Pepperidge, who'd now halted, letting him go by. I'd stopped linear thinking by this time: the left brain was under a kind of random bombardment as data came in to give me the whole picture, adding up the bits and pieces and making them fit, some of them from as long ago and far away as the Brass Lamp in London, with Pepperidge sitting there hunched over his drink with that bloody worm at the bottom. *It surprises you, of course, that anyone should offer this shipwrecked fucking sailor a mission, I see that, I quite understand.* Sitting with his red-rimmed eyes and his thinning hair and his rueful half-smile, and later, *Mean-*

while I shall find someone to take this thing over, because it's too good to miss and I'm buggered if I'll give it to the Bureau.

Loman was coming closer, looking down, watching for the frayed bits in the carpet that might trip him.

Loman.

Long ago and far away in London, *We feel we owe you an apology, Quiller. We—er—deeply regret the circumstances that obviously prompted you to hand in your resignation, and very much hope you'll reconsider.*

Loman, walking towards me, *mincing,* you could call it, wearing, as a concession to the heat and humidity, a light alpaca suit, but with the same black onyx cufflinks and the same regimental tie, Grenadier Guards, what a fucking pain in the arse he must have been to the poor bloody troops, the rage rising inside me, starting in the gut and reaching the throat, blocking it, because he'd conned me, this prissy little shit, he'd *entrapped* me into a mission for the Bureau—*for the Bureau*—and now he'd come out here to lord it over me, bloody London for you, they think they're Jesus Christ.

Got up, I got up as he stopped and stood in front of me, got up but not out of respect for him—for *him?*—but because I wanted to hit him and I couldn't do it sitting down.

Very quiet in here, very quiet. It was the plush all over the place, the red velvet curtains, the carpeting, no echoes, everything very quiet.

"Quiller."

What else could he say?

I mean he couldn't say how are you or it's good to see you again or why don't we shake hands on it, so forth, could he?

I didn't answer, same thing applies, you see, it would have been pleasant to tell him that if he went on standing there just five more seconds his face was going to look like strawberry jelly or of course I could just tell him to fuck off but he'd think that was common, probably right but oh my

God I would've given so *much* to have left him spread all over the floor and walked away, steady lad, steady.

Steady, yes, better get a grip, this is going too far. And surprising how ready I was, so soon after killing a man, to kill another.

Steady. He made you look a bit of a lemon, that's all. Can't take a joke?

Pepperidge standing there, I looked at Pepperidge. He was staring at me with his eyes hollow, haunted, and it made a difference suddenly, gave me comfort, because he'd been a spook in the field and he knew what it was like when the Bureau did it on your doorstep and he felt for me as he watched me being crucified. It helped, because until now I hadn't been feeling terribly fond of him either.

"*Did* they fire you?"

To Pepperidge, not Loman. I didn't even look at Loman.

"No."

Bastards fired me, hunched over his drink in the Brass Lamp, *I'm like you, old boy—sometimes I won't obey orders.*

"That *whole thing* was a setup?"

He didn't look away, stood his ground.

"Yes."

And I don't regret it, you know that? His thin hair lying untidily across his scalp, his moustache at a lopsided angle, sloppily trimmed, his hand shaking as he'd picked up his drink.

"Bloody good actor."

"Thanks." A wintry smile. "I used to be in Rep."

I took a deep breath, and the last wave of the rage eased away. But don't think I was precisely ecstatic.

"A setup." To myself, more or less.

"It was a mission," he said quietly. Another faint smile. "I've known easier."

Poor bastard, he couldn't have cared much for it. He'd been as bad as Loman, really, but I didn't hate him for it. Let me tell you something about Loman: if you ever meet him you'll hate his guts on sight.

"I thought we might have had our meeting tomorrow." His small, calculating eyes on my face like a couple of snails. "You've had a fatiguing day. But Pepperidge told me you weren't ready for sleep."

Civil of him. He's like that. He pretends he's human.

"We don't need a meeting. The answer's no."

He tried to look puzzled.

"The answer—?"

"I'm not going on with the mission. Not for the Bureau."

I felt Pepperidge watching me. I'd do it for him, go on to the objective and bring Shoda down, but not for those bastards in London. But what was I saying? He was Bureau himself. Thought flash and I looked at him.

"Her too? McCorkadale?"

He nodded slowly.

That was why she'd been so useful, so efficient, behind the act she'd put on, *I've never been so near so much drama,* so forth.

And Chen. Johnny Chen.

"Sayako?"

"No."

"Anyone else?"

"No." He turned away and called out—"You there, Flood?"

A man came through the doors, smartly, coming between the tables, looking from Loman to Pepperidge to me.

"Quiller, this is George Flood, our main contact out here."

Medium height, good suit, muscle under it, his eyes blanked off, professional, slight nod of his head.

"Sir."

I nodded back.

"He's manning our station," Pepperidge said.

I didn't answer. It wasn't my concern. I was out of it now. The man took a step back, looking at no one. Chilly reception, yes, but I couldn't help that.

"The station is manned on a twenty-four—" Loman started in.

"Shove it."

Got an echo, even in here.

Loman gave a sigh, hamming it. Pepperidge looked at Flood.

"Go and give it another try."

"Yes, sir."

He left us, clearing his throat to fill the silence, embarrassed I suppose. And I quite agree, I can be terribly common, you know, when the mood hits me, but listen, I'd spent the whole bloody day holed up in a funny farm waiting for a top hit man to come for my head and there'd been two false alarms on the lawn out there and then I'd had to fight for my life in a lavatory and worst of all I'd finally had to take *his* away from him and now *this* bastard, I think you know who I mean, was trying to con me into going on with the mission and *I was fed up to the back teeth,* don't you understand?

"Let's just sit down for a minute, shall we?"

Loman.

So I sat down, dropped, actually, onto the couch, rather fatigued, yes, just as Mr Loman had suggested so courteously just now. I heard a breath come out of Pepperidge, relief I daresay, he wanted this mission to go on because he'd been right in at the beginning and he'd still be my director in the field and earn himself a nice bit of credit if we got the job done.

He sat down on the other end of the couch and caught sight of something pink stuck in the cushions and pulled it out, pair of lace panties, glancing up at us and shoving them in his pocket—"*That* kind of club"—an awkward laugh, Loman sitting there in the velvet wingback chair, face like a po, he probably didn't even know what the bloody things were, can you imagine *Loman* with a *woman,* you must be out of your mind.

He started talking, but I didn't take much of it in, because nothing he could say was going to change my mind; it was just nice sitting down again, that was all, various bits of the anatomy still throbbing, the hand quite painfully, I assumed they knew what they were doing at the clinic when they'd put the stitches in, no risk of infection, we'd been in a lav at the time, after all.

"—And I want you to know in any case," Loman's voice floated in and out of my consciousness, "that this place is under day-and-night observation by undercover officers of the Singapore police, with orders to arrest any loiterers on sight. So this isn't a safe-house, it's a fortress."

Quite impressive. I would have been quite impressed, if in fact I'd needed a safe-house, or even a fortress for that matter.

"Secondly, if you have any misgivings about the death of Manif Kishnar, there will be no repercussions." He was speaking with a lot of care, a lot of articulation, wanting me to understand every word, but the fact *was*, I wasn't interested, it was just pleasant sitting down instead of standing up, and the idea now occurred to me that it would be even more pleasant to *lie* down in a nice soft bed.

"—And you will appreciate that the government of Singapore is every bit as desirous of continuing peace in Asia as every other power in this—"

"Loman."

He stopped. I got up and found some balance and stood looking down at him, and the fact that I was rather tired now didn't diminish the pleasure I was going to get in the next few seconds, because in the next few seconds I was going to blow this little bastard right out of his overweening bloody complacency. I made an attempt to mimic his studied articulation, but whether or not it came off I didn't know and didn't much care.

"I don't want to waste your time, so you should know that I haven't the slightest interest in anything you have to tell me." He sat with his eyes turned upwards in a blank stare. "I do *not* intend going on with the Shoda mission, and *nothing* you can say will change my mind. I repeat—*nothing*."

He went on staring and I went on standing there. Pepperidge hadn't moved. Then Loman did. He gave one of his long-suffering sighs, got his briefcase from the end of the couch, stood up, and without a glance at either of us walked away between the tables and through the doors; and as I watched him I had to fight down a wave of disgust, because everything I'd done since I'd come out here to Singapore had gone for nothing, was down the drain, including six lives lost, one of them ours, gone for *nothing*.

End of mission.

I don't know how long I stood there, wishing Loman would walk out of here under a bus, wishing Pepperidge, a man I'd come to like, come to respect, hadn't conned me into an abortive enterprise, wishing I could go and lie down somewhere and let the throbbing in the blood slow to the delta rhythm of sleep.

"Still can't get her to answer, sir."

Man standing there. Flood.

"She's not at the High Commission?"

"No. They haven't seen her."

Something trying to get through to my attention, but possibly unimportant. Ignore.

"Keep on trying her flat." Pepperidge.

"Will do, sir."

Got my attention now.

"You talking about Katie?"

He looked at me, Pepperidge, face was bleak.

"Yes."

"What's up?"

"She's missing."

28

THE DEAL

"How much does she know?"

"Not a great deal."

He didn't like the way I'd fetched him back.

"So she's expendable?"

Loman hedged. "She's not . . . indispensable."

"So if you can't find her, what're you going to do? Throw her to the dogs?"

Flood had got us some black coffee and I was back on the cutting edge. It was Loman who looked as if he could use some sleep now; it was gone one o'clock and I suppose he was still under jet lag.

"I shall be instructed," he said, "from London."

"London." I thought about that. "Who, in London?"

"Mr Croder."

Oh really. Chief of Control.

Pepperidge eased himself back onto the couch, looking beaten. The last twenty-four hours had been a strain for him too, knowing he'd have to blow his own cover with me and confront me with Loman.

"*Croder* started this?" I asked Loman. "He *initiated* the whole thing?"

It was important to know. At the Bureau Croder ranked about equal to the Holy Ghost.

"Yes." Loman was still standing, briefcase hanging

from his right hand, polished shoes neatly together. "But I rather believe you said you weren't interested in anything I had to tell you."

He'd had to get that bit over and I'd been waiting for it, and he'd put it *exactly* the way I'd known he would, "I rather believe," oh my *God*.

I just ignored it, of course. "When was she last seen?"

"She left her office," Pepperidge said, "soon after ten this morning. Yesterday morning. I've been trying to contact her ever since then because Mr Loman wants her report."

"What report?"

"Just routine."

Fair enough. The London end was out here suddenly and he'd want to debrief everyone in the field as a matter of course.

"Quiller," he said in a moment, "since you are now prepared to listen to me, I have a question for you."

"Well?"

"It's obvious to you that what concerns us is that McCorkadale might have been seized by the Shoda organisation to be held as a hostage in a potential exchange for you. And since you know a very, *very* great deal more than she does, and since you are the sole obstacle standing in the way of the Shoda organisation's projected coup in South-east Asia, my question is this. If the opposition contacts us and offers to release McCorkadale in exchange for you, what would be your decision?"

He was standing with his head lowered, looking upwards at me in an attitude of intense concentration. I was aware of Pepperidge at the edge of my vision, equally intent. A faint singing noise began somewhere and the left brain took a moment off to place it; Flood had left the coffee percolator plugged in on the marble wall-table, and its thermostat had just cut in again. Full consciousness came back to the main issue and I noted Loman still waiting.

"I'd do it," I said.

I heard Pepperidge suck in his breath.

Loman kept his cool. "You would surrender to the opposition?"

"I'd have no choice. If I refused, they'd begin torture and let me know, and they'd finally kill her out of hand in any case."

"She means that much to you?"

"Not really. I've only known her a few days. But she's a woman."

He got impatient now, dropped his briefcase onto the end of the couch and put his hands into the pockets of his jacket, thumbs hooked over the edge. "But surely that's rather Victorian?"

"No, I'm way ahead of my time." I took a step closer to him, pet subject, he'd better keep off. "One day they're going to be thought of as important to us."

He watched me for a bit longer and then sat down in the winged chair, arms across his knees, hands hanging. "Rabid romanticism," I think he said, it was under his breath. Louder, looking up—"And what would you imagine Shoda would do to you, once you were in her hands?"

"Have my head."

"Having done which, she'd then be free to proceed with her projected coup and set the whole of South-east Asia on fire. And you would place *that* as having less importance than the life of one woman?"

"Right on."

Pepperidge put out a cautioning hand. "Old boy, you—" And then saw my expression and drew it back, shrugging.

"Your word on this," Loman said, "is final?"

"Yes."

"So if we receive a message from Shoda, through the British High Commission or the Thai Embassy, that McCorkadale is in their hands and an exchange is proposed, we simply hand you over?"

"Yes. But it doesn't have to come to that, with a bit of luck." I turned to Pepperidge. "She was seen just after ten yesterday morning—where did she say she was going?"

"No one seems to know."

"She leave by car?"

"One of the front desk clerks said she got into a cyclo."

"What's your guess?"

Spread a hand—"It's on the cards that she got a message asking her to meet you, and didn't question it. She was worried about you, because of Kishnar."

"Shoda's got a house here in the city, in Saiboo Street, did you know?"

"Yes. How did *you* know?"

"Sayako told me. That's where I'll have to start."

I was halfway to the doors when I heard Loman.

"Quiller."

Sounded quite urgent, sharp. Made me stop and turn.

"I'll offer you a deal."

"A what?"

"A deal." He was coming towards me between the tables. "I respect your abilities, but how much chance would you say you had of finding McCorkadale and getting her out alive, without playing straight into Shoda's hands and getting killed yourself?"

"Not much."

"I agree. I'd say you have *no* chance at all. But my own resources are infinitely greater, with the Bureau behind me."

"This isn't a case for massive support; it needs just one man to go in. I'm—"

"To go into Shoda's *house?*"

"No. Into the operation, but that's got to be the focus."

"We can have it surrounded by police. We can—"

"What good would that do?"

"The first glimpse we get of McCorkadale, the first hint we get that she's in there and against her will we can—"

"Oh come on Loman, Shoda's untouchable, on a *political* level, you know that. Otherwise we could have destroyed her before now."

He took a step closer to me, very intent, not impatient

anymore, very earnest. "If you try to save McCorkadale you'll be putting it all on one throw, Quiller. You've only got one life—we've got hundreds."

"You told me she's expendable—"

"In terms of policy, she's not indispensable, yes, but—"

"For Christ's sake say what you mean—you're going to throw her to the dogs."

Very fast—"Not if you'll make a deal."

"*What* deal?"

"You'd need to listen for a moment." Tone rather thin, he wasn't terribly fond of me either, you've probably noticed that. "And so far you've shown a certain reluctance."

May God give me patience with this little *prick*.

"I haven't got long, so try and use short words."

He turned away and stood thinking for a couple of seconds. I'd rather thrown him, I suppose, by agreeing to listen at all.

Turned to me—"If you will continue the mission, I will guarantee that the *whole* of our resources will be brought in *immediately* with the object of finding and bringing McCorkadale to safety, with the cooperation of the British High Commission, the Thai Embassy, the Singapore police, and every sleeper and agent-in-place we can mobilise in this city and at once. That is the deal."

I think I started to say something and changed my mind. This thing was too big for emotions to play any part in the decision-making and I'd have to come down off the high or I'd smash things up, no better than a small boy in a tantrum. Loman was a little shit and I couldn't stand him but he was also one of the élite controls in the very highest echelons of the Bureau and he'd run me before, Bangkok and Tangier, and he'd been good in the field, faultless, and he'd got me home alive. So calm down, yes, just let him talk for a minute.

"You would also have the benefit of the Bureau's resources, including the personal supervision of Mr Croder, which carries an importance I'm sure you appreciate."

I didn't say anything. Let him sell it to me, give me the whole pitch, but if he said a wrong word he'd lose me.

"You would still be working officially for the Thai government and would receive whatever remuneration you've agreed on with them. We wouldn't question it." He was watching me hard, hoping to see a reaction, but he was forgetting—a good ferret's got bright black eyes that never show anything, it's part of the job.

"I must tell you, Quiller, that I came out here because we now have only three days left. Mariko Shoda has set a deadline for the launching of her coup—three days from now. In view of this, I hope that you'll decide not to abort your mission at such a critical stage."

He waited. I let him.

Three days. *How the hell could he say that?*

I wasn't going to ask. Not yet.

"Anything else?"

He got an envelope from his pocket and pulled out a letter and unfolded it and dropped it onto the little iron table near him and turned away.

"You may care to read that."

Like someone throwing down the ace. I picked it up.

Very white, very crisp embossed paper, official seal of the Prime Minister, 10 Downing Street. *In view of the very critical issues now endangering peace and geopolitical stability in South-east Asia, nothing must be neglected that might redeem the situation. It is therefore my earnest hope that the agent in question, whose record is well known to me, can be persuaded to proceed with his present mission and bring it to a successful conclusion. You may if you wish convey my feelings to him.*

When I looked up Loman had turned back and was watching me with that deadpan complacency he can turn on when he thinks he's won. I dropped the letter back onto the table.

"Sheer bloody blackmail."

"I'm sorry it strikes you like that."

"What made you think I'd need "persuading" to stay in?"

"I knew that the moment you saw me here you'd start giving us trouble." He came and picked up the letter and put it away. "So you refuse to stay with the mission?"

"No."

The nerves went slack suddenly, relief I suppose, I'd got somewhere to go now.

"Do you mean you'll stay in, under the Bureau's direction?"

"Yes. I'll do what I can. That's all I can say."

I wasn't looking at him, just heard the tone in his voice, nothing triumphant, just very quiet, very cool now. "That's all we require."

He'd done well. He'd put a five-star ferret down the hole again without touching the sides and he hadn't expected to do it and it had left him impressed.

"Just find her," I said. "That was the deal."

"Of course. We shall start immediately." He went across to the double gilt-panelled doors and I heard him calling for Flood, talking about signals or something.

Pepperidge came up, padding quietly. "Good show. I know they're bastards to work for, but can you think of anyone better?"

"Not really."

"Their genius," he said, "is in the way they know their shadow executives." He talked quietly, and I could hear Loman's voice out there on a phone, caught the name Croder. "You've been working under their direction," Pepperidge told me, "since the day you came out here. You know that now. But what I *like*"—he put a hand on my arm—"is the way they just gave you the clues and let you run. It's how you work best, and they're well aware of that. Take the Kishnar situation."

I didn't want to think about the Kishnar situation because the depression was still haunting the psyche but the left brain was catching onto something and I took a look at it and said, "Jesus *Christ*. Was that *briefing?*"

Faint smile. "Yes, old boy."

All right. First-class. First-class direction in the field and not from Pepperidge, not from Loman but from the Chief of Control, London, Croder, because only he had the authority to push the executive for the mission right to the brink and leave him there.

Unless you can think of a quicker way.

Pepperidge, at the clinic. And I'd said I could. And when he'd left there last night he'd known almost for certain that I was going to do the only thing that could be done at this phase of the mission because *whatever* new direction they found for me I wouldn't be able to take it until Kishnar was off my back and out of the way. It had been the first action conceivable and they'd known I'd see that and they'd left me there at the brink to make up my mind and *that* was why Pepperidge had set up a new safe-house—this place—and had it ready for me and got Loman here waiting to put the whole thing on the line.

"First-class," I said.

Pepperidge gave a brief nod. "I rather hoped you'd say something like that. Because it was."

Something else they'd done, but I didn't want to think about that.

"Look," I said, "I need some sleep now. Is there any kind of bed in this place?"

"I'll show you."

He shepherded me through the rooms, solicitous, avuncular, which was what a good local director ought to be, hit a shoulder on a doorway going through, not him, I mean *I* did, hand on my arm.

"Been a busy day," he said. "There's a registered nurse here, by the way, if you need any attention."

"She pretty?" Fell on the bed and slept.

"No. But you should leave that to us."

Damn him.

She went on soaking the blood away.

I'd simply asked him if there were any news of Katie.

"How are you feeling, old boy?"

Pepperidge, on the couch, looking taut, confident. He'd got a ferret to run and felt ready.

"Operational."

"I'm so glad."

Understandable: Loman was going to handle the main briefing in very close liaison with Croder in London but when the final action phase began it'd be Pepperidge who'd have to judge whether I was fit enough to go in.

I was. I'd slept well, nearly seven hours, woke once to find Kishnar bending over me, shadow on the wall that was all, then it was morning and Flood brought me some coffee, life beginning again, I'd come close to losing it.

"I want to assure you"—Loman—"that there'll be no repercussions regarding what occurred last night. Briefly, neither the UK nor Singapore want to see the stability of South-east Asia compromised and they're more than willing to protect the clinic from bad publicity and order the police to hold off. The media never even caught a whiff."

The rest of the dressing came away and she dropped it into the bowl. Same nurse as last night and obviously Bureau or she wouldn't be here.

"I've arranged to have the body of Manif Kishnar delivered in a plain coffin to the house in Saiboo Street. I deemed this not only courteous, since he was in effect an adversary defeated in the field, but also a gesture of the greatest possible provocation to Shoda personally, since she apparently came here to claim your head, not his."

Yes, she'd get the point.

Bitch!

He could have killed me.

"Hurt?"

"What?"

"Sting?"

"No."

Bloody iodine, felt like razor blades.

She began on the dressing.

"You should also know," Loman said, "that early yesterday morning Shoda had the radio station in Laos dive-bombed."

I had to give it a beat.

"Is he dead?"

"Yes."

Cho.

Os, Sempai.

His head lowered over the chipped, grimed shelf of the radio console, a tear falling from his riven cheek to lie there glistening.

He is my father. Sayako, her soft, hesitant voice over the phone at the clinic.

I let out a breath.

"Hurt now?"

"No."

Yes. Hurt now.

In a moment: "I thought General Cho wasn't a threat to Shoda anymore?"

"She didn't think so, until you went to see him. She heard about that."

"How?"

"From the grapevine in the village there."

"You got this from Johnny Chen?"

"Yes."

"If she knew I was there, why didn't she put a hit on me?"

"She tried, but it was too late: you'd flown out."

I'd flown out, leaving Cho with his last few hours to live. First Veneker, now Cho.

Sometimes I hate this trade.

"The important thing," Loman said, "is that this is yet another indication of the effect you have on Shoda, the increasing influence you're developing over her." He stopped pacing and looked down at me, hands tucked behind him, his eyes intent. "Let me tell you something, Quiller. You *frighten* her."

I thought about that.

"Aren't you putting it a bit strong?"

"We don't think so." A glance towards the couch. "Pepperidge has given me a very clear picture of the relationship between you and Shoda—*which is the fundamental axis of the mission,* you understand that?—and I believe it to be absolutely true—you've got her frightened."

Pepperidge had put it in a different way, debriefing me at the clinic. *I think we've found her Achilles' heel, and it's you.*

Loman began pacing again, motes of dust rising from the plum-red Chinese carpet as his polished shoes turned in a beam of morning light. "Let me offer you a picture of our opponent. She wields, behind the scenes in South-east Asia where much of the economy and political infrastructure is centred on the drug trade, a great deal of power. She is also a psychotic. Because of her childhood experiences she is on the one hand consumed by hatred of men to the point of pathological obsession and on the other hand fearful of them to the same degree. This knife-edge aspect of her personality engenders a strong element of superstition, far beyond her orthodox Buddhist faith." He stopped once and looked down at me. "And if this sounds like a psychiatrical diatribe, it is. I am giving you a distillation of the expert opinions of three London psychiatrists of the highest reputation, whom Mr Croder consulted after we'd received a composite picture of Mariko Shoda's behavioural record over the past five years."

Done their homework. Dr Israel had said at the clinic: "One can be obsessed about so many *things,* but the real obsessions are focused on *abstracts*—hate, revenge, life, death, sex, sickness, health." And when I'd asked him if it were something you couldn't stop, he'd said: "Yes. It starts at ten miles an hour and it gets to fifty and then to ninety and you can't stop it. You crash."

"So our opponent," Loman said, on the move again, "is

a classic type in world history, a powerful, dangerous megalomaniac embarked on a sacred crusade. Think of her as an Idi Amin, a Gaddafi.''

Again I remembered Dr Israel, when I'd asked him: ''But someone very powerful, clever, intelligent, authoritative—they can finally lose control, and crash?'' Blowing out smoke from his little cigar—''You have heard of Adolf Hitler?''

Loman stopped again, standing close, his feet neatly together. ''That is the situation, then, in terms of your personal mission and its personal target: Mariko Shoda.'' He didn't glance across at Pepperidge, but I caught a feeling he was doing that. Pepperidge was looking carefully at nothing at all. ''Since you elected to undertake this mission otherwise than under the aegis of the Bureau, I was unable to inform you on the various aspects involved. You should now be told that Mr Croder has a second unit in the field, under the local direction of one of our most talented people.''

He looked up at me and I felt he was expecting a question. I already had a lot so I gave him one.

''What field?''

''Not this one, of course. This is yours.''

''What director?''

''Ferris.''

Oh you *bastard*.

We could offer you rather good ones, he'd said in London, meaning terms, *your sole discretion, for instance, as to backups, shields, signals, liaison, contacts, and so on.* And he'd have asked me to choose my director in the field and you know the man I'd have chosen, don't you? Right—*Ferris*. And I'd have got him.

''So where's their field?'' Nothing in my eyes, nothing in my voice to give him joy.

''It's very flexible.'' He turned away and began walking, like a bloody wind-up toy. But I was listening; I was listening very hard. This was major briefing. ''A consignment of one hundred Slingshot missiles complete with warheads has gone adrift somewhere in the Near East. Our second unit is at present trying to locate it, seize it, and escort it to Thailand, its intended destination.''

I watched him. A *hundred*. A hundred *Slingshots*. Enough to control the whole of the air traffic across Indo-China, military and otherwise.

''But Christ,'' I said, ''what d'you mean by gone adrift?''

Tilted his head. ''A euphemism. We believe that the Shoda organisation has in fact diverted the consignment to a secret destination. As far as we can find out, it's due to reach the Shoda organisation's forces at some time tomorrow; hence the deadline of three days I mentioned to you is now reduced to twelve hours, perhaps less. The significance of this is of course obvious to you.''

I'm sure I don't need to emphasise, Mr Jordan, the devastation this weapon could cause, in the wrong hands. Prince Kityakara, when we'd seen the Slingshot in action. *It means that any armed revolution could proceed with its enterprise in the certainty that it was completely safe from the air. It means that if the Shoda organisation acquired this weapon, it could set Indo-China aflame within a week. And that, of course, is its intention.*

''We await hourly,'' Loman said, ''news from our second unit that the consignment has been found and seized.'' He stopped pacing and stood directly in front of me. ''So you see that your own mission is perhaps even more vital than you might have believed. Whether or not we can keep the Slingshot out of her hands, Shoda *must* be destroyed. With the missile she can devastate South-east Asia, but without it she will continue to present a dangerous element in the area, ready at all times to provoke havoc. We have, of course, something like a trump card. Even if she acquires the Slingshot consignment, I am virtually certain she won't feel able to deploy it while *you* remain alive.'' He turned away, turned back. ''There is therefore no element so crucial, so pivotal, or so potentially decisive as your personal threat to Shoda—and hers to you. I am convinced, in short, that over and above the question of the Slingshot consignment, the outcome of *both* these missions can only be decided by a personal and conclusive confrontation between yourself and Mariko Shoda."

29

TREBLE-THINK

She came in quietly, soon after Loman had finished his main briefing. I didn't see her until she was quite near us, because I'd had my back to the doors, talking with Pepperidge.

"Good morning."

Loman turned. Pepperidge got off the couch. She slung a leather bag from her shoulder; it looked like a diplomatic pouch, probably was.

"The tapes," she said, and gave the bag to Loman.

"All of them?"

"Yes, sir."

"Would you care for some coffee?"

"Please."

Then she looked at me for the first time, just a little swing of her head as if she'd had to make an effort; but the blue-grey eyes were quite steady.

Flood had come in earlier with the message, the "glad tidings" as Pepperidge had called it, going on with the charade for the sake of appearances, because *no one* could now admit the truth.

"She phoned her office," he'd said, "at the High Commission. Her aunt was taken ill yesterday morning, appendicitis, that's why she rushed off without telling anyone where she was going." Loman hadn't been watching him as he'd told us; he'd turned away to do a little pacing. "She stayed at the hospital till her aunt was out of danger." Rueful smile. "All that tra-la for nothing."

Not to embarrass him, I'd said I was relieved.

Facing me now she said very quietly, "Hello."

"How's your aunt?"

"She'll be all right." With a swing of her fair hair, "I—hope you weren't worried about me."

"No."

She looked down, swallowing. "Then I'm glad."

"I knew there wasn't any need."

She looked up quickly, then glanced across to where Loman and Pepperidge were sorting out the tapes, then back to me. "Oh." Puffing out a little laugh, shrugging. "I think I've lost the score."

"It doesn't matter. The game's over now. I'll go and plug in the thing, you like it white, don't you?"

"Yes. Your hand's all right?"

"Everything's fine."

I went over to the percolator and plugged it in. There were lines under her eyes and she looked as if she hadn't slept too well, which probably meant that she'd been briefed about my blowing the safe-house, and why. Otherwise she might have gone along to the clinic and walked right into the surveillance team, and I didn't want to think about *that*.

The thing started singing and I called out to Flood, asking him for another cup. Loman was slotting a tape into the stereo recorder. Katie sat down at one end of the couch, slim in her khaki shirt and slacks, the heavy gold chain at her throat.

It had been treble-think, and Loman and I had worked together like partners in a tennis double, each leaving the ball for the other when that was the next move. He'd been certain I'd want to stay with the mission but couldn't do that, now I knew the Bureau had conned me into it after I'd resigned, so he gave me a way of saving my face and told me that Katie was missing. It was a lie and I knew that, *and he knew I knew,* but I went through the motions of believing it, and agreed to the deal and stayed with the mission. Treble-think, and in case you've forgotten, that's the trade we're in.

"We've boiled them down," Loman said now, "to the bare essence."

The Shoda tapes.

I went over to him. The recorder was on the floor and we sat around it while Katie poured some more coffee.

"These are all translations from the Thai or Cambodian except the one where she's speaking English, presumably to someone whose only language it is. If you want to put questions I'll stop the recorder."

He pressed for play.

I want to stress that we are not mounting a series of isolated revolutionary actions designed to bring in the rabble with us. These are planned as military actions and they will be launched simultaneously as soon as the consignment has been received, evaluated, deployed in the field, and readied for use.

"These transmissions," Loman said, "have been put onto a single tape. There's no continuity—they are separate recordings made at different times."

I will repeat that this agent must *be located and dealt with before we can launch our operations. It would be fatal if we ignored his influence and allowed him to infiltrate our intelligence and jeopardise our plans. There can be no action in any theatre until he is removed.*

"I need hardly tell you"—Loman—"that we for our part are using every endeavour to monitor and harass the various units now searching for you. In point of fact, by midnight last night, London had called in sleepers and local contacts from Hong Kong, Saigon, Hanoi, and Bangkok, and they are now working in the field, liaising with Mr Croder personally through the British High Commission here in Singapore. There is a great deal going on in your support, Quiller, a *great* deal."

Translated: You should never have left the Bureau: look at the resources we have.

Said nothing. He pressed the button.

Our entire action now depends on Kishnar. Until I learn that he has accomplished his assignment there can be no furtherance of our project. Tomorrow I shall go to Singapore and await this information.

"The day before yesterday," Loman said, and lifted the pause button.

The preparations I spoke of are now set up, but our proposed action must await news of an unhampered environment. We must not *underestimate the British-Thai intelligence operations mounted against us.*

Loman played three more tapes, but they were mostly a distillation of the background political aspects of the revolutionary groups deployed throughout Indo-China, some of them under Shoda's command.

"This one," Loman said finally, "is where she is speaking either to an Englishman or an American or at least to someone who doesn't have her various Asian languages. We're trying to find out who he is."

I am told that, pending the now imminent arrival of the consignment, every tactical element is now in place, but there is still no news from Kishnar, and I am now on my way to Singapore. If you need to reach me I shall be airborne at five P.M. *and you can use the radio-phone.*

It was the first time I'd heard her speaking in English. It was clear and almost without an accent. The sibilants were silky and attenuated, as I remembered from hearing her voice in the radio station, and it had the same energy; but there was something in her tone that hadn't been there before; it was a degree of tension, of strain. I had the sense that the world of Mariko Shoda wasn't any longer spinning the way she wanted it.

Loman shut the thing off. "Do you have any comments?"

I got off the floor, wanting movement.

"I hadn't realised things were so close."

He didn't answer, and suddenly I knew why. Things were close only if they could hit me between now and when the Slingshot consignment arrived.

"All right, her operation can't start unless I'm out of the running, so she's going to be throwing the whole thing at me now. She's got no more time to try doing it by stealth, trying to keep it discreet—one man with a bit of wire. If they see me, they'll just shoot, from anywhere—right?"

"That's why we've asked the Singapore police for their help, through diplomatic channels. That's why this place is under guard."

"But for Christ's sake, you can't just keep me cooped up in here so that she's got to put her operations permanently on ice. She might easily lose patience and risk it and have a go regardless."

Loman didn't answer. And nothing from Pepperidge. They'd got things worked out and they wanted to know what my attitude was, because I was the key factor and they'd have to plan according to what I was prepared to do. This was routine direction in the field and that was all right but I couldn't see which way we could make a move, or if there were *any* way at all.

"Have you got any more briefing for me?" I thought he had, but was holding it back for some reason. Pepperidge was looking into the middle distance again and I noted it.

Loman started walking around suddenly: it was like a bloody zoo—we all felt caged up in this place.

"Perhaps you should be informed," he said in a moment, "that in support of your assumption that Shoda will now do everything in her power to 'remove the British agent,' two charter planeloads of so-called tourists have arrived in Singapore this morning, one from Cambodia and one from Laos. Our contacts are reasonably certain that they've been brought in to support the surveillance teams."

Meant hit teams.

"All right. At least we know the score."

I felt Katie's eyes on me. She was Bureau and she'd

probably worked with shadow executives before and she knew what we were going to have to do to get out of the shut-ended situation we were in: we were going to have to take one *hell* of a risk in the hope that it'd come off and leave this little ferret still alive—bloodied, perhaps, but still with its whiskers on; and listen, I'm putting it lightly as I'm sure you've noticed, because at this particular moment I'd started feeling scared and it wasn't very long since the Kishnar thing and my nerves were on a roller-coaster and there wouldn't be a chance of getting them off it until something conclusive was done, something terminal, *finis*, one way or the other, Shoda or me.

It all came down to *that*.

And everyone knew it: Loman, Pepperidge, Katie, and halfway round the world in London, Croder, Chief of Control.

However, *nil desperandum,* so forth, try a few more knee-bends, rough on the left thigh but we need to keep the adrenaline down.

"How long will it be," I asked Loman, "before you hear that your second unit has found the Slingshots and taken them over? If they can in fact do that?"

"We shall be informed at once." He seemed surprised.

"Not through London?"

"Either through London or direct, or both. Why?"

"I'm not absolutely sure." He came and looked down at me; I was at the bottom of a knee-bend, bouncing on the muscles. "But I think it's very important." Sounded lame, but the left brain had started working on something and this was one of the components. "It's important," I tried again, "that *we* should know as soon as possible if and when that consignment has been seized—that's to say has been removed from any danger of Shoda's getting hold of it. *That's* important." I got up and moved around. "It's also *very* important that if the Slingshots are made safe and brought out of Shoda's reach, she doesn't know about it until she and I are face-to-face."

I listened to the echo of what I'd just been saying and

tested it out and found some flaws and tried patching them up and ran it through again, sensing I was getting close to some kind of overkill action but not quite knowing what it was or how it would work.

When I stopped and looked around I saw they were all watching me, not moving.

"There's a *time* thing," I told Loman, "that's got to be thought about. There's a narrow margin of *time* involved."

In a moment Loman asked over-casually, "Have you got anything potentially constructive in mind?"

"What the fuck does that mean?"

Quite a long silence. Yes, I know what *potentially* means and I know what *constructive* means but I'd been way out in the right brain and words like those lose most of their meaning because they're so bloody long that you've got to stop and think what they're trying to say.

"Sorry."

"Not at all."

Toujours la politesse and all that but you know I do wish that little snit would speak the Queen's bloody English when we're all trying to think out how to destroy the objective.

"Let's start from *this,*" I said. "I can't make a hit." Silence again. They needed more data. "I'm not a hired gun, you know that. The only time I killed anyone in cold blood it was because he'd betrayed a woman and she was trapped and shot dead. I'm not"—I found myself staring at Loman, wanting the little bastard to get the point—"I'm not a hit man for the Bureau. Is that understood?"

"Of course." Tone icy.

"So what I've got to do is destroy the objective, Shoda, without killing her. The mission you're running is aimed at the destruction of the Shoda organisation and I'm the executive in the field"—began walking around again—"and we've got our faces shoved right up against the end-phase and we haven't got a bloody *clue* as to how we're going to bring this thing off."

In a minute Pepperidge said very quietly, "I rather think *you* have, old boy."

"What?" I swung round. "Possibly. A very small one. I'm just thinking aloud, trying to get feedback."

I went across and poured some more coffee and put it down again without drinking any because we were in the extreme end-phase of the mission and I was on a collision course with a woman who'd got a small army out there waiting for me and I didn't want to be caught at the wrong end of a caffeine curve, that sort of thing can kill you.

"Another thing"—and I was, yes, thinking aloud but that was good, it was what we were here for, some brainstorming—"is that I can't confront Shoda without getting her *isolated* somehow." And I knew when I said it that it was a key word, *isolated,* though I didn't know why. "I don't mean separated from her bodyguards, I couldn't hope for that. I think I mean away from the public somewhere, in case people get hurt. It's not going to be a tea-party."

Long silence but this time useful, potentially constructive, so forth. And something had got through.

"Isolated," Pepperidge said. He got off the couch and stood with his hands shoved into his pockets looking through the wall. "Not in her house."

"No. I'd never get in there alive."

Loman was staring into the middle distance too but he didn't say anything for a minute, couldn't hit on anything. Then he turned and started walking again and said, "We've got the full cooperation of the Singapore police, but there's nothing they can do against Shoda. She's *politically* untouchable. *Diplomatically*. She could bring almost any democratic government down in Asia simply by hitting its economy or exposing any one of the half dozen corrupt officials in high places." He gave me a direct look. "We can't help you there."

"I understand that."

In any case I couldn't see us going into the end-phase

with any kind of police action. They couldn't touch Shoda. The government couldn't touch her. It wasn't a question of an operation; it was a question of infiltration, very focussed, very specific, just one man going in.

"Would anyone like some lunch?"

Katie.

Loman stopped pacing as if he'd hit a wall and stared at her as if he didn't understand the word. Perhaps she should have said luncheon.

"Good thinking." Pepperidge.

I checked my watch; it was gone noon. "Some kind of protein?"

She passed close to me on her way out, saying softly, "And a little zabaglione?" And left her scent on the air, my God, there's nothing like a woman's presence to bring the tension down, she doesn't even have to touch you.

"Look," Pepperidge said, and didn't finish it because Flood came through the doors just then and told Loman there was a call from one of the contacts in Cambodia and Loman went out to take it and from that minute the final action of the end-phase started running and we were pitched into it headlong.

30

MR CRODER

"Where?" Loman asked them.

We were in the smoking-room off the main salon, reproduction antique brass telephone and plush armchairs and gilt ashtrays and a thin Chinese nude on the wall with exaggerated nipples.

"When?"

Loman looked very calm. One of the things I dislike least about him is that when a mission's in a slow phase he's like a fart in a colander and he can drive you stark raving bonkers but when it swings into momentum again he quietens down and starts running like a well-oiled dynamo. Flood had told him the signal was from our second unit in Cambodia.

"What time tomorrow?"

Pepperidge was hitched on a bar stool, his yellow eyes deceptively sleepy. Flood was standing under a lamp, plaster cherub holding the shade aloft. Flood behaved like a subordinate and called me sir but that was just because he was a bit younger and he probably found the presence of a top control from London intimidating. But I knew who he was now. I'd asked Pepperidge a bit earlier: "Is this man Flood my replacement?"

Pepperidge had looked away, looked back again. "Yes, old boy. But he'll never get the job, of course."

It didn't actually bother me. In fact there was a certain comfort in the knowledge that if I got things wrong in the next few hours and bought the Elysian fields thing at least I'd know they'd got someone standing by to take over.

"Wait a minute," Loman said and blocked the mouthpiece and looked at Pepperidge and me and said briefly, "They've traced the consignment. It's on its way to Prey Veng by air."

"Where's that?" Pepperidge asked him.

"Across the Mekong from Phnom Penh." He looked at me now, waiting. Half the component of the mission was in place and I was the second half and he wanted to know if I had any questions. I did. This was a breakthrough.

"Can they open the crates and switch the contents?"

"Can they *what?*"

"Permission to talk to them." Strictly formal, right out of the book, because he was a control from London and the final decision-making was going to be his or Croder's but I'd got the whole thing in my head now, the end-phase, ready to run, and the timing was so critical that we'd have to work by the minute all the way down to zero and that was why I was being formal with Loman because I didn't want to get his back up and put everything in hazard, not *now*.

He hesitated, then passed me the phone.

"Executive."

"Salutations."

My opposite number.

"Listen, this is fully urgent. Can you switch the contents of those crates and let them go through on schedule?"

Short silence. I hadn't made *their* end-phase any easier.

"You mean shove some pig-iron in them or something?"

"Yes, whatever you can find. We want them to arrive at their projected destination and ETA as if they'd never been touched. That possible?"

Another silence, then: "Like fucking things up, don't you?"

Meant yes.

"Christ," I said, "I wouldn't mind working with you again." He'd got us this end of the mission.

"That's not mutual," he said, "because you've gone and pissed on the chips but I suppose that's life." His tone changed. "All *right,* you want everything left intact, shipping labels, manifest, routing, the whole thing. Yes?"

"Yes."

"And once the crates are there, our end's in the bag and we're completed, that right?"

"Except for getting the Slingshots to the Thai army."

"Oh yes, we shan't be leaving those things around for the kids to play with in the park, don't worry. Look, can I have confirmation from your control?"

"Hold on." I turned to Loman. "You heard what I've asked them to do and they say they can do it and I've worked out our end-phase and it'll give us the only chance we've got, so are you prepared to give me full discretion over this?"

He stood there staring at me with his hands behind him and his feet together and his head on the tilt and I watched him computerising the whole situation including what would happen to him in London if it turned out that he'd let me screw up the mission and drive it into the ground.

Pepperidge had taken a step closer and he was watching me too, his eyes blanked off and his mouth a tight line because he'd catch some of the flak if he let his executive talk his control into a last-ditch spectacular fiasco.

Then Loman made a curt gesture and I gave him the phone and he said, "Control. I am placing the completion of your operation into the hands of the executive here."

Gave me the phone back.

"Thank you, sir."

More than I'd asked for, more than I could have expected, *much* more—he was giving me immediate responsibility for the whole show.

I said into the phone: "What's the ETA for that consignment in Prey Veng?"

"21:14 today."

"Where are you going to make the switch?"

"In Phnom Penh."

"At the airport?"

"Yes, in a holding warehouse."

"Clandestine?"

"We've bought two customs people."

"Not a lot of risk, then."

"Not a lot. I'd say we've got, you know, around ninety percent in our favour."

I whipped through the main essentials to see if I were missing anything, didn't think I was.

"How long is it going to take *them* to unload the consignment and check on the contents, open up a crate?"

"I can't say, sir. I mean it's up to them. But it wouldn't take more than a half hour to get the stuff off the kite and then all they'll need is a crowbar."

So I'd be working inside a time bracket of thirty minutes minimum. But then they'd go through *all* the crates before they radioed Shoda.

"How many crates are there?"

"Twenty."

Think. How long would it take to open up twenty crates and go through the *whole* contents, which was what they'd do before they got on the radio and informed Shoda? An hour. Say an hour. Time bracket, then, of ninety minutes minus an estimated—I looked at Pepperidge—"From here to the airport, how long?"

"Forty minutes, with the escort."

Minus an estimated forty minutes and another forty-five minutes for the Shoda jet to start up and taxi and get to the grid. Bracket of five minutes. *Five*.

Better than zero and I was having to make estimates and I might have longer than that and we still had a chance even if it were shorter, below zero. So take the risk, go for it.

"All right," I said into the phone, "set it up. Any questions?"

"I don't think so."

"Then keep in signals."

"Roger."

I put the phone down and went into the little lav just off the smoking-room and slurped some handfuls of water into my mouth and splashed my face and towelled it and went back and through into the salon and told Loman and Pepperidge what I wanted to do.

"She kill my father."

There was a moth circling the lamp.

"I'm sorry," I said.

"Thank you."

Thank *me* . . . Mother of God, if I hadn't gone there to the radio station she wouldn't have sent the bombers in. *Bitch!*

"You know he die?"

"Yes, Sayako-san."

Moth round the lamp bulb, bumping into it, a powdering of gold dust coming down.

"Kishnar," she said. "What happen?"

"We sent him to Shoda, in a coffin."

I heard her catch her breath. "You do such a thing?"

"Yes."

"Will make her afraid." Silence came in and I waited. Gold dust floating down, are you out of your bloody *mind,* have you got to go on *hitting* the bloody thing?

Couldn't stay away, I suppose. *Don't take this all the way to the brink.*

"I live only now," the soft voice came, "till she die." Meant: *for her* to die.

"I understand."

"She very strong. Very hard. But like glass, one day break easily. You make her break, I think, one day."

"Perhaps."

I'd been wondering why she'd phoned but now I knew. More than anything in the world she wanted Shoda's death, and she thought I might bring it about for her. She'd wanted to talk to the instrument of her heart's most bitter craving.

"Will be graceful," she said. I think she meant that to kill Mariko Shoda would bring grace upon me.

"If it happens, Sayako-san, you will know."

"Yes." Another silence, but for the soft sounds of her crying. "When she die, my father be at peace."

I said something consoling, I don't quite remember what, and then there was a click on the line and it went dead and I suppose she'd just felt she couldn't talk anymore.

I went back into the salon and we took up where we'd left off.

"I don't like your *extemporising*."

Loman.

"It's the only way."

"But surely the risk is high."

"Not so high as if we just wait around till they locate me and wipe me out."

Pepperidge was perched on the edge of a chair and hadn't said anything for a long time. I don't think he liked it. Flood was standing near the stained-glass windows with his feet apart and his arms folded, listening hard but not saying anything either. Katie was manning the phone whenever it rang, coming back to sit apart from us, her face strained. I wished she didn't have to be here with us but it was up to Loman.

Loman hadn't answered so I said it again, trying to sell it to him. "This is the only way."

I'd told them what I wanted to do and how it would have to be handled technically and I'd told Flood to get me what I needed and he'd done that and all we had to do now was wait for our contacts to ring us when Shoda left the house in Saiboo Street for the airport, and that would be when she got the news from Prey Veng that the consignment had arrived there.

Loman still didn't answer. I think he was simply stone-walling so that I'd have to keep on pushing him, and then if

I said something wrong he could pounce on it. That was all right; that was his job. So I went on pushing.

"I know two things. When *she* moves, *I've* got to move, or I'll lose her. And we've got to *isolate* the confrontation, to keep the public out of danger."

Loman still silent. He didn't like this, any more than Pepperidge. A bit earlier Pepperidge had said to me quietly, hand on my arm, "You really are taking this *all* the way to the brink this time." Told him there wasn't anywhere else left for me to go.

Then Loman spoke.

"Very well." He was sitting in the wing-chair with his hands along its arms and his polished shoes together, staring down at them. "But of course I have serious reservations." He swung his small head up and stared at me instead of his shoes and I knew what was on his mind: he could be looking at someone who'd started dying.

"If you can't give me a decision," I told him, "very fast indeed I'd say we've had it. The Slingshot's out of her hands now but she's still alive and she's the target. You can't hope to go on protecting me even with half the Singapore police force because I've got to move into the open for the end-phase *whatever* form it takes and they'll simply pick me off with a telescopic rifle if they can't get any closer."

This situation hadn't happened before: the executive, at present safe and supported by his director in the field and his London control, had a limited life span, and during that span he'd got to complete the mission.

"We are working on *assumptions,*" Loman said. "We assume that when Shoda is told that the consignment has been landed she'll leave the house in Saiboo Street for the airport and take off for Prey Veng, confident that you'll be taken care of in her absence by her hit teams."

"It's logical," I told him. "We're not taking wild swipes."

"I agree. But you've narrowed down the time element to as little as five minutes."

"The time gap's important but it's not critical. If she gets the news that she's lost the Slingshot before *I* can break it to her, we've still got a chance."

He didn't answer.

There was the rustling of paper and I saw Katie clearing away the debris from the sandwiches she'd brought in for us. Flood went across to help her. He looked as if he hadn't been listening to anything but of course he had. He needed to know what kind of mess I might be leaving him to straighten out.

"How do you rate your chances, Quiller?"

Loman was still staring at me with his pale glass eyes.

"Look, if I start thinking in terms of life-and-death percentages it's going to sabotage my confidence. The thing is *this*. We've still got a mission running and the only way I can finish it is to get close to Shoda and this is the last chance we've got."

Waited again.

I hate waiting.

The air was still like steam in here because they'd let the whole place run down and there wasn't any air-conditioning but there was a chill creeping through me as if winter had come.

They're right. You shouldn't take the risk.

Now don't *you* start.

End-phase nerves. Normal, ignore.

You do in fact know what your chances are.

Shuddup and fuck off.

Then Loman said: "I think this is for Mr Croder to decide."

"If it doesn't take all day to get him."

"He is near the signals console at all times." Loman got up and gave his shoes another scrutiny. "Will you talk to him or shall I?"

I thought that was nice of him. A top control in the field from London doesn't normally leave it to the ferret to contact the C. of C. and take part in the decision-making.

"Let me phone him right away," I told him, and the

feeling I had when I made my way round the chairs and tables and into the smoking-room was split right down the middle between total assurance that I could pull off a five-star spectacular and a numbing certainty that this was the day when I was going to the brink for the last time, and right over.

I asked for C. of C.

"Yes?"

"Red Lotus, executive."

I told him what I'd got in mind and he asked me to repeat it and I did that.

He said no.

"Sir, let me put it this way. If I come unstuck, you're not going to lose the mission, just the executive. My replacement's fully briefed and ready to take over."

"He can't."

I pictured Croder, thin, his face cut out of flint with a battle-axe, his black eyes showing nothing but the reflection of the telephone in his articulated metal hand.

"But he's the replacement, sir."

No names.

"Yes, but from the information I've been given, you are in these circumstances unreplaceable. Your personal influence over the opposition is a special case."

Voice like a knife being sharpened.

"That's my original point. I think it's strong enough to bring her down. Look, this isn't just a last desperate throw. I've given it a tremendous lot of thought. And you know my record, sir."

Waited.

The thing was, this was something new. If I'd said I wanted to infiltrate a KGB operation or blow a checkpoint or bring a top-level defector across a frontier he'd have let me. But there was an exotic, untried element to the end-phase of Red Lotus, and its name was voodoo.

"Tell your control I'd like to talk to him."

So I got Loman in and left him at the phone and went back into the salon and stood there with my arms folded and the chill seeping along the nerves because if Croder finally said no I'd lose the day and those snivelling little clerks in the records room would take a pen and fill in the blank space at the end of the operations report, *mission unaccomplished,* and if Croder finally said yes I'd have to go out there and face Shoda, alone and with no backups, no shields, no support, and no escape route, no chance of getting out alive except the one I was ready to take and God knew what it was worth.

I could hear Flood, over by the stained-glass windows, whistling between his teeth. Katie was somewhere behind me; I didn't know what she was doing, I just knew what she was thinking. Pepperidge was standing quite still with his hands in his pockets, head down for a time; then he took a couple of steps towards me and stood close and said softly, "Whatever we go into, old boy, I'll give you full measure."

"I know."

He turned away and gave me room, left me a space to move in if I wanted to. I could hear Loman out there on the phone and thought *Jesus Christ I should've stayed with him and insisted on him selling Croder my plan.* On the other hand Loman would try and do that anyway because he wanted this mission finished so that he could take a plane back to London, *of course the executive didn't have a chance of pulling it off until I went out there,* bloody tin medal for his sparrow's chest, he's always—no, that's unfair, he does a good job, don't needle the poor little bastard.

Nerves, last-chance nerves.

"Would you stop that?"

I was looking across at Flood, didn't really know I'd been going to say it, whistling between his teeth, got on my nerves.

"Sorry, sir."

But of course he'd got a lot to think about too because if I came unstuck he could be pushed into this mission within a matter of hours.

"Can I—"

Katie, close to me, somewhere behind me, but I never heard what she'd been going to say. Could she what? Get me anything, a drink? Could she ask me something and if so what, at a time like this? I never heard it all, would never hear it all, because Loman came in just then and we turned and looked at him.

"We have Mr Croder's approval."

That was at 15:14 hours with the midafternoon sunlight slanting through the stained-glass windows, and we began waiting.

I went through the whole thing in my mind God knows how many times, testing it for faults and unnecessary risks and over-sanguine assumptions, testing it for possible surprises and unpredictable situations, breaking up the overall picture into bits and pieces and changing them around and putting them together again.

Long afternoon, it was a very long afternoon, with Flood manning the phone again, taking periodic calls from our people in the streets, the bell ringing in my guts every time, jangling along the nerves because we were now on a collision course with the deadline and the deadline was 21:14 plus a minute, two minutes for them to radio Shoda with the news that the Slingshots had landed in Prey Veng.

Tea, we had some tea, it revives you, nothing like a good hot cuppa, so forth, even in this stinking heat.

Then at 18:09 when the sun's light began dying in the stained-glass windows we got the signal from the second unit to say they'd flown to Phnom Penh and switched the contents of the twenty crates for obsolete typewriters and at 20:46 they signalled again to tell us the freighter was airborne on schedule from Phnom Penh and at 21:14 we got the final signal telling us it had landed on schedule in Prey Veng and seven minutes later our contacts in Saiboo Street reported that Shoda was leaving the house in a limousine with two escorts.

End-phase running.

31

END-PHASE

Havelock Road, crossing New Bridge.

Loman leaned forward and spoke to Katie.

"What kind of escort has she got?"

Katie unclipped the radio-phone, one hand on the wheel.

"C3. Can you tell me what kind of escort she has?"

Smoked-glass windows, we couldn't see much from inside but I was getting glimpses through the side mirrors.

"Is anyone looking after our tail?"

"Oh yes," Loman said. "Our own escort comprises five unmarked cars, two ahead of us."

I saw a street sign, St Andrews. We were moving north.

C1, please.

"Come in."

She has a car in front and behind.

"Thank you," Katie said.

She half-turned her head and Loman nodded. Pepperidge was on the other side of me. He hadn't spoken since we'd left the nightclub; I didn't know what was on his mind but I suppose he wasn't feeling dissatisfied with his performance: he'd successfully entrapped me into a Bureau operation and had monitored my action in Singapore from Cheltenham, reporting to London and taking his own briefing from them. He'd successfully run me as a director in the field until Loman had flown out here to liaise with Chief of Control and he was now going through the end-phase with me and his job was to watch me like a hawk for any signs of cold feet or dangerous-category paranoia or the more common mood of bravado that will often send an executive right into a trap of his own making, his fear driving him to doing things he wouldn't normally take on.

What I was feeling at this moment was a sense of betrayal, because I valued this man and as the spook he was personally running I should have told him the *whole* of my plan for bringing Shoda down, and I hadn't. I daren't, because he'd have pulled me out right away.

Now entering Nicoll Highway, going north.

Shoda.

Sitting in her limousine among her lethal bodyguards with their black track-suits and their kitten faces and their knives, ready to do anything for her, to give or take life. What was in her mind, as she drove north along Nicoll Highway?

Let me tell you something. Pepperidge. *Shoda is afraid of you.*

She very strong, very hard. Sayako. *But like glass, one day break easily. You make her break, I think, one day.*

Everything depended on that. On her fear of me. It was the only weapon I could take to her. Voodoo.

Katie had swung the wheel again and I saw another sign: Ophir Road.

I asked her: "Where is she now?"

"Ahead of us, on the East Coast Parkway."

"Heading for the airport."

"It looks like it."

There was nowhere else in this direction, except for resorts and tennis clubs.

Take stock and report. The thigh bruise wasn't any real problem—I could run close to the limit if I had to. The laceration to the rib had stopped limiting the lung-capacity two days ago, or I couldn't have worked as I did with Kishnar. The right hand was useless but the arm was perfectly fit, without any degree of paralysis: I could block with it. The sutured artery in the left wrist must have healed to the point of handling very high systolic pressure, or—again—I couldn't have got through the Kishnar thing. Everything else normal.

Hand on my arm. "How—"

"Top line."

Not necessarily telepathy; he'd been waiting for my assessment and report at this stage, within minutes of the action.

He nodded and took his hand away.

C1, please.

"Come in."

Flood's voice. He'd stayed behind at the nightclub to liaise.

Can you give a status report for the board?

Signals board. That was to say Croder.

Loman leaned forward. "Tell him that we're proceeding to the rendezvous as planned, and anticipate effective action."

Took some saying. The man had guts, admit it. He was reporting to C. of C. and there were other ways he could have put it: estimations are sanguine, complications not foreseen at this stage, a nice cosy phrase that would mean that we were all sitting here with our fingers crossed and our sphincter muscles tight and our minds turned away from the unthinkable. The control and the director were, after all, escorting the executive in the field to a deliberate confrontation with the objective, who had put a small army into the streets of Singapore to wipe me out.

C1 . . . C1 . . .

Katie took the phone.

"Come in."

The 727 is being readied for flight. Chinese voice, American-accented English. *Fuelling has commenced and the systems are being checked.*

"Thank you. Please keep me informed." She turned her head. "Did you get that, Mr Loman?"

"Yes."

He didn't speak again until we passed the first of the Changi International Airport signs. Two more calls came in, giving us the present position of the Shoda convoy, and Flood signalled with a request for updated information, obviously for London.

We hadn't stopped at an intersection since we'd left the nightclub; when the lights had been at amber or red there'd been a marked police car standing there with its codes flashing and we'd gone straight through. This was why Pepperidge had said it was a forty-minute run to the airport *with escort*.

I looked out of the windows, trying to get the thought out of my mind that I was sitting in a Black Mariah on my way to the execution block. I wasn't having any second thoughts: if this thing finally didn't work then that would have been written in the stars. There was no other end-phase operation we could hope to pull off and we knew that. The nerves were tightening, that was all, normal at this stage, ignore.

Then Loman spoke.

"It's my opinion"—carefully—"that your estimate of the time factor is on the pessimistic side. I'd say you have more than a five-minute period to work in. There will be quite a little panic when the crates are opened, and they won't signal Shoda's aeroplane immediately. Do you want further briefing on this?"

"No." Beacons were coming up, red lights at the top of radio masts sliding past the darkened windows. "That's all I need." A jet was taking off, its vibrations palpable inside the car.

"If I'm wrong, of course . . ."

If he was wrong it'd blow the whole thing into Christendom. No, not the whole thing, just the executive; but Flood would have a rotten job to take over.

The main tower showed through the windscreen, black against the glow from the terminal lights. The smell of kerosene was coming in through the air-conditioning ducts.

"Gentlemen."

Loman showed us his watch. Mine tallied at 20:13 hours; Pepperidge altered his to synchronise.

I was aware of the outline of Katie's face on the right side, the curve of the cheekbone, the curl of hair.

I wish we could have met before. But then I suppose it wouldn't have worked out.

Slowing. A red light flashed from the rear of the Mazda ahead of us.

"They're taking us straight onto the tarmac," Katie said. "Is that right, sir?"

"Yes."

She slowed again.

Martin, will you stay the night? There's not much of it left anyway.

Another jet went sliding across the roofs of the buildings, lifting clear and leaving its sound filling the night.

She swung the wheel, following the Mazda.

Keep back the dawn. Wasn't that the title of something?

Slowing.

Gates, PERSONNEL ONLY.

Two uniformed guards checking the Mazda, asking for ID's. *Two* guards I suppose because there'd been an attempted hostage situation at this airport a month ago.

Ice.

One of the gates was swung back and the Mazda was waved through. We followed.

Ice along the nerves.

Hand on my arm. "The way you've got things worked out, old boy, it should be a pushover."

"Yes."

Perfect direction in the field, close attention to the minutiae of the situation, tot of rum for the troops, so forth.

Tarmac. Vehicles moving; fuel tankers, baggage trains; security patrols. A jumbo on the main east-west runway, rolling under power, a windsock flying out in its wake, then dropping. The last met report had said still-air conditions at ground level.

A lot of noise now from the jumbo, Northwest Orient. When it had died away Loman asked me:

"You still prefer a police car?"

"Yes."

The High Commission limo would stand out, I didn't want that. The whole thing had to be performed in low key, no rush, no excitement, softlee, softlee, catchee monkee, too much *confidence,* too much bloody *chutzpah,* it's not going to be as easy as *that,* it's not going to be a *pushover.*

Steady, lad.

We slowed and stopped. I could see the 727 standing near the line of hangars, at least I assumed it was the one.

"Is that—"

"Yes, over there," Katie said. "TH-9 J-845." To Loman: "Shall I wait here, sir?"

"See if you can get in there between the fence and the service truck."

We moved off, did a slow turn, and slotted into cover. I could see a limousine standing a hundred yards away, not far from the 727 and flanked by two smaller cars.

C1. C1, please.

"Come in."

Their ETD is down as 20:25.

"Thank you." To Loman: "Sir?"

"Yes, I've got that."

He picked up his field-glasses and focussed them.

Seventeen minutes.

Close, we were getting very close now.

The main taxying-lane was behind us and I could hear the aircraft rolling there; I could see the red wingtip lights on the starboard side reflected in the outside mirrors. The line was almost unbroken.

I've given this a tremendous lot of thought, I'd told Croder, *and you know my record.*

Too much pride? Not really. The way I thought I could handle things, there was a chance. That was all we needed, a chance.

Loman, beside me, suddenly petulant, "I would feel very much better if you would arm yourself."

I think it was just something to say, to fill the silence, break the waiting, because he knew bloody well I never used a gun, those things are more nuisance than they're worth.

Didn't answer.

"This car will stay right here," Pepperidge said. "So if—" And he broke off because we were all watching the limousine over there and an Asian woman in a jump-suit was getting out and opening a rear door, standing aside. At this distance and in this light I couldn't see more than four small figures moving quickly from the car to the steps of the jet. The car didn't move, stayed where it was. Within sixty seconds the steps began retracting and half a minute later the cabin door was closed.

"Two women," Loman said with the field-glasses raised, "and two army officers."

Noted.

A mechanic in overalls and with a sound-muffler on his head walked in front of the aircraft and turned and looked up and signalled, and the first engine began moaning.

A feeling of unreality now, of floating towards a frontier of some kind, not an international frontier with checkpoints and all that, just a quiet, personal boundary, not even physical, perhaps the rather blurred line between doubt and certainty, past and future, life and death. It was quite pleasant, a releasing, I suppose, of the endorphins as I approached the zone where I was going to ask exacting things of myself, and expect to get them.

Then the feeling passed and I pulled myself forward and caught a glimpse of Katie's face as she turned; then I climbed across Pepperidge and snapped the door open and dropped onto the tarmac and went across to the nearest Mazda, got in.

"Jordan."

"Yes, sir."

They were in plain clothes, both Chinese, sitting upright

in the front of the car. I could see more of what was going on now because the windows of the police car were clear glass, not darkened.

The jet began moving. I looked back through the rear window and saw five other aircraft strung out along the taxying-lane, the first of them turning onto the runway. The 727 was joining the line, slowing and turning, coming to a stop.

A call came over the radio for the police car and the passenger responded, said they were stationary.

I leaned forward. "Have you got contact with Mr Loman?"

"Yes, sir. You have a message?"

"No."

Just wanted to know. It was a lifeline, in a way, the link with my control and my director. Soon I'd have to break it.

The second jet was airborne, and the 727 rolled again, keeping station.

20:38. She was due for takeoff in four minutes.

The pervasive burning sensation in the left hand had faded out as the endorphins worked on the nerves. No particular feeling of anxiety: it was too early yet. A sense of suspension, of holding back while the clocks flicked to the next digits, while the big jets rolled again in their orderly line, while life went on.

20:40.

The two Chinese sat stiffly, not talking, not moving, watching the 727. No more calls came through. Another jet turned into line behind the 727, rolling to a halt, Air France.

I could see the High Commission vehicle slotted between the fence and the service truck. Loman sitting inside, Pepperidge, Katie. Were they talking? What are you saying, my good friends, my erstwhile lady-love with your thin shoulders and your blue-grey eyes?

The last aircraft was airborne, the last one before the 727, and the sound came back, surging across the metal bodywork of the car in a wave, passing beyond, fading.

The 727 got the instructions from the tower and rolled

forward, turning onto the runway, its wingtips lifting and falling as the suspension flexed. It stood there, waiting for permission to take off. I could see the main tower with its ruby marker lights. Loman had said the deputy chief of police would be there in the tower itself, and his chief on the tarmac in an unmarked car. The action we'd called for would have been rehearsed during the last hour and we expected it to take place smoothly, especially as the attempted hostage situation of a month ago had brought security bang up to scratch.

The 727 waited, its engines at idling speed.

Saliva came now, a slight onrush, and I began swallowing, waiting for the yawn, letting it happen, normal at this phase, the matador reflex as the bull comes into the arena, fast and enraged.

What we needed was *isolation*. Just the two of us, isolated, Shoda and me.

Kept swallowing. I would have said that at this stage the organism was probably in the best condition we could expect, the odd injury unimportant, the nerves reacting as they should, the adrenaline beginning to flow, becoming copious as the waiting went on.

The driver in front of me started his engine and moved off, turning and stopping, lined up with the slip-road used by the emergency vehicles. He left the engine going.

Sitting and waiting. Not easy, it's not easy, you know.

20:43.

We were a minute overdue but the signal was going through to the flight-deck from the tower and the 727 began gunning up, the scream of the turbines rising to a pitch that cut through the night; then she was rolling, the brakes coming off and the wingtips dipping and lifting as the acceleration-phase went slamming in and the big shape began sliding faster against the line of lamps at a quarter distance along the runway until the emergency order went through from the tower and the green lamps changed to red and the scream of the jets broke and the brakes went on and my driver hit the gearshift and we started forward, the code lamps sending a flicker of red and blue along the walls of a hangar before we reached the slip-road, travelling fast now, moving for the halfway point along the runway as the 727 went on slowing under the brakes, slowing, until I judged the timing looked right and told the driver to pull up here, just here, then I hit the door open and got out and started walking.

32

KISS

It was very quiet now.

The tower had instructed the captain of the 727 to shut down his engines, and he had done that. Since then, the aircraft standing in line along the taxying path had received the same orders, and they too were silent now.

I heard the cry of sea birds beyond the airport, in the waters of the straits. It was humid; the air clung to the skin, heavy with the reek of kerosene. I stood looking up at the windows of the flight deck. One of them slid open and a face appeared there. A voice came, something in Chinese, I didn't know what. Beyond the smooth shape of the plane the lights of the city stood against the sky, and I could see traffic moving along Changi Road, some of the vehicles flashing red and blue; I heard sirens.

The generators of the 727 kept up a low singing; its lights, too, went on flashing at the spine of the fuselage and at the tail section. I could smell the rubber of the tyres, heated by the brakes when the emergency stop had been ordered.

I felt rather lonely.

Waited.

Flash, flash, flash. I looked away, didn't want to become mesmerised. The generators sang quietly. Sweat on my face, partly the humidity, partly the organism producing heat as it stabilised its systems at the level of optimum alertness.

Waited.

The cries of the gulls were mournful, a plaint from the souls of dead sailors.

Then a door opened—a sudden heavy metallic sound and it swung open, the cabin door. Someone standing there, army officer, revolver trained on me.

He called something in Thai. I didn't understand, but it could only have been "What do you want?"

"I want to talk to Mariko Shoda."

Fly on my face; I brushed it away; I can't stand these hot wet climates, you might just as well be in a sauna bath.

The gun hadn't moved. In good English:

"Who are you?"

"Martin Jordan."

He spoke across his shoulder; I could see the blur of a face behind him. He never took his eyes off the target. Bloody things, all they do is make a loud bang, I hate bangs.

She would bring a knife, if she came.

They'd all bring knives, her clutch of athletic young hags. This was one of the assumptions, you understand. The whole operation was designed like a pin-table, a carefully plotted pattern of assumptions, and if each one rang a bell I'd score the maximum, which would be the destruction of Mariko Shoda. I didn't know what the chances were of my losing, the percentages, as I'd told Croder, of life and death, but I knew that of the series of assumptions I'd worked out, each one would have to be right, would have to ring a bell. And this was the first of them: that she would decide to come and talk to me.

I wasn't guessing, you needn't think that. I was relying on the detailed information I'd been given on her character and what I believed to be her present frame of mind. She had set her feline assassins on me in the limousine and I'd confronted her in the temple and she'd tried to have me killed when she'd heard I was in the village in the jungle and she'd thrown Kishnar onto me twice and been sent his body in a coffin and if she could find one single chance in a thousand of finally killing me she'd want to do it *herself,* fierce in her pride, hot in her craving for vengeance, triumphant in the savage, decisive termination of our fateful relationship.

I'd come here to give her that chance.

There was movement in the cabin doorway. Another officer in khaki uniform stood looking down at me for a moment; then they both moved back. They'd be the two military officers Loman had seen earlier from the car. She'd got her own little army, Chen had said.

Another bumping noise and the steps appeared in the doorway, sliding and angling down, the rail rising on the stays until the bottom of the steps reached the tarmac and the movement stopped. Then one of the officers came down, came down steadily, uniform immaculate, short tropical sleeves, polished belt, the shirt open at the neck, a knife sheathed at the hip on the side opposite from the revolver, a short figure, even slight.

Shoda.

She stood for a moment on the bottom step, watching me, her eyes shadowed by her peaked cap. Then she came onto the tarmac.

I stood with my hands by my sides, empty. At the edge of my vision, above her, I noted figures, faces in the cabin doorway. She'd ordered them to stay on board.

Sounds faded, or seemed to fade, and silence fell across us both, containing us, enclosing us, bringing intimacy.

I could see they were all officer rank, by the uniform. Johnny Chen. *Then I put a few things together, the location of the camp and the obviously elite performance going on, and then I got it. That tiny little guy was Mariko Shoda, because believe me there isn't another female colonel in this neck of the woods.*

I'd expected her to be sheathed in silk, sinuous, feline, seducing me into the shades of Lethe with the kiss of her bright blade. But despite the uniform she looked as she had when I'd seen her in the temple, her small face fragile, ivory-skinned, the cheekbones sculpted, noble, her dark eyes luminous, her short hair night-black under the cap.

"You are not armed?"

A light voice, but with the note of harshness I'd heard before, on the tapes, and now something else, a tone of disbelief. Understandable.

"No."

She moved her right hand, a delicate, fine-boned hand, a hand you would want to touch your lips to, and rested it on her gun.

I hadn't expected a gun.

She was looking over my head now, scanning the background for snipers, still disbelieving.

"You have no support?"

"No." I was aware of feedback, and heard that my voice was totally calm. "I don't need arms, and I don't need support."

Totally calm, even though I hadn't expected a gun. There was no trace of panic in the organism that I could detect; it was tuned by its awareness of mortal danger to a pitch where it would have the speed and the strength to save itself if there were a chance.

I didn't think there was one, now. Because of the gun. I'd need to take her through rage before she'd break, and in her rage she'd shoot me.

Sounds coming back, fading in, the high thin whistling of the jets overhead as the tower ordered them into a holding pattern, waiting to land.

Shoda spoke.

"But surely you must realise that I shall kill you now."

Looking at me with her dark eyes shimmering, the eyes of a woman in love, in love with what she was going to do.

But there was something here on the positive side—oh, a bare degree, of course, Christ yes, what can we expect with her hand on that bloody gun, sweat running now, cooling the skin, but at least a degree, a sign of something positive. She wasn't thinking straight. If she'd been thinking straight she'd have realised that a professional agent wouldn't just come here and bare his neck for nothing. He'd come with some kind of bargain to offer, a gesture of tit for tat, you get off my back and I'll get off yours, so forth. But she hadn't even asked why I'd come to her, alone and unarmed. She was too full of her obsession, too eager to rid herself of the one obstacle in her path to Armageddon to think of anything else.

Or I was whistling again, maybe, in the dark.

"There'd be no point," I said, "in killing me."

"Why is that?"

Throw in the first one and watch the reaction.

"Because you've lost the Slingshot."

Without that missile—Pepperidge—*she's finished.* Without the Slingshot she'd struggled from her agonising childhood through the jungles of the Golden Triangle to seize the almost infinite power she'd needed as an antidote for her innermost pain; but now she'd gone beyond that, creating a dream of all Asia in flames, and to make it real she needed a real weapon: the Slingshot. And now she couldn't go back from there, from the heights of her megalomania, to the life of a tawdry narcotics tycoon. She'd have to go on, or break.

I watched the reaction, a faint gold spark in the depth of her eyes: a hit, a direct hit. But what I'd said had shocked her, that was all; she couldn't let herself believe it.

"The shipment has landed," she said, "in Prey Veng. I was informed."

"Yes. It landed at 21:14 hours, on schedule. But your agents are checking the containers now, and there are no missiles. We removed them."

Her hand hit the holster and pulled the clip and drew the gun and I tensed but she half-turned, calling something to the people in the cabin doorway, Thai language and I didn't understand but it was obviously something like *Signal our unit in Prey Veng and ask what's in the containers.*

Then she swung back to face me and now I could see the fear in her eyes, the fear that it was true.

I took the tension off a degree because I needed the calm to work through the project, the end-phase. We'd got the timing right: we'd worked inside the five-minute bracket and that was over now. There wouldn't have been a single chance of breaking Shoda if she'd already heard she'd lost the Slingshot.

It had been essential that I told her myself.

It would give me the power I needed to break her. The news she feared most had to come from this man standing in front of her, unarmed, unassailable, omnipotent. We were to use—it had been agreed by Loman, by Pepperidge, by Croder himself—the psychic chemistry of voodoo.

She waited. She'd do nothing, say nothing, I knew, until she received the signal from Prey Veng, telling her whether I was right or wrong, whether she'd won or lost. *That would be the moment when she'd start to break.*

Or shoot me dead.

I didn't know the weaponry in Asia all that well but it looked like a regulation Japanese army 9mm Hitaki, either five or six shots, I couldn't tell, because the chamber was polished and high-lighted with not much shadow in the grooves. But I saw she'd been trained in gun-handling: her index finger was flattened against the barrel, pointing at the target, and her middle finger was inside the trigger-guard. I couldn't tell if she'd already got pressure on the primary spring but I didn't think it was likely. When the time came she'd do it execution-style, formally, order me to turn my back and kneel, a single shot in the head.

I could hear voices in the near-distance, from inside the jet, one of them distorted, sounding from a speaker on the flight deck.

She was listening too.

The whistling of the aircraft drifted from the night sky as they circled in their holding-pattern, other flights joining them over the minutes.

Seabirds still called from the waters beyond the perimeter road, wakeful in the artificial light. Perhaps they were still fishing, closing their wings and plunging to the surface to pierce the sweet flesh of the prey with their stiletto beaks, one must live, my friends, one must survive.

She went on watching me, Shoda, with her hand on the gun, until a voice reached us from the cabin of the plane, alarm in it, though I didn't understand the words, only their meaning, and I saw the spark come again into Shoda's eyes and flare into rage so I said to her:

"The civilised nations can't afford to let you take possession of a weapon like that. It'd be like putting a live bomb into the paws of a monkey."

She fired and the bullet hit and I blanked out ordinary needs, the temptation to crouch over my diaphragm, the point of impact, to let out my breath, to do anything but stand and watch her, stand without moving and watch her face and see the rage in her eyes change to fear as they widened and her mouth parted and her head tilted back as she stared at me.

The smell of cordite drifting on the air.

"Now that your grandiose ambitions are destroyed, Mariko Shoda, you've nothing left, you *are* nothing, except a sordid little drug-dealer feeding the dreams of the dead-beats on the streets of Hong Kong and Berlin and New York, an ineffective little revolutionary beating with your small fists at the gates of civilized nations. Surely your father, the prince, wouldn't have wanted such a fate for you—"

The gun flashed and I took the shock again and absorbed it, watching her face and seeing the fear change to terror as I went on standing there, not moving.

There's this bullshit of course that you see in the movies when a man gets shot and goes flying backwards as if he's been hit by a train and I suppose it looks cute but work it out for yourself in terms of basic physics, force exerts equal force in the opposite direction, so the gunman would go flying backwards too.

Not that I was actually enjoying myself. I'd told Flood I wanted it proof against *knives* because that was what I'd expected to be getting into if it came to a showdown—a super-spectacular barn dance with half a dozen of those jungle cats trying to do a Julius Caesar thing on me if I couldn't make Shoda fall for the voodoo bit, but obviously it was also proof against close-range 9mm ammunition, a sixteenth-of-an-inch-thick weave of tungsten steel mesh with a covering of toughened nylon, according to Flood's description.

Not, though, enjoying it, no, because she was breaking fast now and if she raised that gun and aimed at my head it'd be strictly no go, *finito,* and a rose for Moira.

I spoke again, telling her what she must be told at this stage in the affair. I hadn't expected a gun when I'd come out here to meet her but there'd been one, so I'd had to change the script. I'd expected her as an Oriental to accord me the execution-style formality so that I could enter Nirvana kneeling in prayer but she hadn't done that because she was now totally dominated by her emotions and all she could think about was pumping the shots into me and focussing on the standard target, the heart, because if she missed it even at this range she'd hit a lung or the spleen or the liver and start death spreading through the system.

So I continued my assault on her psyche because she was now conditioned for it.

"It is not your karma to kill me, Mariko, as you see. This much is now made manifest. On the contrary, you know that by the law of karma the abusers of power must surrender it. This much is ordained."

Flash and in the next millisecond the bang of the gun and then the smoke clouding between us, the third shot, that was the third shot, I'd been counting, but the thing was I didn't know if the chamber held five or six bullets and I was waiting for her to raise the gun and aim at my head and squeeze the thing and *Jesus Christ, I didn't want her to do that,* sweating like a pig, wouldn't you, *waiting for her to do that* in the next second, the next two seconds, blowing my head away, *what happened to Q, oh he never got back, the opposition blew his head away in the middle of a runway on Singapore airport, he'd bitten off more than he could chew, got into some kind of exotic end-phase he couldn't get out of, he was always a bit like that, if you remember,* the fear of Christ in me as I watched her, fascinated, keeping the gun at the edge of my vision and seeing it come up, seeing her lift it and take aim at the centre of my forehead, not, in fact, no, just the nerves, watching her face and waiting for her to do that but she'd gone beyond the point of rational thinking because all she could see in front of her was this man, this *creature,* an animalistic phantasm that was proving itself omnipotent, unkillable, immortal, and, most hideous of all, the incarnation of her own appointed Nemesis.

Watching her face.

Watching her face as she fired again and I felt the impact just above the heart. Fourth shot.

If you had said to an artist, a sculptor, fashion me a mask that will show fear, more than fear, terror, more than terror, the recognition of a force so powerful that the wearer pales before its dread countenance, in thrall to the knowledge of impending death, the death of the mask-wearer, a death that is decreed, predestined, that is fixed by the stars so as to be inescapable. If you had asked an artist, a sculptor, to make you a mask like *that,* then you would be looking into the face of Shoda as I saw her now.

Like glass, one day break easily. You make her break, I think, one day.

Smoke drifting between us on the quiet air.

Bring her down.

Bring her down *now.*

"Acknowledge your karma, Mariko, and obey it. There is nothing more for you here."

Flash and the gun banged and I took the shock and waited. Fifth shot, that had been the fifth shot and there could be a sixth, I didn't know.

Stink of cordite and the echoes coming back from the hangars, the nerves running with fire because of the effort needed to absorb the impact every time it came, the effort to go on standing still, to show her the tranquil mien of an immortal so that the voodoo would work.

Not voodoo, really. I'd told her the eternal truth and she'd recognised it and knew its power.

One last throw, because I had to find out.

"There is nothing you can do now, Mariko, but obey your karma."

She raised the gun and took aim at my head and fired but there was no flash this time, just a click from the hammer, a five-shot chamber, yes, and I watched the final understanding come into her eyes and dwell there, the understanding that this creature was beyond her reach in this world; and then her arms went down and her hand opened and the gun dropped from her fingers and I said, "Go to your father now and be at peace," and turned my back to allow her privacy for this most intimate of acts and heard the knife hiss from its sheath and the soft cry as the blade was buried and I began walking across the tarmac towards the lights.

"When it comes to espionage fiction, Adam Hall has no peer!"
—Eric Van Lustbader,
Bestselling author of The Ninja

Quiller—Adam Hall's world-famous master of espionage, the most deadly man in the British secret service. From the frigid reaches of the Soviet Arctic Circle to the quiet intrigue of 10 Downing Street, he's the all-time classic undercover agent.

__0-515-08415-8 **Quiller**	$3.95
__0-515-08503-0 **The Quiller Memorandum**	$3.95
__0-515-08623-1 **The Mandarin Cypher**	$3.50
__0-515-08678-9 **The Sinkiang Executive**	$3.50
__0-515-09540-0 **Quiller's Run**	$4.50
__0-515-09498-6 **The 9th Directive**	$3.50

Please send the titles I've checked above. Mail orders to:

BERKLEY PUBLISHING GROUP
390 Murray Hill Pkwy., Dept. B
East Rutherford, NJ 07073

NAME ____________________

ADDRESS ____________________

CITY ____________________

STATE ____________ ZIP ____________

Please allow 6 weeks for delivery.
Prices are subject to change without notice.

POSTAGE & HANDLING:
$1.00 for one book, $.25 for each additional. Do not exceed $3.50.

BOOK TOTAL $______

SHIPPING & HANDLING $______

APPLICABLE SALES TAX (CA, NJ, NY, PA) $______

TOTAL AMOUNT DUE $______

PAYABLE IN US FUNDS.
(No cash orders accepted.)

ON SALE IN AUGUST 1988
In Paperback from Berkley Books
PATRIOT GAMES
THE EXPLOSIVE #1 NEW YORK TIMES BESTSELLER
"A high pitch of excitement!"
—WALL STREET JOURNAL
"A bang-up climax..."
—WASHINGTON POST
In Hardcover from G.P. Putman's Sons
THE CARDINAL OF THE KREMLIN
Jack Ryan, hero of Red Storm Rising, heads into the heart of the Kremlin in Tom Clancy's new suspense thriller. A deep-cover CIA mole code-named The Cardinal is about to be exposed, and it's up to Ryan to rescue him—or risk an all-out nuclear war!

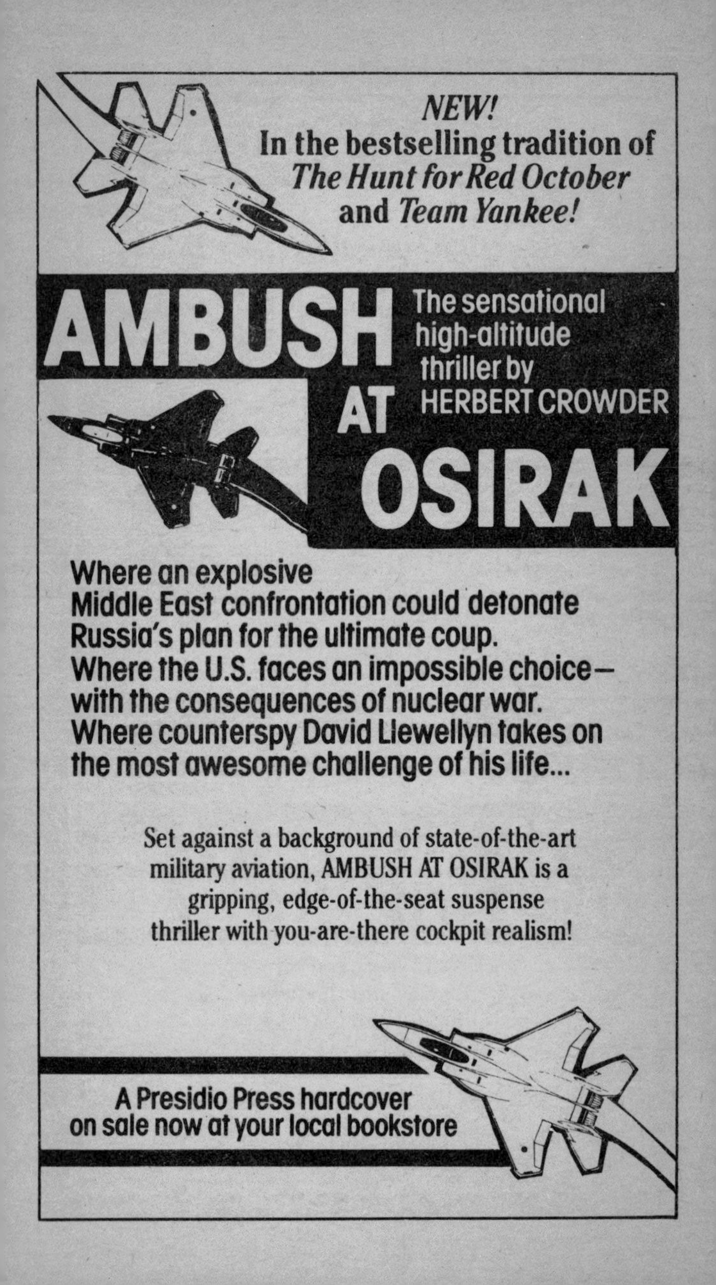
NEW!
In the bestselling tradition of
The Hunt for Red October
and Team Yankee!
AMBUSH
AT
OSIRAK
The sensational
high-altitude
thriller by
HERBERT CROWDER
Where an explosive
Middle East confrontation could detonate
Russia's plan for the ultimate coup.
Where the U.S. faces an impossible choice—
with the consequences of nuclear war.
Where counterspy David Llewellyn takes on
the most awesome challenge of his life...
Set against a background of state-of-the-art
military aviation, AMBUSH AT OSIRAK is a
gripping, edge-of-the-seat suspense
thriller with you-are-there cockpit realism!
A Presidio Press hardcover
on sale now at your local bookstore